For Better, For Worse

June Francis' sagas include *Step by Step*, *A Dream To Share*, *When Clouds Go Rolling By*, *Tilly's Story* and *Sunshine and Showers*. She had her first novel published at forty and is married with three sons. She lives in Liverpool.

Also by June Francis

For Better, For Worse
Where There's a Will
It's Now or Never
Love Letters in the Sand
Many a Tear Has To Fall
Memories Are Made of This
Walking Back to Happiness
Shadows of the Past
Another Man's Child
Someone to Trust
The Heart Will Lead
A Place to Call Home
Look for the Silver Lining

The Victoria Crescent Sagas

Step by Step
A Dream to Share
When the Clouds Go Rolling By
Tilly's Story
Sunshine and Showers

JUNE FRANCIS

For Better, For Worse

1☉ CANELO

First published in the United Kingdom in 2020 by Canelo

This edition published in the United Kingdom in 2022 by

Canelo
Unit 9, 5th Floor
Cargo Works, 1–2 Hatfields
London, SE1 9PG
United Kingdom

A CIP catalogue record for this book is available from the British Library.

Print ISBN 978 1 80032 215 8
Ebook ISBN 978 1 80032 214 1

Look for more great books at www.canelo.co

Printed and bound in Great Britain by Clays Ltd, Elcograf S.p.A.

I

Part 1

July 1934–December 1934

Chapter 1

Liverpool: July 1934

Twenty-year-old Grace Green wiped the tears from her damp cheeks as she neared the stop at the Pierhead. From here she could catch a tram that would take her to West Derby Road and then walk on to her father's house in Lombard Street.

Her aunt, Polly, and her daughters, Marion and Beryl, had wanted Grace to return with them to their Wavertree home in south Liverpool. It was a house Grace knew well, having stayed there a fair amount since she was five years old, when her mother, Hope, had died from influenza in the 1919 pandemic.

Earlier that morning, Grace had been with her aunt and cousins at the port to bid farewell to their brother, Dougie. Polly did not want her son to leave Merseyside, and the atmosphere at the dockside had been strained, even before Grace's father, Norman, had surprised them all by turning up. Norman's dredger had just docked after a long night's work keeping the channels open between the sandbanks in the Mersey, and he'd only managed to get to the docking bay for the Australian-bound steamer just in time. In a rough manner, Norman had wished Dougie success, adding that he looked forward to hearing how his dead wife's nephew found Sydney, given that it had been quite a few years since he himself had set foot in the city himself.

'You've never mentioned having been to Australia before,' Dougie blurted out in surprise.

'That's because my memories of Sydney are ones I prefer not to talk about,' said Grace's father with a strange, twisted smile.

'So, why are you mentioning it now, Dad?' asked Grace sharply. Her nerves were already on edge with Dougie's imminent departure, without an added complication.

'It's to put me off, isn't it?' Dougie said.

His uncle shook his head, tight-lipped all of a sudden. 'You're of an age when you should have more sense than I had when I was there.'

'And what is that supposed to mean?' asked a curious Grace, wondering if this finally was the real reason why her father had been so against her emigrating with Dougie. Maybe he had taken against Australia as a place. It might explain why Norman had refused his permission for them to marry so vehemently – despite Dougie mooting his plans to emigrate with Grace more than eighteen months ago.

In exasperation, Dougie had turned to his mother and asked whether she had known what had happened in Australia. Polly shook her head quickly. 'But I do remember Hope telling me that she'd met a sailor who'd just returned from Australia—'

Suddenly, Norman spoke up again. 'That's right, just before I met Hope, I had been taken on as a fireman on a new ship called the *Medic* – of the White Star line. It was the summer of 1899. The ship had tons of refrigerated cargo capacity, which included space for thousands of frozen carcases from Australia or New Zealand and there were berths for 350 third-class passengers, too! Quite a thing at the time. I remember she had four great masts and one funnel, with bunker space for enough coal so that she didn't have to take on any more during the voyage. She called in at Las Palmas and Cape Town, South Africa, and then various ports in Australia and New Zealand...' He paused, to be interrupted by his nephew.

'What speed was the *Medic* capable of?' Dougie asked, intrigued by the details, he had grown up by the docks, after all.

'14 knots per hour cruising speed,' Grace's father replied instantly. 'Depending on the weather – baring accidents on the ship – the trip to Australia would take approximately a month to six weeks.'

'So, you'd have been away for at least two months,' mused Dougie.

Norman nodded. 'And that's why I never did the Australia run again,' he said abruptly.

Grace looked at her father closely – she was determined to have the whole truth out of him, that evening if necessary, about what had really happened in Australia. So far, she had accepted the excuses Norman had given for refusing to agree to a marriage between Dougie and herself. She knew she was still young, and that Dougie was her first cousin. Although, she was inclined to believe that the nub of it was that Norman would miss her too much if she moved to Australia with a new husband. She was all he had left since her mother had died.

Her aunt Polly had told Grace that Norman had been a lost soul, truly heartbroken, when her sister had died. This was despite him spending most of their marriage away at sea, she had also confided cattily, suggesting that perhaps some of Norman's grief might have been down to guilt. Polly had sided with Norman, though, when he had spoken out against Grace and Dougie marrying. Polly agreed, utterly against her son emigrating.

–

It had been obvious to Polly for years that her son and niece were fond of each other, but she had chosen to believe that her son just felt very protective of his younger, pretty cousin, who, in turn, clearly hero-worshipped him. Then during the summer months there had been an outing to New Brighton and even Wales; her uncle and aunt had gone to Southport and Marion and Beryl had also gone out, by late morning it began to cloud over and Dougie had suggested they stay home and cuddle on the sofa and listen to the radio in peace. Almost before she realised it Dougie had undone her blouse buttons and was fondling her breasts. Grace told him to stop, that it was wrong, but he had said he loved her, and it was what lovers did. He had pushed her down on the sofa and pushed up her skirts. She had told him no but he had forced himself on her. She was mortified when she heard the key in the front door and he had rolled off her, clutching himself as she began to button up her blouse. Her aunt had come in first and it was obvious to Grace it had come as a terrible shock to Polly to find them in such a situation. She had dragged Grace to her feet and hustled her into the back kitchen and told her that it was sinful to lead her cousin on, as well as where it could lead. Later Grace had heard her aunt scolding Dougie for not seeing that his young cousin was besotted by him and didn't realise what she was doing. Grace had waited for him to take the blame for what had happened but all he had said was that he wanted to marry Grace, and that she was unlike any other girl that he had been out with and that they loved each other. He planned for them to leave Liverpool, so Polly and Grace's father would never again interfere in their lives.

From her aunt's behaviour in the weeks that followed Grace was convinced her aunt blamed Grace completely for stealing away her son's affections. Once Polly had realised how things lay, she had attempted to keep them apart, but what with Grace being her sister's only child, and Norman going away to sea at the time, she obviously felt that she had no option but to continue to allow her niece into her home even when she was sixteen and old enough to care for herself. Although, once Norman got a job on the Mersey dredgers, at Polly's instigation, she made sure that her niece, who was nearly eighteen by then, was packed and back in her father's house as quickly as possible.

As for Grace, she had only begun to find her older, blond, cousin attractive when she became aware that Dougie, five years her senior, had started to look at her differently. She had just turned sixteen at the time, and had blossomed in such a way that the local youths now competed to take her to the flickers or to step out for a walk with her. Grace enjoyed the attention, but her head wasn't really turned. Then one day Dougie told one of them, Syd, a kind boy from down the road, to scarper just as he was about to kiss her on the doorstep for the first time. Grace had been annoyed, and told Dougie in no uncertain terms not to interfere as she liked Syd, only for Dougie to punch him on the nose. Later Dougie had told her that he was only protecting her because he cared about her. But then, at Christmastime, she remembered how Dougie had kissed her tentatively, and then with passion, under the mistletoe. After that he started to take her to the flickers regularly and held her hand in the dark. He also took to standing at the top of the backyard when she scurried down to the outdoor lavatory in the dark, kissing her lightly on her return, saying that he was watching out for her in case any of the lads who fancied her sneaked over the wall and took advantage of her. She was flattered at first that her strong, handsome cousin should care for her safety so much, but then she started to realise that the boys that she liked began to avoid her.

Come the following spring, she began to question how Dougie really felt towards her and she felt confused. Although, in the beginning she had thrilled to his kisses, she no longer did so in the same way, and sometimes felt wary about his forceful attentions. She realised that he acted as if he owned her, cutting her off from not only the boys' company she enjoyed but also some of the girls she had known at school. One of whom had told her that her cousin probably found her easy game living under the same roof and her innocence such a change from the experienced women he went out with sometimes. Grace had never spoken to that girl again, thinking so little of her own attractions that she could not blame her cousin for being attracted to women his own age. Fortunately, she still had a friend in Milly who lived in the same street as her father and who was married and expecting her first baby, but Grace was too shy and embarrassed to talk to Milly about her confused feelings for Dougie.

She could not help recalling, too, the argument she had with Dougie when they were window-shopping one evening in town not so long ago; she had pointed out a dress she liked and planned on buying it with some of the allowance her father had given to her aunt for her. He had said that she would be wasting her money as the style was too fussy and girlish for her and she was old enough now to wear the one with the lower neckline. She had immediately recalled how he had slipped his hand down the front of her dress and touched the curve of her breasts. She had been shocked because she had never forgotten her aunt warning her about boys who would try touching her in certain places, and she must always dress with decorum and not to lead them on. Dougie's behaviour spoke to her in a negative way and besides she resented him insulting her taste and wanting her to dress in such a way that her aunt would never trust her again to shop for herself.

He had been furious with her when she had told him she would spend her money on what she wanted and if he did not like it, then he would just have to lump it. His handsome face had twisted and reddened with anger and he had flung the words: 'I thought you loved me and if you did then you would want to please me.' She had replied in retaliation: 'That works two ways and besides which I'm sure your mother and my dad would say I'm too young to know what love is about.'

'But I'm not,' he had said, 'and it's because I'm older and I love you that I know what's best for you and want to guide you in the way that's best for both of us.' He had pulled her into his arms right there on the street and pressed her against him and kissed her as if determined to make her submit to his will. It had been both terrifying and thrilling, but she had felt angry as well and eventually she had kicked him in the shins and once she had breath, she had told him that she hated him and stormed off and went straight to bed when she returned to her aunt's house.

The following day she expected him to cut her dead, as it was what she had decided to do, but instead as he passed her chair at the breakfast table, he dropped a kiss on the top of her head and then sat opposite her and stared at her.

'Did you have a good night's sleep, Gracie?'

'Yes, thank you.'

'I thought you must have been tired from the grumpy way you behaved last night,' he said. 'Even though, I didn't sleep very well because my leg hurt so much, I've decided to buy you a necklace to go with that dress I liked.'

'I'm not buying that dress,' she said icily.

'But you'll look lovely in it,' he said. 'I'll even give you some money to go towards it. You can wear it on the ship when we go to Australia.'

'Australia! What are you talking about?'

'Emigrating. There are plenty of jobs out there and the wages are higher. I could buy us a house and we won't have Mother and your father interfering in our lives.'

Grace thought about what she had heard about Australia and although it had sounded attractive with its beaches and plenty of wide open spaces with plenty of room for large houses and gardens, she loved Liverpool and her father and besides she'd need his permission to marry Dougie.

'We'd have to get married before we could go, and I doubt Dad would give his permission.'

'We could get married when we get there, Gracie,' said Dougie.

'No way,' said Grace. 'Anyway, I don't know how you can suggest such a thing after the row we had last night. I can only marry for love.'

His expression darkened. 'I know you said you hated me, but I don't believe it. Just think of all the fun we've had together and our first kiss under the mistletoe, you can't say you didn't enjoy that!'

'No, I can't,' she said. 'I was only young then and you're so handsome, I felt like Cinderella and you were Prince Charming.'

'Well, there you have it,' said Dougie triumphantly. 'You know how that story ended… happily ever after.'

Grace remembered thinking how at the time she had thought the story ended at the wedding. 'Let's drop the subject,' she said. 'Dad will never agree.'

Dougie shook his head. 'By hook or by crook, we're emigrating to Australia and you'll marry me.'

Grace shook her head and draining her teacup she left the table, undecided whether she was glad or not that her aunt and cousins had not been at the table. Her uncle Douglas had already left the house for work.

The following Saturday, Grace had gone into town and bought the dress she had liked and noticed that the dress Dougie had wanted her to buy was gone. She wore her new dress for church the next day and expected Dougie to change his mind about how she looked, but he kept quiet despite her aunt, Marion and Beryl admiring it.

The following weekend, the whole family had been invited to the engagement party of the son of her uncle's brother. When Grace went upstairs to change, she found the dress Dougie had wanted her to buy on her bed. For a moment she thought that perhaps her girl cousins had chosen it when they had gone shopping for something to wear for the engagement party. Grace spoke to Beryl, the younger cousin about it, only to be told that Marion had bought it at Dougie's insistence, having told her that Grace had liked it but hadn't enough money to afford it, and he was buying it for her as a surprise.

Grace could not help wondering why he would tell a lie.

Marion who had just entered the bedroom, said, 'I must admit I was surprised as he's always broke, what with him enjoying a flutter on the gee-gees and always borrowing money from Mam.'

'He shouldn't have bought it. Perhaps I could return it and get his money back?' murmured Grace.

'It's a lovely dress,' said Beryl, fingering the artificial silk. 'You'll look lovely in it.'

Marion sniffed. 'Don't kid her. It's too old for her.'

'You're just jealous,' said Beryl.

Grace looked at the dress and tried to imagine Dougie's expression when he saw her wearing it and she realised she did not like being out of friends with him and wearing it would please him. He beamed when he saw Grace enter the room and as soon as he was able, he seized her arm and led her out into the garden.

'Admit I was right and give me a kiss as if you mean it, there's a good girl. I spend good money on it and it was worth every penny.'

'Did you have a win on the gee-gees?' she asked, looping her arms around his neck.

'How did you guess?' he teased. 'Now kiss me.'

She kissed him, aware as she did so that he dared to fumble with the zip at the back of the dress. She felt like screaming but did not have the breath and besides, he had spent his winnings on her.

Once she had breath, she murmured, 'Your mother would have a fit if she caught you doing that.'

He whispered, 'Things will be different when we reach Australia.'

'I'm not going to Australia. Father won't give his permission. He'll say I'm too young.'

'That's just an excuse. He wants you to keep house for him, to shop and cook now he's stopped going on those long sea trips.'

'You're right,' Grace had replied after thinking over what he had just said. 'But it's understandable. I'm his only child and he'd miss me terribly.'

'Just like he missed your mother, but still went away to sea for months,' Dougie had sneered in response.

Grace was stung by his words. 'It was all he knew, and it would have been difficult him getting another job,' she said hurriedly.

'He wanted his cake and to eat it,' Dougie had flung the words at her.

'You can say what you like,' said Grace. 'He still won't give his permission.'

'We'll see,' said Dougie. 'I'll get Mother to talk him round. I'll tell her you're pregnant. I could make sure of that now.' He seized hold of her tightly, hurting her.

Grace gasped. She considered it unlikely that her aunt would try and talk her father around or mention pregnancy as that would not reflect well on Dougie. If it had been true, her father would have accused him of taking advantage of her. She decided to say no more and it was several minutes later that Dougie complained, 'I thought you'd jump at the idea of us going off on our own. You said you loved me.'

She sighed. 'You said you loved *me*. If that was true, then you'd have said you'd wait until I come of age when I'm twenty-one.'

'I don't want to wait. I want you now and to emigrate now,' Dougie had wheedled. 'I've heard there's talk of Germany rearming. There could be a war!' He put his arms around her and drew her against him. 'I want you,

Gracie.' He pressed hard against her and she felt the bark of the apple tree through the fabric of her dress. 'Why do you have to keep me waiting like this?'

—

As she hurried to the tram stop, Grace remembered yet again how annoyed she had felt then and on other occasions. 'Dougie! Not this again, get off me! If by that, you mean doing "it", there are several reasons, as I've told you in the past, and just now, they still stand – your mam would hit the roof! And Dad would be so disappointed in me. I would be terribly ashamed if I really were pregnant – what would people say?'

'Well, you wanted it one time, told me you were curious,' retorted Dougie.

'That's only half true! You wouldn't take no for an answer, and when I almost gave in to you because I was curious, and then changed my mind, you got violent. It hurt when you hit me like that, Dougie...' Grace had trailed off, as she remembered how shocked she had felt at the time.

'Women aren't supposed to enjoy it,' Dougie replied. 'They get pleasure by pleasing their husbands and wanting children.'

Grace had half-believed him but still pushed him away, just as she had felt his hand creep under her skirt and ping her garter hard, before kneading her thigh. 'You're not my husband, so it's still no!'

'You'd prefer being left on the shelf, then do you, Gracie?' Dougie had replied with an odd little giggle that irritated her.

'Of course not. But whatever you say, I can't marry you without permission before I'm twenty-one, and so, no, I won't be emigrating any time soon.'

'We'll see.'

'Yeah, we will,' she said as she felt raindrops dampen the shoulders of her jacket as they dripped from one of the trees.

'You have too much to say for yourself,' he said sulkily.

She patted his cheek, feeling fed-up from going over and over the same thing again and again. Hopefully, their being parted would make him realise the sense of them having to wait and give her time to sort out just what she felt about him. One thing was for certain there were times when he really got on her nerves. Perhaps absence would make her heart grow fonder.

'Well, you don't have to listen to me. Thanks, I'm tired, so I'm off home to Dad's. Besides, here comes the rain. Goodnight!'

—

But now, as Grace boarded the tram alone, her emotions were in chaos. She remembered that evening with Dougie so clearly – it had been the last rainfall before the weather had changed and given way to a heatwave. It must have only been a month ago. Grace had thought, almost up to the last minute, that Dougie would change his mind and not go to Australia after all, especially given that his mother wept whenever the idea was mentioned. It had been her father who'd suggested Dougie might go on ahead, and once he had settled in Australia and found a job and a decent house for them to live in, he could then send for her, and Grace could follow him out, once she had come of age.

Dougie's last words to her the previous night, as they had looked up at the Liver birds, on the eve of his departure, were similar to those he had repeated several times over the last year or so: there was no future for him in Liverpool due to the Wall Street Crash causing businesses to go to the wall and mass unemployment and a financial slump even here in Britain, the biggest since 1929. Grace had argued with him, pointing out that he was lucky enough to still be in work, besides she had a part-time job, and the Mersey Tunnel was about to be opened by King George V, which would surely improve business opportunities. But Dougie had shaken his head, saying that the Mersey Tunnel was not going to save Liverpool. Several shipping lines had already left the city and moved to Southampton due to the dockers' Bolshie attitude, and he knew better. After that Grace had given up trying to change his mind, knowing that she was wasting her time.

And, if she was honest with herself, she was looking forward to enjoying the next few weeks without him moaning, anyway – Liverpool was buzzing because the King and Queen Mary would soon be visiting to open the Mersey Tunnel and there were all sorts of festivities and outdoor plays planned. Dougie was so jealous of Grace spending time with anyone other than himself, she doubted if he would have let her go if he was still in the city, and as he was so dismissive of her plays and books, he was hardly likely to come with her himself.

So, today, at the dockside, she had put aside their quarrel, and with a brave face she had kissed Dougie quickly and wished him a safe journey. He had told her to write and promised he would send her a picture postcard and a long letter from every place the ship called in at on the way. He had then looked at her closely and told her she was his, forever. Grace found the intensity of his stare a bit much, so after a final hug she had stepped back, so his mother and sisters could say their farewells – Dougie's father had been unable to see his son off as he was at work.

–

As she sat down on a seat on the lower deck of the tram, Grace sighed heavily and thought of their muted farewell. It had been a mistake telling Dougie that she loved him. But Dougie had said he loved her so often, that it required some sort of reply to stop him getting angry with her. Although, normally he only said it as a preamble to him trying to unbutton her blouse, so Grace had felt a bit wary as to the sincerity of his words. Her friend Milly and her husband Jimmy loved each other, really loved each other, but recently Grace had come to realise that rush of what she had believed to be love at first when Dougie had kissed her was not what she now believed love was and had become increasingly aware that Dougie's and her feelings for each other fell short of her friend's relationship. Truth be told, she envied Milly, and now wondered whether this prolonged absence really might cause her and Dougie to see there was more to love than what they felt for each other.

To distract herself from her confused state of mind, Grace paid the conductor for her ticket as he walked between the seats with his ticket machine and thought back to her father's strange speech at the quayside. There was something odd about his time in Australia, not that Norman had given much away.

The tram passed St George's Hall, and Grace noticed the decorations to celebrate the King's visit for the opening of the Mersey Tunnel later in July. The heatwave still showed no sign of abating, so no doubt the crowds who would turn out to see King George V and would swelter. Right now, the heat was making her feel sick and dizzy, and as the tram swayed down West Derby Road, Grace clung on to a strap as she prepared to leave the vehicle. She stepped down from the tram on to the pavement and narrowly avoided being run down by a small truck. She felt the wind rush as it passed her and for several seconds she froze in her tracks. She stared after the truck which came to a halt a few yards away. A man climbed out of the driving seat and gazed at her.

'Have you a death wish, luv?' he shouted.

Chapter 2

Grace looked at the stranger and bit back the angry words that sprang to her lips.

'Sorry, I didn't see you coming,' she said faintly.

The man inclined his head. 'You gave me a start that's all. Sorry I shouted. I guess I was going too fast. Stupid of me. I have a clean record and I don't want to spoil it. I can't afford to lose my job.' He paused. 'Are you all right?'

Grace nodded, which was a mistake, and she swayed. The man hurried back towards her and placed an arm about her waist and half-carried her from the road onto the pavement.

'Have you far to go?' he asked.

She was about to shake her head, only to remember just in time that wouldn't be such a good idea, so she just stared up into his sweaty, anxious features. His jaw was tense, and his dark hair, which was threaded with threads of silver, was unruly, as if he had been running his hands through it. His hazel eyes were narrowed, and she thought held a look of desperation.

'No, just to that street there.' She pointed. 'I'll be all right.'

'Grace!' called a woman's voice. 'What's going on?'

She recognised the voice of Milly, one of her neighbours, her close friend who was heavily pregnant.

'Milly, if you could spare the time, can you walk with me to my dad's?'

'I'd appreciate it if you could do that, Milly,' said the man who was propping up Grace.

Milly glanced keenly at him. 'I know you?' she asked.

'We have met,' he replied. 'I haven't time to talk now.'

'Ben Evans, that's who you are,' said Milly triumphantly.

His lips twitched in a faint smile. 'You've a good memory. I must go. I've wood to deliver to the site before I go home, and I'm in a rush to get to Alder Hey first.'

His hold on Grace slackened and Milly took his place. They watched him as with shoulders bowed, he walked to his truck.

Milly who was around the same age as Grace, was the first to speak. 'So, how come you're snuggled up to him when you've just been seeing Dougie off to Australia, hey?'

'I wasn't snuggling up! I just missed being run over by him in his truck. I don't know which one of us was the most startled,' said Grace with a shiver. Together they turned the corner into a street of three-bedroomed-terraced houses with lower-bay windows and a small area with iron railings at the front.

'His wife was killed in a road accident,' confided Milly. 'He took it very badly as they had only been married a few years and had a young boy. He had no female relative to help look after little Simon, so he's had to be mother and father to his son and hold down a job.' She frowned. 'Something must have happened to him if Ben's in a rush to reach Alder Hey. It used to be a military hospital during the First World War, but is now a children's hospital.'

'Poor man,' said Grace. 'I hope his son will be all right. How long ago is it since his wife was killed?'

'Probably about six years. Simon's ten now.'

'How come you know him?' Grace straightened up, recalling that Milly was pregnant, which was reason enough for her not to be bearing Grace's weight.

'He knows Jimmy, both are joiners and have been doing some work for Jones, the Welsh building contractor, out past Bootle way,' said Milly. 'I met his wife at the Grafton years ago, we bumped into them when Jimmy and I were dancing, so we had a drink together and got talking. I doubt he gets out much now. In fact, I know he doesn't, because Jimmy told me so.'

'I suppose that's because he can't get someone to sit with his son,' said Grace.

Milly shook her head and her curls bobbed. 'He doesn't want to bother people and he wouldn't leave Simon in the house on his own.'

'Where do they live?' asked Grace.

'Just the next street to us – Saxon Street.'

'Not far then,' Grace said.

Milly smiled. 'It wouldn't be any trouble to me to help him out.'

Grace said, 'I hope his son is all right. You'll let me know when you hear, won't you?'

Milly nodded as they came to a halt outside Grace's home. 'You all right now?'

'Yes, thank you,' said Grace. 'Do you want to come in for a cuppa?'

'I better hadn't. I want to get a casserole in the oven.'

'See you around then,' said Grace, taking a door key from her handbag.

Milly waved and walked away.

Once Grace was inside, she sat down in the armchair for a rest for half an hour or so. Feeling a bit stronger, she then checked the cupboards in the back kitchen and decided to nip to the Co-op grocery store on Whitefield Road, and to May's as well, the corner greengrocers. It didn't take her long to buy what she needed, and she was soon back in the house and had the shopping put away. Grace quickly prepared a pan of scouse and left it simmering on the glowing coals in the black-leaded range while she boiled the kettle and made a pot of tea and a damson jam butty. That done, she sat down with her cuppa and tried to relax, but her thoughts were all over the place.

She relived the scene down at the Pierhead – the quayside had been full of vehicles and people and the river had been busy too, with all kinds of craft, despite the slump, but the large steamer that would be taking Dougie to Australia had towered over them all. Grace thought for a moment about her last sight of Dougie. His fair hair had been blowing in the breeze and his handsome features were alight with pleasure as he had turned and waved to them while standing on the deck. Grace guessed that his thoughts were not on her and his sisters and mother, but were on what lay ahead for him. At least there would be no icebergs en-route, such as the one that had sunk the *Titanic*. Grace sighed, and wished Dougie well, hoping that he would find whatever it was that he was seeking, but there was a small part of her that hoped he would have regrets for what he had left behind: her, his home, family, and all that was familiar – she really did not want what Australia had to offer.

She quickly shut off those thoughts and concentrated on how she had nearly been hit by the speeding truck.

Now she knew about the driver's son being in hospital, she could understand the man's actions and forgive him. For an instant, her thoughts flashed back to Dougie again and she wondered how he might have acted if he had received news that she had been injured. Would he have sent a telegram wishing her a speedy recovery or would he even have left the ship at the nearest port and booked passage on the next vessel home? Probably not, when his mind was filled with Australia, she thought with mixed feelings.

Over the next few days, Grace saw little of her father and forgot about what she was going to ask him about his trip to Australia. She had her job to go to two-and-a-half days a week. It was in a large house on West Derby Road, where she did the housework and prepared an evening meal for the bachelor dentist who lived in rooms over his practice. Her wages came in handy and the hours she worked fitted in nicely now she was living permanently at her father's home. There only being the two of them and the dog, it did not take her long to keep the place clean and tidy, do the washing and ironing, shop and cook, and even walk Fergie.

It was on her way to work the following week that she heard her name being called. She had been thinking of Dougie and remembered those early days when life between them had been sweeter, and had just posted a letter to him, wondering how long it would be before he received his mail and she heard back from him. She was attempting to plot his voyage on a map of the world her father had kept in a drawer in the sideboard for years. She turned to see Milly hurrying towards her. Grace waited until she caught up with her.

Milly was slightly out of breath when she reached her. 'Surely you shouldn't be running,' said Grace, nodding to her pregnant stomach.

'I'm all right,' said Milly. 'I just thought you'd be interested to know that Ben's son is out of hospital, but Jimmy tells me Ben's in a bit of a tizzy because Simon has a cracked kneecap, two broken wrists as well as a damaged nose. He fell out of a tree.'

'Oh, the poor lad.'

Milly nodded. 'Jimmy also said Ben can't afford to stay off work but is concerned about leaving the boy alone in the house all day. A neighbour has offered to look in on the boy now and then, but while he's grateful, Ben doesn't think that's the answer as someone's not with Simon if he needs something.'

'Why not? Can't the hospital keep Simon in longer?'

'No, they need the bed for a more urgent case, so I've offered to have him stay at our house during the day.'

'But won't you find that tiring in your condition?' said Grace.

'I'm not going to run around after him,' said Milly. 'And the school have said they'll provide him with books to read and sums to work out. I'll just make him a midday meal and be company for him. Jimmy reckons he's a good lad, not rowdy at all. It'll only be for six weeks.'

Grace chewed on her lower lip. 'Is there any way I could help out?'

Milly's face brightened. 'That would be smashing.'

Grace said thoughtfully, 'Can he walk at all?'

Milly shook her head. 'He has a splint the length of the leg as he needs to keep the knee straight, so he hops, and he can't use crutches because of his wrists being fractured. What had you in mind?'

23

'I had thought he could walk the dog with me and spend some time at Dad's to give you a break. If he and Ben accept the idea, but if the lad can't use crutches...' Grace sighed and then she remembered something. 'We still have an old bath chair in the back bedroom. It's the sort where someone can sit up but have their legs straight out in front of them. It was my mother's. Dad wanted to get rid of it, but I kept my dolls and teddy in it and used to wheel them about the room. I could take him out in that, if he was willing.'

'I'll suggest it to Jimmy, and he can mention it to Ben and see what answer he comes back with,' said Milly.

On that note they parted, but a couple of evenings later, Fergie began to bark and then there came a knock on the front door. Grace opened it to find the truck driver standing there, with a boy leaning on him, whom she presumed was his son. He had flaxen hair that flopped onto his forehead and grey eyes that looked bruised beneath, while his nose was scratched and out of shape.

'You have been in the wars.'

Ben replied, 'Jimmy told me of your kind offer, so we decided to give you a visit. I hope now isn't inconvenient.'

Grace opened the door wider and, hoping her father had put Fergie in the backyard, she said, 'Do come in. I was hoping you would call, as I've cleaned the old bath chair. Straight up the lobby and second door on the right.' She tried not to stare too intently at Simon as Ben placed a hand on his son's rear and carefully assisted him up and over the threshold. The boy steadied himself, resting a hand on the wall before hopping along.

Ben followed him, ready to help his son if he should lose his balance. Grace had left the kitchen door open, so it did not take as long as she had thought before father and

24

son were settled in chairs and she had placed a pouffe for Simon to prop up his injured leg.

Norman, gazed at the boy and said, 'So how did you come by that, lad?'

'I fell out of a tree,' replied Simon.

'You're lucky you didn't break your neck,' said Norman. 'But boys will be boys.'

'That's what my wife said when he broke a vase kicking a ball in the house. He was only a kid then,' muttered Ben.

Simon remained silent, but Grace noticed him swallowing as if he had a lump in his throat, caused no doubt by the reference to his mother. She could understand how he felt and wanted to help him even more.

'Would you like a drink of lemonade, Simon?' she asked gently.

He said shyly, 'Yes, please.'

'What about you, Mr Evans? Would you like a glass or would you prefer a cup of tea?'

'I'd prefer tea, if it's not too much trouble,' Ben replied.

'No trouble at all. Dad and I were about to have one.'

She took a bottle of R. White's lemonade out of a bucket of water in the back kitchen, where it had been keeping cool and poured out a glass for Simon before removing the kettle from the hob and warming the brown pottery teapot.

Once Grace had drunk her tea with her guests she wheeled in the cushioned bath chair which she had made up with fresh linen. She watched Simon and Ben's faces and guessed what they were thinking. Hurriedly she said, 'It always reminds me of the shape of a *steery*. You do know what I'm talking about, Simon?'

He shook his head, but his father said, 'I do. You're talking about a steering cart – made from old pram wheels, some planks of wood and a bit of rope.'

She smiled. 'I always wanted to have a go of one but the boys in the street wouldn't let me, said that a girl could never control it.'

'They were exciting, but dangerous, more so now there's more traffic about,' said Ben.

Grace's father nodded. 'The only risk with this wheeled vehicle,' he said, 'is getting a wheel stuck in a tramline, but it only happened once when I pushed my wife out in it. Ideal, though, for getting someone having difficulty walking out in the fresh air.'

'Agreed,' said Ben. 'One only needs to avoid tramlines.'

Grace smiled and glanced at Simon. 'How do you feel about it?'

He looked doubtful. 'I like the idea of getting out and about, but not being looked upon as an invalid.'

'But it's only temporary,' said Norman, leaning forward and removing his favourite clay pipe from between his lips. 'And as you've just said, you want to get out in the fresh air.'

'And you could have Fergie with you in the chair until we reach the park,' said Grace, and without another word she went out into the backyard and brought in the black, white and tan Jack Russell. A growl rumbled in the dog's throat, but he calmed down when Grace hushed him and took him over to Simon who held out a plaster-cast wrist and bare hand for the dog to sniff. 'His bark is worse than his bite,' she said. 'Although, he has been known to nip the postman's ankle if he doesn't make it to his bike quick enough.'

'I wanted a dog after Mam died,' said Simon. 'But Dad didn't think it was fair to a dog to leave it alone in the house all day during the week.'

'I don't work every day, all day,' Grace said. 'So, no worries there.' She smiled at him. 'I take it you like animals?'

Simon nodded, holding a hand down to Fergie as he sniffed at the foot resting on the pouffe. The dog hesitated only briefly before climbing up to the boy's lap and making himself comfortable.

Ben eyed the boy and dog before looking at Grace. 'I think this means we gratefully accept your offer.'

'Yes, please,' said Simon.

Before the visitors left, it was decided that Ben would drop Simon off at the house on the days that Grace was not working, bar Sundays, starting in a couple of days' time. Simon would go to Milly's the rest of the time, and that way, Milly could have a bit of a break before her approaching confinement. After Grace had seen them out, she returned to the kitchen to find her father placing the guard in front of the fireplace.

'Well,' she said. 'What do you think?'

'He seems a decent bloke and the lad's not going to be getting into mischief in his condition. Besides, looking after him will help take your mind off Dougie.'

'I'd like to help, and Simon seems a very nice boy, it's nice to be around children, they do make me laugh. Strangely enough, Dougie and I never talked about having children,' she said out of the blue, surprising herself.

'I'd have wanted to visit you in Australia if you'd have children. Getting to know my grandchildren was something I often thought about.'

She was silenced for a moment and then said in a husky voice, 'You never mentioned wanting grandchildren.'

'Most likely because of Dougie being your cousin and it being on the cards your emigrating, so it was unlikely I'd ever get to see any grandchildren. Australia might not let me in and, also, I couldn't imagine Dougie playing with children, just trying to keep them in line. You and he would have more arguments over the children than anything else.'

'Oh Dad!' she said gently, going over to where he sat in an armchair and kissing him. She wondered when she next wrote to Dougie, whether she should mention Ben and Simon's visit, and tell him how much she had enjoyed the boy's visit; ask whether he had given any thought to how many children he would like, or maybe she should wait until he got in touch with her first.

'I've never had much to do with children,' she added.

Not long after that evening, she received a postcard from Dougie with a photograph of Las Palmas on one side. He had not written much, except to say the passage had been smooth and Las Palmas was lovely. He was keeping fit by playing deck games with some friends he had made. He had not answered her question about children, only telling her not to have anything more to do with the boy and his father. She then noticed he'd signed it with, 'Much love, Dougie.' She pulled a face, thinking she no longer had to do what he asked with there being thousands of miles between them. She then took out the world map and unfolded it and placed it on the table. There was a lot of pink on the map, which indicated places that were part of the British Empire. Grace studied it hard and eventually found Las Palmas – it was in Gran Canaria, part of a group of Spanish islands situated in the

Atlantic Ocean. Grace thought that perhaps Simon might be interested in geography, so later on tomorrow after they'd had some fresh air, she decided to show him the map and explain how she was following the voyage of a ship to Australia.

Chapter 3

Grace was about to take a sip of her first cup of tea of the day when Fergie barked and then she heard the letterbox go. She wasted no time hurrying to see what the postman had delivered, doubting it would be a letter from Dougie. Life undoubtedly felt more relaxed with Dougie not around, but she knew her aunt missed him, and had agreed with her that life lacked something in his absence. As she got to the door, she saw it was not the postman, but Simon and his father. They were a bit earlier than she had expected them.

'Good morning,' she said.

'I think it's going to be another scorcher,' said Ben, helping Simon up the step.

'Well, the last thing we want is the weather to break with the celebrations going on for the King and Queen's visit,' she said. 'Will you and Simon be attending any of the festivities?'

'The opening ceremony will be too much for Simon,' Ben said. 'But I have thought of taking him to the pageant being performed at Exchange Flags as he'll be able to sit down.'

'I'm going to see it,' said Grace. 'I've already bought my ticket.'

'Thanks for reminding me,' he said. 'I'll do that today.'

She found herself wondering what evening he had thought of going and whether to mention when she was attending, but decided Ben might think she was wanting his company, what with Dougie away. It wasn't as if she needed company but it would be interesting to discuss with them what they had thought of the performances. She invited them inside and led the way into the parlour, where Dougie's postcard was on the sideboard in clear view. She pushed the invalid chair out of the window alcove into the centre of the room. Ben thanked her, before saying he would carry the invalid chair outside for her, while Simon settled himself in a chair with Fergie on his lap.

She nodded and followed him, fanning herself with the postcard.

'From your boyfriend, is it?' Ben asked, indicating the postcard with his head.

'Obviously, Jimmy told you about Dougie,' she said.

He nodded. 'Said he'd gone to Australia. Quite a distance!'

'Yeah,' said Grace. 'This is from Las Palmas.' She waved the postcard about. 'Have you ever done any travelling?'

He stroked his jaw. 'Outside of Britain, you mean?'

She smiled. 'I think you'd be too young for the trenches, though, or for being in the Navy, like Dad.'

'I had a brother who fought – he was six years older than me. I was born in 1904,' he replied. 'My brother was declared missing, presumed dead. The thing is that he shouldn't have been over in France. He had nervous asthma, but a woman posted an envelope through our letterbox addressed to him. I picked it up and gave it to him, not realising it had a white feather inside, so what did he go and do, but go off to fight somehow or

31

other.' He paused. 'I didn't know then that Mrs Pankhurst was encouraging her supporters to give young men white feathers to shame them into joining up.'

'That's terrible,' said Grace.

'It nearly broke Mam's heart, and she was never the same again. I went to look for him after the war ended, but there were loads of people over there trying to find their missing menfolk. Eventually I had to come home because I ran out of money and it was so difficult getting anywhere. Mam was relieved to have me back and said that she would go by her instincts and carry on believing he was still alive somewhere.'

'I can understand her feelings,' said Grace. 'And it must have been awful for you.'

He nodded. 'She didn't live much longer after he was gone. She got careless and cut herself when opening a tin. The cut got septic and she ended up with blood poisoning and died.'

Tears welled in Grace's eyes. 'That must have been tough.'

He shrugged. 'I wasn't the only one grieving. Anyway, I managed to get an apprenticeship, then I met my wife, and Simon was born a year later.'

She wasn't sure what to say about his wife, but watched as he lifted the bath chair outside over the step as he said, 'I'd help you with Simon, only I'll be late for work if I don't leave now.'

'I understand. We'll manage.' She stood in the doorway and watched him drive off before going back indoors.

'Has your dad gone off to work already?' asked Simon, watching her take a toasting fork from a hook on the chimney breast.

'He's a sailor on the dredgers that are helping to keep the channels clear for the ships entering the Mersey and doesn't get home every day. He should be here the next time you come, though.'

Simon looked pleased. 'I'd like to talk to him about what it's like being a sailor. Has he sailed to other countries?'

She nodded. 'You can ask him about that when you see him.'

Simon fell silent and stroked Fergie, glancing at Grace as she sliced a loaf and speared the first slice on the toasting fork before kneeling on the rag rug and holding the bread out to the fire.

'Can I have a piece of toast, please?' he asked.

'Of course, didn't you have any breakfast?'

'Shredded wheat. I like it, and it means Dad doesn't have to light the fire, saves coal as nobody is going to be in the house until the evening as I'm normally at school.'

'Surely you arrive home before your dad?'

'Yeah, but he's set the fire and all I have to do is put a match to it. I'm very careful,' he said.

'What about a warm drink?' she asked.

'Dad fills a flask with boiling water the night before,' said Simon. 'He's been talking about buying a gas cooker when he's saved enough money. He says it'll make life easier for us.'

Grace did not doubt it and wished she could persuade her father to buy one, but he was inclined to say cooking on the fire was more economical because it provided them with heat, as well, in the winter. She could not argue with that, but what with being the cook in the house she could see the advantages of gas.

'Don't let the toast burn!' called Simon.

Immediately she withdrew the toasting fork and eased the bread off the fork with a butter knife and then buttered the toast while it was warm before toasting and buttering another slice for Simon. She then ate her toast before pouring two cups of tea and making two more slices of toast for them.

Then Grace switched off the wireless and did a quick tidy round before taking her purse from a drawer in the sideboard, as well as picking up Fergie's ball, and an oilcloth shopping bag. She then removed her straw sunhat from a peg in the lobby and led the way to the front door, carrying Fergie. She placed the dog at the foot of the bath chair, and helped Simon outside and with the help of a passing male neighbour, managed to get him into the bath chair. Grace then set off pushing the chair up the street in the direction of West Derby Road and Newsham Park, thinking to go to the park first, and then the shops on the way home.

Grace could feel the warm sun on her bare arms despite the early hour and called out a good morning to a neighbour who was out brushing her front step. She did not stop until she reached the park. Already there were some young men playing cricket on the grass. Simon mentioned that England were playing Australia and wondered aloud how England were doing. Grace had no idea, so remained silent on the subject, but asked if Simon would like to stop for a while and watch the match. He shrugged and then nodded, so she brought the bath chair to a standstill.

They watched the game for a while, and then Grace took Fergie from Simon and threw his ball for him. This game went on for twenty minutes, then Grace brought it to an end by taking the ball and giving Fergie a dog biscuit and Simon a chocolate digestive. She had one as well and produced a lemonade bottle full of water from her bag before she sat on the grass to enjoy the sunshine. She looked up at Simon.

'Say when you want to move on. We can go on to the boating lake. I brought some crusts to feed the ducks.'

'I like the ducks, but I haven't fed them since Christmas Day a few years back when the lake was frozen over. I felt sorry for them slipping on the ice, even though Dad and me couldn't help laughing because they looked so comical, like something out of a cartoon at the flickers. I hadn't seen him laugh like that for ages.'

She said, 'You like cartoons?'

He nodded. 'Felix the Cat is my favourite, although I like all the Loony Tunes' characters. It must be brilliant to be able to draw and think up storylines.'

She said, 'It definitely takes a special talent. Do you like drawing?'

He nodded. 'Dad thinks I could be a draughtsman.'

'He doesn't want you to follow in his footsteps in the building industry?'

'No, he says it's hard – physical work. He wants me to have an easier life than he's had.'

Grace resumed their earlier conversation. 'What would he think about you being a cartoonist?'

'You mean as in cartoons in the newspapers and comics or animated cartoons?'

'I suppose the animated cartoonists started out as cartoonists in comics and newspapers originally,' she said. 'I think film-making altogether is incredible. When you think it's not that long ago since the only moving pictures were those ones you could see at a magic lantern show.'

Simon looked thoughtful and she handed him some water which he drank thirstily before saying, 'Shall we go and feed the ducks then?'

Without further ado, Fergie resumed his place on Simon's lap in the bath chair and Grace steered them onto the path that led to the bridge over the boating lake. There weren't many people rowing, but there were some ducks and Canada geese which made a beeline for them as soon as several morsels of their bread crusts hit the water. The birds had not received such largesse for a long time as most families ate their bread down to the last crumb in these difficult times. But with only herself and her father, Grace had always managed to save some scraps for the birds, having a soft spot for sparrows and pigeons as well as ducks.

Grace was enjoying herself not only because the sun was shining, the park looked lovely and she was having a break from housework, but because she had found her conversation with Simon interesting. She had wondered whether they would both find each other's company boring, but it appeared not, and she had discovered a different side to the boy's father. She would have liked to have seen Ben laughing at the ducks. Had it been Simon or Ben who had suggested a walk in the park on Christmas Day, both of them needing to leave the house which lacked a woman's touch on that special day? She wondered what they had eaten, most likely it would not have been a traditional dinner with all the trimmings. That thought led her on to thinking about Dougie and what kind of Christmas he would have Down Under. Hopefully, he would have made some close friends by then and found a job, as it was four or so months off. Of course, he would meet other emigrants on the voyage. Would he get used to being without her or would he regret their parting?

Grace was interrupted from her musings by a loud splash, and Simon shouting, 'Dog overboard!' She glanced at the boy and her startled eyes met his worried ones. He pointed through the metal bars of the railings to the lake and she leaned over and gazed down and saw Fergie scaring the ducks away as he paddled in the water. One of the geese, though, refused to give way and aimed a peck at him. He yelped and looked for a way to escape.

'Damn and blast!' exploded Grace. 'How did he end up in the water?'

'Sorry, he wriggled out and through the railings and must have overbalanced on the parapet,' retorted Simon. 'I had my arms folded and he was balanced on them. He's not going to drown, though. He's doggy-paddling.'

'He still has to climb out of the water and he only has short legs,' Grace said crossly, bending to put on the brake of the bath chair. But she was in such a hurry that she did not realise she had not put the brake on properly until she glanced back as she made her way down to the water's edge. She quickly changed direction though when she realised the bath chair was moving down the other side of the bridge and picking up speed. Grace was running so fast down the other side of the bridge that she felt in danger of losing her balance and landing flat on her face. She noticed that fortunately there was a man heading towards the bridge and he looked poised to seize hold of the bath chair and bring it to a halt, thank God! He was also with a woman who then took control of the chair. Grace recognised Milly as she got closer, but she could still not stop herself as she drew level with them, only for the man to grab her by the arm and bring her to a swinging halt.

Even so she almost toppled over, he steadied her, holding her by both arms. Panting, Grace sagged against him and tried to get her breath back. Eventually, her breathing eased, she gasped, 'Thank you, there could have been a couple of nasty accidents if you hadn't helped out.'

'It was my good deed for the day,' he said, grinning down at her.

He seemed familiar, but it was not until Milly said, 'Well done, Kyle!' that Grace recognised him as a friend of Milly's and her husband, Jimmy. Kyle was also a volunteer at the Seaman's Orphanage, located not far from the park. He had married one of Grace's old neighbours, Jane Fraser, a few years back. Grace had been friendly with her, and despite Kyle and Jane moving to a bigger house overlooking the park on Newsham Drive, she had tried to keep up with Jane every few months or so with Milly, even though Dougie was not in favour of her visiting a woman she had come to know through Milly who was half-Irish and was friends with Jane's brother, a journalist and his wife Anne. Dougie did not like journalists or the Irish.

Grace glanced in the direction of Simon. 'You all right?' she asked.

His eyes were sparkling. 'I'm fine. It was a bit scary, but exciting. We'd better not mention it to Dad, though.' He paused. 'What about Fergie?'

'Oh hell!' cried Grace, freeing herself from Kyle's hold. 'I'd better go and rescue him.' She hurried over the bridge and down the other side and through the shrubbery to the lake where she could see Fergie a short distance away. She called him and clicked her fingers. The dog spotted her almost immediately and paddled furiously away from the pursuing goose towards his mistress. As he drew nearer, Grace stretched out, but he was just out of reach. She edged closer and felt herself over-reaching. She managed to seize hold of his collar, but her centre of gravity shifted as she grabbed him and her arms went under the water up to her elbows as her shoes slid in the mud on the bank. She swore even as cheers rang out on the bridge. Again, she felt herself seized and dragged away by two pairs of hands. Before she could express her thanks, she heard a familiar feminine voice say, 'It's a good job it was only the dog in the water, and not Simon.'

Grace looked up at Milly and Kyle. 'Did you see all that happened?'

Milly nodded. 'Simon is mortified.'

'So, he should be,' panted Grace, placing Fergie on the ground where he proceeded to shake himself, causing the three of them to step back hastily. 'Have you seen the front of my frock?' she added, gazing down at the muddied garment in dismay.

'You should have held him away from you by the scruff of his neck,' said Kyle.

'He was shivering, and I instinctively pulled him in,' said Grace. 'Anyway, I'm going to have to go back home and change. I'll have to fetch Simon first, though.'

The three of them hurried back up to the bridge with a whining Fergie at Grace's heels. Simon greeted them with a shout and the words, 'I never thought this morning was going to be so exciting.'

'Neither did I,' said Grace tersely. 'Now we're going to head for home. I need to clean myself up, change, and have a cup of tea.'

Once again, she thanked Kyle for his help and taking a good grip of the handle on the bath chair set off through the park, trying to appear oblivious to the curious stares she was receiving from passers-by. Fergie was on his lead now, and if he slowed down, she dragged him along until they reached the main road where she lifted him up and placed him in the bath chair. As she turned left into Whitefield Road, Grace remembered she needed a few things from the Co-op; she did not feel like going home and then coming out again after the morning's adventures. She dithered outside, knowing that she would have to explain her bedraggled appearance to the staff who all knew her. She took a deep breath and went inside, having decided to cut the story down to just rescuing Fergie from the lake.

By the time Ben arrived to pick up Simon, Grace had calmed down and was able to laugh with Simon over what had happened. She was reminded again of how much she had enjoyed his company in the park before the near disaster and decided she would like children of her own one day. Now she and Simon had forgiven each other for their mistakes and were working together on a jigsaw of a London street scene when the knocker sounded. Grace invited Ben in for a cup of tea, but he declined, saying there was a job he needed to do back home. He asked after their day and Grace told him they had been to the park and watched a game of cricket. She felt slightly guilty about not telling him the whole truth, but as Simon had warned her to keep it quiet, she decided not to go against him, as Ben was very protective of his son. As she waved them off, she felt quite restored, and called out cheerfully, 'See you the day after tomorrow!'

But the following evening Ben turned up alone on her doorstep. His expression was such that Grace knew that somehow he had found out what else had happened at the lake. She invited him inside, and at first, he appeared reluctant to accept until she said, 'I refuse to discuss matters with you on the doorstep and have the neighbours listening in.'

He followed her silently into the kitchen. She bid him sit down, but he remained standing, so Grace stayed standing as well to face him. 'So, to what do I owe the pleasure of a visit from you?'

'I'm sure you can guess,' he replied in a tight voice.

She said lightly, 'The episode on the bridge in the park.'

'I can guess why you kept it from me,' he said, running a hand through his dark hair.

'Why was that?' she asked, leaning against the table.

'You behaved irresponsibly. My son could have been badly hurt.'

'I know, and the thought almost frightens me to death. Thank God, he wasn't hurt at all, but seemed to enjoy the experience.'

'No thanks to you,' Ben said quietly.

She flushed. 'Who told you about it?'

'Jimmy mentioned it this morning at work, he thought I knew.'

'So, Simon kept quiet.' Grace moved away from the table and sat down, thinking Milly must have told her husband about it. 'Accidents happen.' She toyed with her fingers.

'I know that,' Ben said fiercely. 'But it's obvious that taking my son out in that chair is too much for you.'

Grace glared at him. 'I agree it's no piece of cake, but everything was going fine and we were getting on well

41

until I heard a splash and I saw that Fergie was in the water.'

'How did that happen?'

'I suggest you ask Simon,' Grace said in a low voice.

'I will! Perhaps it's best if he stays at home in future.'

'You mean all on his own, all day? What if he fell and lay there by himself? And even if he wasn't injured, he can't go without food or drink!'

'I can go home for lunch and check up on him.'

Grace hugged herself and said coolly, 'Won't that be a rush for you?'

'I'll cope,' he replied.

'I'll see you out then, shall I?'

'Want to get rid of me, do you?' he said, making a move towards the lobby.

'I don't mean to be rude – I'm only thinking of Simon all on his own. Has he had his tea?'

'I'll cook it when I get back. I wanted to have a word with you first.'

She stared at him disbelievingly and almost offered to cook for him. 'What was the rush? It's not as if I was leaving the country.'

'Simon would have tried to get me to change my mind. He likes you, your dad and Fergie.'

'I'm sure you could have withstood his pleas,' she said, a smile creeping into her voice. 'We like him, too. Please, let him come and see us?'

'Don't you start,' he said ruefully. 'He's aware you like him and he'll go on and on just like his mother used to when she wanted her own way.'

'Until she wore you down, I suppose,' said Grace, warming to him but determined not to go on and on.

'I shouldn't have brought her into this conversation. I'd best go.'

'Goodnight. Give my best to Simon. I wish things could have worked out. Dad will be home tomorrow and Simon was so good for him.' Just like a surrogate grandson, she mused.

'Goodnight,' Ben said, hurrying away.

She watched him go, and stuck her tongue out at his retreating back, until he turned a corner into the wide entry that ran between their two streets. Then she went back inside and switched on the wireless, thinking she was going to miss Simon – spending the day with him had stopped her from dwelling too much on Dougie, just as her father had suggested it might. It had also made her realise she would like a child of her own, but Dougie not answering her question about children almost convinced her that if she wanted children of her own, she was going to have to look elsewhere, despite his suggestion in the past that he get her pregnant in order to force the parents to agree to an early wedding.

Chapter 4

Grace overslept the following morning as it had been some time before she had nodded off because she had been angry and disappointed. Her mind was too active, going over and over that conversation with Ben.

In the bright light of the morning it all seemed nonsense and she was annoyed to have lost sleep over Ben not giving her a second chance to help the boy. Remembering that her father would arrive home later that day, she climbed out of bed and went downstairs. She let Fergie out into the yard, paid a visit to the lavatory down the backyard herself, washed at the sink in the back kitchen, dressed and brushed her hair quickly and made herself a jam butty before pouring the last of yesterday's milk into a cup and letting Fergie back in and feeding him. Then she cleared out the grate and set the fire ready to light late afternoon to cook a meal for herself and her father.

She did a quick sweep of the floor, a light dust and polish of the parlour, before making a shopping list and checking the money in her purse. She then clipped Fergie's lead on and left the house. After taking the dog for a walk, she planned on dropping in at Milly's to see if she wanted any shopping. She also wanted to see if Simon was at her house for an extra day since Ben didn't think she could be trusted to look after him today.

44

Her suspicions were confirmed, and to Grace's satisfaction she was welcomed into Milly's home and found
Simon partaking of orange juice and a digestive biscuit
in the kitchen. He attempted to half-rise as she entered
the room. Grace unclipped Fergie's leash, and the dog,
wagging his stubby tail, went over to the boy.

'Cup of tea and slice of toast?' asked Milly.

'Thanks,' said Grace. 'How are you this morning?'

'Wishing the baby would come,' Milly replied. 'Being
so big and what with the heatwave still with us I'm finding
moving about exhausting.'

'I could make the tea myself,' offered Grace.

'No. I tell myself the baby will get a move on if I try
and keep busy.' Milly lumbered into the back kitchen and
lit a ring on the gas stove and put on the kettle.

Grace followed her. 'How are you going to cope with
Simon today all day?'

'I had Jimmy buy a comic from the newsagents. He
came back with two. One is a recent publication, in
colour, called *Famous Funnies*. He was reading it himself
last night. By the way, I'm sorry I let the cat out of the bag
by telling Jimmy what happened in the park. Ben told me
when he asked me to take Simon today. I didn't realise it
was such a big thing, it was quite funny really, when you
think about it.'

'That's all right,' Grace said with a shrug. 'I should have
made certain the brake was on the chair, instead of being
in such a rush. Anyway, I can help you with Simon if you
like? I enjoyed his company.'

'I never liked boys when I was a kid,' said Milly. 'I had
this cousin, Liam, I couldn't stand, not that I saw much
of him. But he was rough and used to tease the life out of
me when Mam took me to visit his family.'

'You're like me, an only,' Grace said. 'How will you feel if your baby is a boy?'

'I'll love it whatever sex it is,' replied Milly, keeping quiet about her two younger half-brothers. 'I'd like to have more children and I think it's nice for a girl to have a sister. Besides which, my mother-in-law is wanting a granddaughter. Although, she does say that the most important thing is that the baby is healthy.'

'Agreed,' said Grace, moving towards the stove as the kettle began to boil.

Once the tea was poured out, they returned to the main kitchen and sat down. Simon said, 'Grace, did you finish the jigsaw we were doing?'

She shook her head. 'I was hoping you'd be back to help me, but your dad appears to believe you won't be safe with me.'

'He's overprotective since Mam died,' apologised Simon.

'Your falling out of that tree has to have something to do with it,' Milly said mildly.

Simon blushed to the tips of his ears. 'It was a dare,' he mumbled.

The two women sighed. Then Grace said, 'I remember playing Truth, Dare, Command or Promise in the street with other kids when I was young.'

'Kids have little sense of danger,' Milly said breathlessly.

Grace stared at her. 'Are you all right?'

Milly did not reply but put down her cup and went slowly into the back kitchen. Grace exchanged glances with Simon before following Milly, who was over by the sink and taking deep breaths.

'Something's up,' said Grace, then she noticed Milly was standing in a puddle.

'My waters have broken,' she said, gnawing her lower lip. 'That means my labour has started or will do soon.'

Immediately Grace felt herself panicking. 'What can I do?'

'Fetch the midwife and get word to Jimmy. His boss's phone number is on the calendar above the sideboard in the kitchen.'

'And the midwife's address?'

'That's on the calendar, too.'

'What about Simon? Will I take him to our house when I get back? Dad will be home later today.'

'Yeah, whatever you think,' gasped Milly. Grace helped her back into the kitchen and into a chair while she rattled off to Simon that the baby was on its way and that she was going for the midwife. She then grabbed her handbag and the calendar from the wall and ran out of the house. Grace did not bother closing the front door after her, but left it ajar, and headed for Richmond Terrace where the midwife, Maggie, lived, praying that the woman would be in. Luck was with her, and within less than half an hour, Maggie was on her way to Milly's while Grace headed for the telephone at the Post Office on Breckfield Road North. Her fingers shook as she removed pennies from her purse and dialled the works' number. She managed to put the coins in the slot without dropping any of them. A woman's voice answered, which threw her for a moment as she was expecting a man. For a moment she was lost for words as she couldn't remember Jimmy's surname.

'Who is that?' said the woman. 'How can I help you?'

'I'm phoning on behalf of a neighbour to inform her husband Jimmy that she's gone into labour,' said Grace, her voice shaky with nerves.

'What is his surname?'

'It's slipped my mind,' wailed Grace. 'But he's a carpenter.'

'What's his address, and what's the wife's Christian name?' asked the secretary patiently.

'They live in Lombard Street and her name is Milly,' said Grace in a rush.

'Righteo!' said the secretary. 'I remember her now from the works' Christmas party.'

Grace heard the receiver go down and sagged against the wall of the post office. She rested there for several minutes before leaving the post office and hurrying to Milly's house.

She found Simon alone, struggling to light the gas ring beneath a kettle. 'Where's Milly and the midwife? And what are you doing?' she asked.

'The midwife asked me to boil some water,' he said. 'She's upstairs with Milly.'

'Didn't she realise your wrists were in plaster?'

'She scarcely looked at me,' he said.

'Well, I'll take over now and afterwards we're going to our house… you can help me finish the jigsaw. My father will be home this afternoon and the pair of you can keep each other company while I do the shopping,' she said.

'What about what Dad said?' he asked.

'If he's any sense he'll realise that while Milly is upstairs giving birth you'd be best out of the way, and that means you coming home with me is the wisest option,' Grace replied.

He nodded. 'I want to go with you. Anyway, once the baby is born, I can't come here.'

Grace told Maggie to let Milly know that she was taking Simon home with her. By then it was lunch time and they were on the way out when Jimmy arrived home in a rush. He drew Grace aside and in a low voice told her that he had informed Ben that Milly was in labour and that Grace was the person to let him know and fetch the midwife. 'He had thought of coming back with me and taking Simon home and then rush back to work, but I told him to leave the boy to you and fetch him this evening.'

'He obviously went along with what you suggested,' Grace said.

Jimmy nodded. 'It's difficult for him being father and mother to the boy, but I told him if he doesn't let go a bit, he'll have a rebellious son on his hands.'

'Thanks,' said Grace. 'I like Simon's company and Dad will be home today, so they can have a chat.'

'I told him what he needs is a woman in his life.'

Grace stiffened, realising she did not want another woman in Ben's life and being a mother to Simon. 'And what did he say to that?'

'That he knows he should marry again for Simon's sake, but she needs to be the right woman, so he was taking his time.'

'Poor Simon,' she sighed.

'Hmm!' Jimmy touched her arm. 'I'd best be going. I bet the midwife will chase me out of the bedroom, but I need to be on hand in case I'm needed to fetch the doctor.'

Grace joined Simon who had been leaning against the fence around the small front area and with Fergie on the leash, arm in arm they slowly made their way to her father's house. Norman was there to welcome them and had put a match to the fire and had the kettle on. Grace explained where she had been and that she would have to go out again to the shops for tea things, but she made a pot of tea before leaving her father and Simon huddled over the jigsaw as her father talked about life at sea and the countries he had visited. She was so glad her father was around more. She had always enjoyed his stories as a youngster.

Later, after tea, when Ben called to pick up Simon, he brought the news that Milly had given birth to twins, a boy and a girl. 'Apparently there are twins in her family,' he said with a slow smile. 'Mother and babies are doing fine, and Jimmy has been in touch with his mother and she's already on her way over from New Brighton to lend a hand.'

'I'll pop in tomorrow on my way to work and see if there's anything I can do to help,' said Grace. 'Besides, I'm looking forward to seeing the twins!'

'You like babies?' said Ben, as he stood on the doorstep.

She hesitated. 'I've never had much to do with them. I can't see them being of much interest until they're older. Now your Simon is at an interesting age.'

Ben agreed, 'I just wish his mother was alive to see him.'

She thought he sounded as if he had a frog in his throat, and remembered what Jimmy had told her about his reluctance to marry just anyone. She also thought of her own mother and even her aunt Polly to whom she had been able to turn to for advice as she grew up. Of course, it was different for a son, and naturally it depended on what age a child lost their mother, in terms of how they coped with such a terrible loss. The death of a wife had seemed even more traumatic to her father, just as it appeared so for Ben.

'I'm sure she'd have been proud of him,' Grace said.

'I hope so, I've done the best I can,' he said. 'Although, I doubt anyone can quite replace the loving touch of his mother. Although, he scarcely remembers what she was like.'

'Surely you have photographs of her?' said Grace.

He nodded. 'But he doesn't appear to feel anything inside here,' he thumped his chest, 'when he looks at them.'

'You could be expecting too much of him,' Grace said softly. 'He was so young and the ties he had with her were in their infancy and hadn't had a chance to grow into something deeper. Relationships take time to develop. Do you talk to him about her?'

A shutter seemed to come down over his face. 'I think I'd best leave,' he said. 'I'm sorry I was so rude yesterday. Thank you for keeping an eye on Simon.'

'The pleasure was all mine,' she said gently, aware that she might have said the wrong thing. 'I'll fetch Simon.'

Simon came hopping down the lobby as soon as Grace called him. 'Can we have fish and chips from the chippy, Dad?' he asked.

Ben nodded. 'We'll share a portion and make butties.'

He placed an arm about his son and the boy waved to Grace from the doorway. Fergie followed them out and so did Grace. The dog would have followed the boy into Ben's truck, but Grace called him back. The dog did not respond immediately to her summons and only obeyed the touch of Grace's hand on his head when she went after him. She stood watching father and son until the boy was settled in the passenger seat. He waved again and she returned his wave and called, 'God bless and sweet dreams,' – before returning to the house.

When she entered the kitchen, her father said, 'Ben seemed a touch grumpy this evening. I came out to say hello and overheard you talking on the doorstep.'

'He misses his wife,' said Grace unthinkingly.

'More reason to put an act on and smile. He has a good son there and should show him more affection and appreciation.' Norman then took out his pipe and went through the process of pressing a wad of tobacco in the pipe's bowl before lighting it and settled back in his chair with that evening's *Echo*.

'Have you seen the photo of the King opening the Mersey Tunnel?' he said.

Grace groaned. 'I forgot to go and watch what with Milly going into labour.'

'Understandable,' said Norman.

Fergie followed Grace over and settled on the old man's feet as Grace stared at the newspaper photo of the crowds watching King George V and the opening ceremony. 'I did tell you Milly's had twins?'

Norman smiled up at her. 'Congratulate her and Jimmy for me when you see her.'

'I'm planning on dropping in on my way home from work tomorrow,' said Grace.

'What about Simon? Milly won't be able to look after him now.'

'Ben will have to make other plans,' Grace wondered if she would ever see Simon again. She remembered that she would be going to the pageant, *The Turn of the Tide*, tomorrow evening and it was just possible she might see him and his father there.

Chapter 5

Grace could not wait to leave her workplace at the dentist's house the next day. When she had entered the building, there had been a surprising number of children with their mothers in the waiting room, which upset her as she hated that children should be having their second teeth pulled – their teeth should have lasted them until they were much older. Yet Grace wasn't really surprised, she knew of women who should have had more sense, but who were having all their teeth extracted under gas, including teeth that were not decaying, simply because they believed a set of false teeth looked more attractive and also didn't cause toothache.

Grace stopped on the way home to buy eggs and bacon for the evening meal; she looked in on Milly and her babies on the way back. She was shown up to the bedroom by Jimmy's mother, who had been widowed during the last war. Milly was breastfeeding one of the babies while her mother-in-law was bottle-feeding the other. It was explained to Grace that next feed the twins would be changed around, so that both would benefit from the mother's milk. Grace admired the tiny babies and offered her help over the coming weeks. She handed over a congratulation card from herself and her father before leaving, thinking she would buy a baby present at the babywear shop on Breck Road tomorrow. Then Grace hurried home to cook tea before rushing to get ready to go and see the play.

–

The heatwave was still with them, so Grace chose to wear a floral print dress with blue and red small flowers on a white background. It had puffed sleeves, a high waist and a skirt which flared about the hem to her knees. She had bought it with a gift of money her father had given her last Easter. Her gloves, handbag and small hat, which she set at an angle, were maroon, and her shoes were brown and beige with sturdy heels and double ankle straps. She thought to take a cushion with her and left the house at just before seven o'clock. Grace hurried to the tram stop. The play was due to start at eight o'clock, so she had plenty of time to get there, but she was feeling quite excited because the nearest she had been to seeing an out-of-doors entertainment was the Punch and Judy show that set up regularly in the summer on Saturdays at St George's plateau in Lime Street.

She arrived at the side passage to Exchange Flags behind the Town Hall at twenty to eight and joined a queue and was soon in a seat with time to spare. The Liverpool City Police Band were already playing cheerful music and the Philharmonic Choir were in place. Grace watched eagerly as the band ceased playing and the audience hushed as two traders arrived in a coracle on the stage, which was open to the crowd watching on four sides. The men unloaded a variety of goods from the boat and set out a display of exotic fruit, ornaments and skins. Then for several minutes she was distracted by the sound of more people entering by the way she had come in. She glanced in that direction in the hope of seeing Ben and

Simon, but she could see no sign of them and her spirits fell.

The sound of a horn drew her attention to the stage again. More actors had entered, and the audience started to laugh as a small girl appeared and stole some fruit from under their noses. A woman pointed to an animal skin and her male companion began to argue with the trader and they tussled for possession of the skin; a free-for-all developed on the stage; and a dragon appeared unexpectedly frightening the rest of the players away. By the time the scene had finished, Grace was in stitches.

As the stage emptied, the police band began to play rousing music. Feeling a bit restless from sitting as the night air was still quite close, Grace stood up to have a look around to see if she could spot anyone she knew in the crowd. She thought she might see her neighbours and it would be nice to chat to someone. She suddenly spotted Simon at the end of a row of seats ahead of her. He had obviously seen her before now, because he waved enthusiastically before being checked by his father. Grace was surprised to then receive a friendly nod from Ben, a feeling which was quickly followed by a sense of relief, as she disliked being out of friends with people, as a rule.

The music then changed again and the crowd settled to watch the next scene as a backdrop appeared painted with a dockside and distant sailing ships. The choir started singing 'Blow the Man Down' as townswomen appeared on the stage to affectionately greet some newly arrived sailor sweethearts. Grace found herself humming along to the popular sea shanties and hymns as the drama unfolded on stage. The time flew by, and soon the stage cleared and an interval was announced. There was a buzz of conversation around her and some people began to walk about. Grace applauded the departing players vigorously, thinking of Dougie and his long-distance sea voyage. She was sad that he had missed seeing this treat. She was filled with admiration, not only for the performers, but for the play's author – it felt such a tribute to Liverpool's past given that the growth of the city had been made possible by its link with the sea trade and foreign lands. Grace was impatient to see the second half, and hoped Ben and Simon were enjoying the entertainment as much as she was. She decided to try and see them after the play was over, so she that could talk it over with them.

Soon the second half began. A cheer went up from the audience when a small stowaway aboard a ship was revealed to be Mickey Mouse. The actor playing the sea captain was very angry, but Grace was delighted when a trembling Mickey was made to marry none other than a heavily disguised Minnie Mouse! The Three Little Pigs and the Big Bad Wolf then made an appearance, but the play concluded on a more serious note, with a tableau depicting the Mersey Tunnel and the unloading of merchandise such as oil, tobacco and wool, set to the music of 'The Yeomen of England'. As Grace stood at the end for 'God Save the King', she found herself thinking of Dougie again, and wondered if he might have changed his mind about Liverpool and the opportunities promised by the Mersey Tunnel if he had not sailed for Australia when he did. Her thoughts were interrupted as the people in the seats next to her began to leave. Grace gathered her belongings and made her way to the exit gap. Any hope of finding Ben or Simon was gone, as there was such a crush of people. Grace felt worried for Simon in such a crowd, but quickly reasoned that Ben could carry him if need be. Still humming one of the sea shanties, Grace slowly made her way back to the tram stop. Suddenly she heard her name being called. She thought she recognised a truck a yard or so away through the lines of people, but couldn't be sure.

'Grace! Would you like a lift home?' Ben called.

Given the turn of their last meeting, Grace was surprised by such chivalry, but didn't waste any time hurrying to the other side of the truck.

Chapter 6

Grace was wedged against Simon on the wide seat, on his other side, Ben was making ready to drive off.

'I spotted you, and told Dad it would be gentlemanly to offer you a lift home,' said Simon.

'And I'm very grateful,' replied Grace. 'The tram home would have been so busy with all those people. Did you enjoy the pageant? I enjoyed it. It was a laugh, wasn't it?'

Simon nodded enthusiastically. 'I wasn't bored at all, although Dad told me it was a kind of history of Liverpool and its trading links. I was a bit confused because of the dragon… unless that came from Wales. Them being alive in the olden days and that's why they have one on their flag,' he elaborated.

'Now there's a thought,' said Grace, smiling.

'Some Welsh chieftains were called pendragons,' said Ben.

'But how far does that go to explaining why there was a dragon in the play?' Grace said. 'Unless it symbolised a Welsh pirate raider long ago?'

'I'm part Welsh,' Ben said. 'And I object to that insinuation.'

'I have Welsh blood, too,' said Grace. 'Let's be honest, though, my dad told me in days gone by the English, Welsh, Scots and Irish all made raids beyond their own borders on their close neighbours, until we all settled down and intermarried and traded goods with each other peacefully.'

'Thank goodness,' said Ben.

'What did you think of Micky and Minnie Mouse making an appearance?' asked Ben.

'As well as the Big Bad Wolf and the three little pigs,' Simon said, laughing.

'I'd say they weren't only there to amuse the children,' Grace said drily, 'most likely they made an appearance to remind people of popular films made in Hollywood.'

'We'll pass at least three picture houses on the way home,' said Simon. 'I love the flickers.'

'Me too,' Grace said.

'The growth of the film industry doesn't come without a cost,' said Ben.

'I suppose you mean the loss of some theatres,' responded Grace. 'The Olympia on West Derby Road to name one – it's been converted into a picture house called the Palladium. I'd say, though, that there's an equal number of theatres and picture palaces in Liverpool.'

'I'll take your word for it,' Ben said as they passed the Baptist chapel on the corner of Shaw Street and headed towards Brunswick Road that led into West Derby Road where the Royal Hippodrome theatre was situated.

'I wonder how long it'll be before that becomes a picture house,' said Simon a few minutes later as they passed by.

'Let's drop the subject,' said his father. 'I for one don't want to be thinking of being inside either building in this weather. I'd much prefer sitting on the grass in the park, listening to a brass band playing.'

'Me too,' said Grace. 'I suppose in Australia they spend a lot more time outdoors in the evenings because their weather is like it is here now, but all of the time.'

'What decided your young man to emigrate?' asked Ben, glancing at her.

'The Great Depression... he thought Liverpool was finished. I also reckon he was looking for excitement and to make his fortune,' Grace said slowly.

'What kind of adventure? And where do you fit into his desire for adventure? I'd have thought if he wanted to marry you, the idea would be to settle down together,' Ben said.

For a moment Grace could not think what to say, other than it was none of his business, although the truth of the matter hit home. To cover her confusion, she said brightly, 'Emigrating is a big adventure, don't you think?'

'I suppose some people would see it like that, but I'd say it depends on what kind of life one is going to be living when one gets there. In the last century, of course, lots of blokes went off to Australia because of the gold being discovered and they wanted to get rich. Some went because they didn't have much going on here and were just plain dissatisfied with their lot at home, being told what to do by the toffs and such. Then there were those who wanted to own their own land and farm it, to raise sheep or cattle.'

She was surprised by the detail he went into and murmured, 'You sound like you've given it a lot of thought.'

'I considered emigrating myself when I was a lot younger, but things happened, and as you can see, I'm still here.'

Grace thought sadly about his mother and brother, of his marrying and his wife dying young, and him having to rear his son alone. She became aware that the truck was slowing down and realised that they were almost home.

'I found our chat interesting,' she said, fumbling for the handle to open the door. 'Thanks for the lift! See you both around. Goodnight, God bless.'

'Goodnight, Grace,' said Ben.

'Goodnight,' chimed Simon. 'See you soon.'

'That would be fun,' said Grace, stepping down from the truck and hurrying away. But she did not hear the truck move off until Fergie barked and came rushing to greet her as she opened the front door. The thought crossed her mind that Ben was being a gentleman and making certain she was safely inside the house before driving off, and it made her smile.

Chapter 7

After not seeing any sign of Ben or Simon for a couple of days, and having spent most of the morning doing house-work, Grace thought to take Fergie for a walk around the block before having lunch and going to work. She then decided to drop in on Milly to see how she and the twins were faring. She was also a bit intrigued about what Ben had confided in her last night about the thwarted possibilities of his youth, and she wondered if she could ask Jimmy if he knew anything about Ben's background as a young man. Was it after his mother had died that he had considered emigrating, only to change his mind after he met the girl who was to become his wife? When had she become sickly? Had there been a time when they had both planned to emigrate? Had he given up his dream of adventure in a new country for love of her?

When she arrived, Milly was in the process of tucking the twins in their pram, having already lowered the pram onto the step outside. Grace gazed down at the babies and felt a warmth rising in her chest. One was wearing a pale blue knitted helmet and the other a pink bonnet trimmed with cream lace.

'Gosh, they're so gorgeous,' said Grace. 'I bet your mother-in-law won't want to leave them and go home.'

'She's no choice but to go tomorrow, she has to get back to her job, it's only part-time, but still,' informed

Milly. 'Besides which me mam's coming over from Dublin later today with my stepfather and half-brother.' She began to push the pram along the pavement in the direction of West Derby Road.

'You never talk about your half-brothers,' said Grace.

'That's because my relationship with them is complicated,' Milly said. 'Anyway, how are you? Did you enjoy the play the other night?'

'Yeah, it was marvellous, and guess who I saw there?' Grace's eyes were merry.

'I'm no good at guessing,' said Milly. 'But Jimmy did tell me that Ben planned on taking Simon to see it.'

'He gave me a lift home in his truck,' Grace chuckled.

'So, you and Ben are not at odds, anymore?'

'Well, he and Simon enjoyed the play as well, so we had something easy to talk about, and then we got on to the subject of travel and emigration. Apparently, he had considered emigrating himself when he was young.'

Milly pulled a face. 'You consider him old now?'

'I reckon he's thirty-ish.'

'That's not old,' said Milly.

Grace said, 'He's ten years older than I am and he seems a bit staid.'

'Well, he is a widower and has a child to bring up,' Milly said. 'You surprise me, Grace. He has responsibilities, and even before he married, his life wasn't easy. At least he's reliable.'

'You mean not like Dougie.'

Milly flushed. 'I didn't say that.'

'It's what you meant. I know what you think of him… with his gambling and the like. It's not really his fault, others cause trouble for him…' Grace finished weakly.

'Yeah, but it just slipped out. I didn't mean to hurt you.'

Grace wriggled her shoulders. 'I know. I also know that Ben hasn't had an easy life. He told me about his brother.'

Milly looked surprised. 'How did that come about? Jimmy told me it's something he hardly ever mentions.'

Grace felt embarrassed. 'I wish I hadn't started this. But I suppose it's to do with wanting to help Simon. I feel sorry for the lad, that he has no fun. I was even wondering before whether Ben would agree to my suggesting that Fergie could keep the boy company part of the day when I'm at work.'

'I'm not sure that's a good idea after what happened in the park.'

'If Simon hadn't gone climbing a tree, it wouldn't have happened at all – accidents happen.'

'You can't blame Ben for being overprotective.'

'I don't know why I care so much,' said Grace fiercely.

Milly said, 'It's probably because it's filling a gap in your life with Dougie away – anyway, when did you last see Dougie's mother and your cousins?'

'Not since we waved Dougie off.'

'Have you been in touch with them?'

'No, but they haven't been in touch with me neither.'

Grace knew that was just an excuse, because if the truth was known, she dreaded going to visit the house where she had spent so much time with Dougie, knowing it would cause her to question her deepest feelings about Dougie. She gripped her hands tightly together, feeling guilty, and thinking how good her aunt Polly had been to her in the past. Grace was aware that she wasn't Polly's favourite person of late, but that's because her aunt thought the world of her son, and no one was ever going to be good enough for him.

'That's no excuse,' said Milly, pausing on the kerb, waiting for a couple of cyclists to go past.

'I know,' Grace hesitated. 'I'll drop in there after work and see how they're getting on.'

She bent over the pram and blew a couple of kisses at the babies before turning right and heading towards the shop to pick up some ingredients for a steak casserole that she planned to make for her employer's supper. She then made her way to the large Victorian terrace where she worked.

She did not need to use her key because the front door was open, and the vestibule door was unlocked. She could hear the sound of a dental drill from the waiting area, which made her shudder a little, so she wasted no time climbing the stairs to the upstairs flat, thinking as she did so that instead of being here she could have been with Dougie on a liner heading to the other side of the world, relaxing and playing deck games and they could be getting romantic under a bright moon at night, but would that mean he would expect sex even though they weren't married?

She set about making the bed and dusting and cleaning, thinking now about what Ben had told her about his having considered emigration after his mother had died. She found herself imagining a lonely Ben grieving for his mother and the brother who was missing, presumed dead, wanting to build himself a new life to help him overcome his loss. She wondered if he ever thought about how he would have missed out on having Simon if he had emigrated, having rejected the woman he fell in love with, even though later he was to lose her.

After Grace had washed up the crockery and cutlery from that morning and the night before, she put on the kettle and set about preparing the casserole. She thought of her father and wondered how he had felt after her mother had died and he had to choose between giving up the sea and finding a shore job, which would have been difficult at the time with the lack of jobs available, and care for his young daughter himself or hand her over to his sister-in-law whom he knew did not approve of him. If he hadn't had a relative to look after Grace, would he have married again?

Once the casserole was in the oven, she made a pot of tea and laid a tray with the tea set and a plate of biscuits for the dentist and his staff. She left the tea tray downstairs with Joan, the receptionist. Tired out by all the housework of the day, Grace returned upstairs, drank a restorative cuppa, and busied herself by tiding up behind her and washing the floor. Feeling rather peckish, she shouted a cheery goodbye to Joan as she left the building, intending to stop at the butcher's on her way home to get some meat for herself and her dad's tea.

Grace crossed the main road in Kensington and stopped outside a butcher's and stood for a while in the shade of the striped awning as she gazed in the window. She went inside and bought some chicken giblets, which were going cheap, as well as some bacon bits. Then, via more back streets, she reached Lodge Lane on the other side of which was Wavertree Park, with its lake and botanical gardens, which she had visited often with Dougie and his sisters when she had lived with her aunt Polly and her husband nearby. The day was warm, and Grace was feeling flushed, hot and tired, by the time she banged the knocker on her aunt's front door. She hoped her aunt was in, although if she was not, Grace knew that she could always use the key that hung on a string on the other side of the letterbox and put her meat in her aunt's meat safe.

She had not been waiting long when she heard footsteps coming down the lobby to the front door. 'Who is it?' called her aunt.

'Grace,' she replied.

'About time too,' said Polly, opening the front door. 'Did you forget the way?'

'Of course not! I've been busy.'

'Too busy to come and see your favourite aunt?'

'You're my only aunt and it's only been a few weeks,' Grace said. 'Can I come in? I've bought some meat and would like to put it in your meat safe, please?'

'I suppose so,' said Polly, holding the door wide open and standing aside. 'So, what have you been doing besides going to see the play at Exchange Flags?'

Grace's heart seemed to jiggle inside her chest, and she wondered who had seen her there to report back to her aunt. Feeling a bit strange, but not knowing why, she changed the subject.

'A friend, Milly, gave birth to twins, a boy and a girl. They're lovely. I was visiting her when she went into labour and had to go and fetch the midwife.'

'I'd love a grandchild,' murmured Polly.

'You need to say that to one of the girls,' Grace said. 'It's time at least your Marion was married. You're going to have a wait if you were depending on Dougie and me to provide you with one, since he's in Australia!'

'You don't have to remind me,' said Polly. 'Anyway, have you heard from our Dougie?'

'Just a postcard from Las Palmas. It didn't say much. I wish he'd sent it in an envelope with a letter.'

'Same here,' said Polly, going into the back kitchen. 'I'm his mother and deserve better than just a card of palm trees and a beach with a few lines of writing saying he's enjoying shipboard life and playing games on deck with several new acquaintances.'

Grace followed her, listening, while watching her put on the kettle. 'He said as much on mine.'

'His dad told him he should have applied for a job before he left,' complained Polly.

Grace remained silent, wondering why Dougie had not taken his father's advice. She was annoyed that he had not mentioned it to her. If Dougie had found himself a job before he set off, then her father might have given his permission for her to accompany him to Australia. It made her feel funny to think of that, but she couldn't place why that would be.

'So, did you enjoy the play?' Polly asked, returning to her earlier remark.

'It was great,' said Grace. 'I don't remember telling you that I was going – did Dad mention it to you?'

'I haven't seen your dad. It was my neighbour who noticed you, and saw you climbing into a truck driven by a man afterwards.'

'Oh, that was Ben who lives in the next street. He and his son were at the play and he offered me a lift home.' Grace flushed.

'Was his wife with him then?'

'Oh, he's a widower. His son had an accident, fell out of a tree and broke a few bones, so I've helped keep the boy company a couple of times as he's off school.'

Polly's lips compressed and she darted Grace a stern look. 'You don't want to be too helpful or he'll start expecting it.'

'I doubt it,' Grace said. 'He doesn't trust me to take proper care of Simon. He's very protective of him.'

'How did he lose his wife?'

'She was hit by a car. Ben works with my friend Milly's husband and it's through her that I met Ben's son, Simon. Milly's helping look after him, but I volunteered to give her a hand as she's got the twins to see to.' Grace paused and changed the subject. 'Anyway, I can't stay long. Dad is home again this evening, he's been gone a couple of days.'

'I was surprised when he showed up to see Dougie off,' said Polly.

'It was probably a spur of the moment thing,' said Grace, fiddling with a lock of hair.

'You really think so?' Polly sniffed as she opened a packet of custard creams.

'Are you thinking he was there just to make sure Dougie really left?' suggested Grace, feeling a bit affronted, as she took a biscuit from the plate.

'Well, let's be honest,' said Polly. 'Your dad has always been against you and my son making a match of it. As was I. Not that I could ever understand why you and Dougie would want to make a go of it – you were almost brought up as brother and sister. I still can't understand why he should want to marry you with you being so young or you him. Your relationship was far too close. Your mother wouldn't have approved.'

'But you're not going to stand in my way when the time comes for me to follow Dougie to Australia.' Grace retorted hotly. Although she felt ambivalent about going all the way to Australia herself, she felt duty-bound to defend Dougie's plan for her.

The older woman said, 'A lot could happen between now and your twenty-first birthday next spring, Grace.'

She shoved the cup and saucer across the table towards Grace. 'So, tell me about the babies. What did they weigh?'

'I don't remember exactly, although I thought one of them felt the same as a five-pound bag of spuds.'

'Big enough if one is giving birth to two babies. Our Dougie was eight pounds, two ounces. Such a gorgeous boy. Now you were only six pounds, four ounces, a fact that your mam was glad of, her only being petite.'

'I'm only petite,' said Grace. 'Anyway, enough of this talk. I'll drink me tea quick and get my meat out of the safe, then be on me way to get things ready for Dad.'

Within minutes she was on her way out. Her aunt followed her to the front door. 'Don't be a stranger,' said Polly. 'Your uncle and I do miss you.'

'Give him my love and the same to Marion and Beryl.' Grace pecked her aunt's cheek. 'Look after yourself.'

'And you,' Polly gave her a brief hug. 'And if you need any womanly advice, I'm here for you. I promised your mam I'd look out for you.'

'Thanks,' Grace blew her a kiss as she reached the pavement and wasted no time hurrying home.

—

By the time she arrived at the house her father was already home and standing at the sink washing and peeling potatoes before popping them in a saucepan of salted water on the wooden draining board.

'Where've you been?' He glanced at her hot face. 'You been rushing?'

She nodded. 'I thought I'd best go and see Aunt Polly.'

'You walked there and back, in the heat?'

She nodded. 'I went straight after work and felt in need of air.'

'So how is Polly?' he asked, lifting the pan, and carrying it into the kitchen and placing it on the fire.

'I was going to cook chicken and bacon bits,' she said, having followed him through into the kitchen, trailed by Fergie who was sniffing at her shopping bag.

'Chicken!' he exclaimed.

'It's only chicken giblets,' she said. 'Yer know, hearts, liver, the neck and that. With some scraps of bacon, barley and carrot and onion, it'll be tasty.'

'I bought some sausages,' said her father. 'I thought we could have sausage and mash.'

'All right, have it your way,' said Grace wearily, sitting down and easing off her shoes. 'I'll cook the giblets and bacon bits this evening, though, I don't want them going off in this weather. They'll be good in a soup what with the salt from the bacon.'

Her father stared down at her. 'Your mam used to make lovely giblet soup. Real tasty it was.'

'I wish I'd got to know her better, so I had more memories of her,' said Grace, getting up and setting the table for two. 'Aunt Polly hardly ever talks about her, although she mentioned her today. She was saying she'd like a grandchild.'

'Then she needs to get one of her girls off her hands. Give them a kick out of the door. It's not for you and Dougie to be worrying about, just now.'

'Let's be honest, Dad, there's not many options out there for them – there's still more women to men – despite it being sixteen years since the war's end, most available men are either too young or too old.'

'Or they're crippled physically, mentally or emotionally,' said her father.

She nodded, thinking of Ben and his brother again. 'It's a disgrace, so sad.'

'So, did Polly have anything to say about that boy of hers? Is he still causing mischief, although he's miles away?' Norman asked sharply.

Grace looked at him, surprised by his change in tone. Norman often got like this whenever he talked about Dougie, but he had never come out and said that he didn't like him.

'She's had a postcard the same as me – not a word about missing her – just that he's enjoying shipboard life and has made friends, same as he told me.'

Her father cleared his throat. 'Do you resent my not letting you go?'

'I understand your reasoning. I am your only child.'

'You're not answering my question,' Norman replied, looking at her closely.

'If you must know the truth, I'm glad you gave me some breathing space,' Grace said, twisting her hands together. 'Ever since Dougie and I started being a couple, I was expected to spend every spare minute I had with him, which meant I never got to make friends with anyone else really, other than Milly, but certainly no other fella in particular.'

Her father stared at her in astonishment. 'But if you're in love with someone, you want to spend as much time as you can with them.'

'That's what I've been told by girls when I was at school, but there were times when I wanted to be alone, or in the company of another fella to see what that was like. I mean, what do I really know about love? I need to be certain that what I feel towards Dougie is the real thing?' she paused, a little unsure to be finally putting her emotions into words. 'I mean people say that absence makes the heart grow fonder, so if that's true, my being parted from him should help me to sort out my feelings towards him, isn't that right, Dad?'

Norman scratched his head with the stem of his pipe. 'I wish your mother was here for you to talk to about this kind of stuff... I guess you can hardly discuss it with Polly. Dougie being her son whom she loves the bones of...'

Grace nodded.

'Are you missing Dougie at all?' asked her father.

'Of course! There were times when I loved being in his company, but I'm finding that I'm still enjoying life without him being here. Is that wrong?'

'It's early days,' said Norman. 'And you've plenty of time until your twenty-first birthday to sort your feelings out before you must make a decision about whether to join him in Australia or not.' He stifled a yawn. 'Anyway, luv, has Fergie had a walk today or do one of us need to take him out?'

'I took him out this morning and after walking to Wavertree and back my feet are aching.'

'So, it's down to me,' said Norman. 'I'll take him as far as Sheil Park and back and hopefully he'll do his business and then we can relax and listen to the wireless.'

Grace nodded, her emotions in confusion after telling her father how she felt. She was relieved that he did not broach the subject over their meal of sausage and mash. While her father took Fergie out, she washed the dishes and listened to music on the radio to distract herself. When her father returned, he asked her to tune into the news. Mainly, he was interested in the cricket – the

Third Test Match was on at Old Trafford and it looked like England and Australia were going to draw. Grace wondered idly if Dougie would still support England when he was living in Australia.

'Did you see anybody while you were out?' she asked.

'I saw Ben and his boy, Simon.'

'In the truck?' she asked.

Norman shook his head. 'Ben had his arm around the lad, supporting him. They were out for a breather and going to the chippy afterwards.'

'Did Ben mention me?' she asked, curious as to how he was after his kind behaviour on the night of the play.

'Oh, we were just chatting about my needing to be away for a couple of extra nights on the dredger,' he said casually, adding quickly, 'which led me on to telling him all about Dougie's ship. He asked if you'd had another postcard in the post.'

'And what did you tell him?' she asked, wondering why her father had not mentioned to her about him needing to be away on the dredger longer and why mention it to Ben?

'That there hadn't been time. Next stop after Las Palmas will be Cape Town.'

Grace hesitated before blurting out, 'Yes... although I would have liked a letter as well as a postcard, telling me more about the places he's seen from the ship and about the people he's met. I've written him two letters now and not had a response, although he would not have received them until he arrived at Las Palmas, I suppose.'

'Yes, I suppose that's right, love. Anyway, I suggested that Ben and Simon might like to join us for Sunday lunch as Simon had shown an interest in looking at the map I have of the world and seeing the different places that I went to when I was at sea.'

Grace dropped her fork. 'What did Ben say?'

'He asked was it my idea or yours.'

'And what did you say?'

Norman's expression was bland. 'That it was mine, but you'd be in favour because you're fond of Simon and miss seeing him.'

'Oh, Dad, you forced him into saying yes,' she said with a sigh, unsure of why she felt embarrassed all of a sudden. But she reasoned if Ben had agreed to come, then he must have at least forgiven her for the park incident with Simon.

'And why not,' said Norman. 'You're a good cook and it will be a treat for them both and I'll enjoy talking to Simon about my travels.'

'Which means I'll have to entertain Ben!'

'Nothing wrong with that,' her father said. 'Make an apple pie or a cake and you can find out if he bakes at all.'

Her eyes gleamed in response. 'You can cook, Dad! I can always suggest you give him lessons if Ben confesses to being a lousy cook. What with the times he seems to go to the chippy...'

Chapter 8

The following day, Grace's thoughts kept straying to what she should cook for Sunday lunch. She didn't know why she felt so nervous, but she told herself that they didn't often have guests, so she just wanted it to be extra special. If she was really honest with herself she would admit that she wanted to impress Ben. Generally, she roasted a shoulder of mutton or braised some beef. Maybe, for a change she should roast a decent piece of topside of beef and make Yorkshire puddings, although she had not always been successful at getting them to rise. She planned to bake an apple pie the evening before, as her father always said it tasted better the following day. She would serve it with Bird's custard, so she must remember to buy an extra pint of milk from the dairy. She would have to give the morning service at St Margaret's a miss, but she was sure God would understand given that she had visitors coming. The fire would need to be lit early morning to roast the meat, so it would probably be sensible to eat in the parlour as given the hot weather it would be cooler in there.

On the Saturday when her father got home after his shift, she told him of her plans, so together they moved the dining table and chairs into the front room ready for the next day. Grace had written a detailed list of all that she needed for the weekend meals and she had made the effort to go shopping before going on to her job at the dentist's.

That evening she baked the apple pie, and felt thankful for the times her aunt had taught her to prepare and cook several simple meals. Although, generally speaking, puddings were only served on Sundays, and were often just jelly and custard or rice pudding.

However, the pie looked lovely when Grace took it out of the oven, as did the smaller one she had made with leftover pastry for Ben to take home with him. She set them to cool on the shelf in the alcove at the side of the fireplace and then washed the utensils she had used, before making a jug of cocoa as a reward for herself and finally settling down to finish *Murder on the Orient Express*, a new book which had come out in January. Despite putting her name down at the borrowing library to lend it out in February, it had gone on a list and she had had a four-month wait to get her hands on the novel. Still, it had been worth the wait, and she was already impatient to read the next Agatha Christie due out in September, with her name already down on another waiting list.

Grace was up by seven o'clock the next morning and lit the fire straight away, ate some bread and butter, and then set about preparing the beef to go in the oven once the fire had warmed up. Next, she peeled the vegetables and made the batter for the Yorkshire puddings. Only then did she treat herself to a hot bowl of water carried carefully upstairs to her bedroom for a warm wash. Having cleaned herself with a new, unwrapped block of Lux toilet soap, Grace dusted herself with Yardley's English Lavender talc powder and put on her favourite blue-and-peach floral sundress and tan-coloured sandals. She fastened on a wrap-around pinny to keep her dress clean, before brushing her bobbed flaxen hair and clipping on blue earrings fashioned in the shape of flowers. Pleased with her reflection, she went downstairs again, and only when her father commented on her being all dollied up, did Grace question why she had made such an effort when she wasn't going anywhere.

However, when Ben and Simon arrived just before noon, dressed smartly in what she presumed were their Sunday suits, Grace felt better. She could not get over how good they looked, and was glad she had dressed up a bit for the occasion. She had nagged her father to change into clean clothes, although he had refused to put on his only suit, saying he was in his own home and it was much too hot for that sort of nonsense.

Grace beamed at the father and son from the doorway and hastened to take Ben and Simon's jackets, which they readily handed over. She hung them up and then offered them a cool drink: lemonade for Simon and a pale ale for the men, and a shandy for herself. After some small talk in the kitchen, she suggested her father show Ben and Simon into the parlour, and for them to sit down at the table. Much to her relief, the beef had cooked perfectly as she had followed the butcher's instructions and kept her eye on the meat, so it did not burn. The heat of the oven was difficult to get just right. The roast potatoes also looked good, and who could go wrong with carrots and peas, she thought. Although when she took the Yorkshire puddings out of the oven, they had risen beautifully, but unfortunately their tops were slightly burnt. She could have cried and only hoped her gravy would go some way to making the puddings taste acceptable.

As it was, there was no conversation during the meal, because the three males fell on the food as if they had been lost on the Lancashire moors all night and had not eaten during those hours. Only when she had cleared the dishes away, did her father say, 'That was a good meal, lass. You might have burnt the Yorkshires, but nobody's perfect.'

'I liked it all,' said Simon. 'If I'd been at home, I would have licked me plate.'

His father frowned at him. 'Do you have to let our hosts realise what a little savage you are when you're at home?'

'I should have offered you some bread to mop up the gravy,' Grace said. 'Although, I reckon, Simon, what you said was a compliment to my cooking!'

He smiled at her. 'Are there any afters?'

Ben poked him with his elbow. 'You shouldn't ask, it's bad manners.'

'Leave him be, Ben,' said Grace. 'He's only a boy and you're amongst friends. Did you enjoy your meal?'

He stared at her and their eyes met and held. 'I've cleared my plate, haven't I?'

'Yes, but that could be because your good-mannered and didn't want to hurt my feelings.'

His lips twitched. 'As your father said, it was a good meal. It's ages since I've tasted beef cooked as well.'

She gave him a little bow. 'Thank you, kind sir.' Suddenly she realised she had not removed her pinafore and whisked it off. 'I presume you are all ready for afters.'

'Yeahhh!' shouted Simon.

She realised Ben was staring at her with what she thought was admiration in his eyes, and she smiled and realised she was pleased with the attention. She made to pick up the plates, but Ben beat her to it and carried them out. Grace followed him through into the back kitchen, watching him place them in the enamelled washing bowl in the sink. Then he turned and brushed past her and went into the kitchen and returned with a steaming kettle of water removed from the hob. She watched him in amazement as he poured it over the dishes.

'What do you think you're doing?' she asked.

'What does it look like?' he replied.

'There's no need for you to wash the dishes.' She went over to the sink and attempted to force him out of the way with her hip.

He shoved her back. 'I like washing dishes. It gets my hands nice and clean.'

Feeling slightly breathless, and thinking that Dougie had never washed a plate in his life or rarely offered to help, she said, 'Surely you wash your hands before you eat at home?'

'Naturally, but Simon and I take turns at washing up. When my wife was alive, I always washed up.'

Grace was surprised, but did not ask why.

Ben arrowed her a mocking glance, as if he knew she was wanting to ask why. 'She had rheumatoid arthritis and was inclined to break crockery if she beat me to the sink.'

'That must have been difficult for you both when Simon was born.'

'You can say that again,' he said in heartfelt tones. 'Although, her mother visited every day, she left as soon as I arrived home because she couldn't stand the sight of me. She thought we shouldn't have married and had a child so soon, and blamed me for Simon being born and then later, my wife's death.'

Grace was surprised he was being so open with her. 'But I bet your wife adored him.'

'She did. It was her wanting to wheel him out in his pram because she wanted to show him off that caused her death, though. Her mother was hanging washing out in the backyard. My wife sneaked out and lost control of the pram because of her hands, and that was how she was hit by a car as she was running after it.' There was a break in his voice.

'I'm so sorry! No wonder you were so angry with me because of what happened in the park with the bath chair. It makes sense now...' She reached out and touched his sleeve.

For the briefest moment he covered her hand with his, and she felt a thrill go up her arm, even as he apologised for wetting her hand with his wet soapy one.

She muttered, 'I'd better get on with making the custard or Simon will be shouting for his afters.'

'It was good of you to invite us.'

'I've enjoyed it,' she said. 'It was a challenge and Dad's enjoyed the company of you both.' She paused. 'Anyway, I'd better go and put the milk on for the custard.'

She left him drying his hands on a tea towel and went into the kitchen. When he entered the room, she asked him to get four bowls out of the sideboard cupboard and carry them through to the table in the parlour.

Grace followed him five minutes later with the hot custard and placed the saucepan on the kettle stand and then cut thick slices from the larger apple pie. Later, over cups of tea, the two men discussed the Mersey Tunnel and how much easier it would make travelling to places on the Wirral, as well as Chester and Wales, as most likely buses and charabancs could now leave from the city centre and travel through the tunnel, instead of Liverpudlians having to take the ferry to Birkenhead to catch a bus onwards from there.

After their tea, Norman switched the wireless on to listen to the news. There was talk of the Prince of Wales touring the colonies, and Nazi Germany being the cheapest place to go for a holiday. Something to do with the gold standard and marks being registered, but Grace didn't really follow this. Getting up from the chair, where she was resting after tidying up the table, Grace produced the board game tiddlywinks thinking Simon might enjoy a game, forgetting for the moment the boy's wrists were in plaster. The boy had never played it before, but he soon got excited rooting on his dad against Norman, who won most of the games.

'We need to practise more,' said Simon, glancing at his father.

'You can borrow it,' Grace said.

'You can return it next time you come,' Norman said. 'Me and you can play, Simon, as your wrists are getting better. See if you can beat me next time.'

The boy glanced at Ben. 'Is that all right, Dad?'

Ben said, 'When were you thinking of, Mr Green?'

'I'll check what days I'll be home, and Grace can drop a note through your door,' said Norman.

'It'll be fun,' Simon said.

Norman agreed, 'What about you, Ben? Do you want to join in?'

'I'll let you know when we have a date. Besides I don't want to wear my welcome out,' he said, glancing at Grace. 'Maybe we should wait until Simon's plaster is removed.'

'That's weeks away,' said Simon in dismay.

'More time for your wrists to heal completely and for you to become really proficient,' Grace said, wondering if Ben was having second thoughts about seeing more of her and her father. Yet what he had said made sense, although she did wonder how he would manage with Simon home alone in the day. But she also remembered what her aunt had said about not being too helpful or Ben might come to expect it, so stopped herself from saying anything more. She supposed it was possible he had reasons he did not want to mention.

The visitors did not stay much longer, and both of them thanked her when she handed over the small apple pie that she had made for them.

'Yummy-yum,' said Simon. 'Thanks very much.'

'You're welcome,' Grace said. 'I look forward to seeing you when your plaster is off.' She handed the game of tiddlywinks to Ben. 'I expect you to be a better player next time.'

'We'll see,' he said. 'Thank you for an enjoyable few hours.'

'My pleasure,' she said politely, and waved them off.

Chapter 9

The weeks passed. Although they were on her mind, Grace decided to leave arranging a visit from Simon and Ben for a while. She dropped in on her aunt a couple of times, and the last time, she saw her cousin, Beryl, who held out her left hand to Grace as soon as she entered the kitchen.

'Do you like my ring?' she said.

Grace stared at the garnet ring and said, 'You're engaged!'

Beryl nodded. 'To Davy, you remember him, don't you?'

Grace thought hard and into her mind's eye came a picture of a young man with curling black hair and brown eyes in a kind face. He had a good physique and was a bricklayer. He was one of four brothers and three sisters, and he and Beryl belonged to a ramblers' group – that was where they had first met last spring.

'Congratulations,' Grace said. 'I hope you'll be very happy. When's the wedding?'

'Next June if we can save up enough money and find a place to set up home.' Beryl paused. 'I would have liked you to be one of my bridesmaids, but Mam said you will have left for Australia by then because you'll have had your twenty-first birthday.'

Grace's face fell. 'I'd have liked to have seen you married.'

'Tough luck,' chipped in Marion, the elder sister. Her cousin always liked to put Grace down, especially in the presence of Dougie, and when Grace had lived with them, she found herself avoiding Marion's company as much as possible. She could only think it was because Marion resented Dougie taking so much notice of Grace.

'There'll be photographs,' Beryl said. 'I'll send you and our Dougie one and you'll have to send us one of your wedding.'

'Of course,' Grace said, thinking her wedding seemed to feel more like a dream than reality.

As the heat of the summer faded into the crisp days of autumn, Grace also visited Milly and went for walks with her, taking turns to push the pram to the park at the beginning of September. The heatwave had passed and August had seen several downpours, so the grass in the park was green again, although the leaves on some of the trees were on the change and some had already fallen, creating a rustling brown-and-amber carpet underfoot.

'So, have you seen anything of Simon?' Grace asked Milly, her curiosity finally getting the better of her.

'Not recently, and now he's back at school, so Jimmy told me. I think a neighbour looked in on him. I'm sorry that Ben didn't want you to look after him though.'

'He's able to walk?' said Grace, ignoring her friend's last comment.

'The plaster's off his wrists and he's able to use crutches. His cracked kneecap is pretty well knitted together, so he doesn't need the splint anymore.'

Grace experienced mixed emotions on hearing this news, glad that Simon was so much better, but hurt that

Ben had not informed them of the fact. She tried to hide her feelings, but that night while she was eating tea with her father, she couldn't help telling him what Milly had said, and was unable to keep the hurt out of her voice.

Norman gave her a long, thoughtful look. 'Maybe it's just as well we don't have too much to do with them,' he said gently. 'The boy needs to play with those his own age, and you'll be joining Dougie in Australia in no time at all once Christmas is past. Best you don't get too fond of Ben and take an interest in his affairs.'

Grace could not believe her ears and she placed her knife and fork down with a clatter. 'Why on earth should you think there's a likelihood of me getting fond of *him*?'

'You talk to each other and you want to help him with Simon.'

'That doesn't mean anything,' Grace said fiercely. 'Besides, he doesn't like me interfering – doesn't trust me – he doesn't even like me, otherwise why would he have stayed away so long. He knows about Dougie and my going to Australia!'

Norman looked down at his plate for a moment and carefully cut a forkful of his mutton chop. 'You've got him all confused.'

'I don't understand what you mean, Dad,' she said.

'Ben finds you attractive. I've seen the way he looks at you, so I think he's decided to put some distance between the pair of you, so not to stand on Dougie's toes, like.'

'You're imagining it,' she said, even so she felt all of a quiver, wondering if her father was right. She was convinced that Ben had taken against her for some reason, which was why he had stayed away for so long.

'Please yerself, lass,' mumbled Norman through a mouthful of meat. 'Anyway, isn't it time you were hearing from Dougie again?'

'I'll visit Aunt Polly and see if she has any news of him,' Grace said.

'You do that,' said her father, leaning over and switching on the wireless.

Still feeling a little unsettled by her father's comments, Grace planned to go and see her aunt that evening, but decided she would take the tram part of the way there and back.

–

She arrived at her aunt's house at eight o'clock and found her uncle Douglas in the house on his own. This did not often happen; she did not know him very well as her aunt always took charge of the conversation. He welcomed her warmly, and made her a cup of tea and offered her a biscuit before telling her that Polly had gone to the pictures with a friend to see Evelyn Laye in the musical *Evensong*.

Grace told him that she had come to see if they had heard from their son recently. Douglas nodded his greying head.

'We received a wire from him telling us that he landed in Cape Town a week ago and had decided to stay on in South Africa with some friends he had made on the ship.' Grace, stunned, stared at him wordlessly. 'I know it's a shock, isn't it?' he said.

'What about Australia?' she said eventually.

'That's what I said to Polly.'

'And what did she say?'

'She didn't say anything for ages,' he replied. 'Not until I said, "What's the fool up to now changing his mind like that, and what will Grace say?"'

Grace, suddenly furious, said, 'What's he thinking of sending a telegram that tells you very little, and cost more than a postage stamp, and not getting in touch with me?'

'He didn't even give an address to write to,' said her uncle.

'Can I see the wire? Can I take it home with me to show Dad?' Grace stood up and quickly put her jacket back on and her hat.

'I'll come with you,' Douglas said. 'I'll take you home on my motorbike. I haven't seen your dad for ages. I'll just leave a note for Polly.'

Within half an hour Grace was sitting on the pillion seat of her uncle's motorbike and they were speeding in the direction of Kensington. She arrived home to find Norman on the front step talking to their next-door neighbour. He stared at them, and removed his pipe from his mouth, as he watched his brother-in-law help Grace down from the bike.

'So, what's all this about?' he asked. 'Has something happened to Dougie? Surely the ship hasn't sunk or been attacked by pirates?'

'This is what's happened?' said Grace angrily, waving the telegram under his nose.

Norman grabbed it from her and read it aloud twice, but continued to stare at it for longer. 'I see it was sent from Jo'burg.'

'Jo'burg? What do you mean, Dad?' asked Grace.

Norman smiled grimly. 'No doubt he'll be writing to you telling you all about it soon. Let's go inside and have a drink. I'm parched.' Grace thought that he continued to mutter under his breath, but couldn't be sure, 'Sounds like the boy's up to his old tricks…'

The neighbour had already gone inside his house, so the three of them went indoors. Norman poured out three shandies, and the two men sat down in the kitchen while Grace made some cheese sandwiches.

Once she was seated at the table with them, Norman explained further, 'Jo'burg is short for Johannesburg – it's a city in South Africa where gold and diamonds are mined. But Dougie's ship docked in Cape Town, so he must have left Cape Town for some reason.'

'Looks like my son has gone there hoping to make his fortune, like many another did in the last century when they rushed off to America or Australia,' said Dougie's father.

'He'd be out of luck trying to stake a claim in South Africa. It's not the same,' said Norman. 'If you want to know more, borrow a book from the library.'

Grace resolved to do just that once she received Dougie's letter explaining everything. After all, her father could be mistaken and she didn't want to jump to conclusion, although she felt uneasy about it, as Dougie could change his mind about things so quickly. Maybe he had gambled his money away on the ship playing cards and now he owed these new so-called friends money and they were destined for South Africa and had told him if he stuck with them he could get rich quick. It wouldn't be the first time he had borrowed money which had led to him getting beaten up. Then borrowing money from herself, and his mother lending him money to save him from another beating. That was the situation the last time she had lent him money because he had never paid her back.

It was to be October, several weeks later, before Grace received a letter and a postcard of Cape Town from Dougie. The wait had been agonising, as Grace fretted daily about what might have happened. But when she opened Dougie's long-awaited letter, it offered little in the way of explanation. There was no writing on the postcard, but the letter was two pages long, and told her that he had spent some time in South Africa, but would soon be taking the next ship to Australia, where he hoped to do some business that would enable him to buy a plot of land in Sydney and have a house built, as well as send for her shortly. Dougie claimed he could not wait to see her, as Marion had written to him about Grace having been seen with another fellow at some play. He had closed the letter by saying that she was not to forget that she belonged to him and he didn't want to look a fool in front of the neighbours. Grace felt a strong spurt of anger as she re-read the last paragraph. How dare he speak of her as if she was a possession? She remembered how he had enjoyed showing her off when she was sixteen and she had developed a good figure and her features were no longer so girlish. He hadn't asked how she was in the letter, or how her father was keeping. Typical Dougie, concerned with how things might look to others, without a thought for how she might be doing without him all these weeks. She read the letter to her father that evening, when he returned from another overnight session on the dredgers, to see if he could make better sense of it.

'He makes no mention of Jo'burg or mining,' said Norman, gazing at her.

'Probably he presumes his mother told me about his telegram,' Grace said. 'Do you think he did make some money mining then?'

'He's made some money somehow if he's going to have a house built, and what's this business he mentions, I wonder?' rasped Norman, frowning. 'And he doesn't explain why he left Cape Town originally. There's something not quite right here. Somehow, I did think he'd have spent longer in South Africa. Perhaps things are unsettled there since the Boer Wars.'

'But they were over ages ago,' said Grace.

Norman said, 'Where's the envelope this came in?'

'I put it on the fire. Anyway, he only has himself to blame if I was going out with someone else!' she raged. 'I've a good mind to write back and tell him I've changed my mind about joining him in Australia,' she added, pressing her lips firmly together. '…only I don't have an address!'

'That would suit me,' said Norman. 'I haven't been feeling too good lately.'

'What's wrong, Dad?' she asked, suddenly fearful. 'I have noticed you getting up in the night several times.'

'You're not to worry about me,' he said. 'I wouldn't have mentioned it if it wasn't for Dougie's letter, and you sounding like you'd quite like an excuse to put off going to Australia for a bit longer until you're sure of your feelings, and from what you said the other time when we talked about it.'

'Have you been to see the doctor, Dad?' Grace could not conceal her concern.

'It'll cost money,' he protested.

'We can cut down on food,' she said.

'I like me food,' he said.

'You won't starve.'

'Oh well, if it'll make you feel better, I'll go,' he said resignedly.

'That's a good daddy.' She kissed his cheek. 'It's probably nothing to worry about. He'll give you a tonic and you'll soon start feeling better.'

Norman seized her hand. 'You're a good lass. Far too good for your cousin,' he added darkly.

She eyed him suspiciously. 'You're not having me on, are you, Dad?'

'You mean to keep you here?' He lowered his head and gazed at the floor and the rag rug that his wife had laboured over before she died. 'No, lass, I wouldn't do that. I want you to come to your own decision about this.'

'And you'll tell me the truth about what the doctor says?'

He nodded.

'Cross yer heart,' she said earnestly.

Norman sketched a shaky cross in the region of his heart.

She heaved a sigh and changed the subject. 'Do I go to Aunt Polly's and tell her about the letter?'

'That's up to you. I should think he's written to her as well.'

'I might leave it for a week then. I don't know why she can't come and visit us for a change. She could come over on the motorbike, just like I did.'

'She hates the motorbike, used to be for ever nagging Douglas to get rid of it,' said Norman. 'But give him his due, he's stuck to his guns and kept it. He loves that machine and knows what he's doing. He's raced in the Isle of Man and during the last war he was a dispatch rider.'

'I didn't know that. She probably worries about him having an accident now he's getting on.' Grace relived those moments riding pillion when Douglas was travelling really fast.

'I think it's more that she worried that young Dougie might decide he wanted a motorbike too, like his dad.' Norman yawned.

'Would you like a cup of cocoa, Dad, before going to bed?'

'Better not, I'll be up in the night more than ever if I do,' he said. 'Don't let me stop you having one, lass.'

'Thanks, Dad, goodnight. God bless,' said Grace as she went into the back kitchen to fetch the tin of Bournville cocoa.

—

The following evening, Grace was crossing West Derby Road with Fergie on the lead, when she heard her name being called. She waited until she reached the pavement on the other side, before looking about her. Then she felt a tap on her back and Fergie let out a welcoming yelp. She turned and saw Simon grinning at her. She beamed at him.

'Look at you now,' she said, noticing that the crutches had gone, as well as the splint and plaster casts. 'I bet you're feeling good.'

'It's great! I can play footie now and help Dad out at home. How are you, Grace, and how's your dad?'

'I'm fine, although my dad isn't well, so he's going to see the doctor.' She paused. 'We miss you, so why don't you drop round and see us sometime?'

'I'd like to do that,' Simon said, bending to stroke Fergie.

'And your dad doesn't have to come if he has something better to do,' she said.

Simon nodded. 'Tarrah!' he called as he set off with a run that Grace was glad to see.

She wondered if she had really needed to have said what she did about his dad. It sounded unfriendly. She could have said that his dad was welcome to come too. After all, her father would have enjoyed talking to Ben.

When she arrived home, she was expecting to find her father already there as he wasn't due at work that night, but the house was empty. She wondered if he had managed to see the doctor. There was no appointment system and you just had to go along and wait to be seen, so it might be taking a while. But when Norman had still not arrived home an hour later, Grace could feel herself becoming more and more worked up.

She paced the floor, before giving herself a stern talking to and busied herself making something to eat should her dad arrive home hungry. A few minutes later, thankfully, she heard a key in the latch and hurried out of the kitchen to greet her father. Despite his smile, she knew it was bad news as soon as she saw him.

'You're late,' she said.

'I was one of the last to be seen and then on the way home I got talking to a couple of people.' He brushed past her and hurried up the lobby. She followed him and watched as he sank wearily into a chair.

'I met Simon,' she said. 'He looks great. But never mind that now, what did the doctor have to say?'

'He wants me to go and see a specialist at the Royal Infirmary in Pembroke Place.'

Grace felt the colour drain from her face. 'It's something serious, then?'

'Might be or it might not that's why he wants me to see the specialist,' Norman said, stroking his chin. 'Make us a cuppa, lass, and something to eat?'

Grace didn't say another word, but arranged the corned beef hash that she'd made on a tray for him, along with a bottle of HP sauce and a strong cup of tea.

'Did he tell you anything at all?' she asked as she handed it over.

'I'd rather not talk about it,' he said.

'But, Dad, I need to know!'

'You don't need to know all the ins and outs,' he said wearily. 'Let's wait and see what the specialist has to say.'

Grace was not satisfied, but knew better than to push her father further – she would have to accept what he had said for now. So, she finished eating her meal, and then switched on the wireless, before picking up her mending basket and proceeding to darn her father's socks, all the while praying fervently.

Chapter 10

Simon dropped by the following evening, and told Grace and Norman that Ben was working overtime, adding that his father hardly ever had the chance to earn extra money. As the job was urgent, Ben had gratefully accepted the opportunity, despite meaning that Simon would be on his own for longer after school.

'I left him a note saying I was visiting you, so he won't worry about where I am,' he concluded.

'We're pleased to see you, it's been a while,' said Norman. 'And is that the tiddlywinks game you have under your arm?' The boy nodded.

'I'll be able to play now,' he said, placing the box on the table. 'I got bored at home sometimes. Mrs Jones next door would look in on me and make me drinks and bring me sausage rolls from the bakery and she'd natter on about her daughter getting married. Then sometimes her husband would keep me company. He works nights as a cocky watchman, where some new houses are being built and electricity is being put in. He talks about having to chase youths and tramps away from his brassiere now the nights are getting colder because he wouldn't put it past them to pinch stuff, but what he really likes to talk about is darts.' He paused for breath. 'He goes on about how many double tops he's scored. He also likes fishing in the canal and catches enormous fish. I think he exaggerates. I much prefer being left alone to read the comics that the twins' dad sends me.' He paused. 'I know I must sound ungrateful about Mr and Mrs Jones, but Dad says they mean well and I must be polite and always thank them.'

'What about your school friends, don't they call in to see you?' asked Norman. Simon nodded.

'Not as much as they did at first and when they do come, they don't talk much but read my comics. Dad takes me to the flickers some evenings and I enjoy that.'

'At least you're better now and can get out and about,' said Norman.

'Let us have our meal first and then we can play,' Grace said. 'Would you like some dinner, too?'

'If you have enough,' he said. 'I've only had a jam butty and a drink of milk.'

'Well, you're in luck, because I've made a mince and onion pie,' said Grace.

'That sounds the gear,' said Simon. 'Dad said you're a good pastry cook. We really enjoyed that apple pie.'

'Thanks for the compliment,' said Grace, with the slightest of curtseys.

She fetched an extra plate and cutlery, and then cut three slices out of the pie and added mashed carrots and fried potato scallops before pouring glasses of water and sitting at the table. She watched as her father and Simon dug into the food.

They had just finished eating when there came the sound of the knocker at the front door. Grace stood and went to see who was there. She had a feeling it might be Ben and was aware that her heart rate had increased. Her intuition was right. Simon's father stood on the step, still wearing what appeared to be his working clothes, with sawdust clinging to his hair and his eyelashes.

'I thought it was going to be you,' Grace said, her grey eyes meeting his treacle-toffee brown ones. 'He's here. You'll come in? I'm sure Dad will enjoy a chat with you.' She stepped aside and held the door wide open.

'Only your dad?' he said.

'Don't be daft! You and Simon are always welcome.'

He raised his eyebrows interrogatively. 'I thought you might have had enough of us.'

'Why should you think that?' she asked.

'Well, you don't owe us anything. It's not as if we're family or neighbours.'

'I'd hope you would regard us as friends,' she said.

'I'd like to be friends with you if your boyfriend wouldn't object.'

'I don't care if he does,' she said with an edge to her voice.

Ben's eyes narrowed. 'Has he still not written to you?'

'He's written, but it's more about what he doesn't say that annoys me.'

Ben looked puzzled.

'Dad can explain.' She smiled and indicated that he step inside. 'I guess you haven't eaten.'

'You guess right. Does that mean you're offering to feed me?' She nodded.

'Seeing as I've heard how you complimented my pastry skills.'

Grace followed him up the lobby, admiring the broad spread of his shoulders beneath the light gabardine jacket. Norman nodded a welcome, and said, 'I hope you're not going to rush the lad away. He's determined to beat me at tiddlywinks.'

Ben said, 'I'll watch. I've hardly stopped all day and I'll be glad to relax for half an hour. Before you and I have a chat, Norman.'

The older man blinked at him and then nodded.

As Simon and Norman settled down to play, Grace drew out a chair for Ben at the table and bid him sit down before serving out the remainder of the pie. 'Eat up,' she said, moving away and putting the kettle on before stacking some of their dirty plates and cutlery out of Ben's way. 'So, you're being kept busy on the new housing estate out Seaforth way, are you?'

'It's Litherland, which is the same stop on the Southport train, but we're building houses on land that was farmland – for the workers of a tannery up that way overlooking the Leeds–Liverpool canal.'

'I've never heard of Litherland,' Grace said.

'Well, it's been around for quite a while. On this side of the canal there are quite a few older terraced houses and a Bryan & May match-works... and a number of shops and pubs. There's talk of a library being built. There's a Methodist church too, I think.'

'I suppose the air is fresher out that way.'

He smiled. 'Depends on which way the wind from the Mersey is blowing. Tanneries can be smelly places at times.'

Grace bit her lower lip. ''Course, I wasn't thinking.'

'There's lots of villages around Liverpool, but they're all growing now.' Ben paused. 'Anyway, that's enough from me.' Ben forked a potato scallop and fell silent.

Grace feeling flustered, turned away and carried some plates into the back kitchen. Ben gazed after her for several minutes, before glancing across at Norman, who suddenly appeared to be very engrossed in a tricky tiddlywink manoeuvre.

'Have you told Grace you're ill, Norman?' he asked.

Norman nodded, watching Simon flip his counter into the container in the centre of the board.

'Is that why she doesn't want to talk about the boyfriend and suggested I talk to you about him and Australia? I wouldn't blame you if you preferred her to stay in Liverpool.'

'I don't know yet how bad I am,' said Norman. 'I'll know more after I've seen the specialist in a couple of days' time.'

'I see,' Ben said. 'You'll keep me informed, won't you?'

'Oh yes!' said Norman grimly. 'I could do with your help. I'd rather not have Grace have to depend on my sister-in-law, Dougie's mother. I'll tell you more before you and Simon leave.'

Ben asked no more questions, only finished eating, before carrying his plate and cutlery into the back kitchen.

Grace glanced at him over her shoulder as he came towards her. He smiled and dropped the plate and cutlery into the washing-up bowl. 'Thanks for the dinner. I really enjoyed it.'

She found herself thinking, Well, you know what they say? The way to a man's heart is through his stomach. Then she wondered why that thought should come into her head and quickly pushed it away.

Ben picked up a tea towel and began to dry the dishes.

'You don't have to,' she said. 'You've been working all day and need a rest.'

'I thought it would give us the chance to talk privately,' he said. Grace stilled, her hands motionless in the washing-up water, but her heart was beating fast.

'What about?' she asked, with a tremor in her voice.

'Your dad! I take it that you won't have asked him about his illness.'

'You know!' She stared at Ben, her eyes wide with surprise and apprehension.

'He told me a while ago. He needed a friend and wanted to spare you for as long as possible. I told him you'd want to know and to support him. Anyway, he'll know more after he's seen the specialist.'

Her shoulders sagged. 'Do you think he'll be honest with me?'

'Yeah, for better, for worse. He doesn't want you going to Australia, does he?'

She shook her head and gripped the sink. 'He thinks there's something not quite right about Dougie and the job he had with the friends he made on the ship. They left Cape Town where the ship docked and went to Johannesburg to make their fortune and he wants to buy a house in Australia. My aunt and uncle knew about his scheme in South Africa before I did.'

'Whatever it was, it must have been well paid if he can afford to buy a house in Australia.'

Grace nodded. 'Dad and I have just been hazarding guesses.'

Ben said seriously, 'Well, whatever it was, I think you're making the right decision staying here with your dad being taken unwell.'

'I wonder what my aunt Polly will say when I tell her.'

'Are you close?'

'We used to be. She's my mam's sister.' Grace shook herself and finished washing the dishes. 'She's inclined to be bossy and I don't want her barging in and telling me what I should or shouldn't do. I want to continue looking after Dad whatever...' Tears shone in her eyes.

Ben dried the last of the cutlery. 'He asked me would I help him if need be.'

'He did?'

'I said I would... and you've both been so good with Simon.'

'That was for selfish reasons – we love spending time with him,' said Grace. Ben placed a hand on her shoulder.

'He's very fond of both of you, too. You should have heard him talk about the two of you this last month gone, while his wrists and knee healed. Now, I think I will go and sit down.' He suddenly seemed to notice the pile of newspapers in a cardboard box by the door and picked one up. 'All right if I take this?'

'Of course, but don't be surprised if it's an old *Echo*. I save them for lighting the fire.'

'It's ages since I've bought a paper,' he said, leaving her wiping the draining board as he left the room.

When Grace entered the kitchen, it was to find that her father and Simon had set up to play another game of tiddlywinks and Ben was sitting back in an easy chair reading the newspaper he had picked up. He glanced up at her and said, 'You're right about this, it's from August! Apparently, back then, the film star, Maureen O'Sullivan, arrived in Liverpool with her fiancé, John Villiers Farrow – he's a film director at MGM.'

Grace wondered if Ben was telling her this to lighten the mood.

'She has to have some Irish blood with a name like O'Sullivan,' said Norman.

'I wonder if the wedding is soon,' Grace said. 'Maybe they've just landed on the Irish ferry and are going to America on a liner for the wedding.'

Ben glanced at the clock on the mantelpiece. 'I think it's time we were on our way, son,' he said.

'Ahhh! We haven't finished this game, Dad!' said Simon.

'You can finish it when you come again,' Ben suggested.

'Give it a couple of days, eh,' said Norman. 'I'll be working, so I'm not sure exactly what time I'll land home.'

–

The following day Grace called in on Milly to see how the twins were coming on and whether there was anything she could do for her as the weather was turning colder. As she arrived, Milly was just leaving the house again with the twins.

'Grace! I'm glad to see you. I've been meaning to ask if you and your dad would like to come to the twins' christenings,' Milly said.

Grace said, 'I'd love to and I'm sure Dad will as well. Where are you having the service?'

'St Margaret's. Jane and Kyle have offered their parlour for the do afterwards because their house is much bigger than ours. There's quite a crowd coming – Jimmy's aunt and her husband from Essex, and then there's the Irish lot, and my relatives on Dad's side.'

'When is it?' Grace asked.

'Not for a while, next year, due to us wanting to make sure all the people we wanted there had plenty of warning. We also wanted nice weather, so it's Easter Sunday, 21st April.'

Grace thought what a good job she wasn't going to Australia as she would have missed the christening because her twenty-first birthday was exactly a month earlier, on 21st March, the start of spring.

'Listen, instead of taking the twins out in this weather, can I get whatever you need?'

'I'd appreciate that,' said Milly. 'You could help me get the pram inside, though.'

'Have you thought of using the back way? I know the alley can be a bit smelly what with cats and rubbish dropped by the bin men, but it will be easier getting out of the house,' said Grace.

Milly screwed up her face. 'Now, why haven't I thought of that?' she paused. 'We might as well go now. By the way, I just want some stamps from the post office and some invitations posted.'

'That's no trouble,' said Grace.

The two women walked to the nearest opening that led into the next street where Ben and Simon lived, and halfway along it they turned into a narrower alley that ran alongside the back of the houses, and went along it a short way before stopping at Milly's back door. She lifted the latch and pushed the door open to wheel the pram in before turning and taking out several envelopes and her purse from her bag. Milly handed Grace the envelopes and two florins from her purse.

'Thanks,' Milly said. 'And drop in for a cuppa on the way home.'

'Thanks, I will,' promised Grace.

Grace turned back the way she had come along the alley, and found herself idly wondering which back door might be Ben and Simon's. She had no time to go and check it out now though, as she needed to get to the post office and shops straight away, but it did put her in mind of her conversation with Ben last evening about PO boxes – she wanted to visit her aunt as soon as possible and discover whether she had heard from Dougie again. She also felt duty-bound to inform her aunt that Norman was ill and that she might not be able to leave him and go to Australia as planned.

–

Grace was back at Milly's house within half an hour and then enjoyed holding the twins one by one. 'They already feel heavier,' she said, cuddling the little boy.

'I know,' said Milly. 'My mother-in-law will really notice the difference. Jimmy and I are going to take them over to New Brighton to see her. She sprained her ankle a couple of days ago, so we want to see whether she has all she needs with her having difficulty getting out.'

'Dad has health problems, too,' said Grace.

'Nothing too serious I hope?' Milly said.

'Could be! He's going to the Royal Infirmary to see a specialist,' replied Grace, as her voice cracked.

Milly's expression was sympathetic. 'Let's hope for the best – I'll light a candle for him next time I go to church.'

Grace murmured a thanks before saying she'd best be going as she was planning on visiting her aunt. Milly saw her out and wished her all the best.

She went home and put away her shopping. She left a note for her father, saying where she had gone, in case he should arrive home while she was out. Then she left the house and caught a tram part of the way to her aunt's house and walked the rest of the way. She was in luck, as Polly opened the door this time, and smiled down at Grace.

'Hello, stranger! I was wondering when we'd see you again.'

'It hasn't been that long since I called. You were out, Uncle Douglas saw me home.'

'To what do we owe the pleasure of a visit from you now? Have you heard from our Dougie?'

'Yes… I've been wondering if you have, though.'

Polly smiled. 'I'd have thought he'd have definitely got in touch with you the same time as he did us, given the circumstances.'

Grace stepped over the threshold. 'What do you mean? Can we go and sit down, please? I'm tired.'

'Sorry, of course! I don't know what I'm thinking of, keeping you on the doorstep.' Polly said absent-mindedly.

'It appears to me you've a lot on your mind. Is it to do with Dougie? He hasn't changed his plans again, has he?' Grace asked anxiously.

Polly did not reply straight away, but waited until she had brewed a pot of tea and the pair of them were sitting in front of the fire. Then she put down her cup and said, 'The latest news I've had from Dougie is that he's changed his mind about staying in Australia and is on his way back to England on a merchant ship to London.'

Grace choked on a mouthful of tea as it went down the wrong way. When she was able to speak again, she said, 'I didn't know that − I can't believe it after the way he went on and on for years about everything being finished in Liverpool and Australia being the only place to be!'

'Well, I would have thought you'd be pleased he's coming back to England. You never wanted to go to Australia. He's just doing what you want,' Polly said firmly.

'Rubbish!' said Grace, sipping her tea carefully this time. 'Something has happened that he's not telling us about.'

'And what do you think that is about? Everyone always thinks the worst of our Dougie and he only ever tries his best,' said Polly defensively.

'How should I know? But I don't see how it can be anything to do with me. Not really, he was so set on going, regardless of what I felt about it.'

Her aunt looked at her coyly. 'Our Marion has written to him a few times. She might have mentioned that bloke you were seen with after the play on Exchange Flags.'

'So she did, and Dougie mentioned it in his letter to me. Talk about making a mountain out of a mole hill. She was always trying to cause trouble between us.'

'She might have resented you and Dougie getting together. They were close even when they were little,' said Polly. 'She probably wrote to him as she thought he might like to come home for Beryl and Davy's wedding.'

'I doubt it. He was never struck on Davy and wasn't exactly kind to Beryl growing up. You won't remember how he removed the head of her doll and Marion smashed it with a hammer, then there was the time he put a spider down the back of Beryl's frock and Marion called her a cry baby and threatened to take the top off her hot water bottle in her bed if she told Mum and Dad. I told her she was mean and managed to rescue the spider. I was threatened, too, by Marion, but I told her I'd tell my dad if she dared burn me with a match.'

Polly's thin lips tightened. 'I think we should change the subject. Children can be very cruel to each other, but they grow out of it.'

'That's no excuse.' Grace said, with a toss of her head. 'I came to tell you that Dad's not well. He's having to go and see a specialist at the Royal Infirmary.'

Polly looked surprised. 'Despite his smoking like a chimney he's always seemed as fit as a fiddle. What's wrong with him?'

'He didn't tell me. He's waiting to see what the specialist says. I think he also said that he'll be having some tests.'

'Well, it comes to us all sooner or later,' said Polly.

Grace felt as if she had been slapped in the face, and said defiantly, 'Milly, my friend, is going to light a candle for him.'

'A lot of good that'll do,' said Polly, rolling her eyes.

Grace sighed. 'There's no need to be like that, Aunty, just because you're not a believer.'

'Your mother was, and a lot of good it did her,' muttered Polly.

Grace felt her anger rising again and deliberately placed her empty cup on the saucer and stood up to take her leave.

'Thanks for the tea and the information about Dougie. I'll be seeing you,' she said, as she stalked out of the room.

Chapter 11

Grace entered the house, her mind still going like a whirl-wind. She lit the fire which she had set that morning. The note she had left for her father was still there and appeared not to have been touched. She wished he was home as she desperately wanted to share with him what her aunt had said about Dougie. She stared through the kitchen window at the foggy backyard, aware of the faint sound of fog horns on the Mersey as she drew the curtains and hoped that the weather would mean he might be home earlier than planned. As luck would have it, she heard the front door open just as she was boiling an egg. She rushed out of the room and flung herself at her father.

'Oh, I'm so glad you're home.' She pressed her cheek against his shoulder. 'I'll put a couple more eggs on to boil. I've made a pot of tea, so you can have a hot drink straight away.'

He hugged her and then held her away from him at arm's length. 'What's up? You're not worrying about me, are you?'

She did not reply but said, 'I've been to see Aunt Polly and—'

'I suppose you told her about me going to see the specialist and she's upset you?'

'It wasn't only that,' confessed Grace. 'She told me that Dougie is on his way back to England from Australia on a merchant ship going to London! She's had a letter from him.'

Norman was silent and she thought he must be as shocked as she was at the news. Grace waited, but he didn't say anything further. She went to add more eggs to the water boiling in the pan on the hob, while he removed his coat and cap and sat down with a cuppa in his hand. She then went to sit down opposite him.

He said, 'It sounds odd to me.'

'Me too,' said Grace.

'Polly said that he's coming home for me, because I didn't really want to emigrate. I said that was nonsense. Then she said it could be because Marion had written to him about me having been seen with Ben, after the play. She then went on that it could be because Dougie wants to be home for Beryl and Davy's wedding next June. I said I didn't believe that because I know he doesn't care much about either of them. That's when Polly decided to change the subject… and I told her about you not being well. But I really believe there's something fishy about the whole thing with Dougie.'

'Too right,' said Norman. 'Anyway, what about the eggs?'

For a moment Grace could only think what did eggs have to do with their conversation, but then she noticed the saucepan was steaming merrily away, and snatching up a thick cloth, she removed the pan from the fire and placed it on the hearth. Then she reached for the toasting fork to toast the bread she had cut earlier.

Norman took up the saucepan and went into the back kitchen to drain and cool the eggs. A short while later, the toast was buttered, the eggs were peeled, and father and daughter were sitting at the dining table enjoying their late tea. It was not until their appetites were eased that they picked up on their earlier conversation.

'Dougie can't have been in Australia long,' said Norman. 'I wonder if he was deported?'

Grace was flabbergasted. 'What on earth for?'

'I have my suspicions, but I don't want to slander the boy without proof. I think he's been led astray by these so-called friends he made on the outgoing voyage. They might have persuaded him to stop off in South Africa and maybe he was then caught out when he entered Australia.' Norman paused to top up their teacups.

'You're thinking that he's done something illegal?'

'Possibly, but I don't know anything for sure, but I'm guessing that if he was on a merchant ship, he was forced to leave fast and he's probably broke and working his passage back to Blighty.'

'I'm surprised he hasn't decided to stop off at South Africa again,' Grace said, still hardly able to believe that Dougie could be such a fool as to become involved in something illegal. She knew he could be a little irresponsible, but he wouldn't break the law, would he? Yet, as her father said, he was only guessing, and Dougie could be innocent.

Her father touched the back of her hand which was resting on the table. 'Forget him for now, love, and tell me what else you've done with your day?'

She cleared her throat. 'I visited Milly and she's invited us to the twins' christening, but it's not until next Easter.'

'That's a long way off,' he said, sounding dismayed.

'I thought the same, but it's because she wants to give those that she wants there plenty of notice as they are coming from far off, and hopefully the weather should be nicer.'

'Fair enough! Do you think I should buy a new suit seeing as we'll be going to church at Easter?'

'Can you afford one?'

He smiled. 'I haven't had a new one since your mother's funeral, fifteen years ago now.'

Grace drew in her breath with a hiss. 'Then you could do with one, but I suggest we wait until nearer the time, and in the meantime, we save up as many pennies as we can.'

He nodded. 'Fair enough, lass. I can always go to Great Homer Street market and see what's on the second-hand clothes stall.'

That said, he switched on the wireless and smoked his pipe while attempting to empty his mind of his worries.

–

A couple of days later Grace received her own letter from Dougie telling her that he had changed his mind about settling in Australia and was on his way back to England. The letter reported that the ship would be docking in London and he had decided to stay in the capital for a while and see what jobs were available. He suggested that she come down to visit, and that they could have some time together and set a date for their wedding. She could also see what she thought about living in the south, as it would not be as far away from her father as Australia would have been. She noticed that Dougie had given an address where she could write to him in London.

Grace seethed inside, it sounded like he had it all cut and dried. Could he possibly be in London already? Or had he given her the address of a friend? She shoved the letter behind the clock on the mantelshelf, thinking she would tell her father about it later. She hoped he was getting on all right at the hospital, as today was the day he was seeing the specialist. Grace sent up another prayer for his well-being before putting on her outdoor clothes and checking her purse was in her handbag.

Recalling that Simon and Ben might visit that evening, she wondered whether she should drop a note through their door putting the visit off for another evening. But as she left the house quietly by the front door, she thought it might be good for her father to have a visit from them.

She stopped in at the butcher's, and came out with two parcels of meat, and finally decided to leave matters as they were as she hurried to her workplace. Most of the time while she worked, her thoughts had veered between Dougie's letter and how her father was getting on at the hospital. Now and again the thought of Ben and Simon's visit lightened her mood, as did the future christening of Milly's twins. She left a note for her employer on the kitchen table about his evening meal, and not forgetting her belly pork in the meat safe, she took it out and left the building and hurried home, intending to take Fergie for a walk. She hoped that her father would be back from the hospital.

But Norman was not home and Grace started to worry that the specialist had decided to keep him in the hospital. If only they had a telephone, she could have phoned the hospital. As it was, Fergie was bouncing around desperate for a walk, so she fastened on his leash and took him out. To her surprise she was just passing an entry between two streets, when Fergie dragged the leash out of her hand and shot up the opening, barking excitedly at a figure running through the opening. She recognised Simon and paused – 'You off for a run around the park?' she asked.

'Nope,' he said breathlessly, crouching in front of the dog and fondling his ears. 'I've been sent to tell you that your dad is at our house, so he'll be a little late home.'

Grace's heart performed a somersault in her chest. She could think of only one reason why her father should call at Ben's house and the thought made her feel sick and dizzy.

'Can you walk with me to your dad's house?' she said.

'If that's what you want,' Simon replied, grabbing hold of the leash.

'It is. You don't think your dad will mind me dropping in?' Simon stared at her as if he could not believe she needed to ask such a question.

'Why should he? The times we've dropped in on you and your dad.' Suddenly he surprised her by slipping his hand through her arm. 'You seem a bit wobbly. Your dad was the same when he came into our house.'

Grace was convinced then that her father had received bad news and tears clogged her throat. He must have felt the need to talk to another man, but why choose Ben when he could have unburdened himself to one of his fellow workmates?

It took less than five minutes to reach their destination and just as long for Grace to pull herself together on the doorstep before she gave Simon the go-ahead to bang the knocker. Naturally, it was Ben who opened the door. She thought he did not appear to be surprised to see her and without a word he took hold of her shoulders and helped her up over the threshold.

'Welcome to my home,' he said, ushering her along the lobby, where he paused at the bottom of the stairs. 'It's time I had the chance to return your hospitality. Norman was looking a bit down in the mouth when I saw him get off the tram, so I suggested he come back here and have a glass of ale from a jug I'd had filled at the off-licence at the pub. Simon, can you go see how he's doing, please?' Grace moved out of the way as Simon carried Fergie by her into the kitchen.

'That was kind of you, thank you' Grace mumbled. 'Did he tell you why he was looking miserable?'

'The results of the tests haven't come through yet, but he doesn't find the wait easy, and is expecting the worst,' Ben said, squeezing her shoulder gently. 'He's worried about telling you.'

'So, what do I do?'

'Difficult as it is, I think his thoughts need to be led in a different direction.'

'He already has something else to distract him, but that's another worry.' She gazed up at him. 'I don't suppose he mentioned Dougie having changed his mind about settling in Australia?'

Ben frowned. 'He did mention him, but I didn't quite catch what he said because I was still getting my head around what he'd told me about his visit to the hospital.'

'Is it cancer?' asked Grace, a tremor in her voice.

'It's a possibility, but it's not definite.'

'Where is it if it is? It can't be his lungs because he'd surely have shown signs of having difficulty breathing.'

Ben hesitated. 'It's the prostate.'

She looked puzzled.

'It's a man thing,' he said quietly.

'Oh!' she exclaimed, none the wiser.

He changed the subject. 'So, where is Dougie now?'

'He could be in London or still on a ship on the way there.'

'Would you mind if he settled in London?'

'He wants me to go down there and is thinking we could set a date for the wedding then.'

'And how do you feel about that?'

'It's the last thing I want,' she said with passion, coming to a halt and gazing up into Ben's shadowy features.

'So you won't be going down?'

'He'll try and persuade me that he's really come back to please me, but I don't believe that – neither does Dad. I think he's hiding something.'

'Is it your dad being ill that's caused you to change your mind about Dougie?'

'It's a good excuse to give him,' Grace said hesitantly, 'but… the truth is… my feelings towards him have changed. I no longer admire him… and I don't particularly trust him either. He's always been a bit of a gambler but I do believe he hasn't been honest with me about the extent of the risks he took with money. Even without any proper proof I do believe he's addicted to gambling and that he'll never be able to financially support us both. If the truth were known, I think he believes Dad has a nest egg tucked away and I'll inherit it. He believes he can twist me around his little finger and I'll give and forgive him anything.'

'I take it that means you no longer love him?'

'I don't think I knew what love was when he started taking me out. I was only sixteen at the time, and I think my head was turned by his good looks. He can be charming, but, I don't know, he can be quite mean as well – he was always telling me what I could or couldn't do. I think I wasn't just something that looked good on his arm on Friday night, but I could be someone who could fund his addiction in the future,' she sighed, and then she continued wearily, shaking her head slightly. 'Sorry, why am I telling you all this?'

'Because I asked you,' Ben said softly.

She caught the gleam of his eyes and could not look away. When she spoke, the breath caught in her throat.

'Is it because of Dad you wanted to know?'

'Partly, I want to ease his mind, so I have a proposal to put to you,' he paused a moment. 'Would I be right in thinking that we both like and admire each other?'

'I like and admire you,' she admitted, a little taken aback.

'And I like and admire you,' said Ben, his arms finding her waist. 'I think together we could support each other through difficult times.' He paused. 'Please, marry me, Grace? I can assure you, I'm not after your father's money.'

For a moment she did not know what to say because his proposal had come out of the blue, and there had been no mention of love, so she could only presume he was proposing a marriage that would be convenient to them both. Then he lowered his head and kissed her. She felt her heartbeat increase and she tingled all over as she returned his kiss. She would have liked the kiss to have lasted longer, but as it was, she was needing to take a breath when he ended the embrace.

'Well!' she exclaimed, resting her head against his chest. 'You'd better ask Dad's permission.'

'I take that for a "yes" then,' Ben said, and he kissed her lightly on the lips as gently as the flutter of a butterfly's wing on a flower.

He then helped her remove her coat and hung it on a peg on the wall and led her by the hand into the kitchen. She was aware of her father's and Simon's eyes fixed on their clasped hands.

'Norman, I'd like to ask your permission for Grace's hand in marriage,' said Ben without any preamble.

Her father's face lit up and his gaze passed from Ben's to his daughter's flushed countenance. 'I'm delighted to give it, as I suspect from her expression she is in favour of this match.'

'Yes, Dad!' said Grace. 'I believe Ben and I will rub along together nicely. I only need to ask Simon if he is in agreement?'

Simon's expression answered that question, but if there had been any doubt the hug that he gave both his father and Grace said it all.

'Can the wedding be before Christmas?' he asked.

'Let it be as soon as it can be arranged,' Norman said.

—

And so, despite still being in a bit of a daze, Grace heeded Norman's advice, and when she went to church on Sunday morning, she made an appointment with the vicar for her and Ben to talk to him one evening that coming week. They wanted to arrange a date for their wedding and having the banns read. The marriage service was arranged for one o'clock on Sunday 9th December 1934 and the banns would be read three Sundays before at the Sunday morning services.

Grace resolved to write to Dougie as soon as the date was set, knowing her marrying Ben was the right path to take; her feelings for him were so different from those she had felt towards Dougie. What she had felt for Dougie had just been youthful infatuation, not love, so it would be a mistake for her to marry him, and she did not believe Dougie truly loved her or he would not have messed her about so much.

As she wrote the letter, Grace felt calmer than she had in weeks; it was as though all the confusion and turmoil that she had felt since Dougie had departed had slipped away overnight. She went on to tell Dougie that she was breaking things off with him also because her father was seriously ill and she couldn't bear to leave him. Besides, she had met someone else, a thoughtful, caring and responsible man, who had asked her to marry him, and she had accepted his proposal. Then Grace posted the letter to the address in London straight away.

That done, and feeling as though a huge weight had been lifted from her shoulders, Grace went and told Milly her news. She wanted to ask Milly whether she would be her matron of honour, knowing that Ben intended to ask Jimmy to be his best man. Milly's pleasure at her friend's news was obvious. She agreed instantly, and after placing the baby she had been dressing in the pram, Milly removed a bottle of sherry from the sideboard, and despite the early hour, poured two small glasses to toast the happy couple. She then asked Grace eagerly for information on how Ben's proposal had come about and whether she had written to Dougie yet.

'I posted a letter off this morning,' said Grace, sipping her sherry. 'But I've yet to let my aunt and cousins know.'

'That won't be easy, given the time you've been promised to each other,' Milly said sympathetically.

'No,' said Grace, pulling a face. 'I'm seriously thinking of writing my aunt a letter, but it seems cowardly. Despite her not really being in favour of the match given that we are first cousins, she'll hate me for rejecting Dougie. Especially when she's convinced he's given up his plan to settle in Australia and make something of himself just because of me, although, she never wanted him to go to Australia in the first place.'

'Would you like me to come with you to see her?' Milly suggested. Grace hesitated and then shook her head.

'I'll speak to Ben about it and see what he thinks.'

She then told Milly some more of what had taken place last night before checking the time and realising she was late for work. As she rushed off, her head slightly giddy from the sherry, Grace realised cheerfully that she would have to inform her boss of her forthcoming marriage, as it would be expected that she would give up her job once settled, especially as she would have to look in on her father regularly. While she walked along, Grace thought about how there had been times when she had felt a drudge – but earning her own money had come in handy. Her father had been generous with the housekeeping, but she had no idea what Ben would be like. He might be similar to some husbands she had heard about and demand to know where every penny she spent went. However, what must be, must be, and she would be needed in her own home going forward. So, Grace made peace with herself and waited until she had performed all her tasks before she went to break the news to her boss. To her surprise, he took it well, saying that he had expected to lose her to some man sooner rather than later, adding that it was probably time he thought of getting married himself.

–

That evening Ben and Simon came round, and over celebratory cups of tea and homemade scones with margarine and jam, the talk turned to living arrangements after the wedding. Grace had been dreading this conversation, as she hated the thought of leaving Norman, especially with him not being well. However, once again Ben surprised her, as he suggested straight away that Norman move in with him, Grace and Simon as soon as the couple were married, adding that there was plenty of space, as his house had three bedrooms. Ben quickly justified the idea by saying that it would mean less work for Grace, because otherwise she would be going backwards and forwards between the two homes. Grace caught his eye over the table and she felt a rush of such emotion and wanted to get up and kiss him, thinking what a lovely man he was, understanding how much her father meant to her. She could not help comparing his gracious attitude against Dougie's uncompromising behaviour about her reluctance to emigrate earlier in the summer.

'I'd like that,' said Norman. 'As long as I'm allowed to pay my way.'

'Of course,' said Ben. 'You can pay a quarter of the living expenses.'

'A half,' said Norman, his expression determined.

'No,' said Ben. 'I'll be supporting my wife and son.'

'But you could make more money from a lodger.'

Ben smiled. 'But you're family and I'm not out to make money out of you.'

Norman let the subject drop, thinking he could always treat the family with a special something now and then. He went over to the sideboard and removed the box of snakes and ladders.

'Who's for a game?' he asked.

Grace cleared the table and Norman set up the game. The four of them pulled chairs up to the table and sat down to play while the wireless played music in the background. When the nine o'clock news came on, Ben stood up and said, 'Time for bed, son, and no arguments – we have to go.'

The boy removed his coat from the back of a chair, shrugged the garment on, and removed his cap from a pocket and put that on.

'Thanks for the tea and scones,' he said.

'Thank you for coming,' said Norman and Grace.

Grace drew Ben into the lobby. 'I wanted to tell you that I've written to Dougie telling him I won't be marrying him and that I've met someone else,' she said in a low voice.

'Good,' said Ben, hugging her. 'Anything else you want to tell me?'

She breathed in the scent of him, a combination of wood, wool, a hint of perspiration and soap which she recognised as Wright's Coal, as her father used it as well. She was still getting used to being so close to him, it made her feel giddy. Yet it also felt so right.

'I told Milly we were getting married and asked her to be my matron of honour.'

'That's fitting, seeing as how I have spoken to Jimmy today about being my best man.' He paused. 'What about your female cousins, will they be put out?'

'Well, one of them is getting married herself next year, so I don't think she'll be bothered, as for her older sister, Marion, I don't care what she thinks. It's my aunt who I'm bothered about. She'll take it as a slight. I was wondering if you'd come with me, when I break the news. I mean you're going to have to meet them sooner or later.'

'If you need moral support, then I'll come,' he said with a wry smile. 'Although, don't you think it'll be easier if you and your father invite them to yours for Sunday tea and Simon and I will be there, as well?'

Her spirits lifted. 'Of course, why didn't I think of that! I can ask my uncle, as well.'

The kitchen door opened at that moment and Simon appeared. 'Are we going then, Dad?'

'Sure, son! Grace and I had something to discuss,' said Ben, moving apart from Grace and taking his son by the shoulder and directing him towards the front door. She followed them, intending to wave them off. As they reached the pavement Ben turned and said, 'Do you fancy going the flickers on Friday if your dad can put up with Simon, Grace?'

'I'd like that,' she replied. 'I'm sure Dad will be delighted to have Simon's company.'

She waved again and then went inside and found her father sitting in an easy chair with his eyes closed. She gazed down at him, noticing the fresh deep lines on his face and the sallow colour of his skin. She wondered if the new lines had been brought on by pain. She knew something of the distress the disease could cause as her hairdresser had succumbed to it. Yet she had heard of others who had survived and gone on to live for at least ten years more due to the new forms of treatment. She touched her father's shoulder gently.

'Cup of cocoa, Dad?' His eyelids fluttered and then closed before opening wider.

'Yes, thanks, love.'

Grace ran water into the kettle and put it on to boil before making the cocoa paste. Then she sat down by the fire with him. 'I need to talk to you, Dad.'

'Go ahead,' he urged, sitting up straighter.

She cleared her throat.

'I need to tell Aunt Polly and the girls I won't be marrying Dougie. Ben's suggested I invite them here for Sunday tea and he and Simon will be here, as well, to break the news together. What do you think?'

'It'll be easier for you spilling the beans here than going along to their house.'

She nodded. 'I'll drop the whole family a line and hopefully they'll all come. I've already written to Dougie telling him I won't be marrying him and that there's someone else.'

'You've made the right decision, lass,' Norman said.

'There's one more thing,' Grace said, getting up and taking the kettle off the heat. 'Ben wants to take me to the flickers on Friday evening, so could you look after Simon?'

'Of course,' he said. 'Now hurry up with that cocoa.'

While she drank her cocoa, Grace perused the *Echo* for what films were showing on Friday and discovered that *Tarzan and his Mate* was being released again as it had been so popular when it was first released. She noticed that Maureen O'Sullivan was in it and decided to ask Ben if they could go and see it on Friday.

Chapter 12

The following day, Grace wrote and posted her letter off to her aunt and uncle; she caught the first post and then she put it to the back of her mind and thought instead of going to the pictures with Ben to see the Tarzan film. As it happened Simon dropped by after school to see Fergie and she mentioned the film to him.

'Dad and I have seen it,' he said.

Grace was disappointed but decided not to mention it to Ben when he called for her on Friday. She had also received a reply to her letter from her aunt that day which was brief, simply saying that the four of them would be there. Grace decided not to mention it to Ben until after their outing to the flickers.

As it was, Ben asked her did she like Clark Gable and Claudette Colbert. She certainly liked Clark Gable and so answered in the affirmative. So, he told her that Jimmy had mentioned going to see a film called *It Happened One Night* which was fun, so off they went to the Paramount on London Road to see it.

The film was enjoyable, romantic as well as witty, but Grace enjoyed Ben holding her hand throughout the film even more. On the tram home she told him that her aunt, uncle and two cousins were all coming to tea on Sunday.

'I'd best get baking,' she said.

'So, I can look forward to having some more of your delicious scones,' he said, squeezing her hand.

'And cake and sandwiches,' she said, gratified by the compliment.

–

The following day she withdrew some money from her post office saving account to buy the extras she would need, such as the best boiled ham and a tin of Canadian salmon, as well as extra eggs and mayonnaise for the sandwiches, not forgetting the sugar, butter and dried fruit for the scones and cake. On the way home she realised she was looking forward to the feast and showing her relatives that she was capable of plotting out her own life, whatever came her way. She just prayed that the oven would behave itself. She would have to make sure it did not get too hot, but she would bake that evening, so that if anything went wrong, she could make some more scones on Sunday morning.

Her father thought it would be a good idea if he lit a fire in the parlour and everyone could sit in there until Grace was ready to serve tea in the kitchen. 'What about using up the coal?' she fretted. 'We could run short before the next delivery and we can't afford to buy extra from the coal yard, not at their prices.'

'Stop worrying,' he said. 'We can keep our coats and hats on or go to bed early.'

With that settled Grace set about making scones having decided to bake a dozen fruit ones and a dozen plain. As for cake, she would make a fruit cake and two dozen fairy cakes. Hopefully, that would be enough with the sandwiches as well. She would have to make sure everything was put safely away out of reach of Fergie whose curiosity might lead him into mischief. Could be best if she took him for a quick walk before bedtime and then have his basket in her bedroom overnight.

–

Happily, everything went to plan that evening, and the following morning Grace was able to do a quick tidy around before having a lunch of sausages and mash and taking Fergie for a run in the park after which he curled up in his basket and fell asleep. She then boiled some eggs and mixed them with mayonnaise, mashed the salmon with salt and pepper, and made the sandwiches and placed them into greaseproof bags. The boiled ham sandwiches she decorated with slices of tomatoes and put them on plates on the table covered by an embroidered Irish linen tablecloth. She asked her father to place everything else on the table, as she took Fergie with her upstairs and changed into her best tweed skirt. It had a lovely green, beige, and red pattern, which she matched with a pine-green sweater. Grace brushed her hair and fastened it back with two slides, before applying a light rose lipstick and face powder. She took a final look in the mirror at herself and then left the room followed by Fergie.

The first thing Grace did on entering the kitchen was to check the time on the clock on the mantelshelf and saw that it was three o'clock. She had an hour to check everything was in place before Ben and Simon made an appearance.

Ben did not come empty-handed, but brought three bottles of beer, one of sherry and a bottle of dandelion and burdock. She thanked him and drew him and Simon inside and led them into the parlour and invited them to sit down. The bottles she placed on the sideboard and then she took glasses out of the cupboard beneath and a bottle opener out of a drawer.

The door knocker sounded, and she excused herself and went to answer its summons, leaving her father to see to drinks. As she expected, her aunt, uncle and cousins stood on the step along with Beryl's fiancé, Davy.

'Come on in,' said Grace, stepping aside and holding the door wide open. 'Go into the parlour.'

Polly led the way with her husband Douglas close behind, followed by their daughters and Davy. Grace closed the front door and followed them into the parlour. The three men were on their feet while Simon was on the rug playing with Fergie.

Her aunt sniffed. 'I forgot you had a dog – who's this young man on the floor?'

'I'm Simon,' said the boy, uncurling and rising to his feet. 'My dad is going to marry Grace and they are going to come and live in our house.'

Grace stared at her aunt, whose mouth had fallen open, and waited for the explosion. But it was Marion who said, 'That's a right turn up for the book! You're a right secretive bitch.'

'Language, girl,' rebuked her father. 'Remember you're a guest in this house.'

'Yes, Marion,' said her mother. 'Keep a civil tongue in your head.' She looked across at Ben. 'I take it I'm right in believing you are this young man's father?'

'You are, missus. I'm Ben Evans.' He proffered his hand.

She hesitated and stared at it before taking it and shaking it. 'I presume you do know that Grace was supposed to be marrying my son?'

'Yes, and that they are cousins, and that you and her father were not in favour of the match.'

Grace could not doubt that Ben's words had taken the wind out of her aunt's sail. The next minute her uncle was shaking Ben's hand and congratulating him and welcoming him to the family. Then Beryl and Davy stepped up and shook Ben's hand and had a conversation with him that Grace could not hear. Marion held back and looked on with a disapproving expression as the rest made friends with Ben and his son. Grace asked her father to pour out some drinks. She was relieved that this first meeting between Ben and her relatives had passed with little unpleasantness.

Suddenly her aunt was at her side. Polly made a point of saying to her, 'Have you been in touch with Dougie telling him of your plan to marry someone else?'

Grace smiled and handed Polly a glass of sherry. 'I sent a letter to the address in London that he sent me a couple of days ago. Although, whether he's in London yet I don't know. I also told him that Dad was ill, and I couldn't possibly leave him right now.'

'I see,' said Polly. 'Norman is obviously in favour of you marrying this Ben Evans.'

'Yes, he and Ben and Simon get on like a house on fire.'

'They must if he's prepared to have Norman living with you after your wedding,' said Polly. 'But if Norman is seriously ill, it won't be for long will it?' Her aunt's words and her tone infuriated Grace.

'Well, he'll have the best care we can provide and a good Christmas. The wedding is planned for Sunday 9th December at one o'clock in St Margaret's Church.'

'So soon! You're not pregnant, are you?'

'Certainly not! Dad didn't want us to wait and we thought it would be lovely to spend Christmas Eve under the same roof, so we can watch Simon empty his stocking and open his presents. Unlike Dougie, Ben has a sense of family. Anyway, I'd best go and put the kettle on,' she excused herself. 'Food's ready in the other room, I just need to make a pot of tea.'

As Grace made to leave the room, she was aware that Marion had hurried across to her mother and the four men were in a group talking avidly about the political situation in Germany. The British press were taking a great interest in what was going on in Italy and Germany as the aged German president, Hindenburg, had died a short while ago and it looked likely that the fascist Chancellor, Adolph Hitler, was likely to take over that powerful role. In Italy, fascist Mussolini was in power and it was said that Hitler was a great admirer of the dictator.

'Hitler is a fanatic – he is growing too big for his boots,' she heard Ben say. 'He needs to be stopped. Chamberlain has done his best to bring peace to Europe, but even he agrees there's a lot of dissatisfaction in Germany since the last war and the terms of the Treaty of Versailles.'

'You don't think there'll be another war, do you?' Grace asked, alarmed, from the doorway.

'I bloody hope not,' Ben said vehemently. 'Nobody wants another war, even the Germans, I should imagine. There's no use in worrying about it. We can only leave it to the government and the diplomats and hope for the best.'

'If there is another war,' said Norman. 'It'll be very different to the last one.'

'I wish we hadn't started this conversation,' wailed Grace, worried about losing Ben just as they were about to get married.

'Go put the kettle on for tea,' interrupted Ben, and Grace left the room determined not to worry about such rumours, especially on such an important day like today. She believed that the British government would do anything to prevent another war, so she set aside her fears and got on with making a pot of tea and removing the food from the greaseproof bags. That done she returned to the parlour and told everyone to come through into the kitchen.

Some of her guests seated themselves at the table, while others stood, and Grace handed round plates and told them to help themselves to more food. Ben had saved a chair for her next to him, and once everyone had some food, Grace poured tea into their best china teacups, which were decorated with dark red roses and had belonged to her mother.

'Good spread,' Ben said. 'You must have really worked hard.'

'It's a special occasion,' Grace responded.

'Our wedding will be more special, but I wouldn't expect you to prepare the wedding breakfast or make the cake,' he said with a smile.

'I'll ask Milly for the name of her caterers, although I suppose ours will be a smaller affair as neither of us have a big family like her and Jimmy.'

Ben agreed, 'Just some friends and those of your relatives who are here. Where shall we have the wedding breakfast?'

'We can't afford to hire a hall,' she said.

He agreed, adding that the Co-op hall and the Tudor Rooms would be too large and expensive.

'I'd suggest the church hall,' said Grace. 'But being so close to Christmas, it's probably going to be used for a party for one of the organisations or refreshments after a carol service.' She paused. 'I'll ask Milly and see if she can come up with any ideas.'

She turned away and began to talk to Beryl about her and Davy's wedding plans. As she did so her uncle said, 'Nice food, Grace. The scones are deliciously light.'

She smiled and said, 'That's thanks to Aunt Polly, she taught me.'

Polly smiled across the table at Grace. 'You were a good pupil.'

It was not until her aunt, uncle and cousins were leaving that Polly asked who Grace was having for her bridesmaids. It was a question that Grace had been dreading, and in a voice as calm as she could make it, she replied, 'No bridesmaids, only a matron of honour, my best friend, Milly.'

Her aunt looked as if she had sucked a lemon, but she managed to refrain from voicing her feeling, and simply said, 'Goodnight and thanks for the lovely tea.'

Grace stood on the doorstep, waving until they were out of sight, then she closed the door, rested her back against it and sighed with relief before hurrying into the kitchen and putting on the kettle.

'Anyone for cocoa?' she asked.

Ben and Simon were clearing the plates away, but they each put up a hand. Her father had lit his pipe, but he took it out of his mouth and said, 'You sit down, lass, and relax.

I'll make the cocoa. I must admit that went off better than I thought it would.'

'Everything got eaten,' Simon said forlornly.

'Not everything,' said Grace, going over to the sideboard and taking out an old biscuit tin. She removed the lid and revealed various goodies she had set aside. 'I thought we'd want something to eat with our cocoa.'

The three men grinned and blew her kisses.

Chapter 13

Grace gazed about the room; Milly and Jimmy's friend, Kyle Anderson, had obtained permission from the Seaman's Orphanage for Grace and Ben to use it for their wedding breakfast. Kyle did voluntary work for the orphanage and had paid the hire fee as a wedding present for the couple. The room was just right for their fourteen guests. Ben had considered the gift too much, so had offered his carpentry skills for any future work that the orphanage might need during the coming year.

The last month or so had passed so quickly, and the wedding was in just three days' time. Grace turned to Mrs Audrey Turner, who was in charge of the caterers recommended by Milly, and checked again if there was anything else she needed to do before the big day.

'What about flower arrangements for the tables?' asked Audrey. 'The tableware, food and wedding cake are all organised, but at this time of year there isn't much in the way of flowers for decoration.'

Grace thought about the Christmas Fayre she had been to a few weeks ago in the church hall and remembered the stall with Christmas arrangements created by a couple of the church flower arrangers.

'I'll see what I can do,' she said, thinking to ask the vicar for the addresses of the flower arrangers. She knew their names because she had spoken to them about the wedding flowers in the church.

Grace and Audrey left the orphanage and went their separate ways after arranging to meet the day before the wedding. As she felt the damp kisses of a flurry of sleet on her cheek, Grace prayed for a dry day on the 16th December. When she arrived home, it was to find her father inspecting his suit for the wedding; they had chosen it together from the fifty-shilling tailors. Brand new and of good quality, an extra pair of trousers were given free.

She hoped he would not wear them just for best because she wanted him to get his money's worth out of them. When the results had come back from the hospital last month, they had not been welcome. Norman did have cancer, and a large part of the prostate had been cut away, but one good thing was that an X-ray seemed to show that the cancer had not spread beyond the prostate. The specialist had suggested radium treatment as a small infected area was still there, as it had been difficult to get at during the operation. Norman's treatment would begin in a month's time. Happily, he was grateful for what had been done for him and for the further treatment that was planned, despite there being some side effects after the operation, with others likely to come. There was the possibility of him having a few days convalescent in a rest home in Colwyn Bay on the coast of North Wales in a fortnight's time paid for by the Seamen's Mission, after Grace and Ben returned from a two-day honeymoon in Southport.

Grace thought how fortunate that her father had been thrifty over the years and he had also paid into the seamen's union scheme that helped pay for medical bills. As for the wedding, Ben had savings and Grace's boss gave her a bonus when she finished work and she also had money in her post office savings account. Her uncle Douglas gave her a postal order for twenty pounds.

'At least I've been given more time,' Norman said. 'A hundred years or so ago I'd have been a gonner by now.'

'Isn't medical science marvellous,' said Grace, giving him a hug. 'Could be in another hundred years all cancers will be treatable.'

After urging Norman to take it easy, as he was still recovering from his operation, they had a cup of tea together, and then Grace said that she had to go out again to see some ladies about flower arrangements.

–

That evening Ben and Simon called, and not for the first time, the two men and Grace discussed what Norman and Grace wanted to take with them to their new home and what they wanted to sell. Ben planned to move some of his furniture out too to make room for that of his future wife and father-in-law. He had decided to get rid of his double bed and buy a new one for starters. It was all go, but fortunately Ben had the use of his work's truck to move bulky items for when the households came together.

Grace would have enjoyed shopping for new bedding, but Milly reminded her that it was possible she and Ben might receive bedding as a wedding present, so best to wait and see. When Grace mentioned to Milly that she was feeling apprehensive about her wedding night, and sharing a double bed with a man for the first time, Milly told her that was natural to feel like that, and that it was extremely pleasant snuggling up with the man she loved on a cold night.

'But surely there's more to it than simply snuggling up?' said Grace, quite liking the thought of snuggling up in Ben's arms. Was it possible that it was love she felt towards him?

'Of course! Where do you think babies come from?' Milly went over to her sideboard and riffled in a drawer and removed two books. 'Read these as soon as you can.'

Grace gazed down at the front covers of the books and saw that the authoress was a Marie Stopes and the books were called *Married Love* and *The Human Body*.

'She's written more books – they are a tremendous help for women on subjects that have been taboo for our mothers and grandmothers. Even if your mother had not died, she might not have been much help to you, but Marie explains it all.'

Grace said, 'I can't wait to get reading.'

Milly said, 'If you don't understand anything and need help with it, ask me. There are things that could shock you, but if you remember Almighty God made us the way we are and for a purpose, you'll feel better about it.'

Grace felt a bit odd when she heard that but thanked her anyway. She turned over several pages of *The Human Body*. Her eyes widened, and she decided she would be best reading the books in the privacy of her own bedroom. She realised she was unlikely to get through both books before the wedding, but she maybe could do so while Ben was at work after they were married, as she was uncertain how he would feel about her reading books like these.

That night she read parts of the first book and skipped through the second. There were words she just did not understand and decided to ask Milly about them when she came to help her dress for the wedding. A shiver ran through her, just thinking that in a couple more days she would be married and most likely in bed with Ben in a hotel in Southport.

When she could not keep her eyes open any longer, she placed the books under the bedclothes and tried to sleep, but she found it difficult, as her mind was too active. It was the same the following night, but eventually she managed to drift off and woke to find Milly at her bedside with a cup of tea and a couple of slices of buttered toast on a tray.

–

Milly helped her to sit up and placed the tray in front of her.

'Come on, rise and shine! You're getting married today.'

Grace groaned and dragged the two books from beneath the covers. 'Could you put these in my suitcase under my clothes, please?'

'No wonder you're tired if you stayed away half the night reading,' said Milly. 'Although, I think I'd be best taking these home and you can pick up on your reading in a few days…'

'There are words I don't understand,' said Grace, sipping her tea. 'And I'd rather take the books with me.'

'I should imagine there's more than a few words,' Milly said. 'But right now, I think you need to eat your toast and drink your tea and then get up, wash and dress, and we can talk while I pin up your hair.'

Once Grace had eaten her breakfast, risen from her bed and had a thorough wash all over, she carefully put on the white silk underwear and stockings she had treated herself to from Marks & Spencer. Then she turned to the foot of the bed where Milly had placed the box containing the dress she had worn for her wedding along with a veil and headdress which she had offered to Grace as her something borrowed. Grace had been delighted to accept the kind offer, as she had often admired Milly's dress, and the only addition she had made, was to wear an angora rabbit fur-edged wool bolero on top due to the weather being cold. She wore last winter's leather ankle boots for warmth and comfort.

By the time she was dressed, her father was knocking on the bedroom door asking was she ready, as time was really getting on. Milly opened the door with a flourish and hummed the wedding march; Norman gasped as his daughter appeared in the doorway.

'You look beautiful! I just wish your mother could have been here to see you.'

'So, do I,' said Grace, slipping her arm through his. 'But I'm so happy, Dad, that you're here to give me away.'

Norman led the way down the stairs and into the parlour, saying, 'Your and Milly's bouquets were dropped off a short while ago. Polly, Douglas, Davy and the girls have already left for the church.' He peered out of the window. 'And, if I'm not mistaken, here comes your wedding carriage to take the three of us to church.'

Grace could not help giggling as her wedding carriage was the milkman's cart, with a couple of extra planks for seating, decorated nicely with white ribbons and artificial white flowers. Alf, the milkman, climbed down and assisted the bride and her attendant up into his cart. He also helped Norman up. Then, once Alf was perched up on his seat again, he cracked his whip and told the horse, Old Tom, to walk on.

Grace enjoyed the short journey to the church; she surveyed the pavements both sides of the cart and waved back to those who shouted good wishes. They arrived at the church to be greeted by a crowd of sightseers outside. She caught sight of Kyle with his camera at the ready inside the grounds. She slowed, and she, Norman and Milly posed for him before he darted inside the church and signalled to the vicar that the bride had arrived. The organ burst into sound and the congregation rose to their feet.

'Here we go,' said Norman, with his daughter's hand tucked through his arm.

As she walked slowly up the aisle, Grace's gaze was fixed firmly on Ben's broad back, willing him to turn and look at her, but it was not until she was a yard or so away that he turned his head. Even through her veil, she was aware of his eyes meeting hers. The service seemed to go by as if she was in a dream, but several parts stuck in her mind: the words spoken by Ben, '…*with my body I thee worship*…' and herself replying, '…*love and obey*…' then there was the part about '…*until death do we part*…'.

Awe-inspiring words, she thought, as she left the church on Ben's arm. Would she be able to keep the vow to love and obey him? And what did it mean that he would worship her with his body? Maybe she would find something about that in the books Milly had lent her. It was then she remembered that Milly had forgotten to tell her about those words she did not understand. But then that thought went out of her mind as Kyle called to her and Ben to take a couple's photograph. Grace realised that she was going to have to concentrate on all that was happening in the here and now and put her worries for the night ahead aside.

Ben squeezed her hand. 'What are you thinking about? You seem miles away.'

'No, my thoughts are here with you,' she said, smiling up at her husband, aware of a sense of relief that not for one moment during the service had she given thought to Dougie who was miles away, thank God. The last thing she wanted was him turning up out of the blue and spoiling her and Ben's special day. It was something he might have considered doing, she realised. Perhaps he was not in London yet, so did not know about her wedding as she had not received a letter from him ranting about her letting him down by betraying him with another man.

Instead, she had been able to enjoy outings with Ben, visiting Otterspool in south Liverpool and walking arm in arm along the promenade. She had never given any thought to how it got its name, but now Ben had told her that there used to be otters that played in an inlet of the Mersey that had eventually formed a pool. They had also visited Chester and walked along the River Dee and taken the train to Parbold and walked up the hill where there was a fabulous view of the southern Lancashire plain where one could just about catch the gleam of the Irish Sea in the distance. She had enjoyed those scenic and peaceful moments in Ben's company when their moods seemed to be in complete harmony. Dougie would not have enjoyed just standing and staring but would have wanted to either rush back to the city where there was what he called plenty of things happening; she realised how often he had bullied her into doing what he wanted. There were times when Ben would help her over a stile and draw her gently into his arms when a chill wind blew and kiss her warmly, but there was never any hint of cruelty in his embraces.

Of course, there were evenings when they went to the flickers and enjoyed sitting close in the warmth of the auditorium while outside the wind whipped the rain into a frenzy. There was no embarrassing fumbling in the dark, but she enjoyed the feel of Ben's arm around her shoulders and the scent of his shaving soap, as well as his fingers lacing with hers as they shared a bag of nut brittle while their eyes were fixed on the screen. Afterwards they would fight their way home against the wild weather, laughing but also discussing the films they had watched as well as voicing the hope that the weather would be better on their honeymoon.

Once the wedding breakfast had been eaten, the cake cut and glasses raised to toast the happy couple, the happiness of the day could have been easily soured. As Jimmy, the best man, read the cards and telegrams that had arrived to congratulate the newly-weds; he opened one of the telegrams addressed solely to Grace, and then discreetly put it aside. After waving the bride and groom off as they departed to catch their train to Southport he gave it to the care of his wife, Milly, for safekeeping. Later, they read it again at home together, and burnt it. As they fed the twins, husband and wife pondered on how the telegram would have mortified Grace, and possibly have shaken the foundations of her new marriage.

Unfortunately, they had not accounted for the spitefulness of Dougie's sister, Marion.

Part 2

December 1934–1936

Chapter 14

'Do you fancy a walk along Lord Street before we turn in?' asked Ben.

Grace was in the act of laying out the white negligee embroidered with pink flowers around the scooped neck-line that she had bought at Marks & Spencer on the double bed, and Ben's question and the feel of his hands on her shoulders from behind startled her, causing her to bang her foot against one of the bed's casters. She stumbled and would have fallen onto the bed if her husband had not caught her against his chest and pressed his lips against the nape of her neck.

Grace was tempted to kiss him, but already Ben was moving away from her and reaching for his overcoat.

'If that's what you want,' she replied in a low voice. 'I suppose some fresh air and exercise will clear my mind.'

'I can guess how you feel, conversations buzzing inside your head. One of your cousins asked me had you read the message her brother had sent you.'

Grace sat up. 'I bet it was Marion. She hates me and would like nothing more than to cause distrust between us. There is no message from Dougie. I've not heard from him since I sent him that letter telling him I was marrying you.'

'Why does she hate you?' Ben stared down at Grace.

'I'd rather not talk about it,' she murmured.

'If that's how you feel, it's all right by me.' He began to button up his overcoat. 'Move yourself and let's go for our walk.'

She stood up and fetched her new green winter coat with its beaver lamb collar and her tan gloves and tan felt cloche hat. As they left their bedroom on the second floor of the Prince of Wales hotel, Grace felt near to tears. It was not that she would not enjoy a walk, especially when the shops and Lord Street were decorated already for Christmas with lights and looked wonderful when it was dark – she felt hurt by Ben's eagerness for a walk. It was probably because he was in no rush to make love to her – he was most likely remembering his first wife whom he had been madly in love with, and still was, deep within his heart. How could this convenient match with herself compare? Well, they were just going to have to make it work for Simon's sake, if not their own, because they were tied to each other till death they did part, she thought.

Then, of course, there was this so-called message from Dougie that Ben had mentioned. She had to admit she had been surprised, if not relieved, when Dougie had not responded to her letter back in October. Knowing how he hated to be slighted, she had expected him to rant at her, in a letter, if not the flesh. Dougie had always been so possessive about her, Grace had been bracing herself for an outpouring.

Suddenly, she was aware that the wind had risen. She glanced sidelong at the silent Ben and wondered what he was thinking. She found herself saying, 'The only thing I find wrong with Southport is that it doesn't have what I call a proper "front".'

'It has a pier,' Ben said, looking down at her from beneath the brim of his trilby.

'Piers are interesting,' Grace said with a shiver. 'But it takes some time for the tide to come in here. I wonder why that is. Surely, it's the Irish Sea that washes Lancashire's shores. I mean we can see Blackpool Tower along the coast from here and the tide rolls up the beach there.'

He reached out and took her hand and drew it through his arm.

'Write into the *Echo*, I'm sure they'll find out for you. Because there's bound to be others who've asked themselves the same question.'

'I'll do that, although I wouldn't be surprised if Dad knows, him being a sailor.'

'Perhaps it has to do with the coast being curved along a huge bay between here and Blackpool, and that's why we can see the tower.'

'Shall we go and have a look to see if the tide is on its way in?'

'No, you're shivering. Let's turn back and ask at the hotel for two mugs of cocoa and go to bed.'

'Good idea! Just what I need,' she said, hugging his arm.

Once back in their bedroom, Ben rang for room service and asked for two mugs of cocoa. While they waited for their drinks, Grace went along the corridor to a bathroom for a wash. She did consider having a bath, but decided there were people who might wish to use the lavatory in a hurry. She changed into her negligee while in the bathroom and then hurried back to the bedroom with her clothes under her arm.

'What's this? Changed already,' said Ben, taking her clothes from her and placing them on a chair.

Grace noticed the cocoa had been delivered and that Ben had removed his wedding suit and was wearing a light blue and black patterned dressing gown. She was unsure what he was wearing underneath because his muscular calves were bare.

'I'll just nip to the lavatory,' he said. 'Drink up your cocoa. Don't let it get cold.'

She took the mug and placed it on the cabinet on the right side of the bed and climbed beneath the covers and pulled them up to her shoulders and reached for her mug. She leaned back against the pillows and said a prayer for her father and Simon and gave thanks that everything had gone off well that day so far and asked that she and Ben would please each other.

The door opened and Ben entered just as she placed her empty cocoa mug on the cabinet. He drank the remains of his cocoa and placed their mugs back on the tray. Then he removed his dressing gown and she saw he was wearing a nightshirt that was unbuttoned at the neck and reached to his knees. He slid into bed on the left side and said, 'I presume you always sleep on the right side of the bed?'

'I normally sleep in the middle of the bed, but face right,' she replied. 'Why, do you want to sleep on this side?' She made to get out and moved to the other side. He shuffled to the centre of the bed, watching her. She climbed into the left side of the bed and nudged him to move over with an elbow. He did not move. 'I'm going to be squashed,' she said. 'You need to move over.'

'I know your game,' he said. 'Do you know the song, "There's two in the bed and the little one said, 'Roll over, roll over?' They both rolled over, and one fell out.'"

'You've altered the words,' Grace said, laughing.

'Of course, I have to, it suits the situation we're in.'

'Are you saying if you roll over to give me more room, you'll fall out?'

'What do you think?' he asked.

'That you'll only fall out if you move too far.'

'Then I suggest we both stay in the centre of the bed,' said Ben.

Grace said, 'We both can't stay in the centre of the bed.'

'We can,' he said, turning to face her. 'All we have to do is cuddle up close. It's cosy that way.'

Grace could feel her heartbeat accelerating as his arms embraced her and he drew her closer. She stammered, 'Of course, you have experience of this. You've been married before.'

'I have, but you're forgetting my wife was not a well woman and there's been times when I've wondered how we managed to conceive Simon. Lovemaking wasn't often on the cards.'

'That must have been difficult for you,' Grace said sympathetically, slipping an arm about his waist over his nightshirt. She realised he had no underpants on beneath the nightshirt and suddenly she was shivering with nerves.

'I appreciate that, but you're a virgin, so how can you know of my frustration?' He slackened his hold of her. Grace tensed, afraid that she had said the wrong thing. Ben misreading her expression asked quickly, 'Or am I mistaken and you're not a virgin—'

Grace felt anger rising inside her and drew away from him, only for him to pull her close again and said jokingly, 'Tell me what you have to say for yourself?'

'What a thing to say! You insult me, Ben. I'm no innocent, but I am a virgin.'

'No innocent – what does that mean?'

'Free me and I'll show you,' Grace said, struggling in his grasp. He released her and watched as she went over to her suitcase and began to take clothes out and place them neatly on the dressing table. Then she produced what looked to him like books and she brought them over and hesitated slightly before tossing them in his direction. She did not get into bed but stood at the foot of it, watching him.

He picked up the first book and read the title, *Married Love,* and then the other, *The Human Body.* Ben raised his eyebrows and grinned, 'Have you read both?'

Relieved that he was not cross, Grace climbed into bed. 'Not completely and there are sections I just don't understand. Milly lent me them a short while ago. I had no mother to go to, and my aunt would have thought the worst of me if I'd asked her for advice, especially how things stand with us after my breaking with Dougie.'

'You never thought we could do just what came naturally? Why didn't you ask me?'

'That might have worked if…' she hesitated '…if ours was more than a convenient match.'

'I can see how it could have seemed like that to you,' he said, and then was silent for what seemed an age to Grace.

'I'm sorry if I've upset you,' she said.

'No, there's no need for you to say you're sorry. I have to admit that our marriage is convenient for me but I thought you would find it convenient as well.'

'But I made a vow to love you,' she said.

Ben drew her down close to him. 'I think we'll grow to love each other over time and as we get to know each other better. As it is, we like and respect each other.'

He started to kiss her, partly covering her body with his. Her arms went up around his neck, and it was not until he removed them and planted little kisses down her throat and upper curve of a breast did it occur to her that they were doing what came naturally and she wanted it to go on for ever. Then to her surprise, he lifted himself off her slightly and said playfully, 'Perhaps now's the time to read those books?'

–

The following morning, they woke to the sound of rain on the windowpanes.

'Blast!' exclaimed Grace sleepily. 'It's raining.'

'Then let's stay in bed,' Ben said cheerfully.

She gazed into his twinkling brown eyes. 'That sounds lovely, but I'm hungry.'

'Madam, can have both,' he said. 'I asked if we could have breakfast served in our room.'

She kissed him. 'Oh, you are clever.'

'I knew that would please us both,' he said. 'And later, rain or no rain, we'll go and see if the tide is in and if it isn't, we can walk on the sand and then along the pier if it's open.'

After a breakfast of cornflakes, bacon and egg, and toast and marmalade, Ben tossed one of the books to her and suggested in all seriousness that they read parts of them with their pot of tea.

'No doubt Jimmy, as well as Milly, have read them, and they seem happy enough.'

'And now they have the twins who are adorable,' said Grace.

Only later as they walked along the beach after the rain had stopped did they share some of what they had read. They also talked of other things, such as the wedding and their guests, but soon the talk turned to places they would like to visit, their favourite foods, films and the games they played as children. They held back from discussing what the future might hold, as both were aware of Norman's recent operation, but they did remark how nice it would be to have a new house with a bathroom and indoor lavatory as well as a garden. Grace then asked Ben about his job and whether he really enjoyed it. Ben nodded.

'Although, I would like a change from making window and door frames, but that's where the demand is, so I have to stick at it.'

'What about furniture?'

'I occasionally turn my hand to making something more creative. I've made some of the furniture in the house as well as some toys for Simon. I enjoy carving and I'd do more of it if I had the time to market it. It was my brother who taught me. He was really creative.'

'I can't wait to see what you've created with those nimble fingers of yours. I like embroidery, but I haven't done much since I moved back in with Dad and started my job at the dentist's.'

He reached for her hand and gazed down at the shiny new wedding ring on her work-worn left hand. 'I wish I could have bought you an engagement ring.' He drew her hand through his arm. A chill wind had risen and was whipping the sand up, as well as fluttering her tartan woollen headscarf.

'Thank you for the thought, but I don't need one. I'm content with this golden band.'

'I'm glad about that,' he said. 'Shall we go and find a nice, warm cafe and have some fish and chips?'

'Yeah, that sounds great.' She hugged his arm. 'Could we go to the flicks this afternoon?'

'I was going to suggest that as it'll be warmer than walking along the pier.'

'Great minds think alike,' she said.

But when they asked in the cafe, it was to be told there wasn't a picture palace in Southport and it was suggested that they visit the Garrick Theatre, although it was doubtful there would be a matinee performance on a Monday afternoon. They decided to gaze in the shop windows under cover of the Victorian wrought-iron and glass arcade along Lord Street. They saw little to tempt them and returned to the hotel to be told by the receptionist that there would be a tea dance in an hour in the hotel's ballroom.

The pair rushed upstairs and had a rest and a cuddle on the bed before changing into something more suitable for dancing. Grace pulled on a floral organdie frock with a cream cotton underskirt which she had bought in a sale at Lewis's. The underskirt had some of the stitching undone. She admitted the only dancing that she had ever done was barn dancing in the church hall. As he watched her, Ben replied that the only dances he knew were the waltz and the polka.

'We can always just watch and see whether we can pick up the steps,' Grace suggested.

'Agreed,' he said, offering his hand. 'Let's shake on it.'

So, they did, and walked downstairs hand in hand. Tables for two were set out in a circle around the dance floor in the ballroom. They chose one not too close to the band, a waiter came up to them immediately bearing a pot of tea and teacups and saucers.

'I can scarcely believe this is me sitting here,' said Grace. 'Is it real?'

'Of course, it's real!' Ben paused, his head cocked to one side. 'How about a dance? If my ears don't deceive me the band have just struck up a polka.'

He rose to his feet and held out a hand to her. Grace placed her hand in that of her husband and in no time at all he was whirling her around the dance floor. At first, she almost fell over his feet and Ben had to lift her up by the waist to prevent them both from losing their balance. Then Grace caught the rhythm and by the time the dance came to an end, she was breathless with laughter.

They sat out the next dance and had a cup of tea, and shortly after they danced the last waltz and then went upstairs to have a rest before getting ready for dinner. She did not know what Ben might have had in mind when they lay side by side on the bed in their underwear, but she found herself drifting off and when she regained consciousness, it was to the feel of his arms around her and her head against his shoulder and she could hear his steady breathing and guessed that he had fallen asleep as well. She lay there, unmoving until she realised his breathing had changed and sensed that he was awake.

'I suppose we should be making a move,' he said.

She agreed, but added, 'But I'm so comfortable.'

'Me too, but I'm hungry.'

Reluctantly they disentangled themselves and dressed and went downstairs. Over a meal of cream of vegetable soup, game pie and fried potatoes, they discussed whether they should go straight home after breakfast in the morning or spend the morning in Southport and aim to be home in time for Grace to cook a dinner for the four of them.

'I think I've seen enough of Southport,' said Grace, after swallowing a mouthful of tasty game pie. 'What about going to Formby on the way home and walking along the beach there and watching the waves crashing on the sand?'

'That's a smashing idea,' Ben said.

She beamed at him and managed to hold back from saying that it was a place that she and her cousins, Dougie and the girls, had visited with her aunt and uncle by train as young children. She recalled how Dougie had challenged her and her sisters to leap off the top of a high sandhill. Grace had not wanted to do it as she was scared of heights. Dougie had called her 'a scaredy boots!' and pushed her over the edge. She remembered the feeling when she had plunged into the hard sand below. How was it she had allowed the bullying actions of Dougie as a child to have slipped her memory? How had she allowed herself at sixteen to be so infatuated with him as not to see what he was really like?

'You look miles away,' said Ben. 'What are you thinking?'

She hesitated briefly. 'I was thinking of Simon and Dad and how much they'd enjoy a trip to Formby beach.'

'Then what about just the two of us going to Formby this time and we'll take Simon and Norman another time when the weather is warmer?'

Despite a chillness about her heart, Grace agreed, hoping her father would still be alive when the weather warmed up.

–

Before they left the hotel, Grace made a point of asking the receptionist whether there was anywhere in Southport she could buy a game pie. She hastened to add, 'I'm sure your chef makes his own, but I'm sure my father and stepson would enjoy any game pie when we arrive home.' The receptionist smiled and said she would look into it.

An hour later a maid knocked on their bedroom door and handed a well wrapped package to Grace. 'The chef sent this with his compliments and with his wishes that your family enjoy it and that we have the pleasure of serving you again.' Grace was almost overcome, but managed to express her gratitude, and to wish her and all the staff a happy Christmas as she handed over a large tip.

She explained to Ben and he felt the weight of the package and said, 'I reckon there's plenty enough there for the four of us. Kind of him. Wrapped as it is and what with the cold weather it should be fine, even with us going to Formby.'

Chapter 15

The newly-weds enjoyed their time on the Formby shore, having managed to leave their luggage with the station master before setting out on the walk to the beach a couple of miles away. The tide was on its way in, so they walked down to the water's edge and despite the cold, removed their shoes, socks and stockings to have a paddle. When they could bear the temperature no longer, they ran hand in hand along the sands whooping like children before settling on a low sandhill to watch the waves.

'I enjoyed that,' said Grace as they brushed the sand off their feet and then set out for the station where they reclaimed their possessions and caught the Liverpool train home.

'Me too,' Ben said. 'I felt carefree, just what I needed before having to settle down to earning a living again and coping with ordinary life.'

She darted him a questioning look. 'But it won't be the old ordinary life, will it? Not now we're married and living together with Simon and Dad.'

'You're right, but we won't be able to spend the same amount of time like we have, just the two of us having fun,' he said seriously.

'No,' she said. 'We'll have to try and make time, but I don't suppose it'll be easy.'

'We'll have more demands on us.'

'Yes, I realised that a while ago – it's why I gave in my notice at the dentist's,' she said. 'I'd be no use to you, Dad and Simon, and even Fergie, if I were exhausted all the time.'

—

When they arrived in Liverpool, they headed for Elliot Street and St John's Market to buy special ingredients for their first meal at home with Simon and Norman. Inside it felt colder than outside, so they quickly bought vegetables, fresh bread and cream buns, bananas and a couple of large 'Jaffas' to share. Then they caught the tram to West Derby Road and got off by Saxon Street where Ben's house was situated. Grace felt strange not returning to her dad's, but Norman had moved into Ben's while they had been in Southport.

Ben took his door key from his pocket and opened the front door. Then he placed suitcases on the step and lifted the surprised and giggling Grace off her feet and carried her over the threshold with the shopping bags swinging from her arms. They almost hit Ben in the face as she linked her hands behind his neck.

'Ye daft ha'porth,' she said, a choke in her voice. Then she heard Fergie barking. The kitchen door opened, and the dog squeezed through the gap past Simon.

'You're home,' he shouted, then added over his shoulder. 'Granddad, they're home!'

Without waiting for a response from Norman, the boy rushed down the lobby and flung himself at Ben and Grace. Unfortunately, Grace chose that moment to unclasp her hands and Ben felt her slipping from his grasp. The next second the three of them ended in a heap on the floor, almost squashing Fergie to death. The dog managed to worm his way out from under and immediately sought out Grace and began to lick her face. Ben seized Fergie and handed him to Norman who had arrived on the scene, just in time to prevent the dog from dragging out a package from one of the shopping bags. Norman then helped Simon to his feet with his free hand, while Ben hoisted his wife upright.

'Well, that was some welcome home,' said Grace, seizing both shopping bags and leading the way to the kitchen, pausing only to plant a kiss on her father's cheek before entering the kitchen. A fire glowed red in the black-leaded range and a table covered with her best table-cloth and set with cutlery and plates for four, was another welcome sight. For a moment she could only wonder if they had cooked dinner for them, but she could not smell anything on the hob.

Then her father said, 'I hope there's dinner in those shopping bags, lass.'

'Of course,' she replied, shrugging off her coat and removing her scarf and gloves before unpacking the shopping.

–

The meal was devoured in no time despite the four of them talking almost non-stop as they shared their news. Afterwards, Simon volunteered to do the dishes while Grace and Ben went upstairs to unpack; Norman relaxed in front of the fire with Southport's local paper. The layout of the house was pretty well much the same as the house her father had rented in the next street, although it was on the other side of the street, and of course, Grace would no longer be sleeping in the middle bedroom that overlooked a backyard, but in the larger front bedroom that gazed over the street. She had expected the bedroom to be very much a man's bedroom, but as it was there was a floral eiderdown on the double bed, and the pillows were covered with frilled pillowcases. There were two doors in the alcoves each side of the bedhead.

'You've blocked in the little fireplace,' she said.

'Well spotted,' said Ben, placing the suitcases on the bed. 'I had no need of it, and besides, I couldn't afford coal for two fires.'

There was a dressing table in the bay window space in front of which there was a chair. On the dressing table was a cut-glass trinket bowl and two candlestick holders with white candles. There was also a washstand with a bowl and a pitcher underneath and on the rails either side of the stand were towels. There was a gas lamp on a bracket attached to the wall opposite the bed, as well as two pictures, one of a seascape and another of a path running through a wood.

'Did you make the washstand?'

He nodded. 'And the dressing table and the two built-in cupboards.'

'You are clever,' she murmured, going over to have a closer look of the pictures. 'Did you paint these?'

'No, my dad did.'

She whirled round. 'He was talented.'

'Yeah, my brother Martin was, too.' He opened a cupboard and took out a couple of carved animals. 'He carved these for me when I was just a kid.'

She peered closer at the paintings before taking the wooden animals from him. 'These are so realistic, just like the paintings. I feel like I could walk into those woods and swim in that sea.'

'Dad went to Liverpool Art School. They thought he could have won a scholarship to the Royal Academy in London,' said Ben quickly. 'But he wouldn't have gone, his parents couldn't afford it, and besides, it takes some doing making a living in the arts. Now, let's drop the subject.'

Grace stared at his closed-off face, she went word-lessly over to the bed and opened her suitcase and started removing clothing. She wanted to ask which cupboard and drawers she should take, but Ben's expression was still off-putting, so she tried a door and found its interior was empty but for several items on a top shelf, under which was a rail to hang coats, dresses and the like.

She removed a coat hanger and hung up a dress, then a skirt and a blouse and cardigan. Her nightdress she placed under the pillow on the same side of the bed she had slept on their honeymoon. She then thought of the clothes she had not taken on honeymoon and wondered where her father had put them, as she would need to sort and unpack them as well. She doubted they were still in the other house. Perhaps Ben would know. She glanced in his direction and their eyes met and she realised he must have been watching her every movement.

'Do you know where the rest of my clothes are?' she asked.

His expression relaxed. 'Probably in the Gladstone bag in the parlour,' he said. 'Shall I go and fetch it for you?'

She smiled. 'Yes, please.'

Then she glanced about her. 'This is a nice room.'

'The sun will wake you up mornings.' He paused. 'I'm glad you like the room. I wasn't sure the wallpaper would be to your taste or if you'd prefer something fancier.'

Grace had not noticed the wallpaper, but now she took a proper look at it. Pale orange with a silvery white pattern on that was not small or fussy and didn't it hit you in the face. It was a good background for the pictures. She checked the curtains, which were patterned in geometrical shapes of brown, beige, and cream, and decided she didn't like them with the wallpaper. She thought the curtains from the old house would match better, but she would not say anything now, perhaps she could change them next week and see if Ben noticed. As for the floor that was covered in linoleum in a pattern that looked like wood grain. There was a rag rug either side of the bed in a mixture of fabrics and colours. They appeared well-worn and she wondered if Ben's first wife had made them.

As if he could read her mind, he said, 'Me mam made them for me.'

'It must have taken her a while,' said Grace.

'We'd knock on the back doors of posh houses asking for any old rags they could spare. So, what do you think? I know the rugs don't go with the décor.'

She reached out and took his hand. 'I was thinking of making two new ones… but now knowing they are precious to you, I suggest we wash them in a tub once spring arrives. And while we wait, I could crochet a fringe with orange wool on both, so they match each other and the wallpaper.'

'You can crochet!'

'Of course, you silly man! I wouldn't have suggested it if I couldn't.'

'Who are you calling silly?' he teased. 'I married you, didn't I? I reckon that was clever of me.' He pulled her close and hugged her. 'Who taught you to crochet? Your aunt?'

'No, I've only learnt since Dad's been home more often. He used to crochet and knit when he was away on long trips. Apparently, he found it soothing, so I asked him to teach me. I could already knit.'

Ben said, 'Perhaps you could teach me, and we could do a rug each and maybe Norman would help too.'

She freed herself from his grasp and knelt on the linoleum to inspect the edge of one of the rugs. Her opinion of Ben was now even higher – some men would have bridled against assisting in such a task – Dougie, for instance. She thanked God that he was hundreds of miles away and for her lucky escape. She prayed that he would meet someone who would suit him better.

Chapter 16

As Grace went about her household tasks during the days after her return from Southport, she sang as she swept and washed floors, and polished the furniture, thinking how the four of them had settled down so well together. Only occasionally did she wish herself and Ben back in Southport, just the two of them together. Then she told herself how fortunate she was in having a good home and husband, and her father looking so much better, content in Ben and Simon's company, and in seeing his daughter settled.

A few days later Grace woke early. She left Ben fast asleep and stealthily slid out of bed and went downstairs and set and lit the fire, put the kettle on and made Ben's carry-out of corned beef and Branston pickle butties and then mixed some tea leaves with condensed milk and wrapped it in greaseproof paper. Then she placed the lot in his knapsack along with a tin mug. She had just brewed a pot of tea when she heard footsteps on the stairs. A minute or two later Ben entered the kitchen. His thatch of hair was an untidy mess and he needed a shave.

'What are you doing up so early?' he asked. 'It's not even light yet.'

'I woke early, and you were fast asleep, so I thought I'd get a start on the day and have a fire ready for you and do your carry-out.'

'That was good of you,' he said, warming his hands by the fire. 'But didn't you think I'd have liked a cuddle?'

'You fell asleep straight away last night, so I really thought you needed your sleep,' she said, offering him a cup of tea.

He took the cup and placed it on the mantelshelf and drew her towards him, slipping his warm hands up the back of her jumper and beneath her camisole, then he bent his head and kissed her.

The feel of his warm hands on her bare skin was delightful and she responded to his kiss with enthusiasm, then a voice said, 'Morning, can I have a cup of tea and a warm by the fire, please?' A startled Grace almost jumped out of her skin, and Ben withdrew his hands quickly, but still holding his wife, he manoeuvred her away from the fireplace.

'You're up early, son,' said Ben, reaching out for a cup of tea.

'I wouldn't have been if you'd let me stay up later,' grumbled Simon. 'Granddad suggested me and him going into town and visiting the museum, then having something to eat out before going to the flicks.'

'That sounds like a fun-packed day.' Grace moved over to the table and poured tea into a cup and indicated that the boy add milk and sugar. She was still struggling against an urge to giggle, so left the room and went into the back kitchen where Fergie was standing by his feeding bowl. She decided once she had the house to herself, she would do the housework before taking Fergie for a walk and then do some shopping. She knew that she should go and visit her aunt, but she was just not in the mood, knowing that she would be bombarded with questions that she did not wish to answer, aware that what she said might be reported to Dougie.

Later on that day, Grace was taking Fergie for a walk before she tackled the day's shopping, when she met Milly pushing the pram with the twins propped up either end, taking in the world around them.

'Gosh, they're all there, aren't they?' said Grace.

'Yes,' said Milly proudly. 'Jimmy's mother is so made up with them and now the weather has turned unseasonably mild, she's suggesting we take them over to see her in New Brighton, so she can show them off to her friends over there.'

'It would be a nice break for you, and you could take the pram if you go by train or ferry,' said Grace. 'You'll have to walk into town, of course.'

'We'll definitely do that,' said Milly. 'We could even go on the beach if the weather continues mild. When you think it snowed in November and now it's like early spring!'

'Simon was hoping it would snow for Christmas,' Grace said. 'I think he's going to be disappointed, though.'

Milly said, 'How was Southport?'

'Good, the food in the hotel was really tasty, and we had a nice bedroom.'

'All went well, then?'

'Mmmm… we both read part of the books you lent me.' She paused. 'My eyes have been opened I can tell you!'

'Ben didn't take against them?'

'Not when I told him that you and Jimmy had read them,' Grace smiled.

'I wonder if he'll mention doing so to Jimmy,' said Milly thoughtfully.

'Would he tell you if Ben did?' asked Grace, feeling a tug on the leash as Fergie began to get impatient.

'I'm not sure. Men aren't like us women, are they? Men talk is exactly that – for men only.'

Grace did not deny it, but said that she had better be on her way as Fergie was getting restless, so they parted, with Grace agreeing to pop round later once she had run her errands. She went to the park first, and then she went to buy wool and crochet hooks and meat for their evening meal.

She was just returning from the shops when she heard her name being called. She looked about her and caught sight of her cousin Marion, and groaned. She was one of the last people she wanted to see and wished her to the other side of the world; she was bound to ask how her honeymoon had been and whatever Grace said was bound to be repeated to Dougie. Grace remembered it had been Marion who had seen Grace out with Syd all those years ago and believed it was her who had told Dougie.

'What are you doing here?' Grace asked.

'That's a nice welcome that is,' said Marion.

'Well, it's not often you show your face round here,' retorted Grace. 'Are your mam and dad all right?'

'They're fine,' Marion said, as she flicked a strand of dark hair away from her left eye. 'I'm just wondering if you got to see the wedding telegram our Dougie sent you?'

'What telegram?' asked Grace with a sinking heart. 'Are you trying to cause trouble like you have in the past?'

Marion punched her on the shoulder, quite hard. 'Why should you think that?'

Fergie growled and would have gone for Marion if Grace had not pulled him back.

'Don't you hit me,' said Grace, rubbing her shoulder. 'I'm not a little girl that you can boss around anymore. If there had been a telegram from Dougie the best man would have mentioned it.'

'Not if he thought it would upset his friend,' chortled Marion.

Anger flashed in Grace's hazel eyes. 'I take it you read it, then.'

Marion sneered, 'Of course. Dougie sent it to me first and then I put it in with the other messages to be read out. You should be ashamed of yourself, Miss So-called Innocent.'

'What are you talking about? I've had enough of this,' said Grace, turning on her heel and walking away, pulling on Fergie's leash.

Marion shouted, 'I remember word for word what it said, and I'll write it down and send it to Ben. You'll just have to hope you'll get to it first.'

Grace halted and said, 'Why do you hate me so much?'

'I don't hate you. I've heard it said that one needs to have loved first to hate and I've never cared for you. From the moment you came to stay in our house I loathed you. Always going around and taking all our mam's attention, just because your mother died.'

'You'd have wanted attention if your mother had died when you were my age and had no brothers and sisters. I never did you any harm,' said Grace.

'You wouldn't understand, poor little motherless girl,' taunted Marion. 'When our Beryl was born, she got the attention Mam had given me – even Dad was made up when I was born, having a daughter after a son. Then Beryl arrived on the scene and babies always get spoilt. I was just the piggy in the middle. Happily, Dougie resented her as much as I did, as he'd had his nose pushed out of joint when I was born, so he and I joined forces when Beryl was old enough for us to lord it over. The last thing we wanted was another kid getting all the attention, as well as joining forces with Beryl.'

'You're sick in the head,' Grace muttered.

'What did you say?' asked Marion, bringing her face up close to Grace's. She drew back and hurried off to Milly's and did not wait to be asked inside but stepped straight over the threshold, dragging Fergie with her. Once inside she rested against the lobby wall and took deep breaths.

Milly stared at her. 'What's wrong? Is it your dad?'

Grace shook her head and signalled to her friend to wait until you got her breath back.

Milly took her by the arm and helped her into a seat in the kitchen. 'Now take your time and I'll make you a cup of tea.'

'Thanks,' Grace managed to say before leaning back in the chair, a hand gripping Fergie's collar. He was sitting at her feet, staring at the twins propped up with cushions in a playpen, each holding a fluffy toy, one a teddy and the other a small white dog. There were other toys nearby and one of the twins was bouncing in a way that caused her to move a little towards a counting toy. A low growl rumbled in the dog's throat causing Grace to rebuke him, even as she lifted him onto her lap and held him tight. When Milly entered the room carrying a tray, Grace asked whether she should put Fergie in the backyard.

'If you think he'll be all right there,' said Milly.

'He should be, and we won't stay long,' Grace assured her.

'So, what's upset you?' asked Milly.

'My cousin Marion – she told me that Dougie had sent a wedding telegram and asked me if I'd seen it. She suggested that there was something horrid about me in it…'

'Oh, that… Yes, there was a wire from Dougie. Jimmy hid it, and then we destroyed it on the night of the wedding thinking Dougie was just being spiteful and out to spoil your marriage,' Milly confessed.

'Oh, thank you,' said Grace, pleating her skirt with restless fingers. 'But even so, Marion is still out to blacken my name. Dougie sent it to her apparently, and she read it and put it with the other telegrams. She remembers what it said and is going to send a copy to Ben! She said if I don't want him to read it, then I'll have to intercept it, that won't be easy because Dad or Simon might pick it up and put it aside for Ben to read when he comes home from work…' She paused for breath. 'My head's in a whirl. I don't even know what it said! I'm confused and don't know what's best to do. I want to save our marriage, as things are working out so well, but I know what Dougie is like, he can be so mean-spirited if he wants to be…' A sob escaped her. 'Marion has always had it in for me, and I know why now and it's so childish.'

Milly hushed her and poured out tea and milk into cups before handing one to Grace. 'Jimmy and I don't believe a word of what Dougie wrote,' she said soothingly. 'Besides which, surely Ben will know by now you were a virgin on your wedding night?' Here her voice softened, 'In the telegram, Dougie accused you of being a slut and throwing yourself at Dougie and being damaged goods and that he is glad that Ben has taken you off his hands, but that sort of slur only had power to ruin your marriage before your wedding night, it simply doesn't matter now. For some reason Marion has not realised that.'

Grace stopped crying and wiped her damp cheeks with the back of a hand. 'But what will the neighbours think if it got out?' she whispered. 'It's all lies, all of it, but you know how people talk around here. And it would shame Ben if he thought that I was putting myself around before I married him. He would still think I was damaged goods, or he'd been tricked into marrying me. And what about my dad? It's awful!' she groaned.

Milly nodded. 'I understand, but I think you're worrying unnecessarily. If Ben was to see the words that were written on the telegram, I consider him intelligent enough to know what Dougie and Marion were up to. And to ask you about it... he knows the girl he married,' she said gently.

Feeling much calmer and reassured by her friend, Grace dried her eyes and drank the remains of her tea before fetching Fergie from the backyard to go home. She thanked Milly profusely, who handed Grace her shopping and then gave her a hug goodbye. Once home, Grace made herself an early lunch of toast and brawn and fed Fergie scraps from her plate. Then, with the dog on her lap, exhausted by the day's revelations, she fell asleep in front of the low-burning fire.

She was wakened by a banging on the front door and still half asleep, staggered to the front door. Cautiously she asked who it was before opening the door. Her spirits plummeted when a voice called out, 'Police.'

Chapter 17

Grace whipped the door open and stared at the bobby who had a serious expression on his young face. Standing beside him was a worried-looking Simon.

'Mrs Evans?' said the bobby.

'Yes,' replied Grace, her eyes wide open now.

'Your father is Norman Green?'

She nodded, reaching out a hand to Simon. 'Has there been an accident?'

'No, but your father has been taken to the Royal Infirmary after collapsing in the museum,' said the policeman.

'We were standing in front of a huge spider crab,' said Simon. 'Suddenly, he swayed and reached out to me. I grabbed his hand, but I didn't have a proper hold of it,' Simon gulped. 'He fell to the floor. I tried to help him up but wasn't strong enough and one of the attendants came running.' He paused. 'Granddad's not going to die, is he?' he whispered.

'Shush, lad,' said the policeman. 'I could take you to the hospital in the police car now, Mrs Evans, if you wish to see your father.'

'Of course, thank you,' Grace said. 'If you'll give me a few minutes. I was having a nap and your knock woke me. I'd like to splash some cold water on my face and put my coat and hat on. Do come in,' she said, leading the way up the lobby. 'Simon, perhaps you should stay here with Fergie. I'll ask Mrs Shaw next door to keep an eye on you.'

As soon as she was ready and had spoken to Mrs Shaw, Grace went with the policeman in the shiny black police car to the hospital. The building had been constructed in Victorian times and its outer walls were blackened with the smoke from chimneys over the years. Grace was shown into a long ward with high windows on either side. To her relief she found her father awake, although he looked pale and anxious. She sat on a chair at the side of the bed and covered his hand on the bedcover with hers, before asking if he had seen a doctor.

Norman nodded. 'He reckons I've been doing too much.'

'It's my fault. I shouldn't have gone on my honey-moon.'

He shook his head. 'Don't be daft. I was glad you were away. I wasn't going to tell you but I had a nasty letter from Dougie. He went on about why couldn't I have got sick and died six months ago. Then you'd have been on the ship with him and he wouldn't have got into debt and you wouldn't have been forced into marrying another man because you were pregnant with his baby.'

'The lying swine!' She shivered, even as she attempted to control her nerves, thinking what a day it had been so far. 'He's despicable. Have they given you any idea how long you'll be in here?' she asked.

'I should imagine I'll be home tomorrow.' Norman paused. 'Don't feel that you have to come and see me again today. You have enough to do with having Simon and Ben to look after.'

'Should I let Aunt Polly and Uncle Douglas know you're here?'

'No, not worth it.' He closed his eyes. 'You can go now, lass. I feel like having a doze.'

Grace kissed his cheek. 'Behave yourself. Don't be flirting with the nurses,' she joked.

'I wish! Bye, lass. Take care!' he murmured.

Grace walked slowly out of the ward and caught a tram almost straight away. When she arrived home, she found Simon peeling potatoes.

'That's good of you,' she said, giving him a hug. 'I bought some mutton chops and carrots and a turnip earlier. I'd bought a chop for Dad, but you and your dad can share it.'

'How's Granddad?' Simon asked.

'He thinks he'll be home tomorrow,' she replied. 'They're of the opinion he collapsed due to him doing too much.'

Simon's face lit up. 'Goody, I'm glad they're letting him out.'

'Me too,' said Grace.

Ben took the news about Norman in his stride, but over dinner, he decided that he would go and see his father-in-law and hopefully have a word with the doctor and try and arrange for him to go to the convalescent home straight away. Grace thanked him, knowing that if there was anything else her father was keeping back from her, Ben would get at the truth simply because those in authority were more likely to talk to him because he was a man. Irritatingly it was a fact of life and something women were still fighting against.

When Ben returned from the hospital, he stood watching his son and wife playing snakes and ladders. Grace's mind was not completely on the game and her husband's presence caused her to lose her concentration utterly.

'So, how were things?' she asked hesitantly.

'Your dad was pleased to see me, and we had a good chat.'

'What about the doctor? Were you able to speak with him?' She was guessing her father had not mentioned Dougie's letter by the tone of her husband's voice.

'No, apparently it's his daughter's birthday and there was to be a party, so he had to leave.' He paused. 'But matron did verify that Norman will be allowed to go home at eleven o'clock tomorrow morning. I think you should be there and arrange for a cab to pick you up at the hospital and bring you both home.' He delved into his trouser pocket and produced two half crowns. 'I don't know how much it'll cost. Hopefully, this will be enough.'

Grace hoped so too, and thanked him as she took the money.

–

The following morning, she was up early, as was Ben, who had the fire blazing before she arrived downstairs. He had also prepared his carry-out of cheese and pickle butties and had the kettle on. Simon came downstairs soon after and the three of them sat down together and ate cereal followed by toast and jam. Ben left first at a quarter to eight and Simon at eight thirty after Grace had ironed his footie shirt and shorts for the last school game of the term. After she had seen him off at the door, she set about doing her household chores.

She had scarcely finished and was putting the kettle on before going shopping and taking Fergie for a walk when there came a knock on the door. She hurried to answer it and there was Milly with the twins in the pram on the doorstep.

'Hi!' she said. 'I thought I'd call and see how you were. I've also something to tell you that you won't want to hear.'

'That sounds ominous,' said Grace. 'I'll be going out soon, but I'm about to have a cuppa, so come join me.'

Milly put the brake of the pram on and leaving the front door slightly ajar, she and Grace went indoors.

The kettle was boiling, so Grace made two cups of tea and they both sat down. 'What have you to tell me?' she asked.

'Firstly, have you spoken to Ben about the telegram and what Marion threatened you with yesterday?'

'No, because Dad collapsed and was taken to hospital, so it went completely out of my mind.' Grace took a sip of tea. 'They're letting him out today, so I'll be going there before lunch.'

'He must be all right then,' Milly said.

'They reckon he'd been overdoing things.' Grace drank more of her tea. 'So, what's this news I won't want to hear?'

Milly hesitated and then said in a rush, 'I could have sworn that earlier I saw Dougie or someone who looked very like him.'

Grace thought of the mean words in Dougie's telegram and all that he had threatened to do to her standing in the community and of the letter he had sent to her father and her heart plunged into her stomach.

'I hope you were mistaken. I would have thought Aunt Polly would have let me know if he was coming home for a visit.' Her voice shook. 'I'd like to kill him.'

'He could be out to just get on your nerves,' mused Milly.

Grace pondered on her words. 'He already does that.'

'Has he a job in London?'

'I really don't know. Anyway, I'm going to have to speak to Ben.' Grace nibbled her lower lip and was about to refill their cups when she thought she heard one of the twins crying. She was about to make a comment, when Milly stood up.

'That sounds like my son crying.'

'How can you tell the difference?' asked Grace, following her to the front door, only to hear Milly say in a scared voice, 'The pram's gone!'

Chapter 18

Grace hurried outside after her and onto the pavement where Milly stood looking left and right. Several children were playing rounders on the road and a couple were running after what looked like a large ball flying off in the direction of Whitefield Road. Milly ran after them. Grace realised that the ball was actually the pram, which was now only a few yards from intersecting the cobbled road ahead and was busy with traffic. She sprinted after her friend as fast as she could. Milly must have put on a spurt, because as Grace watched, Milly managed to grab the handle of the pram just as it reached the corner of the street. Then she turned on the children who had been chasing the pram too, to tell them off.

Grace caught up with Milly, and said breathlessly, 'I saw you put the brake on! Did some of these children take it off, thinking they'd like to wheel the babies?'

'They deny it,' gasped Milly. 'Thank God there was no traffic.'

'I've never seen you run so fast.'

'I was desperate.' Milly fussed over her babies who appeared none the worse for what had happened.

Grace frowned down at the children. 'Are you telling the truth?'

'Yeah, missus,' responded a girl with two short plaits tied up with rags. 'Me and me friend only went and looked at the babies. Then a man came along and asked would we like to take them for a walk.'

'We thought he must be the father,' said the plump girl with a mop of curly red hair. 'We couldn't move the brake.'

'It was stiff,' said her friend. 'So, he took it off for us and wheeled it to the pavement and gave it a big push.'

'To get us started, he said,' muttered the other girl.

'Where did he go?' asked Milly.

'I don't know,' said the girl with plaits.

'We were too busy chasing the pram,' informed the red head.

'Perhaps those boys playing rounders might have noticed,' said her friends.

'Why aren't you at school?' Grace asked, thinking these children were younger than Simon, but even so…

'It's closed because of an outbreak of measles,' said a girl. 'There was hardly anyone in school. Besides which we'll be finishing for Christmas tomorrow.'

'Then surely you all should be at home in quarantine, not playing out?' said Milly, although she noticed that none of them had spots, but that was not to say that they weren't infectious.

'Some of us have already had it,' commented another girl. 'We can't catch it again.'

'I hope those who could have it, haven't breathed on the twins,' Milly said, wheeling the pram away from the girls. 'I think I remember having it when I lived with my grandma.'

Grace followed her. 'I can't remember. Perhaps the strange bloke, whoever he was, might catch it,' she said.

'Whatever, I won't be leaving the twins outside again. What sort of behaviour is that from a grown man?' Milly said. 'Anyway, I'd better leave you to get on, as you're going to the hospital. Give your dad my love.'

Milly left, carefully wheeling the pram, and Grace collected together her coat and hat and headed out alone, thinking Fergie could have his walk later.

—

She dashed around the shops and then hurried home to put away the pasties that she had bought. Then she went out again to catch a tram and walked up to Pembroke Place where the hospital was situated. It was only when she reached her father's ward that she remembered about the taxi. She mentioned it to the staff nurse, who phoned the taxi firm for her.

Her father seemed frailer today, and hung on to her arm as they made their way to the waiting taxi. The driver helped him inside and it was not long before they arrived home. She helped Norman inside and settled him in front of the fire, where he slumped in his chair. While she was putting the kettle on and placing some of the pasties in the oven to warm, Simon arrived home. He volunteered to take Fergie out for a short run while the pasties and baked beans were warming up.

While he was out, she told her father about Milly's visit earlier and what had happened with the pram, the children and the strange man. Norman looked taken aback.

'That's odd!'

'You don't think he could have been a dirty old man, do you?' she said, thinking aloud, but almost immediately, she added, 'No, that's daft! He'd want to catch one on their own.'

'It could be that he was watching the kids and choosing one to follow and pick on later.'

'I never thought of that,' said Grace. 'While I remember, Dad, do you know if I ever had measles?'

He looked thoughtful and eventually said, 'You'd have to ask Polly. Anyway, what about those pasties I can smell?'

Grace took the pasties out of the oven. She hoped Simon would not be long, not wanting his food to get cold. As it was, he entered the house ten minutes later, washed his hands and sat down at the table. She told him about the children and the measles and asked had the outbreak affected his school at all.

'There's a couple in our class who've been sent home and last week apparently one mother sent in a note saying she was keeping her son Billy at home because he had a temperature and a few spots on his face and throat.' Simon bit into his pasty. 'You don't have to worry about me, though. I've had measles. It was horrible. I was burning hot before I had any spots and felt tired. Anyway, I was up and about within days, but didn't go back to school for more than a week. It was great!'

'That's a relief, anyway,' said Grace. 'What about this outbreak, are you allowed to return to school this afternoon?'

'Yeah, we have important exams, and I'm all right, so I can go.' He reached out for his cup of milk and took a long draught.

'How did footie go this morning?' Grace asked.

'Good enough, although I can't see me ever playing for Liverpool or Everton.' He hesitated. 'Has Dad mentioned it's me eleventh birthday on Friday? It's just that I'd like to have some of my mates round. I don't mean to have a big party, but just cakes, pop or ginger beer and crisps.'

'I'm sure we can manage that,' Grace said, wondering why Ben had not mentioned Simon's birthday to her. It must have slipped his mind with the wedding and moving, but she would need to go shopping again that afternoon. She'd waited until Simon had left for school before asking her father would he be all right on his own for an hour.

Norman nodded. 'Don't worry about me.' He fumbled in his pocket and produced a handful of coins and a ten-shilling note. 'You can spend all that. Buy what you need for his little party and a present from me. Just leave the front door ajar so Simon can get in without me getting up.'

She thanked him and took the money and then left, remembering to leave the door just pushed to behind her. She was away longer than she had planned due mainly to choosing a present for Simon. Eventually she chose a two-hundred-piece jigsaw from Norman, one with a scene of Ancient Egypt, and from herself she bought a box of chocolates.

When she reached her doorstep, Grace entered the house in a rush because she could hear Fergie barking inside. Then she caught the sound of raised voices from the kitchen. The sound of one voice shocked her so much that for a moment she froze. Then she pulled herself together, and despite her rapidly beating heart, strode into the kitchen.

Dougie stood in front of the fireplace, threatening Fergie with a poker. The dog was in front of Norman's chair and was obviously determined to defend his master come what may. If the torn material on the leg of Dougie's trouser was anything to go by, Fergie had made his move before Dougie had seized a weapon.

'What are you doing here, Dougie?' Grace cried. 'Put that down at once!'

'And let that animal attack me again?' he yelled. 'Not bloody likely. Anyway, don't you be giving me orders – it's your shilly-shallying that's messed up my life and caused this!'

'Don't blame me for your mistakes,' said Grace. 'Now put that poker down before you hurt somebody.'

'You heard my daughter, lad,' Norman raised his voice over the noise of the dog who was dancing and yelping around Grace now she had arrived home. He was struggling in vain to stand unaided, but Grace could tell from just looking at him, how much pain he was in.

'I'll put it down once one of you gets control of that dog.' Dougie struck the brass fender with the poker.

Grace seized the back of Fergie's collar and lifted him up against her chest. 'I suppose Marion gave you this address,' she said through pursed lips.

'You suppose right. Then you did me a favour of leaving the front door open so I came in to say hello.' He grimaced, as he said it. 'I came round earlier today, but when I saw the two babies in the pram, I realised your friend Milly was visiting.' He looked at her bitterly. 'Mum wrote to me about the twins, hinting about grandchildren and whatnot. Not that that is likely for us now, is it, Gracie...'

'So, you decided to get her out of the way by playing that stupid trick with the young girls in the street,' said Grace accusingly. 'You're a dangerous idiot.'

His eyes flashed angrily. 'It wasn't my fault the girls let the pram run away from them. Anyway, Milly's husband should have read out my telegram. Marion told me all about how you didn't get my message – Milly and her husband stuck their noses in where they weren't wanted.'

'A telegram of lies! How dare you try and ruin my reputation like that and send a horrible letter to Dad! Get out of my life, Dougie and stay out of it. I've made a new life for myself and I was of the opinion you'd done the same.'

'But you b-belong to m-me! If I can't have you, no one can!' he roared.

'I do not! I never did. I'm not sixteen anymore, Dougie. I can make my own decisions now. You can't bully me. Now, leave!' Grace ordered, pointing to the door.

Dougie moved forward, but only to brandish a fist in Norman's face. 'This is your fault, old man! Why couldn't you have got sick a year ago and died! Instead of keeping us waiting around!'

Fergie scrambled down from Grace's arms and went for Dougie again. He raised the poker and aimed a blow at the dog, but already Grace was there to block it as she grabbed his arm. The blow went wide and caught her on the hip.

The pain was so bad that she felt faint and lost her grip on his arm. She slid to the floor. She tried to get up, but Dougie kicked her to the ground. Norman roared with frustration and anger and managed finally to push himself upright out of the chair. He took a couple of steps forward and aimed a fist at Dougie, only to miss his target and lose his balance. Dougie thrust the poker into his groin and Norman screamed in pain and blacked out.

Then the poker slid from Dougie's grasp and he covered his face with his hands for a second. As he made to pick up the poker again, Fergie went for him. Grace managed to drag herself to her feet while Dougie screamed in pain, his hand clutched to his chest, the poker lying on the floor where he had dropped it.

'You've done it now, Dougie,' she said. 'You're for it.' Dougie stared wildly at her, his face white and strained, before he stumbled out of the room. Grace heard him trip down the lobby. She quickly picked up the poker and hid it in the sideboard, before she bent over her father and checked his pulse. Then she gathered up her skirts and ran.

Chapter 19

When Grace returned to the house after using the telephone at the corner shop, it was to find her father slowly coming around, a little dazed and confused. She made him as comfortable as she could on the floor, having told him she had sent for their doctor. She then made a pot of weak tea for him, and feeling sick and headachy, settled down to wait beside him.

Half an hour later the doctor arrived, and it was only when he had inspected them both, did he demand answers to how they had come by their injuries. If it had only been herself who had a severely bruised hip, Grace might have said less for the sake of her aunt, but she was furious at the way Dougie had treated her father.

Immediately, the doctor became grim-faced and said this was a matter for the police, as it was assault. Of a sick man, to boot, he added in a disbelieving voice. He left the house, and told them he would call for an ambulance on the way to the police station, leaving orders that Norman must have an X-ray to check for further damage.

–

When Ben arrived home, he was in complete agreement with the doctor's assessment. When a constable turned up on the doorstep a while later, Ben invited him in and made a cup of tea while the copper took statements from Grace and Norman and asked if they wanted to lay charges.

Norman replied in the affirmative immediately, and Grace hesitated because she was thinking how it would affect her aunt and uncle having their son arrested for assault and battery. But then aware of Ben's stare and how not so long ago she had wanted to kill Dougie for his spitefulness, she said, 'Yes!'

Fortunately, before they had to face her relatives, Norman was carted off to the hospital in an ambulance; Grace promised to follow him as soon as possible.

Polly and Marion arrived an hour or so later and they were so angry that Grace would not have been surprised to see smoke coming out of their ears. As it was, it was Ben who asked them in icy tones what Dougie had to say for himself. Polly replied that he had arrived home earlier and set about packing his suitcase. He had told them he had to get back to London in a hurry.

'So, he didn't tell you that he attacked Dad and me with a poker!' cried Grace.

'I don't believe it, not of our Dougie,' said her aunt. 'The policeman only told us that they needed to speak to him about an incident here, which is why we came round straight away to find out what wicked falsehoods you've been spreading about him.'

'So, he's run away back to London,' said Ben, in a scornful voice.

'He was very hurt when Grace threw him over for you. They've been together for years, promised to each other since she was sixteen – all Dougie did was work hard for her and their future, like the good lad he is, only to be disappointed by her flightiness as soon as she had to show some backbone and wait for him for a few months—' said Polly, turning on Ben.

'That's no excuse for his behaviour,' put in Grace wearily.

'Did you give the bobby his address in London?' asked Ben.

Mother and daughter were silent.

'No matter,' said Grace. 'I can give it to them. He's not getting away with the way he treated Dad, me, and even Fergie! Family or not. Dad's had to go back in hospital, you know. He had only come out today. Now he needs an X-ray to see what damage Dougie has done.'

'I can see we're not going to get any satisfaction here, Mam, only a host of lies from this one,' Marion burst out. 'Come on, let's get home.'

No sooner had they departed, than Ben insisted on Grace telling him Dougie's London address. He put on his coat and hat.

'I'm going to the police station to give them this address straight away. You can bet that Marion will be in touch with Dougie without delay to warn him about the police wanting him.'

Grace nodded. 'Simon's not home yet. What do I tell him when he arrives?'

'The truth, of course. I wonder why he's late.'

'Yes, I left the door open for him. He could have gone to a friend's and be playing out in the street,' said Grace.

As it was, Simon came in a few minutes after his father left, sounding breathless, with his knees scratched and slightly bloody. 'Sorry I'm late in, but me and some of the kids in Alec's street were playing Truth, Dare, Command and Promise.'

'And what were you dared to do?' she asked.

187

He hesitated. 'You don't want to know.'

Grace frowned. 'Did you see your dad on the way here?'

'I waved to him. He was on the other side of the road.'

'Well, you're going to have to tell him what you've been up to, because he's bound to ask you when he sees those knees.'

'Couldn't I put my pyjamas on ready for bed?' Simon said persuasively. Grace decided that she and Ben had had enough to cope with that evening and agreed Simon could put his pyjamas on.

'But not until I've had a look at those cuts.'

Simon agreed with a sigh, so after she had cleaned the cuts and put iodine and plasters on them with trembling hands, he washed his face and hands and put on his pyjamas, while she served up his dinner. He gobbled the food down and then suddenly seemed to notice that Norman was missing.

'Where's Granddad?' he asked.

'He had to go back to the hospital for an X-ray.'

Simon scrambled to his feet. 'Why, has his condition got worse?'

'My cousin Dougie sneaked into the house because the door had been left open and he attacked Dad, me and Fergie with a poker,' she replied in a trembling voice.

'Why?' His voice was pitched high with shock.

'Because he was furious that I rejected him and married your father,' she said. 'The doctor called in the police, but Dougie has already scarpered back to London. Your dad is on his way, now, to the police station to give them his London address.'

'I hope they catch him,' snarled Simon. 'If Grandad dies because your cousin hit him, he'll really be in trouble.' The boy went over to Grace and placed his arms around her waist. 'He's wicked.'

'Yes, he is, and a selfish bully. I should have realised it a long time ago.' She rested her cheek on her stepson's head and sighed deeply, thinking what a fool she had been to hero-worship Dougie for all those years. At least she had not gone with him to Australia – thank God.

When Ben arrived home later, he told her that the Liverpool police were going to phone through to the Met in London and they would act as quickly as possible to arrest Dougie.

'He'll be brought back to Liverpool to face charges here,' he added.

'It means Dad and I will have to go to court, doesn't it?' Grace said fretfully, wondering what the neighbours would think.

'Of course, you're not regretting bringing charges against him, are you?' said Ben.

'No, he deserves to be punished for how he threatened us and for using a poker to hurt Dad. And how careless he was with Milly's babies...' she answered. 'I just can't help thinking of how I used to be part of the family and how they'll suffer. Polly was good to me when my Mum passed.'

'Don't worry about them, they only care about protecting Dougie now,' said Ben bluntly. 'They'll disown you quick as – I know they're your relations, but Simon and I and your dad are the only family you need now.'

Grace did not argue with him, even though she knew she would always care about her aunt and uncle and Beryl. She decided to go to bed early as her hip was hurting and she wanted to rest. Ben followed her up the stairs, ready to catch her if she fell as she was still unsteady on her feet. She slipped once and he prevented her from falling, whispering that he would always be there for her. Grace felt comforted because at this moment, all she wanted to do was cry, as she felt almost overwhelmed by a sense of panic. She knew rationally that Dougie needed to be taught a lesson, and she had been badly frightened at how vengeful he was.

Ben left her to rest, but Grace could not get comfortable – she could not clear her mind of Dougie's accusations that everything was all her fault and that she had ruined his life. At last she drifted off, and despite waking up the following morning in Ben's arms, she had no recollection of him coming to bed. She stayed as still as she could, not wanting to disturb Ben's sleep. She thought of how hard he worked to support her and Simon, and to provide a home for her father and counted her blessings. She was also pleased that his having put his arms around her meant that he must have forgiven her for hesitating about bringing charges against Dougie. The last thing she wanted was her husband thinking she had any warm feelings still towards her cousin. Although she was dreading having to go to court and be a witness in a process against a member of her family.

Gradually, Grace relaxed and fell asleep. She was wakened by Ben attempting to get out of bed without rousing her. Immediately, she said in a whisper, 'I'm already missing your warmth.'

'I make a good hot water bottle, do I?' he said hoarsely.

'The best, because you're not made of stone.' She stretched out a hand to him. 'I'm sorry to bring trouble to you and Simon.'

'You more than make up for it by the way you warm my bed and care for Simon.'

'So, I'm a handy hot water bottle too.' She chuckled, throwing back the bedcovers. 'I'll come down with you and cook breakfast.'

'You don't have to,' he said. 'The bed is still warm. You could have a further rest. The coming days are going to be difficult.'

'But we have to celebrate Simon's birthday on Friday and Christmas next week,' she said.

'So we do,' he said, catching her to him and kissing her. 'He told you when it was?'

'Yeah, he wanted to have some friends here for cake, crisps and pop. I was shopping for them yesterday when Dougie called round.'

He kissed the top of her head. 'I'd best make a move, or I'll be late.' He released her.

A quarter of an hour later she followed him downstairs. He had lit the fire and the kettle was on. She made scrambled eggs and toast. They sat across the table from each other and she poured the tea.

'I thought I might buy some balloons for Simon's birthday. I'm sure he and his friends will have fun with them.' He delved into his pocket and produced some coins, but she shook her head.

'The balloons and crackers will be my treat.' As she collected their plates and cutlery, she said, 'I wonder when the trial will be.'

'It's a straightforward case, so I imagine, as long as Dougie doesn't do a disappearing act, it'll be soon.' He hesitated a moment before saying, 'I hope they put him away for years for all he's put our family through. Our family, Grace, that's you, me and Simon and your dad, not your aunt Polly, Dougie and Marion. I like your uncle and Beryl and will be okay with you keeping in touch with them.' He took a deep breath and held up a hand as she was about to speak. 'Dougie sent me a copy of the telegram he wanted read out on our wedding day. I threw it on the fire and your father told me about the letter he received from Dougie. So, you have a straight choice, Grace. When you think of your family it has to be this one who live under our roof. I care for you and for better, for worse, I want our marriage to last and that means us being honest and loyal to each other. Not for a moment did I believe your cousin's insinuations because I've got to know you so much better since we wed – I think we can make our relationship be a blessing to us both, Simon and Norman.' He paused. 'So, what do you say?' By the time Ben had finished speaking, Grace could not answer as she was choked by tears.

Eventually, she was able to pull herself together and said, 'I say that I already feel blessed being your wife, and I love you and our family and the home we've made together.' She hiccoughed, accepted a large white hand-kerchief from him and wiped away her tears. 'Can I have a big hug and a kiss now,' she added shakily.

He enveloped her in his arms and kissed her long and sweetly.

Ben was right about the case, and as soon the police had consulted with Norman's doctor, Dougie was appre-hended and transferred to Liverpool, and the trial was fixed for the coming Monday morning, which was Christmas Eve.

Grace steeled herself for the forthcoming ordeal as she focused on welcoming her father back home. Luckily the X-ray hadn't shown further damage, but Norman was increasingly frail and Grace worried about him having to take to the witness stand. Norman was determined to go through with it, though. He had said little about her cousin when Grace had first started spending more time with Dougie, trusting her to see sense; however, she suspected that he had disapproved of his nephew for a long time and now some of his long-held resentment towards Dougie's bullying behaviour and lack of respect towards himself and Grace was finally coming out. Norman was adamant that Grace should at last put Dougie in his place and speak out in court of his shocking behaviour.

Chapter 20

Simon's birthday turned out to be a happy day, although he and his friends mourned the absence of snow. Even so, they enjoyed themselves indoors, playing various games and eating the party food.

By keeping her ears open as she served the treats, Grace discovered how her stepson had come by the scrapes on his knees. Apparently, he had accepted a dare to climb a street gas lamp and hang a rope over one of the bars to make a swing. Unfortunately, he had slipped on the way down and landed on his knees. Grace was a bit annoyed to hear this, given his recent broken bones, but she didn't want to spoil his birthday, so resolved to take it up with him later. The boy certainly knew how to survive various scrapes.

On Sunday morning the four of them went to the morning service at St Margaret's Church and saw Milly and Jimmy with the babies in the pram as they entered the church grounds. Ben could not have the following morning off work, but luckily the couple were already aware that the court case was the next day, and Jimmy's mother was coming over from New Brighton to look after the twins as Milly wanted to be in court to support Grace.

-

The following morning Ben held Grace tightly as he was about to leave for work and whispered encouraging words in her ear, telling her the trial was about getting justice for her father more than anything else. He wished he could be by her side, but he would be with her in spirit. He kissed her several times before tearing himself away and climbing into the van.

Simon cooked her breakfast and washed up afterwards. He wanted to go to court with her, but she insisted he stay out of it and look after Fergus.

'Things could get nasty and you might find it difficult remaining silent and we don't want you being charged with being in contempt of court.'

She kissed him and went upstairs to decide on what she should wear for the ordeal ahead. She thought of wearing the dress she had bought years ago, having chosen it over the one Dougie had wanted her to buy as a gesture of defiance, but decided it was much too cold, and instead she took out a pin-striped skirt, pink blouse and pin-striped jacket. When Milly arrived she told Grace that she looked smart and like she meant business which bucked Grace up. She asked Milly to pin her hair up as she had done on her wedding day and she wore the hat she had worn later that day. As she, Norman and Milly glanced out of the bus window at St George's Hall on Lime Street, Grace was thinking of Dougie having spent the last few days in the cells below and she wondered if he was regretting his violence towards her father, as well as writing those insulting words he had written about her and his desire that his uncle had sickened and died a year ago.

Despite the butterflies fluttering madly in her stomach, Grace managed to get through giving her evidence to the judge without breaking down, even though she was aware of her aunt and cousin's disapproving looks as she recounted what had happened. Grace guessed that her uncle Douglas had to work that day, so could not be there. She felt proud of her father when Norman took the stand and gave his oath, followed by his evidence. Dougie had decided to plead not guilty, despite legal advice, claiming that he had acted in self-defence as Fergie had attacked him. Nonetheless, he was found guilty of unlawful entry as he came into the house premeditated to cause harm to his cousin and her father. The judge sentenced him to five years' imprisonment, based mainly on the fact that he had attacked Norman, who was defenceless and frail.

Grace was stunned by length of the sentence; she had wanted Dougie to suffer for what he had done to her father, but she had not thought he would be imprisoned for so long. She did not need to glance in either Dougie's direction or that of his mother to imagine their horrified expressions. Instead, she gazed at her father, who said in a low voice, 'Don't you dare blame yourself! He's brought it on himself. He always was an unpredictable chancer and he's fortunate that I'm a tough old bird, otherwise, he could be facing a charge of manslaughter.'

'Let's get out of here, Dad,' Grace pleaded, her mind reeling. 'I don't want to come face to face with Aunt Polly on the way out.'

Unfortunately, Grace could not rush her father, because he was not as tough as he thought he was and could only walk at a snail's pace. Luckily, Milly managed to reach them and helped to support him from the court-room. As they reached the steps outside the building, that they were approached by Polly and Marion.

'How could you?' demanded a weeping Polly. 'After all I've done for you since my sister died! She'd hate you both for turning against your own flesh and blood. You're to blame for his problems and behind his behaviour.'

'Your son is not my flesh and blood,' retorted Norman in a quavering voice. 'And I paid you for caring for my daughter. The boy threatened us and would have done worse had the dog not stopped him. Now get out of our way before I call a bobby.'

'Don't you speak to my mother like that,' Marion yelled, thrusting her face into Norman's. 'You'll regret this day.'

Norman drew back his head. 'Not as much as your brother is regretting taking a poker to me and my daughter in that shameful way,' he countered.

'And he could have caused my babies to be injured!' burst out Milly.

'What are you talking about?' spluttered Polly.

'He took the brake off their pram and pushed it off the step and set it going down the street,' said Grace. 'If it hadn't been for some girls playing nearby and Milly tearing after it, the pram could have ended up in the road and been hit by a car. I think Dougie wanted to be sure that he had the right address and see who came out of the house, but who knows why he did it – probably as a way of trying to get back at me somehow. Or maybe Milly...'

'But why should he want to hurt Milly?' asked Polly bewildered.

Milly said, 'Most probably because my husband did not read out the nasty telegram he sent to Grace at the wedding reception which threatened to spoil things for her. Ask Marion if you don't believe us.'

'What!' Polly glanced at her daughter. 'What do you know about this?'

Marion did not answer, but dragged on her mother's arm. 'Let's go!'

Polly allowed herself to be pulled away, and Grace, Milly and Norman went in the opposite direction, heading for the Kardomah Cafe in Church Street where they were fortunate to find a table available; it being the last day for Christmas shopping. They ordered a pot of tea and buttered toasted teacakes, and ate and drank in silence. As they watched what was going on around them, Grace felt herself slowly relaxing. Milly ordered a jug of hot water and another four teacakes. When they had finished, as if by an unspoken agreement not to mention the court case and its aftermath, they left the cafe and went to catch the tram home. There was a queue for the tram, but fortunately they managed to get on it, although Grace and Milly had to stand. Norman would have given his daughter his seat, but she insisted he sit down and rest. She and Norman parted from Milly and strolled up the street to their home where they found Simon eating a tin of heated-up oxtail soup with Fergie sitting at his feet, eager for a sop of bread.

'So, how did it go?' Simon asked.

'As I expected,' said Norman. 'He won't be out of prison for a while.'

'Good,' said Simon. 'Now we can forget him and enjoy Christmas.'

Grace thought that was easier said than done. But she knew she was going to have to put her best face on and make it a really good Christmas, as it might just be her father's last. She could not deny that Dougie's attack on Norman had taken it out of him.

Chapter 21

The snow which Simon hoped would arrive on Christmas Day did not materialise. Instead the weather was quite mild and after breakfast and the opening of presents, Grace shooed Simon and Ben out, so the boy could have a kick about with his new football in the park while she could get on, in peace, preparing lunch. She had installed her father in an armchair to one side of the fireplace and had switched the wireless on, so he could listen to Christmas music. Later they would all listen to the King's Christmas message.

In the meantime, she stuffed the capon and placed the bird in the oven before peeling the potatoes and placing them round the capon in the roasting tin. She made brandy butter for the Christmas pudding and then set the table with the damask, lace-trimmed tablecloth that had been a wedding present. She did so while thinking about her aunt and uncle and cousins and how they must be feeling this Christmas with Dougie in Walton prison, not so very far away. She wondered if prisoners were served Christmas lunch, and whether Dougie was now having regrets for his violent behaviour.

Ben had said that he had received what he deserved and had only himself to blame, adding, 'We can put him out of our minds now for the term of his imprisonment and get on with our lives. I can't bear the thought of him sniffing around you, like he owned you. There's something not quite right about it.'

Grace had agreed with him and knew she had to make the most of having her father with them. Every time she had looked at Norman over the last few days her heart sank, because he was simply not the man he had been a year ago.

–

Christmas passed and the start of the new year of 1935 came and went. Spring arrived and with it the news that Grace was going to have a baby in the September. Ben was delighted, as was the expectant mother, and Simon and Norman. Grace prayed every day that he would live to see his grandchild born and that her aunt would forgive her and there could be peace between them.

She was able to pass on the news to her aunt via Beryl who was now married to Davy and no longer lived at home, but rented a house in Troughton Street, which was not far from Wavertree Road. Grace sometimes ran into her in St John's Market in the city centre. Their first meeting had been awkward, but Beryl didn't seem as keen to disown Grace as the rest of her family and proclaim Dougie's innocence, something that Grace put down to Dougie's harsh treatment of his younger sister when they were children.

'It's not a big house,' said Beryl, 'but it means we can have our own place. Mam suggested we live with her, but if I'm honest, I wanted to get away from our Marion and from Mam's moodiness and nagging. We're also nearer to Davy's mam who lives on Chatsworth Street, and we're not far from the *Pivvie* on Lodge Lane if we wanted to go out one night.'

Grace smiled, remembering visiting the Pavilion theatre to see a pantomime years ago with her aunt and Beryl. Marion and Dougie had considered themselves too old for pantomimes, saying they were for children.

'So, a good move,' she said.

Beryl nodded. 'We're really happy.'

'Your dad all right?'

'He's fine, and tries to buck Mam up, reminding her that she wouldn't have been seeing anything of Dougie if he'd gone to live in Australia or if he'd decided to live in London and not near her. At least now she can go and visit him in prison here.'

'Does she go regularly?'

Beryl nodded. 'Once a month. She doesn't really talk about it, though.' Sensing Grace's discomfort, she changed the subject quickly. 'So, what sex do you want the baby to be?'

'I don't mind, just as long as it's healthy.' Grace smiled. 'I suspect Ben would like a girl, as he already has a son.'

'I'd like a girl, so I can dress her up in pretty frocks,' said Beryl dreamily. 'Besides, if there's a war in the future a boy could be called up.'

Grace stiffened. 'Why do you say that?'

'Because that there Hitler and his gang have broken the Versailles Treaty several times – they've reinstated their air force and are rearming and have brought in conscription – according to my fella who reads the newspapers and listens to the wireless.'

'That wouldn't affect any babies we have,' said Grace, thinking gloomily that it could affect their husbands, though. 'Our government should take a firm stand and protest at the next League of Nations meeting.'

'Too right they should,' said Beryl. 'It fair makes me shiver to think that there could be another war. Wasn't the last one supposed to be a war to end all wars?'

Grace nodded. 'Let's hope for the best and not think the worse,' she said.

That evening she mentioned to Ben and her father what Beryl had told her. They exchanged glances.

'No use worrying about it,' said Ben. 'It won't change things. We just have to hope and pray that our government reacts wisely and puts the wind up Hitler. We can't depend on Italy because Mussolini is another extremist, but France would side with us.'

'What about Russia and other countries in Europe?' she asked.

'Don't let's get ahead of ourselves. We'll have more pleasant things to think about soon,' he said nodding towards her stomach.

Grace let the subject drop and took up her knitting and carried on with the matinee coat she was making for the baby. Milly had been thrilled with the news of the baby and she offered her hand-me-downs from one or the other twin for when the baby was born. Grace had accepted gladly and made up her mind to do what Ben had said and think only of pleasant things.

-

In May, the country celebrated the King's Silver Jubilee, and Grace remembered the Royal visit to Liverpool last year. It seemed an age ago since Grace had waved Dougie off to Australia and had nearly been run over by Ben later that day on her way back. She smiled to think of the pageant in Exchange Flags and how Ben had offered her a lift home. Now here she was settled with Ben and having his baby, although truth be known she would be happier if her father's health was not failing so badly. She was concerned that he might die before the baby was born and she didn't think she could bear it.

One day, Grace left the house to take Fergie for a walk after she'd made sure her father was comfortable by the fire. She planned to drop in on Milly to tell her that she had felt the baby quickening; that was what she had heard it called when the baby stirred. Milly had made cups of tea served with freshly baked scones, and not for the first time, they had discussed what Grace could expect as her pregnancy progressed. Milly recommended that she read Marie Stopes' *Radiant Mother* and *Wise Parenthood* before she gave birth.

'You might be able to borrow them from the library. If not I'll lend you my copies, but I wouldn't want you to hang on to them too long as I like to dip into them,' Milly added. 'There could be parts in the books that bother you, but we can always talk about them.'

Grace took in all that Milly said to her but she did not rush to order the books from the library, aware that if the two books mentioned were anything like Marie Stopes' other books, she would need to bring to bear all her concentration – and she had such difficulty concentrating at the moment.

Spring quickly turned to summer and Grace's days fell into a slightly different routine. Ben insisted that she behaved sensibly and put her own health and that of their baby first. It caused an argument one day in July when she had grown quite big, and Ben found her sprucing up the bath chair with the intention of taking her father out in it to the park to enjoy the fine weather.

'But I'm strong and it's so dull for Dad being indoors day after day.'

'Well, you taking him out in the bath chair is not the answer. You're being foolish. It'll be too much for you. You could strain yourself, and you don't want to risk losing our baby,' Ben thundered protectively.

'Don't shout at me,' she cried. 'You don't understand!'

'Of course, I do! But I lost my parents, a brother and a wife,' he replied. 'I don't want to lose you and the baby as well because of a whim. How do you think it would make Simon feel? He's so looking forward to being a big brother.'

'All right! You've made your point. But have you any ideas on how to make life a little less dull for Dad?'

'I'll talk to him,' said Ben resorting to his normal tone. 'In the meantime, you make sure you have enough rest and some *sensible* exercise. Now, I'm off to work. I'll see you later.' He kissed her cheek and left her staring after him as he went downstairs and opened the front door. Grace could feel the tears coming, but was conscious that Ben had not shouted at her since the episode in the park last year with Simon and the runaway bath chair.

–

The following morning, the sun was streaming into their bedroom as Ben slipped out of bed so as not to disturb Grace. But she was awake already and said, 'It looks like it's going to be nice morning.'

Ben agreed, 'If you want to get your dad up and make sure he's wrapped up warmly and bring a couple of cushions, I could run you both to the seawards side of the Customs House where the old salts gather on the steps, to look out towards the docks and the Mersey and to reminisce. Norman would enjoy that.'

'Oh, that sounds like a plan! But how do we get back home? You surely don't expect us to stay there until you finish work?'

'Kyle has offered to pick you both up in the motor he bought with some of his winnings from the Irish sweepstake the other year. He's given up working as a driver and is helping out at the orphanage full time.'

'How kind of him. How's Jane and their little boy? I miss her living round here. It's ages since I've seen them.'

'He's a good bloke. As soon as I mentioned it was something your dad might like, he wanted to help. He won a packet on that sweepstake. He said their little boy is thriving. He also suggested you drop in and see Jane soon.'

Grace agreed, 'I'll go next week, if they'll have me.'

Grace dressed and then went to see to her father with Ben's help. When Simon woke up, the four of them had breakfast together; he said that he would like to have gone with Grace and Norman but as it was the school holidays, he had already arranged to meet his mates and have a game of cricket in the park.

So, the three adults left the house leaving Simon making himself another slice of toast. Within half an hour, Ben had dropped off Grace and Norman outside the Customs House in Canning Place which was on the landward side of the road from Canning, Salthouse and Albert docks. As it was early in the morning, they had no difficulty finding a place where they could rest their backs and sit down. Grace did not stay still for long because the ageing ex-mariners gathered round and wanted to speak to her father. She excused herself and slowly went on her way to do that day's shopping. An hour or so went by and as Grace was returning to her father, a car pulled up and Kyle stepped out and took the bags from her, before helping her and her father into the car.

Grace breathed a sigh of relief as she leaned back in the passenger seat. 'Are you all right, Dad?' she called over her shoulder.

'Fine, lass. I'm in clover. I really appreciate you giving us a lift, Kyle,' he said.

'My pleasure,' Kyle assured him. 'Have you enjoyed your outing?'

'It was the gear!' exclaimed Norman. 'And tomorrow I'm to have a visit from your uncle Douglas, Grace. Apparently, he mentioned to Ben at the wedding that if Ben ever needed to get in touch with him, he was to ring him at work and he gave Ben his work's phone number.'

Grace was flabbergasted. 'I knew nothing of this. Why did Ben telephone him?'

'Well, you do now, lass. I think Ben just wanted me to have a new visitor to talk to, and he knows how fond I am of your uncle.'

'What about Aunt Polly? She still won't have anything to do with me.'

Norman said, 'She doesn't have to know anything about it, so keep your gob shut and don't say anything to Beryl if you see her out hereabouts. She just might let it slip and I don't want Douglas getting into trouble with Polly.'

'All right, Dad. I had planned to be out tomorrow.' Grace turned to Kyle. 'Do you think it'll be fine for me to drop in and see your Jane and little one tomorrow afternoon?'

'I should think so. We've got Anne and the children staying with us up from Essex,' he said. 'You might like to give Milly that news and she and the twins could come along as well. Come for tea. You do remember that Anne's husband is Jane's brother. You probably know, too, that Milly met Anne and Andrew on a ferry across the Mersey.'

'Will do,' said Grace distracted for the second with the idea of Uncle Douglas's visit.

–

The following morning, having left her father in bed longer to recuperate from yesterday's outing, Grace baked some fairy cakes for her dad, uncle and Simon to have as a special treat while she was out. Grace would take some cakes to Jane's as well. She set out at three o'clock to collect Milly on her way and waved to her uncle as he rode past her on his motorbike. Milly was waiting for her on the step with the twins.

'You've baked too,' said Milly. 'I've made a walnut and coffee sponge cake.'

'Lovely,' Grace said. 'I've baked fairy cakes.'

'It's going to be a right feast,' said Milly. 'The kids will scoff plenty!'

Grace and Milly hurried along, chatting of this and that all the way to Kyle and Jane's home, which was a large house overlooking Newsham Park. Kyle helped to lift the pram into the entrance hall before opening the second door on the left and standing aside to let Milly and Grace go ahead of him, as he carried the twins inside. A fireguard was in place of a glowing coal fire, so the twins were leaned against Milly's legs near a scattering of toys and the other children who were playing on the hearth rug. The largest child, who was Anne's daughter, picked up a rag doll and handed it to Milly's daughter who was dressed in a pretty pink frock, white leggings and a cardigan.

'Here, you can play with this,' she said, and a delightful smile lit up her heart-shaped face framed by flaxen curls. 'I'm five and will be going to school this year. My name's Chrissie.' Her blue eyes stared up at Milly. 'What are your babies' names?'

Milly lowered herself to the girl's level and said, 'John and Mary.'

Anne, Jane's sister-in-law, came over at that point and said, 'It's incredible how they've grown.'

'Time does fly past. I mean Chrissie's just told me she'll be going to school this year,' said Milly.

'I know. We're reached another stage in life and I'm going to have to reschedule my days to fit in with taking her to school and picking her up, feeding the baby and giving some of my time, as well, to housework and shopping,' said Anne. 'I've told Andrew I don't think I could cope with any more children.' She faced Grace. 'You look as if you haven't far to go now. When is the baby due?'

'September! I'm praying all goes well and that my dad lasts at least that long.' Grace gave a shuddering breath.

Anne's expression altered and became grave. 'Milly told me. I'll put you and your family on my prayer list.'

'Thank you,' said Grace, kneeling on the rug and reaching for some coloured wooden blocks and showing baby John how to build with them.

It was not long before the women were able to leave the children playing reasonably amicably with Chrissie watching over their fair play; the women sat at the table and enjoyed a cup of tea, sandwiches and cake. Anne's husband, Andrew, also joined them. After the first cup of tea they saw to the children, although Chrissie had already begged for two fairy cakes, one for her and one for her brother.

Anne had told her daughter to mind her manners, but Jane had given way to her niece's plea and then made up plates for the other children and drinks of milk in beakers with straws.

'Do you and Andrew have any time to yourself?' asked Milly.

Anne said, 'We're fortunate in having Jimmy's aunt living next door to us in Southend, as you know. She's willing to babysit once a week, so we can go to the flickers or the theatre.'

'Andrew, you're a newspaper reporter, is that correct?' said Grace.

'Yes, why do you ask?' said Andrew.

'I just wondered what you thought about what was going on in Germany,' Grace said.

Andrew frowned. 'I don't like what I'm hearing from our Foreign Correspondent over there. Hitler started conscription earlier this year. He's definitely looking for trouble.'

'But surely the League of Nations can do something to stop him?' said Grace.

'No country wants outright war so they're putting their hopes in diplomacy,' interjected Anne. 'Now that might work if Hitler was a reasonable man, but he's not.'

'So, what do you think will happen next?' asked Milly, glancing at her children, and then back at Andrew.

'Hitler will lie through his teeth, biding his time until he has trained troops and weapons of war ready, and then he'll make his move and other countries will be caught on the hop. Churchill is right and we should be preparing for war.'

The three women looked horrified. 'What about the German people, surely they don't want another war?' said Grace.

'Germany's economy is in a mess and anyone of note standing against Hitler and his gang disappear, most likely murdered. As for the ordinary people, they're suffering and still smarting after being defeated in the last war and losing their colonies abroad. The Jews are being persecuted because Hitler is blaming them, saying they've got rich at the expense of the German people.'

'So, our next government needs to do something,' said Grace, thinking of the forthcoming general election later in the year.

'We need someone with courage, who is also patriotic and honourable and can stir our nation to do what is right,' Andrew said. 'What we're likely to get is an appeaser because most British people don't want another war… and then there are the British fascists, who admire Hitler and Mussolini.'

'Such as Sir Oswald Mosley,' said Milly. 'I've read about him in the *Echo*.'

Andrew nodded, and then said in a low voice, 'I suppose I shouldn't be talking to you like this, worrying you.'

'Ben and Dad discuss Hitler and Germany between themselves,' said Grace. 'I know they think such things should be kept from women, but what is happening over in Europe will affect us too if the worse comes to the worst.'

'Yes, women had their part to play in the last war,' Anne said. 'We need to be prepared for the fight on the Home Front.'

'Kyle lost his father in the last war,' said Jane. 'We really do need to stop Hitler now before it's too late.'

'Ben's brother Martin was declared missing presumed dead,' said Grace.

The women looked at Andrew, but he was silent, and it was left to Jane to say, 'Let's be prepared for whatever happens, while at the same time making the most of the time we have now and live in hope and pray for righteousness to triumph.'

'Here, here!' said Grace firstly, with tears in her eyes, thinking that she could at least be thankful that it was unlikely her father would live to see the horrors of another war if peace went to the wall.

The mood was altered by John knocking over the building blocks and Mary, his twin, bursting into tears. The adults now gave their attention to the children once more. After all, it was the children who were the future.

Chapter 22

Liverpool: September 1935

Grace was thinking about the threat of war, it seemed a long time since that tea when Jane's brother had talked about what was going on in Germany and she soon put it out of her mind when her waters broke, and she went into labour on a Saturday evening towards the end of September. Fortunately, Ben was home, and he ran to fetch the midwife, Maggie, who lived a few streets away. Ben was obviously stressed, so, feeling sorry for him, Maggie returned with him straight away bringing along her black bag. Maggie then proceeded to give Ben firm orders to boil a kettle and to make a pot of tea for the whole household, including the mother-to-be and for herself. He was then to boil another kettle and air the baby's vest, nightie, matinee coat, nappy and shawl, before removing himself from the bedroom and staying out of the way.

Norman, who was just as on edge as Ben, suggested the pair of them and Simon get on with crocheting the border of the rug for Ben and Grace's bedroom, which had been forgotten about since the households had moved in together. Meanwhile, Grace was settled as comfortably as possible in bed, while the midwife sat at her bedside having set out the instruments she might need. Grace remembered Maggie from Milly's labour, and tried to listen to her as she told her not to worry and how to breathe through the contractions.

'I don't think you're going to take long,' Maggie said.

Grace just did her best to let the pains pass over her like waves on a shore. She tried to distract herself by remembering that time on the beach with Ben on their honeymoon, but it was impossible. Then suddenly the pains altered and she had an urge to push before she felt a fierce pain and was told the baby's head was out. Grace tried to see her child but found it difficult as she had the urge to push again. Then a few minutes later she heard the baby cry.

'What is it?' Grace asked.

'A darling little girl,' said Maggie.

Not long after, Maggie wrapped the baby in a towel, and placed her in the crook of Grace's arm against her breast so that Grace was able to feel for herself that her daughter had twenty tiny fingers and twenty perfect toes. Her hair was damp; Grace could not decide whether it would be blonde or light brown, but her eyes were blue and there was a dimple in her dainty chin.

'Oh, she's beautiful,' murmured Grace. 'Can my husband come in and see her now and then my father and stepson?'

'Shortly,' replied Maggie. 'We haven't quite finished here yet.' She latched the baby's rosebud mouth onto a nipple and watched, occasionally adjusting the baby's position, until the tiny mite suckled. 'That first milk is extra special.'

Five minutes later there came a knock on the bedroom door and Grace heard Ben asking if he could come in.

'Just a minute,' said Maggie, and as she spoke, she placed the baby still wrapped in the towel, into a Moses' basket on a stand. 'Have you brought your daughter's clothes?'

'I have a daughter!' exclaimed Ben, a choke in his voice.

'That's what I said,' replied Maggie, opening the door wide, so he could enter.

He handed her the baby garments and then went over to the bed and bent and kissed Grace. 'Are you all right?'

'Now I am. I thought you might like a daughter, what with already having a son.'

'I'm delighted to have a daughter, but more importantly you have both come through the ordeal safely.'

'Go on and see her then,' Grace laughed.

Ben turned away to where Maggie held out the baby wrapped in a shawl. 'I've yet to dress her, but you have a hold of her for a few minutes.'

Grace watched her husband's face as he gazed into their child's face in wonder. 'She has my mam's dimple. How she would have loved her.'

'I hope Simon will love her,' she said.

'I have no doubts about that,' said Ben, handing the baby back to Maggie. 'I'd better go and tell him and your dad.'

Ben did not have to go far because Simon and Norman were halfway up the stairs.

'A precious little girl,' Grace heard Ben say.

'Can we see them?' Norman asked.

'In a few minutes, the midwife is just dressing the baby.'

'All went well – is Grace all right?' asked Norman.

Ben smiled and nodded.

Maggie opened the door. 'Come on in, gentlemen.'

Grace was sitting propped up with pillows and the baby in her arms. 'Say hello to the latest member of the family,' she said, a smile in her voice.

Simon was at the bedside first and reached out and took hold of one of the baby's hands. 'Hello, little sister,' he said, gently shaking the hand. 'Gosh, how small your hand is compared to mine.'

Norman sat down in the chair Maggie had vacated, and, with tears in his eyes, he kissed his daughter's cheek. 'All's well,' he said. 'I feel truly blessed. A daughter, a son-in-law who is like a son to me, a grandson, and now a granddaughter.'

'Oh, Dad, I'm so grateful.' Grace wondered whether she would ever be as happy again as she was in that moment.

Chapter 23

Grace lifted her daughter out of her cot, changed her nappy and dressed her, then put her to the breast. Irene was now almost four months old and had been christened at the beginning of November, a fortnight before her grandfather had passed away in his sleep. Norman had lasted longer than Grace had thought possible, despite the fact that he had stopped the radiation treatment some time ago, complaining that it made him headachy and sick. To alleviate the pain of the growing cancer, he had paid for morphine injections, which a visiting nurse had administered. She had felt lost and disappointed, having convinced herself that he would still be on the scene for his granddaughter's first Christmas. Simon had experienced his loss deeply especially on his birthday and at Christmastide comparing it to last year's, but the boy took some solace in his new important role as big brother to baby Irene. Grace had found strength in her Christian faith and Ben's emotional support, having already replaced her father as her rock since their marriage. Yet she could never forget the years her father had supported her.

Grace rested her chin against her daughter's fine blonde hair and swallowed a lump in her throat, thinking it was a sad start to the year as the King had died yesterday,

20th January 1936. His second son, the handsome Prince of Wales had been proclaimed King Edward VIII. The Prince was popular and even the anti-monarchists were looking forward to the celebrations when he would be crowned king. The country even had hopes of a wedding to a suitable bride soon, as Edward was forty and still unmarried.

Later in the day, she met Milly for a walk to the shops and the talk quickly turned to the new monarch. 'I had a letter from Anne recently, and she wrote that Andrew told her that the new King has been seen around a lot with an American woman who is married, but also a divorcee. It is rumoured by some that Edward wants to marry her, and she is in the process of divorcing her second husband – a Mr Simpson. The press have known for a while, but were told to keep it out of the newspapers and off the wireless… but it's been reported in the American newspapers and some of the European ones too.' Milly confided.

Grace's mouth fell open and her eyes widened with shock. 'He must be mad. The prime minister and the Church aren't going to allow the King to marry a divorced woman!'

'Apparently he's in love with her and isn't prepared to give her up,' said Milly.

'So, what does Andrew think will happen?' asked Grace.

'Well, he thinks there won't be a coronation until the government have their say. It'll be in all the British and Empire newspapers this week. He says Edward's had affairs with married women before he met Mrs Simpson…'

'What's her first name?' asked Grace.

'Wallace. Peculiar name, isn't it?'

Grace nodded. 'I wonder what she looks like.'

'No doubt her picture will be in the *Echo* tomorrow.'

'Has she any children?' Grace asked.

'If she has, Andrew didn't mention them. She's one of those socialites who mix with the rich and famous, and just think of having a good time.'

'I bet she doesn't have children then,' said Grace laughing. 'They'd have stopped her gallop, and so would her first husband, if there had been children around.'

'If she has, it'll be in the papers,' Milly said, stopping outside the butcher's on Whitefield Road.

Grace stopped as well and put the brake on the pram, thinking she could keep her eye on the pram through the butcher's window. She bought stewing steak, thinking to make a casserole, and as soon as she paid for her purchase, she hurried outside after Milly who had bought three mutton chops and a quarter of mince.

'Have you a visitor for dinner this evening?' asked Grace.

Milly nodded. 'Jimmy's mam is coming. The mince is for the twins—' She paused and glanced about her. 'Where's Fergie, by the way?'

'I left him at home because he didn't budge from in front of the fire when I called him,' said Grace. 'He went out with Simon after school yesterday and rolled in the wet grass apparently, so I'm wondering if he has a chill. I'd hate to lose him. After losing Dad, Simon would be miserable all over again.' She paused. 'Anyway, I'd best nip along to the post office and buy some stamps. Beryl's had a baby boy and I want to send her and Davy congratulations.'

'Did Davy come and let you know?' asked Milly.

Grace nodded. 'I suppose it's asking too much for Aunt Polly to come by. I just hope she'll have some pleasure from having a grandson now.'

'I'm sure she will,' said Milly. 'Perhaps she'll stop going to see Dougie in prison so often. Didn't Beryl tell you it gets her real down every time? Surely Marion could go in her place, alternate fortnights say?'

'You'd think so, wouldn't you, because the pair of them used to be close,' said Grace. 'Anyway, thinking about all that business still makes me feel funny – I just wish Aunt Polly and I could be friends again, but she didn't respond to my last Christmas card or the invitation to Irene's christening. I just got replies from Beryl and Davy. Ben's not in favour of me paying her a visit either. I thought Aunt Polly might come around with a bit of time, once she'd had a chance to think it all over, but the rift's still there,' Grace said sadly.

Soon the friends parted and Grace carried on with her shopping. As she visited the greengrocers she wondered how much more of his prison sentence Dougie had to serve and whether he would stay in Liverpool when he was released. She hoped he might return to London. She doubted he would be able to go back to Australia, worse luck. She dreaded the thought of him remaining in the city and bumping into him when she was out. Still, no point in worrying about that now. Besides, she had Ben to protect her.

That evening she began to tell Ben the gossip Milly had told her about the King, but he stopped her, saying that Jimmy had already told him. 'I'm not interested,' Ben added. 'I just hope that all that nonsense doesn't distract the government and end up allowing Mosley and his British fascists to grow too powerful. We don't want another Hitler or Mussolini over here.'

'Thinking of Germany,' Grace said. 'It's the Winter Olympics next month over there.'

'We never win much in the winter ones,' he grumbled, 'but I suppose we'll still be taking part to keep face with Hitler.'

However, despite Ben's dismissal of the King's growing attachment to Mrs Simpson, Grace found herself increasingly transfixed by the affair. By the time Irene's first birthday had past and autumn was well underway, the nation was in turmoil. The late October headlines reported that Stanley Baldwin, the Conservative Prime Minister, had met with the King to confront him about the growing constitutional crisis centred on his relationship with the glamourous socialite. Grace could not believe it when a few days later, the news came that Wallace Simpson had divorced her husband. Both she and Milly were agog to hear what would happen next. They did not have to wait long, as a fortnight later, it was reported that the King had informed the prime minister that he intended on marrying Mrs Simpson. Mr Baldwin told the King that the British people would never accept the twice-divorced American as queen.

When Grace and Milly met the next day at Milly's house, they could not conceal their shock and unease. 'Do you think the King really means to marry her?' said Grace.

'Jimmy says the King knows that as the Prince of Wales he was popular and maybe he believes the people would forgive him for marrying the woman he loves.'

'Some might, but the majority wouldn't. It's not as if she's British, is it?'

'I suppose now there'll be talks behind the scenes, until somebody backs down,' said Milly. 'Cup of tea?'

'Thanks,' said Grace. 'And have you a biscuit for Irene? She didn't eat all her breakfast this morning.'

'What about half a Farley's rusk? I'm out of biscuits.'

'Ta, that's fine,' said Grace. 'Well, I suppose we'll know what's going to happen with the King and Mrs Simpson before this year's out.'

Grace's premonition proved right, as by the beginning of December, the Bishop of Bradford gave a speech in which he hinted that the King might abdicate if the government did not agree to his marriage to Mrs Simpson. Following the speech, early that evening, Ben, Jimmy and their wives, discussed the turn of events over a fish-and-chip supper at Ben and Grace's house, while the little children played with Simon in the parlour.

'I think there must be some truth in it,' said Ben. 'But if so, even *considering* abdicating in order to marry an American divorcee is a slap in the face for us. It feels like a betrayal for our own King. I can't imagine it can come to this, he'll think of his people first.'

But three days later, Ben, Grace and Simon huddled around the wireless, as did most of the nation, to hear an address from the now former King, as he informed the nation that he had abdicated that very day; he explained that he had given up his throne for the sake of the woman he loved.

'So that's that,' growled Ben, turning off the wireless set with a snap. 'He hasn't told us anything that we didn't already know.'

Grace said, 'The Royal Family must feel that he's let them down, as well as us.'

'That means the Duke and Duchess of York are now King and Queen, I suppose,' said Ben. 'It's not going to be easy for them, but at least the Duke has a good wife at his side, by all accounts.'

'And they have two children,' murmured Grace, thinking of Simon and Irene.

'I wonder what other unforgettable events might happen next – it seems like so much is changing so quickly,' interrupted Simon suddenly. 'When you think that these days aviators such as Amy Johnson are flying singlehanded through the skies – across oceans even! I'd like to go up in an aeroplane...'

'Thank God, you're too young,' said Ben. 'In Spain, cities are being bombed from the air. Attacks from the air are a reality if war does come—' he stopped speaking abruptly.

'And by their own countrymen!' Grace wailed. 'Civil war is so much worse than an ordinary war. Though if Hitler did cause another war, his air force would try and bomb us into submission.'

'Of course, it'll be a war like no other before...' Ben looked grim, as Grace cuddled Irene against her breast instinctively. 'Let's change the subject,' he continued hastily, turning to look at Simon. 'It might never happen, eh?'

Grace glanced at her husband, thinking that despite his cheerful manner, Ben was beginning to believe that there was a real possibility that Hitler would start another war, and soon. If that happened there was bound to be conscription, but with Ben not far off forty, then surely he would not be in the first batch of men to be called up, especially as he was married with children? She could only hope he would not volunteer. Grace checked herself, as her thoughts were running away with her. Her heart sank though, as she couldn't believe that after the casualties of the last war there would ever be another one so soon. She quashed her worries realising that it did no good. In fact, it was positively harmful. Britain and their Allies had to prevent war whatever the cost.

Part 3

1939–1941

Chapter 24

Grace and Milly and the children had been invited over to Jane and Kyle's house for tea. Kyle was out for the day, working at the orphanage, but the women were just sitting down at the tea table when the telephone rang. Jane rose and went over to pick up the receiver. She checked on her way through the window that the children were playing nicely together in the back garden. The other two women could not help hearing Jane's end of the conversation. They did not have long to wait before Jane returned to them and then asked politely, 'Do you want a refill?'

Grace and Milly nodded and waited while she poured the tea. 'That was Anne on the phone. Apparently two bombs have gone off at two London Underground stations.' She paused. 'And no, it wasn't the Germans, but the IRA!'

'Hell!' exclaimed Milly. 'What are they playing at? Jimmy said that the Republic of Ireland got what they wanted last April with that trade deal, where the navy had to withdraw from trade ports in the south. It's bad enough that if there is to be a war and German U–boats are bent on destroying British shipping in the Atlantic then the lack of a friendly port for the British in the south of Ireland could really aid the Germans. I'm sure the Irish government wouldn't side with Germany, but who's to say what the IRA might do – they hate the English. Let's not forget that they tried to assassinate our King in the summer of '37.'

'Well, I hope the IRA have not now made a pact with the devil and his henchman, Hitler…' agreed Grace. 'If so, they should lock them away and throw away the key.' She was suddenly reminded of Dougie. 'Was anyone hurt?' she countered, pushing the thought of Dougie from her mind. She hadn't heard from her aunt for a couple of years now and their estrangement continued to weigh on her mind.

'Nine people injured, two seriously,' said Jane.

'I'm surprised they haven't set off bombs in Liverpool,' said Grace. 'They could escape on a boat back to Ireland quicker than from London.'

'Give them time,' Milly said. 'I suppose the plan is to unnerve our government and take their minds off what Hitler will be up to next.'

'It's not going to work,' said Jane conspiratorially. 'You can bet we have spies over in Europe, keeping their eye on things. That's what Andrew says – Anne told me.'

'I wonder when Hitler will make his next move,' said Grace, 'Ben doesn't agree with Chamberlain. He thinks Churchill's got it right and Hitler can't be trusted and that we'll be at war with Germany sooner or later,' she added, thinking with a chill about the last year of worrying political news and Ben's growing anger at the dinner table, which was, more often than not, directed towards the new Prime Minister, Neville Chamberlain. The elderly statesmen had tried to stave off war honourably in the face of mounting Italian and German aggression. Following the shock of the abdication, events had followed swift and fast during the course of 1938, and Grace had felt as though she couldn't quite keep up: Italian armies had invaded Ethiopia and Germany had annexed Austria, making it a part of the German nation again, against the pact made in Versailles after the Great War.

At fourteen, Simon had also become increasingly interested in the world news and Grace had overheard hushed conversations between him and Ben late at night when they thought she wasn't listening; so not to worry her. Rumours were also coming out of Germany that the Jews were being persecuted. Hitler was a bully and a tyrant, and he needed to be stopped, that much was clear, but Grace still hoped in her heart for peace, despite what her menfolk thought was likely. But since the autumn just gone, she was becoming more fearful, as Britain felt precariously on the brink of war. Alarming headlines greeted her on what seemed like every street corner. Hitler had turned his eye on a part of Czechoslovakia called the Sudetenland, and despite Chamberlain's assurances that he had appeased Hitler at a big summit in Munich in September 1938 – heralded as 'peace in our time' – even Grace had grave misgivings by now.

'It can't go on,' agreed Jane. 'But I suppose the longer Chamberlain can appease Hitler, the more time we have to prepare and step up rearmament, but in the meantime other countries suffer.'

–

The tea party ended quite soon after that and Grace, feeling blue, made her way home with Irene. Both of them carried gas masks with them as they were issued to all British civilians last July. Even Irene received a mask which was supposed to resemble Mickey Mouse. Grace found herself thinking back to the show when the Mersey Tunnel was opened by the old king and how a player dressed up as Mickey Mouse had appeared. How that had made her laugh! She was only twenty-six, but she felt about a hundred years old with all the warmongering news at the moment. Irene's mask did not even really resemble that player's mask, she thought sadly. She just prayed that they would never have need to wear them.

Grace had carried a partied-out Irene the last bit home, and Ben was in from work when she got through the door. Grace told him about the call that Jane had received from Anne and how their talk had turned to the likelihood of war. Ben agreed wholeheartedly with Jane's gloomy assessment.

'But surely you don't want a war, Ben?' said Grace heatedly.

'Of course not, but neither do I want fascism and a dictator gaining power in Britain,' he replied. 'Which is what could happen in Europe. Hitler started rearming a while ago – we're way behind, and I bet France is, too. It looks like Hitler and Mussolini have signed some sort of pact and are out to gain as much territory as they can. Chamberlain has to realise that Hitler and Mussolini are toying with him and we can't believe a word they say! We don't want our young men to suffer the same as the previous generation, but we just can't allow the fascists to have their way, Grace.'

'You've really thought about this, haven't you?' said Grace, calming down.

'Of course – I think there will be war because Hitler will go a step too far and he'll have to be stopped,' said Ben grimly.

'You won't go and volunteer, will you?' Grace's voice trembled.

He gazed down at her and his sleeping daughter in her arms, and his face softened. 'No, I'll bide my time until I'm called.'

'Oh, Ben, I know it's right, I just don't want to lose you. *We* need you.'

Ben placed his arms around them both and hugged them. 'I'm going to be here for you both and Simon as long as I can. We're not alone in this situation, so we have to stick together and help each other. We need to be of good courage, Grace.'

Somehow, his words did give her courage and Grace blinked back the tears that threatened. She took a deep breath. 'Shall we see if there's any music on?' she said as she relaxed into his hold.

Ben kissed her before moving over to the wireless and fiddling with the knobs until lively music flowed out. 'Let's dance,' he said.

The two of them, with Irene caught up between them, danced slowly around the kitchen until Irene woke up and began singing nonsense. They were all still dancing when Simon entered the kitchen after college. He laughingly removed Irene from her perch between her parents and placed her arms about his neck. The four of them danced alongside each other in time to the music.

Chapter 25

Ever since Grace had thought of Dougie while she was at Jane's for tea she was conscious that she must go and see Dougie's sister, Beryl, to find out how her parents and Marion were. Grace still saw Beryl intermittently out and about, and occasionally for tea, but there had been no contact between the warring sides of the family for years. Making amends to her aunt Polly felt increasingly unlikely, but it still troubled Grace, especially when she thought of the kindness her aunt had shown her when her mother had died. And although she shied away from the idea, Grace was curious to find out if Dougie was out of prison. She had lost count of time, but suspected that his jail term was coming to an end.

As it turned out Grace did not need to visit Beryl, as the following day, she turned up at Grace's house, looking obviously pregnant, with Sammy, her two-year-old son who had his father's light brown hair, in tow.

'I didn't know you were having another baby,' said Grace. 'Congratulations!'

'Thank you, it's due in June. I hope you don't mind my calling, I was passing nearby.'

'Sit down and make yourself comfortable.' Grace removed several toys from a chair by the fire and went to put the kettle on. At the same time, she removed a cardboard box of toys from behind the sofa and placed it on the floor. She wondered idly what it would be like to be pregnant again. Ben and Grace did make love, but he was not taking the chance of getting her pregnant just yet. Secretly she was glad about that because although she wanted another child, she had seen Milly struggle with controlling two young children. It would probably be easier if they waited until Irene was a bit older and had started school. Let alone worry about being pregnant at an uncertain time like this.

Instantly Irene began to empty the box, watched by the younger lad. She offered Sammy a stuffed rabbit, but he tossed it away and joined her in emptying the box. Once everything was thrown out, he tipped the box on its side and crawled inside.

'I should have brought some of his cars,' Beryl said. 'He's mad on cars, but his favourite is a fire engine that Dad bought for his birthday.'

'How is Uncle Douglas getting on? I've not seen him in passing since he kindly popped round to catch up with my dad in his last days.' Thinking about Norman made Grace feel emotional all of a sudden and she knelt on the floor and began to gather the scattered toys in one place in order to hide her face.

'Fed up! Mam's kicking up a fuss about our Dougie because Dad wants him out of the house—'

'So, he's out of prison!'

'Oh, yes – he's been out for months, just lounging around their house. I didn't realise you didn't know, sorry. Dougie says he'll return to London and stay with his mate if Dad kicks him out.'

'Your dad should put his foot down, especially if Dougie is back to his usual nonsense,' Grace said bluntly. She stood up and went to fill the kettle in the back kitchen. She heard a sudden yelp and hurried back into the kitchen to find Irene attempting to drag Sammy out of the box.

'Stop that, Irene,' she said.

Irene shook her fair curls. 'It's my box and I want to get inside.'

'It's big enough for two of you,' Grace said. 'Sammy just needs to move to one side.' She smiled down at the boy. 'Come on, sunshine, move over.'

He folded his arms across his chest. 'No!'

The boy's expression and obstinacy reminded Grace of Dougie and her spirits sank. She turned to Beryl. 'Could you tell him to share, please?'

'Waste of time,' she said. 'Anyway, they'll just fight if they were both in the box. They'd be squashed.'

Grace decided that there was only one thing for it, and she lifted the struggling child out of the box and quickly replaced all the toys in the box before returning it to behind the sofa.

Beryl stared at her. 'So, what are they going to play with now?'

'They can have some orange juice and look at a couple of Simon's old *Dandy* and *Beano* comics. He's moved on to *The Wizard* and the *Adventure* comics now he's older.'

'Do you still get on well the pair of you now he's reached a difficult age?'

'We rub along fine the three of us,' replied Grace. 'I just hope there won't be a war that lasts long enough for him to be called up.'

Beryl frowned. 'What about our husbands?'

'I know, it's a worry. Ben's promised he won't volunteer, but if he's called up, he'll have to go.'

'I bet we don't get many volunteering this time.' Beryl placed a hand on her bump. 'I tell you, I wouldn't be having this baby if the prime minister hadn't come back from Germany waving that bit of paper and saying we'd all have peace.'

'I suppose he tried his best because nobody wants to go to war.'

'Dad thinks there'll be a war. Mam's just worried her precious son will be called up.'

'It's going to be a different kind of war to the last one. The air force will play a major role, that's what Ben says.'

'Davy agrees—'

The women looked at each other, both thinking the same thing about falling bombs. Beryl then watched as Grace poured tea into two cups and gave the children their juice and comics.

It fell silent, but the peace did not last for long, as Sammy ripped one of the comics and Irene landed him a smack and snatched the comic from him and held it up for her mother to see.

'Look what he's done, Mam. He's a naughty boy, isn't he?'

'It's only an old comic,' said Beryl, lifting her crying son onto her knee.

'It's Simon's and he collects them,' piped up Irene.

'You shouldn't have hit Sammy,' Beryl said. 'It's you that's naughty.'

'These things happen,' said Grace. 'It's my fault, I shouldn't have given them Simon's things. Some paper and crayons would have been more sensible.'

'It's too late now,' said Beryl. 'Look at the red finger marks on Sammy's arm.'

Grace looked and saw that the marks were already starting to fade. 'He'll live,' she said.

'Of course, he will, but that's not the point. You should punish her.'

'I think this is six to one and half a dozen to the other,' Grace said. 'Let's forget it. Another biscuit, have a chocolate one, Beryl.'

Beryl said, 'Don't— I think it's time we get going.' She put her son down and stood up.

'Don't be like that,' said Grace. 'I don't want to fall out with you.'

'I don't want to fall out, either, but let's call it a day for now.' Beryl put on her son's coat and buttoned it up.

Grace held out the chocolate biscuit she had intended on giving to Beryl. The boy took it and crammed it whole into his mouth. The cousins looked at each other and broke into giggles.

'Kids,' they burst out.

Grace and Irene saw them out and waved them off before going back into the kitchen and the warmth of the fire. Grace sat down and reached for her unfinished tea.

'Can I have a choccie biscuit now, Mam?' asked Irene in a wheedling tone.

'You were naughty,' said Grace severely.

'So was he,' said her daughter.

'That's no excuse,' Grace rested her head on the back of the chair and closed her eyes. She was exhausted by the visit, but at least for a short while she had managed to forget about the possibility of war.

She could not forget, though, that Dougie was out of prison. She started worrying about whether he might come around and pester her when Ben was at work.

She was reluctant to mention Dougie to her husband, as Ben got all hot under the collar whenever his name was mentioned, but decided it was something she could not keep from him. As it was, it was a good job she had decided to mention it to him, as Irene babbled to Ben about the naughty little boy who had visited with his mammy that day. Ben raised his eyebrows and gazed at Grace, so, over dinner, she told him of Beryl's visit, and her being due again in June. Grace stood, as though to clear the table, and then added the news that Dougie was out of prison.

Ben frowned. 'I've been thinking about his being released, as I thought it might be around now. Let's hope he doesn't stay in Liverpool. If he does... and dares to show his face here – if I'm out of the house, you're best informing the police and have them warning him off. I can't be here all the time, protecting you and the kids...'

'I'm praying he'll return to London,' she said.

'If he's heard about the IRA setting bombs off there, I doubt he'll go,' said Ben. 'Anyway, I'll telephone your uncle and tell him if Dougie starts making a nuisance of himself, my next stop will be the police.' Grace agreed that was the sensible action to take, and tried not to think about Dougie.

–

Her mind was easily distracted, because a few days later, at the beginning of March, there were other worrying things to occupy her as Germany invaded the rest of Czechoslovakia. This expansionist move broke the Munich Agreement that Chamberlain had secured with Hitler in Munich last September. Within days Chamberlain broadcasted to the British nation that Herr Hitler could not be trusted to keep his word. Britain warned Hitler against invading Poland, saying they would declare war on Germany if he did. A few weeks later on the 1st April, the Spanish Civil War ended, and the fascist, General Franco was on the winning side which meant that Hitler could withdraw the forces he had supplied to the fascists in Spain. Preparations for war were set in motion and the Royal Armoured Corps was formed and the Women's Royal Naval Service, which had been disbanded after the Great War, was set in motion again.

During the school holidays, Simon was one of the volunteers turning up on a Lancashire beach to fill bags with sand. Cities and towns expected to be bombed from the air by the Luftwaffe and some construction workers were put to work building air-raid shelters, and councils began to make plans for children to be evacuated. Simon had already told them he was too old to be ferried off to the countryside, as he believed he could be of some use in Liverpool if the city was bombed. The King and Queen visited Canada and the USA. The Military Training Act was passed for men between twenty and twenty-one who were to undertake six months' military training.

Grace's fears came to a head at the beginning of June when tragedy struck close to home in Liverpool Bay. Something went horribly wrong on a recruits' trial for the submarine HMS *Thetis* and the lives of ninety-nine men were lost. Grace wept bitterly for the grieving families, especially for the mother and sisters of one of the young men: Syd, who had grown up in the next street along from her, whose father had lost his life in the last war, when his ship was torpedoed by a U-boat in the Atlantic. She remembered fondly that Syd had been the first boy to try to kiss her, before Dougie had rudely intervened on the doorstep. Grace knew she was not alone in feeling a growing sense of horror as the misery of war promised to unleash itself – the devastation caused by the deaths of so many Merseyside mariners during the Great War was still fresh in the city, and the people of Liverpool were now filled with dread at the thought of being denuded of their young men once more when war was to come.

–

Soon after this tragedy, a visit from Beryl's Davy lifted Grace's spirits. Davy had called by with the welcome news that Beryl has given birth a day or so ago to a healthy girl whom they had named Elizabeth after the princess. Beryl was doing well and Grace made arrangements with Davy to visit the mother and baby the following day. She asked Milly to watch Irene for a few hours so that she could help Beryl, undistracted, during her visit.

Grace had taken with her some of Irene's early baby clothes, thinking they could come in handy for Elizabeth and save Beryl and Davy some money. She was busy sorting out the clothes and showing them to Beryl when she was surprised by the sound of her aunt calling her daughter's name from downstairs.

Her mother snatched the clothes away from Beryl's outstretched hands and said, 'You don't need cast-offs from the likes of her. She betrayed your brother!'

Beryl glared at her mother. 'Keep your nose out, Mam. Besides, there's some really pretty dresses amongst those, and I appreciate Grace giving them to me for Elizabeth, so—'

'How dare you speak to me like that, you ungrateful little madam,' spluttered Polly. 'After all I've done for you.

Marion warned me that you might try and make friends with this one again.'

'What have you done?' countered Beryl. 'Dougie's always been your favourite.'

'I've brought you up, haven't I?' snapped Polly.

'That was your duty. I didn't ask to be born,' said Beryl. 'And I bet I had to wear cast-offs…' she muttered sulkily.

'I think I'd best be going,' interrupted Grace. 'I'll see you another time, Beryl.'

She hurried from the room and placed the bundle of baby garments in the parlour on her way out for Beryl to find later. Shaken from her encounter with Polly, and not sure what to make of the intensity of the older woman's anger, she ran down the street, not wanting her aunt to catch up with her and resume her shouting in the street.

It was as she turned the corner, and was looking over her shoulder, that she almost collided with Dougie. She swerved to avoid him, and drew herself up short, but he managed to catch hold of her arm.

'If it isn't my dear cousin,' he drawled, digging his fingernails into the pale skin of her upper arm, below the sleeve of her summer tea dress.

'Let go of me,' Grace gasped, breathless with rushing.

'How unfriendly, and such a pretty one still, too, I see,' he murmured, leering slightly and catapulting her tight against him, so she could feel his breath on her face. 'Although, I'm not so surprised you don't want to see me after the way you behaved, putting me behind bars. First you play with me, throwing yourself at me for years, then you reject me when you think your next gravy train has arrived. Though I can't see why he'd want to marry used goods like you—'

'You deserved it, Dougie,' she said, struggling to free herself. 'You're a bully – just like Hitler!'

Instantly, he slapped her across the face. 'Don't you compare me to him!'

She swore at him. 'Bugger off, you beast,' she shouted up into his face.

Dougie was so taken aback at her outburst – so unlike the quiet Gracie he thought he knew – that his grip slackened, and with a hand to her stinging cheek, Grace fled.

Chapter 26

By the time Ben arrived home from work, the red marks of Dougie's fingers had faded, although Grace's cheek was still slightly swollen. She hoped no one would notice, as she made the evening meal. She had felt quite proud of herself for shocking Dougie into letting her go, but it had taken her some time to calm down when she'd got back to the house, and Grace had been careful to lock the front door, in case Dougie had decided to follow her. After agonising over a pot of tea by the fire, Grace had come to the painful decision to not mention her encounter with Dougie to her husband. She felt too on edge to talk about it properly, and she knew that Ben would confront her family immediately about Dougie's behaviour. The encounter with her aunt Polly at Beryl's had also upset Grace, and she wasn't sure if she was ready for further confrontations – not just yet in any case. She knew it was most likely inevitable, but again found it hard to dismiss the kindness of her aunt's family following the years after her mother's death; this was just something that Ben would not understand. However, the idea of omitting the truth to Ben just didn't sit comfortably with her; she tried to tell herself that Ben had only instructed her to call the police if her cousin approached the house, and technically Dougie hadn't done that...

The violence and anger of that day continued to play on in Grace's mind over the coming weeks, as her sense of unease about not being completely honest with Ben grew. However, her personal troubles diminished, as the sheer scale of world events threw a shadow over their daily lives.

Meanwhile, as Britain prepared for war with Germany by getting more women involved in the forces, and by creating the Women's Auxiliary Air Force, on the other side of the world the Imperial Army of Japan blockaded Britain's trading ports into Northern China.

The Mersey Ferries stopped the ferry from Liverpool to Rock Ferry on the Wirral and the women's land army was reformed to work in agriculture. Towards the end of August, army reservists were called up and the Civil Defence Service was put on the alert.

On 1st September, Germany and Russia invaded Poland and at eleven o'clock, the prime minister broadcast the news to the nation. Operation Pied Piper was put into operation, and so began the evacuation of children from the main cities into the countryside. Grace had known about evacuation because Jane and Milly had spoken about it. Neither wanted to be parted from their children, but Milly's mother and stepfather had suggested that Milly and the twins stay with them at their house in Dublin, But she was reluctant to do so, not only because she did not want to leave Jimmy, but in August another IRA bomb had been exploded in Coventry and there had been five fatalities and seventy people injured. Jimmy's mother had suggested that the twins stay with her in New Brighton. Jimmy and Milly decided that she would have to stay with them in New Brighton, having decided that the two children would be too much for his mother to cope with and that Jimmy would stay over there at the weekends. Jane and her two children were to accompany Kyle and the staff from the orphanage with the orphans to a manor house in the Lancashire countryside. Grace and Ben decided to stay in Liverpool with Irene. On 3rd September, Britain declared war on Nazi Germany.

–

After that during the next fortnight, several events took place so that Grace found it difficult to remember in what order they happened. Mobilisation of the armed forces began and the National Service Act for men between eighteen and forty-one was passed by Parliament. The new BBC Home Service was people's lifeline to news, as were the newspapers. Within days a blackout was enforced, and the British Expeditionary Force sailed for France. The British civilian liner, SS *Athenia*, was torpedoed and sunk by a German U-boat and ninety-eight passengers and nineteen crew were killed. Aircraft carrier HMS *Courageous* was torpedoed and sunk with a great loss of life in the Western Approaches.

'The Royal Air Force has bombed the port of Wilhelmshaven,' said Ben, as he came in from walking Fergie during the last week of September. 'Hopefully, it will go some way to preventing the German U-boats wreaking more havoc on Allied shipping and invading us.'

Grace glanced up from mashing potatoes. 'Jane told me that Andrew had heard that the prime minister has formed a war cabinet.'

'He should have listened to Churchill and done that ages ago,' complained Ben.

'Churchill is to be the First Lord of the Admiralty,' Grace said, pleased that Jane was able to update her on the latest news, as she added a knob of butter to the potatoes.

'Good, he has some experience of what is needed from the Great War,' said Ben.

His words were of some comfort to Grace, but Ben's face was serious as he sat at table. 'I hate to upset you, luv, but I've heard that all pets are having to be put down.'

'You're joking,' Grace cried, reaching out and stroking Fergie.

'I wish I were, but apparently they could prove a worry when the bombing starts, and feeding them will be a problem, too. Sooner, rather than later, rationing will come into force, and having enough food to feed people isn't going to be easy with German U-boats stopping our food supplies getting through.'

'But we couldn't do that with Fergie... I couldn't give him up to be put down!' protested Grace, tears in her eyes.

'I don't see how we have any choice. We have a dog licence, so that will be on record.'

'Can't we hide him somewhere?' she pleaded.

Ben covered her hand on the table with one of his. 'Don't you think lots of dog owners will want to do that? Anyway, where do you suggest?'

Grace could not think of anywhere, but then she had an idea. 'Presumably, they won't be putting down dogs for the blind. Maybe I could pretend to be blind?'

Ben gazed at her and his lips twitched. 'Grace, you're not thinking straight. Blind people are registered, as are the dogs.'

Grace banged her fist on the table. 'Oh, why do you have to have a sensible answer for everything?'

'Because your suggestions won't work,' he said gently. 'We all have to make sacrifices in wartime, and this is just the start.'

'Damn Hitler and the Nazis!'

Ben nodded. 'Anyway, let's just carry on caring for Fergie as long as we can. Who's to say, the scheme might only be carried out for so long, and then the men might be called away to do something more vital to the war effort.'

Grace sighed. 'I hope you're right. Anyway, where's Simon?'

'Probably at one of his mates', discussing which service they'll join when they're old enough to be called up,' said Ben grimly.

'Bloody hell,' said Grace. 'I hope to God the war will be over by the time he's eighteen.'

'That'll be 1943,' murmured Ben. 'We've a helluva fight ahead of us if that's to happen and we're to come out victorious.'

'Rule Britannia,' Grace said softly. 'Britons never, never, never shall be slaves.'

Ben came around the table and reached out and drew her close to him. 'That's the spirit. We're all in this together, and no doubt, just like the last war, we'll get through the fight.'

Chapter 27

Grace was often to think of that evening as the early dark days of the war passed with several more Royal Navy vessels and merchant ships being sunk by German U-boats. Thankfully, the anticipated air raids on Liverpool had not yet materialised, and nobody had called to put down Fergie, but Grace soon accepted that life for herself and millions of other Britons and her Allies was going to get tougher.

Since the end of the previous year, identity cards had been issued to all citizens and petrol rationing had been introduced, which meant Ben could only use his work van for essential trips. To Grace's relief he was not in the first batch of men to be conscripted. She listened with growing dread as the new year saw more than two million British men aged between nineteen and twenty-seven called up. Dougie was to be one of their ranks. Grace had finally gathered up enough courage to call on Beryl again to see how baby Elizabeth was doing, and Beryl told her that her mother was almost out of her mind because Dougie had been conscripted and was now training at a camp in Scotland.

'What about Davy?' asked Grace quickly, hiding her feelings.

'He's joined the merchant navy,' Beryl's lips tightened. 'He thinks it's less dangerous than being on a battleship.'

Grace could only think to say, 'Let's hope he's right.' She did not believe for a moment that merchant ships were any safer than battleships. Food rationing had been introduced and the German U-boats would have orders to prevent non-combatant ships from reaching British ports with food, tools or armaments from America.

–

Halfway through the first month of the year the weather turned cold and Grace bundled Irene in as many layers as she could before she sent her out to play in the street. It was, in fact, so cold that the lake in Newsham Park iced completely, and the Thames, in London, also froze over for the first time since 1888.

Over the winter, the cold weather continued, but it was not as bone-chilling as January had been, and still there was no sign of German bombers over the skies of Lancashire or even the south of England and its capital. Some evacuated children returned home, including Milly and the twins from her mother-in-law's in New Brighton, and Grace's frayed nerves grew more settled. She began to hope that the war would end well before Ben and – in her darker moments – Simon, could be conscripted.

At the beginning of April, Chamberlain had declared that Hitler had missed the bus. Ben called him a fool. Soon afterwards there came news that British forces were in Norway; Hitler's army had invaded neutral Norway and Denmark. British forces occupied the Faroe Isles to prevent the Germans getting a foothold there.

At the beginning of May, the British and French troops were evacuating Norway which triggered criticism of

Chamberlain's handling of the war and so he resigned as prime minister. Winston Churchill replaced him as leader of a coalition war cabinet.

Ben switched on the wireless as soon as he arrived home. It was well known that Hitler's army had swept through the Low Countries and over the border into France. Despite defending the defensive line, the Germans broke through and the British Expeditionary Forces were in danger of being swept up as they retreated before the larger forces of Germany.

It was through Anne that they heard Churchill had made a speech in the House of Commons, saying, 'I have nothing to offer you but blood, toil, sweat and tears.'

'Well, at least we know where we are,' said Grace. 'But what's he going to do about rescuing the Expeditionary Forces?'

Within a short space of time they knew what had been decided. Beryl told Grace that Davy had sent her a wire that she picked up at the post office, which said that all boats and ships of any size were needed to help rescue the British Expeditionary Force from France and bring them home.

It was days later that they read in the *Echo* of 'The Miracle of Dunkirk' in which even a Mersey ferry boat *Daffodil* had played a part, as did the Isle of Man ferry boats, and lots of other boats from all over the country. The RAF had battled in the air over the beach and its approaches with the Luftwaffe. Sadly, some British forces were captured by the Germans as they fought a rear-guard action and some ships were sunk, but 330,000 troops were saved, including some Polish, Belgian and French.

'"We will fight them on the beaches… we will never surrender…"' Grace slowly read Churchill's words in that day's *Echo*. She was sitting by the kitchen window enjoying the longer days, before she tidied the kitchen for the night. It was June and the air was warm, filled with the promise of sunnier days ahead. There had been rumours reported in the press that Hitler wanted to have peace talks with Britain, and the Foreign Secretary, Viscount Halifax, was in favour, but Churchill was standing firm saying that there would be no negotiations and had persuaded the war cabinet round to his way of thinking. Grace had been following the reports in the papers and looked up at Ben while she said, 'Stirring words, but is it now that we can expect to be bombed into submission and then invaded?'

'You can bet your life that'll be Hitler's plan if we don't agree with his plans for a peace agreement with us,' said Ben grimly. 'Can you see him retreating from Poland and Austria, and what about the Low Countries he's just invaded and France?'

'He'll probably try for a peace agreement with France, do you think? And where's Russia in all this?' said Grace. 'I mean they invaded Poland when Hitler did. They are allies.'

Ben did not reply straight away, but looked thoughtful. 'I should imagine Russia and Germany won't stay allies for long. Communism and Fascism don't mix – both leaders are greedy for power and land.' He paused. 'Anyway, let's try to leave all that for now and live in the moment. I'm still hungry.'

'There's no more dinner,' said Grace. 'You can have a couple of jam butties.'

'If that's all there is,' he said, sinking wearily into an armchair.

'I've tins, but I want to use them for proper meals when things get worse.' Grace had come to terms with using ration books, but meat had begun to be rationed in the spring and that made cooking meals that were tasty and nourishing more challenging. Fortunately, during last summer, Grace had begun to buy a tin of food, such as corned beef or luncheon meat, once a week for her store cupboard, so now she had something to fall back on, but she was wary of using her supply all at once.

'Then jam butties it is. What kind of jam?'

'Raspberry.'

'My worse favourite jam,' he said.

'I know, the pips get between your teeth,' she said. 'But that's all there was left in the shops.'

'All right, there's worse things than pips between your teeth,' Ben said. 'I think I'll go up and see Irene.'

'Don't wake her up,' cautioned Grace.

'I just want to look at what we'll be fighting for...' Ben had enrolled in the Civil Defence and Simon had volunteered as a messenger.

Grace listened to his feet on the stairs and sighed. Then she told herself to count her blessings and pray for those in Europe already suffering under the Nazis.

—

During the long summer days, as news of the war felt increasingly desperate, Grace took Irene to the park in the afternoons to make the most of playing with her daughter in the peace and quiet of the fresh air. She tried not to dwell on the news, but she felt overwhelmed again by the scale and speed of events.

Italy had declared war on Britain and France, and British troops had just crossed into Italian Libya, marking the start of a desert warfare campaign. Despite a Franco–British War Agreement formed in the autumn of 1939,

France, fearful of a repeat of the atrocities it had suffered in the last war, had agreed to an armistice with Germany. Meanwhile General de Gaulle, the leader of the Free French army, continued to broadcast from London to France rallying French resistance.

To cap this, Churchill had just cautioned that the Battle of Britain was about to begin. Grace's eyes were often lifted to the skies; every time she left the house, tugging Irene along with her, even when she was queuing up outside a shop. If she was in the park, at the first sound of an aircraft, she would dash with the four-year-old for shelter in some trees, only to emerge ten minutes later laughing at herself. The sense of anticipation grew unbearable, and as early summer passed into August, it came as a peculiar relief to her to hear the news that industrial Birmingham had been bombed, followed by nearby Birkenhead.

'So, it's started,' said Grace to Ben, fearfully. 'I supposed we'll be next.'

'Maybe, or they might target London or Southampton,' Ben said, thinking the Luftwaffe could have intended bombing the Liverpool docks, but might not have got their aim right when they hit Birkenhead.

'They might target both,' said Grace, a shiver going down her spine. 'I suppose our ports are their prime targets though.'

'And our airfields, army camps, ammunition factories, machinery – the list goes on,' said Ben. 'They'll also be aiming to destroy our morale. But, whatever the case, you need to be prepared – have a bag ready with a torch, some food and drink, extra clothing and head for the air-raid shelter. Failing that, get you and Irene to some sort of cellar, even the cupboard under the stairs...'

'Should I take some bandages, plasters, iodine and such, do you think?'

'If it makes you feel better,' he said, smiling. 'And don't forget the gas masks.'

She returned his smile. 'You're thinking if anyone did get hurt, they'd need more than plasters and iodine, aren't you? I hate the masks, the smell of rubber and the feeling I can't breathe.'

Ben put his arms around her. 'Just think as you go – be aware, be careful where you put your feet and watch for buildings or walls toppling.'

'You too,' she said, resting her head for a moment against his chest. 'Now how about some toast and dripping before your night shift?'

'Sounds good,' he said, releasing her.

The dripping was from roast mutton, so was tasty spread on the bread toasted close to the fire's glowing embers. Simon came downstairs, drawn he said, by the savoury smell. He was just in time to eat the last slice.

'Fortunately, bread's not on ration,' said Grace shaking her head.

'I'm still hungry,' Simon said, 'Should I go and get a loaf?'

'You might as well,' said Grace, fetching her purse. 'But you'll have to make do with having just jam on it. Although, we're going to run out of that soon.'

'Sugar's not rationed, is it?' asked Simon.

'No, so we could start thinking of going blackberry picking once they're ripe and I could have a go at making my own jam,' said Grace.

'We could make a day of it,' said Ben. 'We could either take a tram out to Kirkby or the train to Formby. They'll be plenty of brambles either way.'

But in the following weeks, blackberry picking went completely out of Grace's mind, as one night, like some sort of nightmare, she was awoken by the distinctive screech of the air-raid siren. She roused a bewildered Irene from her sleep, and still dressed in her night clothes, met Milly and her children on the street outside. With heavily beating hearts, they headed for the nearest shelter, even before the local warden could usher them there. Nobody slept a wink that night; Milly started up a singsong to try and drown out the sound of the overhead planes and distant explosions. When the All Clear sounded in the early hours, everyone trooped out of the shelter silently and headed home, breathing in air that was heavy with the smell of cordite and brick and plaster dust.

Grace and Milly were relieved to find their streets still standing and undamaged. Once inside, Grace found Fergie hiding under the dining table. She gave him a saucer of bread and milk, annoyed with herself for forgetting about him. When Ben arrived home, followed by Simon, straight from delivering messages to various warden's posts on his bicycle, they were both mucky messes. Ben had been helping to dig people out of the ruins of buildings, some of whom were thankfully still alive. Grace tutted when she saw the state of their uniforms, and made a fuss of putting the kettle on to hide her eyes, which were wet with tears at the sight of her men – home, safe and sound.

Chapter 28

The air-raid sirens sounded again the following night, and with a sinking heart Grace and Irene hurried to the air-raid shelter. There she found Milly settled in with the twins. The children dosed back into a fitful sleep, and as the might of the Luftwaffe could be heard droning overhead, Grace confided in Milly about a plan she had to create a little bed to grow some vegetables in the backyard. Milly excitedly reported that as luck would have it, Kyle and Jane had had a similar idea. Since they had been evacuated to the countryside with the orphanage they were worried that their large garden which overlooked the park might be running wild. Kyle had phoned Milly's husband, Jimmy, earlier that day and asked if Milly and Grace would like to use the space to grow vegetables for themselves as Jane and Kyle found it hard to get away regularly. He also suggested that they keep a few chickens for eggs, adding that if Jimmy could meet him in Ormskirk he would be able to bring him some chicks to rear.

'What about feeding them?' Grace asked.

'He said he'd provide some food to get them started,' answered Milly. 'I lived on a farm for a while as you know in Ireland, so I know a bit about rearing and caring for chickens.'

The women were so engrossed in their plans, they had almost forgotten about the raid, and were startled when the All Clear sounded.

'Thank God that wasn't very long,' said one of the older women in the shelter, making for the door.

Milly and Grace, woke the children and hurried out to the cool night air. Grace was not home long when Ben and Simon arrived. As Ben removed his jacket he said, 'That was only a light raid, hardly any damage, and no casualties where I was.'

'That's a relief,' she said. 'Shall we have a cup of cocoa?'

Father and son agreed, and while they drank their cocoa and had a biscuit, she told them what Milly had said about the garden. 'Do you think they'll share the chicks with us?' asked Simon.

'I should think so,' Ben said. 'And they'd probably appreciate some help digging vegetable patches.'

'I'm game,' said Simon.

However, when Grace and Milly and their families arrived at Kyle and Jane's home that weekend, it was to discover that the back garden had already been dug over, including the lawn, and tidy rows upon rows of vegetables had been planted. Some looked ready to pick. The adults exchanged glances.

'I wonder who's done this,' said Ben.

'Perhaps we should go next door and see if they know anything about it,' suggested Grace.

'Which next door?' asked Milly.

'How about the one where there was an old woman peering around a curtain?' said Ben.

'We all shouldn't go,' said Grace. 'We might scare her.'

It was decided that the two women should investigate, so while the younger children played in the garden, Milly and Grace went and knocked on the neighbouring door to the right. They had to wait some time before the door was opened by a small, dumpy, wrinkly-faced woman. Her hair was concealed by a tartan scarf tied in a turban and she was dressed in a cream blouse with the buttons in the wrong holes and a tartan skirt.

'Canna help ye?' she asked in the slightest of Scottish accents.

Milly explained the situation.

The woman nodded several times before holding the door wider and invited them in.

'It was ma son, yer ken, who dug over the ground and planted tatties, cabbages and beans, only then he was called up and had to go. We didn't think Kyle and Jane would mind, as they are away. I managed to pick some beans, but I haven't the strength to start digging the tatties.'

'Our menfolk can do that,' said Milly, and explained what Kyle and Jane had suggested.

The woman's face lit up. 'I'd appreciate that, as there'll be too much for me, so you must take some for yerselves. It would be kind of them if they could also do some digging in ma garden after picking the rest of the veggies. I'm Mrs Alice Burns, by the way, but ye can call me Alice.'

So, Milly and Alice shook hands and made friends, and Grace went and told Jimmy, Ben and Simon what had been decided. In the meantime, Milly had learnt from Alice that she was a widow and her son was her only kin. He was twenty-eight and a newly qualified doctor in the Royal Navy on a convoy ship.

'Did she mention the air raids, as she's living on her own?' asked Ben.

'I asked her how she managed,' replied Milly. 'She told me that she couldn't be bothered with going to the shelter, but went down into the cellar.'

'Wasn't she frightened being all alone?' Simon asked.

'Not frightened, only a wee bit lonely, apparently. She sings hymns and she'd like someone to sing along with her...'

'Surely someone from St Margaret's would stay with her and sing?' said Simon.

'She doesn't attend there, says it's too high. She's a Presbyterian.'

'There's a Presbyterian church in Kirkdale,' said Ben. 'Only that's a bit far for her to go to, I suppose.'

'I'm surprised she ever left Scotland,' said Jimmy.

'She married a Scouser, he was a shipmate of her brother who was killed in the last war,' said Milly.

'You've found out a lot about her in a short time,' said Jimmy laughing as he shook his head.

'She wanted to talk, and once she started, she couldn't seem to stop,' Milly said.

'So, what are we going to do to help her?' asked Simon.

'What she could do with is a lodger,' said Ben thoughtfully. 'So she's not by herself late at night with the air raids. And Kyle could do with a caretaker in his house as well. I don't like the idea of it being left empty for so long.'

'I'll give him a ring,' Jimmy said. 'And perhaps the girls could speak to Alice about taking in a lodger.'

'I could speak to her now,' said Milly thoughtfully, 'but she might want some time to mull it over – and she might not like us sticking our noses into her business.'

As it was, Alice said that she would need to send a wire to her son as it was his house, but confessed that a lodger was something that she had been thinking about.

'In the meantime,' she said, indicating to Simon with a nod of her head, 'maybe, this young man could stay and that way he could also keep an eye on Kyle and Jane's place.'

'Now there's a thought,' said Simon. 'Can I bring our dog, Fergie? He could come with me and I could take him for runs in the park as it's just across the way!'

Ben and Grace agreed to think about it, and came to an agreement together overnight that Simon should go; so things were set in motion. It was with a heavy heart that Grace watched Simon pack his things, but there was no question that helping others came first, a lesson that Grace had had drummed into her from a young girl.

Grace saw little of Ben, and even less of Simon during that autumn, as Simon settled into living with Alice as a permanent lodger. He seemed happy enough from what Grace could tell from her regular visits.

Meanwhile, Grace continued in her daily household routine, but often found her spirits flagging – it seemed to her that bombing raid followed bombing raid, with just the odd day's reprieve. Of course, she knew that London was being severely targeted, but at the close of November, Merseyside underwent a real baptism of fire as Hitler's forces attempted to destroy the city's docks. Wave after wave of bombers attacked. Grace huddled in the shelter at night with Irene, frantic with worry, as Ben and Jimmy went out on fire-watching duty to face the destruction. Luckily, both men returned home. They were exhausted, eyes red-rimmed from smoke and dust, but unhurt. Grace again counted her blessings as Ben reported that intense fires still burnt on the docks and hundreds of Liverpudlians were made homeless as their homes were destroyed overnight.

Later that afternoon, Grace was sitting at home with Milly knitting socks for the troops and discussing the bomb attack, when Beryl surprised them with a visit. Beryl had Sammy and little Elizabeth with her, and as Grace opened the door, she was taken aback by the sight of her cousin's dishevelled and filthy appearance. Beryl was normally so careful about her appearance.

'Whatever's happened?' Grace asked, dragging her cousin inside quickly with the children.

'Davy's ship has been torpedoed and he's missing, presumed dead!' wailed Beryl in a tight voice, pale beneath the dirt streaked over her face. 'It seemed unreal after what happened last night as well!'

Grace pushed her down into a chair in front of the fire and took the baby from her. Immediately, Sammy climbed onto his mother's lap. Grace sent the twins into the parlour with some toys, and then said, 'Milly, make a pot of tea, please?'

Milly hurried into the back kitchen and put on the kettle. She got out cups and milk and sugar before hurrying back into the kitchen in time to hear Beryl say, '—Mam's in the Royal Infirmary now. She was taken to Smithdown Road hospital first, but it was full.' She paused. 'Dad had just helped me to get the kids out and was holding us back on the other side of the street. We were staying overnight with them – the raid started and we knew it was going to be a big one. We didn't have a chance to get to the shelter before we heard the bombs going off—' She gulped back her tears and it was several minutes before she was able to carry on. 'Mam was stupid. She ignored what Dad was saying, and ran across the street back into the house, saying she must fetch something. Dad was going to go after her, but a fire engine had just managed to get through and a fire bobby dragged him back. Dad was talking away at him, nineteen to the dozen, frantic like, but...'

Grace felt sick, able to see the horrible scene in her mind's eye. 'I presume a fire bobby went in and rescued Aunt Polly?' she whispered.

'Not immediately! The chief wouldn't let him because gas pipes had been damaged in the nearby blast and he couldn't enter until he was wearing the right clothing and had the right equipment.'

'But he managed to rescue her?' said Milly.

Beryl nodded. 'But I don't think she'll recover.' She closed her eyes.

'Is there any more tea?' asked Grace, at a loss for what to do.

Milly rushed into the kitchen and topped up the teapot with hot water. When she returned to the room it was to find Grace and Beryl in tears. The boy was howling, and Grace was rocking the baby. Milly took charge and told Grace to sit down. She then asked the boy kindly to shut up making that nonsense. He stuttered to a stop and asked for his daddy.

Milly handed a cup of tea to Beryl and then to Grace. She gave Sammy a drink of milk with an encouraging smile. 'So, where's your dad now, Beryl?'

'Still at the hospital, I should imagine.' Beryl rubbed her eyes with the back of her hand. 'He told me I was to come straight here and let Grace know. He thought she might need to see Mam.'

Grace gulped her tea too quickly and burnt her mouth. After a few minutes she said, 'Where's Marion?'

'She wasn't home. She and her best friend have been called up and have joined the WAAF,' Beryl said. 'Dad said she's stationed at an airfield near Southport.'

'That's probably Woodvale. Does he have a number he can phone the base on in emergencies?'

'I think so. What about Dougie being told?' Grace said hesitantly.

'Dad's going to telephone his commanding officer.'

'Most likely he'll be given compassionate leave,' said Milly, who had been all ears.

'Is your dad going to stay with you at your house while he sorts things out?' asked Grace.

'I don't know what he's going to do yet,' said Beryl. 'And, as you know, our house is only small…'

'Anyway, first things first,' said Milly, taking charge again. 'You'll want to go to the hospital, Grace.'

Grace nodded. 'I'll probably have to walk. How did you get here, Beryl?'

'I walked. It's the only way, unless you have a bike.'

'You must be exhausted,' said Grace. 'You stay here with the kids. I don't know what time Ben will get in, but if he's in before me, can you explain what's happened and where I've gone? Listen out for Irene in case she wakes. She's having a nap upstairs.'

Milly stayed with Beryl, thinking she might be glad of the company, and Grace hurried off to the hospital, hoping her aunt would still be alive when she arrived. The closer she got to the city centre, the thicker the air seemed with dust and the smell of smoke and charred wood. The roads were littered with debris, but she guessed it would be even worse nearer the docks.

Grace felt uneasy as she entered the hospital grounds, as not only were there injured people wandering around in a daze, but several ambulances were coming and going. She spotted Douglas standing in the entrance and ran towards him. Grace placed her arms around her uncle and hugged him hard.

'I'm not too late, am I?' she cried.

'She was still alive when I left her, muttering away to herself,' he said. 'Earlier on, she pulled off the oxygen mask suddenly and gasped at me, "Douglas, you have to let Dougie know." Then before I could say a word, she'd stopped, and her head flopped against the pillow. I thought that was it, Grace, so I called a nurse, but before she arrived, Polly had gathered her strength again and whispered, "I must see Grace before I go."'

'Have you managed to get through to Dougie's commanding officer?' asked Grace.

'A doctor did it for me,' said Douglas. 'He was from Edinburgh and said he'd make himself understood quicker than I would. Real kind of him considering how busy he was.'

'Did the doctor manage to speak to Dougie as well?' Grace asked, moving aside to allow several people to pass into the hospital.

'No, but the officer told him that Dougie would be on his way in no time. He was going to send him by car with a driver as there are delays on the railway due to raids further south that have damaged the tracks.'

'How kind some people are,' agreed Grace, despite knowing she would rather not have to see Dougie in the days ahead. But first things first, she had to make things right with her aunt Polly. Hand in hand with her uncle, he led her into the hospital and past reception and along passages and through doorways until they came to the room where Polly was lying in bed with an oxygen mask covering her mouth and nose. Her hands were swathed in bandages, but Grace could see where her hair had been singed by the heat of the fire and ointment smeared on the burns on her forehead. Tears ran down Grace's face and she threw herself down beside her aunt and cried, 'Oh, Aunt Polly, please forgive me. I'm sorry I hurt you and I've missed you so much.' Polly's eyelashes fluttered and her eyelids opened, and she attempted to focus on her niece's face. 'Hope, is that you?' she whispered.

Grace glanced at her uncle and he shook his head and wiped his eyes with the back of his hand.

'No, it's me Grace,' she said.

'Grace,' Polly's mouth moved as if she was tasting the name. Then she reached out one of her bandaged hands. 'You came. I'm sorry too. I let your mother down. Forgive me.'

'Of course,' said Grace. 'I love you.'

'Dougie, I was wrong...' Her voice trailed away.

There was the sound of a door closing, Grace glanced over her shoulder and saw a woman in uniform. 'Marion!' she uttered, struggling to her feet to make way for her cousin.

Marion helped her up and said, 'I'm sorry too for all the times I was horrible to you in the past. Please forgive me?'

Grace's emotions were running high and all she could do was to squeeze her cousin's hand. Then she left the room, desperately in need of Ben's arms around her.

Chapter 29

Liverpool: December 1940

Grace was woken by Ben on the morning of 6th December as he put a cup of tea and a slice of jam toast gently down by her bedside. She gazed up into his clean-shaven face and smiled.

'You are good,' she said. 'Does this mean that you're attending the funeral with me?'

'I wouldn't let you go alone,' he said.

'I'm glad,' she said, placing her arms about his neck as he carefully moved the breakfast tray on the bed beside her. She brought down his head and kissed him. He returned her kiss and then freed himself and stepped away from the bed. Going over to the wardrobe he removed the only black dress from its interior and placed it softly on a chair. She thanked him and reached for the cup of tea.

'At least Dougie'll be going back to Scotland this evening and we've found Uncle Douglas, Beryl and the children a place to live together.'

Grace thought thankfully how there had not been an air raid on Merseyside since the beginning of December. Most of the citizens on Merseyside had been able to sleep through the night, although the trials of the November bombing had been great, especially for her family – when Beryl had returned to her street after informing Grace about her aunt Polly's condition and Davy's presumed death, it had been to discover that several houses, including her own, had been near-destroyed by the blast of an incendiary. Beryl and the children had returned to Grace's house in a state of total despair. Not only had she lost her husband in a day, but also her home and her mother.

When Grace had returned from the hospital accompanied by her uncle Douglas, she had found Beryl in pieces, being comforted by Milly. Instantly, Grace had thought of Kyle and had hurried to Milly's house with her friend. A phone call was put through to the relocated orphanage up in Lancashire and Grace was able to speak to Kyle and explain the situation. Without hesitation he agreed to his house being used by her uncle, cousin and children, as they were now all homeless. Grace had thanked him profusely, grateful that her family didn't have to squeeze into her small house or take refuge in the local church with the other bombed-out families. She returned home to make the arrangements with her cousin and uncle.

–

Again this morning, thinking back to that terrible night, Grace mouthed silent thanks that Ben and her children had survived and for the kindness of friends. She prayed for the bereaved and injured, and her heart was heavy as she dressed for her aunt's funeral. Her aunt was to be buried in the plot that held Grace's maternal grandparents and her mother and father. Milly was looking after Irene and Beryl's children while the funeral was taking place at Anfield Cemetery Chapel.

Grace thought back to the day her aunt had died. It had been several days after the bombing attack. Polly had rallied for some time, but had not been able to overcome the extent of her burns. Dougie had eventually arrived and spent a few minutes with his mother before she passed. He was in tears but pulled himself together. Douglas was also at his wife's bedside and he was able to tell them that Grace had managed to find him and Beryl and the children somewhere to live.

'Where is this place?' Dougie asked.

'It overlooks Newsham Park and belongs to a friend of hers. They know her friend Milly really well. He and his wife are up Lancashire assisting with the children from the Seaman's Orphanage.'

'Oh, I know who you mean,' said Marion. 'They're called Kyle and Jane.'

'That's handy for Grace, isn't it?' sneered Dougie. 'She lands on her feet all right – first she rejects me, as we're not good enough for her, now she gets to play saviour to our family, and after all the trouble she's caused.'

'Ben's son is lodging next door with an elderly neighbour whose son is away with the Royal Navy. Helping her out and such,' said Douglas, ignoring his son's remarks.

'How old is the son?' asked Dougie pointedly.

'I think he's coming up to sixteen,' said his father. 'But that's all I know. Anyway, I've matters to see to, so I'll see you later.' He walked away.

Grace knew this because her uncle had told her, she had only seen Dougie once since his return and for that she was relieved; although she did feel sorry for him, knowing how dear he had been to his mother.

Grace tried to put these thoughts out of her head as she linked her arm through Ben's as they walked along Belmont Road in the direction of the cemetery. She could not help but think of her father and his funeral. Ben suddenly squeezed her arm against his side.

'You're thinking of your dad,' he said.

She nodded, feeling too emotional to speak. She wondered how he would have coped with another war if he had lived to see it. Would he have joined the Home Guard, wanting to do his bit? It would have been tough having him to worry about as well during the bombing. Worrying about Ben was enough, let alone what Simon was up to... She forced herself to think of something else.

The funeral service was short, but Dougie embarrassed the family by making as if to throw himself in the grave after his mother's coffin had been lowered. It was Marion who pulled him back, hissing, 'Silly boy, that's the last thing Mam would want you to do. She would want you to make something of yourself, to make her proud.'

'She was always proud of me,' sniffled Dougie. 'I failed her by not giving her a grandson.' He threw daggers at Grace across the grave. She pretended not to hear, not wanting to argue at a graveside in front of others. She was aware of his eyes fixated on her as she stood alone, while Ben spoke to her uncle and the vicar after the service. He seemed about to approach her, only for Ben to shake hands abruptly with her uncle and the vicar and step towards her.

He gripped Grace's hand and said in a low voice, 'We're going now. I've explained to your uncle that I need to get home. I'm wanted this evening in case there's a raid.'

'You think there will be?' she asked, a tremor in her voice.

'I hope not, but I don't believe Hitler's finished with us just yet,' he said grimly.

There was no raid that evening and neither in the weeks approaching Simon's sixteenth birthday. Simon had voiced a desire to go to the flicks, but the film he wanted to see, *The Thief of Bagdad*, which starred Sabu, was not to be shown until Christmas. A promise was made for him to see it later, and in the meantime, on his birthday Ben and Grace would take him to *Busman's Honeymoon*, as they had all missed it the first time and it was now being re-released. That evening, they remembered to take gasmasks and torches with them and hoped there would not be an air raid to spoil the show. They were happy, as they came out of the cinema, having enjoyed the film, to find the sky clear. They returned home for a birthday celebration of cocoa and homemade Victoria sponge. Simon then returned to his lodgings, laden with half of the Victoria sponge to share with his landlady, Alice, and his extended family next door.

–

Four evenings later, just before six o'clock, Ben, having received word that a heavy raid was on its way and fearful that the local shelter would be overcrowded, decided to escort Grace and Irene to Alice's house through the blackout. Ben told Simon that a raid was on its way and that he should report for duty as a messenger. Simon scrambled to gather his uniform and Grace kissed and hugged them and told them to be sensible as she waved them off. She fought back tears as she watched them until they were out of sight, Simon wheeling his bicycle alongside his dad.

As she knocked on her uncle's door, the air-raid siren started up. Her uncle opened the door and started in surprise at the sight of her. Before he could speak, she told him that she would be next door with Alice in the cellar.

'I'd join you and Beryl, only Alice won't shift, she has hers just as she likes it. See you in the morning.'

She wasted no time hurrying back to Alice in the cellar just as she heard the drone of planes and then the thud of an incendiary landing nearby. Alice already had the kettle on her primus stove in the cellar and soon they were enjoying a cuppa and a broken biscuit each, while Irene enjoyed a rusk in milk out of a mug. For a while the raid didn't give them much cause to set their teeth on edge, but just after eight o'clock the noise grew almost unbearable. Alice began to sing the 23rd Psalm and they continued singing until eleven o'clock. The noise outside lessened, but did not die away completely and continued until four in the morning when the All Clear finally sounded.

Irene had slept through some of the noise, clasped tight against Grace's chest. She stirred when Grace stood up and went upstairs to look outside. There was a glow in the sky that told of many fires still burning. The neighbouring door opened, and her uncle stepped out and waved.

'That's the worst of the raids I've experienced, even the one that did for our Polly,' he called.

Grace agreed, 'I hope Ben and Simon are all right. They'll have been kept busy and will still be at it, so I can't expect any word from them for hours.'

Much to Grace's relief Ben arrived at noon, badly in need of a change of clothes and a wash. He had already had something to eat and drink, supplied by the canteen run by the Women's Voluntary Services. St George's Hall on Lime Street had been set alight and damaged slightly. Roads were choked by debris and fire engines and rescue worker's vehicles had had difficulty trying to get through. Simon arrived back shortly afterwards.

Alice told Ben he could have a bath in the bathroom upstairs, so Grace rushed to draw the water. She noticed how painful it was for Ben to lift his arms and offered to wash his back. He did not refuse and so she also helped him undress and get clean. He hugged and kissed her. She held him tight, saying that she wished he didn't have to go out again.

'So, do I,' he said huskily. 'Oh, for a night in bed together.'

'It can't go on for ever,' she said.

'No, but this one's not over yet,' he said. 'Keep safe,' as he went out again in the early morning to assist in clearing rubble.

That evening there was another raid and this one seemed to go on for much longer. Just like the night before, Liverpool, Bootle and Seaforth were bombed and Birkenhead, Wallasey and the docks on both sides were damaged, as well as homes and municipal buildings. Again, Grace was a nervous wreck, despite doing her best to put on a brave face for Irene as she sang hymns with Alice in the cellar.

About an hour into the raid, Simon had turned up on his bike to tell them that Mill Road Infirmary had been hit and that was where Ben was helping to rescue patients and staff. Grace asked him if he had seen any sign of Jimmy, Milly and the twins on his travels. Simon had shaken his head, had a quick cup of tea and a luncheon-meat butty, before heading on his way with a message to the Auxiliary Fire Service post in Anfield where it was known that lots of houses had been hit.

The long night wore on; Ben did not arrive back until three in the afternoon the following day. When he got home, he just sat in a chair, gazing into the fire without moving or speaking. Grace sat opposite him, watching as he slumped in the chair and fell asleep. She had decided not to wake him, but suddenly the sound of their own guns in the distance started up with the wail of the warning sirens accompanied by the sound of enemy planes returning. She watched as Ben sat up and rubbed his eyes. He stared across at her as she stood up with Irene in her arms. He kissed her and their daughter, squeezed Simon's shoulder, and then was gone. It was not long after that Simon left, leaving the women alone once more.

Chapter 30

A couple of hours later, Grace caught the sound of banging at the front of the house. She wondered if it was a bomb landing. She stepped back to the inner wall and waited in what she always thought of the lull before the next bang. Then she heard her name being called, and handing Irene to Alice, she went upstairs to hear someone kicking the door. For a second, she wondered if the Germans had invaded. Telling herself she was being stupid, as how would they know her name, she opened the door. Simon stood on the step with a bandage around his head and his arm in a sling.

Grace dragged him inside and slammed the door shut before asking, 'What's happened?'

He did not reply straight away, but sank onto the bottom stair. She sat beside him and placed her arm about his shoulders, listening to his breathing steadying. 'I got caught in the blast of a bomb exploding and it blew me off my bike into a wall. A warden found me and took me to the nearest First Aid Post.' The young lad paused. 'They wanted me to stay there, but I wanted to find what had happened to me bike and come back here, so I scarpered.'

'Did you find your bike?'

He nodded and winced. 'It's a mess. I'll never be able to ride it again.'

'Never mind. You've well had your worth out of it and Christmas is coming.' She took hold of him by his uninjured arm and lifted him to his feet. 'Let's get you to the cellar and into a chair – you need to rest.'

Simon did not argue with her, but leaned against her as they went down the steep cellar steps. Alice exclaimed in horror when she saw him. He gave her a wan smile as he was lowered into a chair, leaned back, and closed his eyes.

Grace covered him with a blanket and prayed for Ben. She wished he would arrive back safely – soon. She was on pins for the rest of the night and then all morning and for most of the afternoon. As the evening drew on, she gazed at Simon who was jogging Irene on his knee. She was aware that his eyes kept wandering to the clock to check the time, just as she was doing. She was not only on edge because Ben had not arrived back, but she was waiting for the siren to wail its next warning of approaching enemy planes. Thankfully, it was the All Clear that they heard, and Ben arrived back half an hour later, exhausted. A smile lit his mucky face at the sight of them, until he spotted his injured son. He rushed over to Simon and soon had the tale out of him. Then he told them that there had been a light raid over on the Wirral, but the planes had been chased off, and hopefully it looked like there was not going to be a raid over Liverpool that evening.

'Tomorrow's Christmas Eve,' said Grace. 'Maybe we'll be left in peace over Christmas.'

'You won't be able to buy much in the way of presents,' said Ben. 'The city centre is a mess. At least we're still here to celebrate Christmas together. There's so many who have lost their lives or family and homes.'

'Which reminds me,' said Grace. 'What about Milly, the twins and Jimmy and our street?'

'Our house is still standing, well, it was when I was coming back here,' said Simon. 'In fact, our street and Milly and Jimmy's were undamaged.'

'I must go and see if they're all right, it went on such a long time,' said Grace, reaching for her hat and coat.

'It wouldn't be sensible going there in the blackout, but maybe you're right,' said Ben. 'I'd enjoy sleeping in my own bed tonight. We could all do with having a meal and an early night. I'll be back helping clear up again tomorrow. The docks and factories have to be able to carry on working as soon as possible.'

As Grace snuggled up to Ben later that evening in their own bed, she sighed contentedly. 'Is it wrong of me to feel happy despite knowing so many people have lost so much?'

'No, you've got to make the most of the moment. It's not as if you've stood on the sideline. You've faced danger along with the rest of them, and were a comfort to Alice.'

'It was good of Simon to stay with her, while we came home,' she said. 'He needs to rest, though.' Ben agreed in a sleepy voice and then within minutes Grace realised he had fallen asleep.

–

Come morning after an undisturbed night, Grace did not rush to get out of bed, but lay in the curve of Ben's arm, aware of his breath fluttering the hair on the crown of her head. Then she felt his arm tighten about her and turn her over to face him. He began to kiss her, and then in no time at all, they were coupling. It was not until they rolled apart after making love, did she tell herself that he had not taken any precautions. A different kind of thrill went through her as she dared to dream that they could have another child. A war baby!

A few hours later she was on her way to visit Milly to check everything was okay. Ben accompanied her and Irene, making up silly rhymes with his daughter as he did so. He left them outside Milly's, and carried on to Newsham Drive to see Simon. After that he would report to the nearest post for orders.

Grace watched him go before knocking on Milly's front door. It was a while before she heard footsteps coming down the stairs and the door was opened.

'Oh, I was hoping it might be you,' Milly said, seizing Grace's sleeve and dragging her inside.

'Are you all right?' asked Grace alarmed; she had Irene by the hand and half-lifted her over the threshold. 'Are the twins well, and Jimmy and his mam?'

'The twins are a bit cranky because they haven't had their breakfast yet. Jimmy is in bed with a broken leg!' Milly's voice shook.

'What happened?' asked Grace, seizing her friend's hand and holding it tightly.

'He was helping out with rescue work when a wooden beam holding up a ceiling gave way and landed on the back of his legs. One leg caught the force more than the other, so is just badly bruised, the other has been put in plaster.' She paused, tears in her eyes. 'They wanted to keep him in hospital, but he refused and signed himself out.'

'So, how are you coping?' Grace asked.

'It's early days yet, and he's already wanting to come downstairs and sit in a chair with his leg up on a stool. I'd have difficulty getting him down though, and wondered if Ben could give us a hand.'

Grace sighed. 'He came this far with me, but then carried on to Alice's. I could ring hers from here and ask him. Although, won't you have trouble getting Jimmy upstairs to bed?'

'I said that to him, but he said he could stay down here and sleep on the sofa. He thinks it'd be safer if there was a raid.' Milly bit her lower lip. 'I said how will I manage to get him and the children to the shelter?'

'And what did he say to that?' said Grace aware that Jimmy was probably not thinking straight.

'That we didn't have to go to the shelter! But we don't have a cellar, just like you, so I don't know what he's thinking!'

'What did he say to that?'

'That you pays your money and takes your choice.'

'What?' cried Grace.

'He rambled on about direct hits on shelters, and cellars only being safe if the walls and ceilings are strengthened with iron or steel supports,' she said.

'Oh, my God,' whispered Grace. 'I suppose he has a point. I haven't told you yet, but Simon was blown off his bike yesterday and has a broken arm and a head injury.'

'At least they're both alive,' said Milly, rubbing her forehead. 'But what am I going to do about Jimmy if there's another raid?'

'Let's see what Ben says,' said Grace, 'Why don't you feed the twins while I telephone him now?'

'Of course,' said Milly. 'I should also phone Jimmy's mother.'

'Later,' Grace said. 'You don't want her rushing over here once you tell her Jimmy's injured.'

Milly agreed, 'Perhaps we should go over to Dublin and stay with Mam.'

Grace nodded. 'Although, I'll miss you,' she added. 'And it's possible I'll need you.'

'Why?' asked Milly.

Grace did not answer but went and lifted the phone receiver and dialled Alice's number. A male voice answered with the house's number. Grace did not recognise it, and she gave her name, and asked who was speaking. The man on the other end said, 'I'll fetch your husband.'

A few minutes later Ben came on the line. 'Hello, Grace, is there something up?'

'Yes, but who was that on the phone?'

'Alice's son. His ship's in dock for repairs up in Scotland, so having heard about the raids on Merseyside he decided to take some leave he was due and come down and find out how his mother is. He couldn't get through the other day on the telephone as the lines were down, so he was worried.' He paused. 'So, what's wrong?'

Grace told him all that Milly had said about Jimmy being stubborn and what he'd said about the safety of shelters. Grace paused for breath as she heard Ben swear softly.

'So, what do you think?' she asked after a minute or so.

'He had no right to put the wind up Milly like that, by making her believe nowhere is safe, but I can understand him wanting to be at home. One thing is for sure, he won't be passed medically fit if he gets his call-up papers any day soon.'

'That's a lot of help,' said Grace. 'But what advice should I give her?'

'I should tell her to go to Dublin and take Jimmy's mother with them to help Jimmy manage the journey. Only one questions how safe that is with German U-boats lurking about.'

Grace heard a male voice in the background and then Ben's answer in reply. 'What's going on?' she asked.

'It's the doc… he said that if they were on board a Republican ferry, they should be safe, because the ship would be recognised as being Irish and neutral.'

'When you say "the doc", do you mean Alice's son?'

'Yes, you'll probably get to meet him because his ship is going to be in dock for a while. He's volunteered to help out in a hospital here while he sees something of his mother.' He paused. 'Anyway, give my regards to Milly and Jimmy and tell him that he needs to stay in bed for now and hopefully I'll drop in and see him later.'

'Thank you… before you go, do you think you'll have time to do some Christmas shopping with me?'

'I doubt it. Anyway, you watch your step. There's still a lot of rubble around. See you later, luv.'

He ended the call and Grace placed the receiver down. She turned and saw that Milly was helping the twins to sit at the table for their late breakfast.

'So, what did he say?' asked Milly.

Grace repeated most of the conversation. Milly said, 'Alice must be over the moon, having her son home.'

'I imagine so, especially as it's Christmas tomorrow. He had a nice voice,' said Grace. 'So, what do you think you'll do?'

'Think about it, and then in a few days I'll speak to Jimmy and his mam and see what they think. But how do the U-boats know about the nationality of a ship?' She paused. 'Anyway, what did you mean when you said that you might need me?'

Grace bit her lower lip and said, 'You'll think I'm daft, but I'm hoping we could have another child.'

'Gosh, what a time for it to happen!' said Milly.

'I know! I'm thinking that I shouldn't mention it to Ben. It's far from certain yet, and I don't want him worrying about me.'

'He probably worries about you, pregnant or not,' said Milly.

'Well, worry more then,' Grace said laughing. 'Anyway, I thought I'd go to Breck Road and see what I can buy for Christmas.'

'You'll be lucky,' said Milly.

'I'm not worrying about a fowl because Simon and my uncle Douglas have been looking after the chickens at Alice's – they've promised me one for Christmas dinner.'

'I'd forgotten about them,' said Milly. 'Anyway, I need to phone Jimmy's mother and see what she wants to do for Christmas now Jimmy's injured and we won't be able to go to hers.'

'Is there anything I can get you? Would you mind looking after Irene for a while, there's a few things I want to pick up for her.'

Milly nodded. 'I'll wait and see what the mother-in-law has to say. No problem about Irene, the twins can play with her, while I see to Jimmy.'

Grace nodded. 'I'll see you when I see you then. I won't be long. Give my love to Jimmy.'

–

Grace found that there was little to buy in the shops, although she did manage to buy some dolly mixtures in a box that looked like a little shop, and chocolates from the little sweet shop on Whitefield Road. There were no tangerines to be had, but there were apples, potatoes, carrots, onions, sprouts and bunches of sage for stuffing in a greengrocer's on Breck Road. In a toy shop on Lower Breck Road she managed to find a few puzzle toys and a small teddy bear with one arm for Irene. The shop assistant was able to produce the missing arm, so Grace bought the teddy and the arm at a reduced price. The bakery had no Christmas cakes, but they did have some crusty loaves. Grace bought two of them, along with the single bun loaf that was left, thinking it would be nice with custard. She had secretly been knitting a jumper for Ben and a pullover for Simon, but she could not find wrapping paper for love nor money.

When she arrived home, after collecting Irene on the way, it was to be greeted by Simon sitting in the kitchen. 'Are you staying now?' she asked, delighted to see him. She missed having him and his belongings around the place. Things weren't the same with Ben out all hours with his volunteering too. 'How's your arm and head?'

'They're okay, they look worse than they are. I am just staying for tonight and for Christmas lunch and then they'd like me to go back to the house, if that's okay.' Simon took the shopping bags from her with his good arm and placed them on the table. 'I brought you a few things from the doc and his mam as well. He's really grateful for what we've done for Alice. I've got some veggies from the garden and he gave me some treats from Scotland – shortbread and Edinburgh rock!'

'I love Scottish shortbread,' said Grace. 'Perhaps we should save it for New Year's Eve.'

'He also gave me a miniature Scotch liquor Drambuie for you and a bottle of whisky for Dad. Dad said he must know the right people,' said Simon.

'What did he give you?' she asked.

'His old bike,' Simon said with a big grin. 'Although, it's not that old, but he bought himself a motorbike just before war broke out. He's going to ride it when he returns to Scotland. It's a bit hard to ride the bike with my arm like this, but I managed all right.'

'Well, that's really kind of him,' said Grace. 'I know I don't have to ask you whether you thanked him on all our behalf.'

He grinned again. 'Of course, I did. He was just sorry that he didn't have anything for Irene, but his mam has made her a tartan frock with a white collar and cuffs.'

'It sounds lovely!' said Grace. 'Did you bring it with you? It will be lovely for her to have something new to wear tomorrow. It's so hard with rationing these days.'

'I brought everything with me in a knapsack, as I rode the bike,' said Simon, smiling afresh.

'Good for you,' said Grace, with a warm feeling inside her. She prayed that there would not be a raid that night or for weeks to come, and that the Luftwaffe would take time off for Christmas and New Year.

'Where is your dad?'

'He's gone to see Jimmy and Milly.'

Grace wondered whether to follow him there after she'd unpacked the shopping and had a look at the goodies the doc and Alice had sent. Mostly she could not wait to see the frock that Alice had made for Irene. However, when she saw the chicken Grace decided it was best if she stayed home, as the chicken needed its feathers plucking and insides removing. Once she'd sorted that messy business, she set herself to making mince pies.

Ben arrived home later than she had expected, but the state of his clothes convinced her that after having visited their friends, he must have returned to help clear the streets again.

'What's cooking?' he asked.

'You hungry?' She removed her apron and went over and kissed him.

'Don't ask daft questions. Of course, I'm hungry. I'll go and get a wash and change,' he said.

By the time he reappeared, washed, shaved and wearing clean brown corduroy trousers, a cream-and-black check shirt and a Fair Isle pullover, there were bowls of soup on the table and a plate of sliced crusty bread.

'This smells good,' he said, leaning over to say hello to Irene.

'Giblet soup,' she said.

'So, you got the chicken.'

'Of course, amongst other things,' she replied. 'We can have a drink later with a mince pie.' She watched as he spooned up some of the soup along with a chunk of liver. She dipped a slice of bread into her soup. 'So, how did you get on with Jimmy?'

'I told him he was an idiot,' he replied in a rough voice. 'He should have stayed in hospital. He's not talking right. He's not making sense and he won't send for his GP.'

'Milly must be out of her mind.'

'She's furious with him, not that she's showing him how she feels.'

'So, what's she going to do?'

'She's been in touch with his mother, and she's coming over.'

'She won't persuade him to go back to hospital. She hates hospitals. Perhaps he'd listen to the doc,' suggested Grace.

'I don't think it's medical etiquette to get a doctor to do that,' said Ben, screwing up his face. 'I don't know what's best to do. Perhaps you should mention it to the doc.'

No sooner were the words out of his mouth than Simon said as he came into the room, 'What's that about the doc?'

'Nothing for you to worry about, son,' said Ben.

'I'm not worried.' Simon sat at table and reached for a slice of bread. 'Can I have some soup, please?'

'Help yourself,' said Grace.

'I'd rather you did it,' said Simon. 'I don't want to be accused of pinching all the meat.'

'There isn't that much, and we've already had our share,' she said, filling a bowl for him. 'We were talking about Jimmy. He's not himself.' She told him more about the situation.

He looked thoughtful and said, 'I think Doc could help. You say he hasn't had a knock on the head and it's his legs that are injured?'

Both nodded.

'Right,' he said. 'Doc and I have had some real interesting talks, so I have an idea what might be going on with Jimmy.' He dipped a chunk of bread in the soup.

'What?' asked Grace.

'I'm not saying. I could be wrong, but I'll have a word with Doc tomorrow.'

No more was said, and as the siren had not sounded, they all trooped upstairs to sleep in their own beds. Grace cuddled up to Ben. 'This is lovely,' she said. 'I hope Jimmy and Milly are all right.'

'Hmmm!' murmured Ben. 'I think tiredness is the biggest battle that those who have been under attack have been fighting. I know I've had a struggle keeping my eyes open during the day, but the clearing up has to go on – we've got to help each other.' His voice had dropped, and Grace guessed he was falling asleep.

She drew his head down on her breast and whispered, 'You poor love. Rest now and maybe tomorrow we can go to the Christmas service and sing carols.'

He lifted his head and kissed her. 'That would be nice. I'm sorry, but I haven't much of a Christmas present for you.'

'You're here, alive and well, and that's good enough for me,' she said closing her eyes.

–

The following morning Grace used the last of the butter ration that she had saved especially for this morning's toast. The tea ration had been increased for Christmas, so they were able to have two decent cups of tea each. Then she produced her knitted presents for Ben and Simon, and after exclamations of delight, Ben handed her a pair of pearl-drop earrings in a small grubby box. She stared at him in amazement.

'I thought you hadn't been able to buy me anything.'

'I didn't buy them in a shop,' he confessed. 'I found them in a gutter one night and I showed them to the other people around the bombsite. One of the men recognised them, and said he'd bought them for his mam, but she was killed in a raid… so I bought them from him—'

'I'm sorry about his mam, but I appreciate the gift,' Grace said, fingering the pearls.

'Do you want me to put them in for you?' asked Ben.

She handed one to him, glad she'd had her ears pierced in her teens.

Once fastened, Ben led her over to the mirror to have a look at herself. She moved her head, so the earrings swung gently. 'I really like them. Thank you.'

'It's my pleasure,' he said. 'You've shell-like ears, so pearls are fitting.'

'What a nice thing to say,' she smiled up at him.

He smiled back and there was an expression in his eyes that made her feel as if her heart flipped over. Grace thought back to when they first married and how she worried that they might not love each other.

It was Simon who broke the spell, saying, 'I bought your present from Alice,' he said. 'She'd had them in a drawer for ages, making her clothes smell nice.' He handed her a paper bag.

She thought from the smell, the bag would contain lavender bags, but to her delight it held two tablets of Yardley's lavender soap. 'Oh, that's wonderful,' she said, thinking about how hard it was to get hold of soap these days.

'Your dad managed to get tickets for the Everton match today,' she said.

'Tommy Lawton is a guest player,' confirmed Ben.

'I couldn't ask for a better Christmas present,' said Simon, giving his dad a hug.

'I'm treating us to go and see *Thief of Bagdad* this evening as well,' said Grace.

'That's good too,' said Simon.

Grace said, 'So, we're all happy.'

'What about Irene?' asked Simon. 'Has she emptied her stocking yet?'

Grace put her hand to her mouth. 'She's been so quiet that I haven't checked her.'

'I'll go and fetch her,' said Ben.

'Who's going to look after her while we go the flicks tonight?' Simon asked. 'We can't expect Aunt Milly to do it with Jimmy not well.'

'We'll take her with us,' said Grace. 'I've seen mothers with young children in the flicks before, and it is Christmastide, the season of goodwill.'

So, it was settled, and the four of them sat down while Simon helped Irene empty her stocking. He appeared to gain more pleasure from it than she did, although she screamed with delight when the small teddy was produced. Grace then bathed her daughter in the kitchen sink and washed her hair before dressing her in dainty underwear trimmed with lace and putting on the tartan frock Alice had given her. Ben produced a forest-green ribbon and Grace tied it around Irene's hair and fastened it in a big bow. Then she took a small box from the sideboard cupboard and produced a pair of black leather strapped shoes and white socks.

'Gosh, she looks a picture,' said Ben.

'We should take her to Newsham Drive for Alice to see her in the dress,' said Simon.

'You're right,' said Ben.

'We'll go about two,' Grace said. 'But we won't be able to stay long with going to the flicks.'

'Did you have to book seats?' Simon asked.

She nodded. 'They were expecting a crowd wanting to see it on such a special day, so I had to buy the tickets in advance.'

'Surely some parents would be taking their kids to see a pantomime,' said Simon.

Grace agreed, 'Even so, they'll be plenty of older children, like yourself, preferring to see a film.'

They had their lunch at twelve and were on their way to visit Alice and Doc at a quarter to two. They were welcomed with open arms. Simon updated Doc on what he thought about Jimmy, while Ben and Grace and Alice chatted. Alice was enchanted by Irene's appearance.

'I love the bones of my son, but I would have liked to have a daughter as well to dress up,' she said.

'Maybe he'll marry and provide you with a granddaughter,' said Grace.

Doc, who had stopped conferring with Simon, overheard their conversation and said, 'I'm making no plans until the war's over.'

'Sensible,' said Ben.

Doc shrugged. 'We need to get the job done, defeat Hitler, Mussolini and the Japanese – courtship and marriage would be too big a distraction.' He paused. 'I must admit I can't get your friend Jimmy out of my head. I would need to have a consultation with him to be sure, but you must have heard of shell-shock from the Great War.'

Ben and Grace nodded.

'Most people are inclined to think it's something that only happens to men on the battlefield, especially in the trenches, but I consider that people of a certain disposition can suffer when the sound of the bombardment goes on and on and shatters their nerves. More often than not, they suppress how they feel when they're involved in rescue work or firefighting and try to put the fear they feel for their families and for their own safety to the back of their minds.'

Ben said, 'You think that's what's wrong with Jimmy?'

285

'I believe it's possible that's he's reached a point where his nerves just can't cope with the intensity of the work he's doing. He and his family need to get away completely for a while, or he could end up having a breakdown. I've been doing a lot of research into this area.'

'Well, would going to Milly's mother in Dublin be a good idea? Milly was hoping to take Jimmy's mother with them, too.' said Grace.

'I suspect not, and for two reasons. Escaping to a country that is neutral might make him feel even more of a coward than he believes himself to be now. The other reason is that his fear might cripple him on the journey because he could well convince himself that a torpedo could blow up the ferry.'

'So, what do you suggest?' asked Simon.

'He needs to feel that he is safe, and that his family is too. At the same time, his morale needs building up,' said Doc. 'Is there anyone, preferably based somewhere rural, that he could go and stay with for a while?'

Ben and Grace exchanged glances. 'I think Jimmy and Milly could go and stay and help Kyle and Jane with the orphans for a while,' Ben said slowly.

'Sounds like a good plan to me,' Grace said.

The doc agreed, 'From what I've heard from Simon and my ma about them, that sounds ideal. You'll have to sound them out. I suggest Ben does it from here on the telephone and then I can speak to Kyle as well to let him know more about the condition.'

'But what about Jimmy's mam?' asked Grace.

'She does have a sister,' said Ben. 'Maybe she'd prefer to stay with her – Jimmy's aunt, in Southend-on-Sea.'

Once that was decided, Alice suggested they have tea and cake right away as Simon had told her that they were going to the flicks. As they ate and drank, Doc talked about Scotland and how he would like to settle there once the war was over. Grace told him that Milly had visited Edinburgh and so had her friends Anne and Andrew who lived next door to Jimmy's aunt. Simon went and fed the chickens, while Grace excused herself and went next door with Irene to wish a Merry Christmas to her uncle, Beryl and children.

Grace was surprised to find Marion there with a new boyfriend, Roderick Sanderson. They had popped in briefly to see Douglas, and Grace learnt that Roddy, as he liked to be called, had been in the same Scottish training camp as Dougie, although he was now based down in Yorkshire. He looked at her keenly when they were introduced, but did not get into conversation with her, other than chucking Irene under the chin and remarking what a beauty she was. Marion said very little, beyond admiring Irene's frock, and Grace was glad when it was time for the couple to take their leave.

After Marion and her beau had left, Grace listened as her uncle told her they were surprised to see Marion as much as Grace had been. Grace got the impression that Marion didn't call round that often, and she felt sorry for her uncle given the loss he had suffered earlier that year. Apparently, Marion had met Roddy when their family home had been destroyed and her mother had died, having promised her mother to keep an eye on her brother.

'He's quite good-looking,' Grace said. 'But then I'd expect Marion to only go for someone with looks. I take it that he and Dougie are friends, and that's how Marion met him?'

Beryl glanced at her father, who frowned and said, 'Apparently, Roddy's father is in business, and not short of a bob or two. He, Dougie and another two soldiers play cards regularly together.'

'Presumably for money,' said Grace drily, thinking back to how Dougie couldn't resist what he called a 'sure bet'. She'd lost much of her wage packet from the dentist's doling him out of gambling scrapes in the past.

'What do you think?' said Beryl. 'Remember how he used to cheat when we played Snap when we were kids? He hates losing.'

'Dougie's not sensible. He can't afford to lose, – Roddy can. I wonder if the other soldiers in their playing circle can,' mused her father.

'I reckon Marion brought Roddy to this big house to make him think we have money,' said Beryl looking around her. 'It is a lovely house, and maybe Marion thinks that Roddy will be prepared to play for higher stakes if he thinks we have goods to back it up. No doubt Dougie will find a way of cheating him out of his money, given what he's like…'

'It's a big risk,' said her father, breathing heavily. 'But then he's always been one to take risks, just like our Marion, although she's nicer since joining the WAAFs. Your mother admired them and was always ready to help them out. I was the saver, the careful one, and no doubt they thought I'd go first, and she would get her hands on my savings and they'd manage to convince her to give them a share.'

'Don't get yourself worked up, Dad,' said Beryl, placing an arm around him. 'They won't get their way.'

'But you do need to make a will, Uncle Douglas,' cautioned Grace. Her eyes had been opened as to how

Marion and Dougie operated together, as she remembered back to how they tried to destroy her reputation following her marriage to Ben. She just didn't trust them. 'Otherwise, those two being the oldest, they'll take control when you do go, and probably try and fiddle Beryl and your grandchildren out of what's theirs.'

Douglas smiled as he gazed at her. 'I've already seen to that, lass, don't worry – soon after your aunt died. I saw a solicitor and had Ben and you named as my executors.'

Chapter 31

Grace rolled over in bed and gazed at the bedside clock. It was seven o'clock. Her stomach heaved, but she managed to control the need to vomit, and slid out of bed, hoping not to disturb Ben. She staggered over to the bedroom door and opened it and went into Irene's bedroom, where she picked up the basin on the floor and was a little sick. She wiped her mouth with a cloth and looked over to where Irene was still sleeping in her cot bed, with one leg hanging over the side down where the bars were lowered. She was too big for it now really, and they needed to find a suitable child's bed for her. Ben had just decided to make her one when his call-up papers had arrived. That had been three weeks ago at the beginning of February – there had not been a raid since the first weeks of January and even those had been nothing compared to the ones in December. The people of Merseyside had used the lull in the attacks to get the docks functioning again, and had resumed the relentless task of clearing away the bomb damage and finding lodgings for the newly homeless. The struggle to win the war continued.

Milly, Jimmy and the twins were now staying up past Burscough in Lancashire, helping out with the orphans. Jimmy's mother had not accompanied them in the end, or even gone to stay at her sister's by the sea, as she had been injured in a late December raid, and along with several neighbours, had been transferred to a convalescent home in North Wales.

Doc had returned to his ship in the new year and Simon remained at Alice's, helping with the gardening and caring for the chickens and collecting eggs alongside his volunteering. He was able to keep them up to date with what was happening with Grace's family next door, especially regarding any visits from Marion or Dougie. Both households, trying to do their bit for the war effort, had taken in some homeless people. Alice's new lodgers were a mother and daughter who had been bombed in early January. Simon and Alice didn't see them much – the mother, Joan Taylor worked shifts at a local ammunition factory and the daughter, Barbara, who was of a similar age to Simon, was training to be a nurse. Grace's uncle and cousin had taken in an elderly couple who had lost their home down by the docks, where they had lived all their married life.

Grace had yet to tell Ben that she was three-months' pregnant. She had been intending to do so, only to be distracted by the arrival of his call-up papers. Now, as she sat quietly on her knees in the early morning light coming through Irene's window, she slowly shook her head. Her instincts about falling pregnant in December had been right, but she could hardly believe another baby would be here come the beginning of September. Now Ben was due to report at a training camp near Haverfordwest in Pembrokeshire tomorrow. Grace was not looking forward to him leaving, but had decided to look on the bright side, comforting herself with the thought that his life was likely to be in less danger in rural Wales than it would here, especially if there were more enemy raids planned for Liverpool. She would miss him terribly, but she steeled herself, accepting that she was just one of millions of women having to carry on without a man at their side.

She returned to their bedroom and was about to climb into bed when Ben said, 'Is Irene all right?'

'She's fine. I woke and thought I'd just go and check she wasn't getting ready for mischief.'

Ben squinted up at her. 'And you? You look a bit peaky. You're not worrying about me going away, are you?'

'I'm already missing you! Irene and Simon are going to be beside themselves. I can imagine her saying every day, "Where's Dadda?"'

'Don't!' Ben said roughly. 'It's going to be tough enough saying tara.'

Grace climbed into bed and snuggled up to him. 'I don't know how I'll bear it.'

'You'll bear it because you've no choice.'

He kissed her, and after that there was no conversation for a while, and then she said, 'You've done it again.' She wrapped her nightie tightly about her and reached for her wrap. 'I'm going down to put the kettle on. You stay there and rest for a bit longer. I was wondering if I should ask Simon to come home now that Alice has lodgers.'

'You'd like it better if he were here to look out for you, if there was a raid?'

'Is that selfish of me?'

'No, and what did you mean by, "You've done it again?"'

'I'm not making it easy for you,' she said, removing some clean underwear from a drawer and taking her outer clothes from a chair. 'Use your brains.'

She left the bedroom and hurried downstairs, had a wash down in the back kitchen before she dressed and lit the fire and put the kettle on. She took a couple of arrowroot biscuits from a tin and let the tea brew. Then she sat down in front of the fire and ate the biscuits and drank the tea. Only when she felt able and the fire had a glowing heart did she slice some bread and reach for the toasting fork, still undecided about whether she should tell Ben that she was pregnant before he left for Pembrokeshire.

Twenty minutes later and feeling much better, she placed a plate of jam toast and a mug of tea on a tray and carried it upstairs. 'You've dressed,' said Ben, sitting up further in the bed.

'You are observant,' she said in a teasing voice. 'It's gone eight o'clock and I thought we could have a walk around the park before calling on Simon and Alice.'

'That's fine by me,' he said, getting out of bed and putting on his dressing gown over his nakedness. 'I'll have the tea and toast downstairs after I've had a wash. You'd better get Irene ready.'

It was not until Irene was running around nearby and they were standing on the bridge overlooking the lake that Ben said, 'I didn't take precautions, did I? That's what you meant earlier.'

'No,' she replied, glancing at him.

'And from what you said — it's not the first time.'

'You've only forgotten once before.'

'When?' He gazed into her eyes.

'Try and remember,' she said, letting go of the bridge's railing with one hand and reaching for his hand and clasping it firmly. 'When we went to bed, you were exhausted.'

He said slowly, 'The raids just before Christmas. Was it the morning after?'

'Well done!'

He frowned at her. 'Why didn't you remind me?'

'I was enjoying myself and so were you. We'd both been through a lot and it would have spoilt the moment. Besides, I want another baby.'

He looked away and stared at the surface of the lake. 'There's a war on, Grace, luv.'

'I had noticed,' she said mildly.

'So… are you pregnant?' he said huskily, squeezing her hand.

'I think so, although I haven't seen a doctor yet.'

'If he confirms it, and I'm gone, you'll let me know right off?'

'Of course! I only kept quiet about my suspicions because I didn't want you worrying.'

He took a deep breath, held it for a second, and then let it go in a rush. 'I wish I could take you with me.'

'You mean I would be a camp follower like in an historical novel where the soldiers' women stayed nearby? Like I read in *An Infamous Army* by Georgette Heyer, about the soldiers at Waterloo?'

'What novel was this?' Ben asked with a wry smile. He shook his head at her. 'The things you read. I take it the women didn't have children to look after as well.'

'Not that I remember.' She smiled. 'I don't have much time to read now I've a husband and child.'

'You'll be even busier when this baby is born,' he said dryly. 'Which will be September, if I've got my sums right and all goes well.'

She nodded. 'September seems an awful long way away.'

'Yeah, it would be wonderful if the war was over by then. I can't see that happening, though—'

'No,' she agreed sadly. 'But I'd settle for there being no more bombs over the British Isles and our ships safe from torpedoes as well.'

He nodded. 'Anyway, isn't it time we were heading for Alice's?'

'Don't go telling her about the baby,' said Grace as they turned about and called for Irene, ready to make their way to Newsham Drive.

When they arrived, Simon told Grace that Marion and a soldier were visiting next door.

'I suppose we should drop in and see them,' suggested Ben.

Grace sighed, thinking of her cousin's attitude towards her, but reluctantly agreed adding, 'The soldier's most likely the boyfriend we met at Christmas – yes, you should probably go and introduce yourself if Marion is serious about him.'

Grace was correct, Roddy was the gentleman caller, and she was interested to see that Ben and him appeared deep in conversation shortly after being introduced. The female cousins didn't have much to say to each other, but Grace was hopeful, as at least Marion made no mention of Dougie.

After they returned next door to Alice's, Ben took Simon off discreetly and spoke to him about returning home to keep Grace company while he was gone. He suggested that the young lad would be able to help her with Irene and everyday tasks, as the new man of the household. Now that Alice had the lodgers to keep her company, Simon was happy with this arrangement, although he suggested that he continued to visit Alice several times a week to check on her and to help in the garden, as well as to give Fergie a good run out in the park.

That decided, they helped Simon pack a few belongings, and all said their goodbyes before returning home as a family. They left Fergie behind with Barbara, the trainee nurse, who promised to take him for walks in the park when Simon could not. At now sixteen, Simon had grown into a strapping young man, and Grace half wondered if he was sad to be leaving the lodger's daughter, who had nice features and a curvaceous figure with slender ankles. On their first meeting Barbara had seemed a little shy, but that had now passed when Grace had made the effort to draw the girl out and had encouraged her to talk about her training.

Later that evening, a strained atmosphere descended on the house as Grace made certain Ben had packed all he needed for his departure tomorrow. In an attempt to lighten the mood, after Simon had unpacked, they listened to a crime programme on the radio called *Gang Busters* before going up to bed. Grace and Ben talked far into the night as they cuddled up together. Ben insisted that Grace promise she would not book into Mill Road Hospital to have the baby. She promised, knowing that he was thinking of the night when he had helped out rescuing survivors when it was bombed last December. She prayed that the raids would be over by the time she went in labour. Her thoughts were interrupted when Ben asked her not to see him off at the railway station tomorrow, but to write regularly. Eventually, they dozed off in each other's arms, only to wake up an hour later for a final coupling, before Ben rose and went to fetch his daughter who could be heard stirring in the room next door. They all fell to sleep again and Grace rose at seven o'clock to light the fire.

To her relief she did not feel bilious today. Singing softly, she went downstairs, and put the kettle on. As a treat for Ben, she cooked the entire week's bacon ration and one of the eggs they had brought with them from Alice's. She fried a couple of slices of bread in the bacon fat and then placed it all on Ben's breakfast plate on the table before calling him down.

Hearing Ben's heavy tread on the stairs, Grace felt her breath catch, as she thought she would not hear that sound for a while. If ever again, said a voice in the recesses of her mind. She ordered the voice to go away, and thought instead of how since the days they had returned from their honeymoon in Southport Ben's strong footfall had always filled her with a sense of security. She told herself firmly that being pessimistic never did anyone any good, and that now, more than ever, she must look on the bright side of life. As Gracie Field sang in 'Sing as we go' she thought – something about life's worthwhile with a smile and a song, even if skies are grey. It's true that singing does make one feel better, she thought.

As Ben entered, carrying Irene, Grace smiled and said, 'Aren't we blessed?'

'That's the last thing I expected you to say when I'm leaving! God only knows when we'll see each other again,' Ben grumbled.

'I know, and as you said yesterday, there's a war on, but just think since war was declared, through the good times and the bad we've been together – and we've survived I don't know how many raids, and so have our children. Now we must be strong in body, mind and spirit and keep hope alive.'

'You little optimist, you,' he smiled as he passed Irene to her. 'Is that my breakfast?'

'Who else's would it be?' Grace turned away from the table as Simon entered the kitchen. 'Could you look after Irene's breakfast while I make your dad some sarnies for the journey?'

Simon took Irene and swung her in his arms. 'All set then, Dad?'

'I'm ready as I'll ever be,' Ben rapped his son on the knuckles with his fork as Simon put Irene down and made to pinch a rasher of his bacon. 'Gerroff, that's mine.'

'Meanie,' said Simon.

Father and son exchanged smiles. 'I bet you'll be well fed, Dad, in the training camp. You'll need to be fighting fit.'

'I doubt I'll be doing any fighting for a while, son.' Ben nudged the bit of bacon towards the edge of his plate, and Simon snatched it up, and said, 'Thanks, Dad.' Then went into the back kitchen and prepared two bowls of cornflakes before returning and placing them on the table. He called Irene to the table and supervised her breakfast.

Ben smiled across at them and then, with a glance at the clock, finished his own breakfast. He carried his plate into the back kitchen to talk to Grace. 'I'm going to make a move, luv.'

Grace nodded. 'Your sarnies are ready and there's a slice of sponge cake.' There was an odd break in her voice as she handed the package to him. He swept her into his arms and kissed her fiercely. 'Keep singing and stay safe, you, and the kids.'

She hugged him tightly. 'No heroics. You've risked your life volunteering too many times already.'

They kissed again and then returned to the kitchen. Ben rammed his sarnies and cake in a pocket, collected his pack from the parlour and headed for the front door, followed by Grace with Irene in her arms, and Simon. He hugged and kissed the three of them, and then with a smile, walked out the door.

Grace watched from the doorstep with Simon, until Ben, halfway along the street, turned and waved. She helped Irene to wave back and said a silent prayer. Suddenly Simon bolted after his father. They hugged for a final time and she saw Ben whisper into Simon's ear. Then the tall young man squared his shoulders and walked towards her and Irene, without looking back.

Chapter 32

There were times during the following days when Grace found it difficult to smile or sing, but then she received a short letter from Ben saying that he had arrived at his camp safely and was settling in. Apparently, there were a couple of blokes from Liverpool, but he had heard other accents spoken that he was unfamiliar with, although he thought the Sergeant Major was a Brummie. He was missing her and the kids already, and hoped she would write back with all her news. He sent his love with kisses.

Grace clutched the letter to her chest when she had read it, but could not think what she was going to tell him in reply, because there was no real news, daily life had continued much as before. Thinking that maybe Ben would be content with just hearing from her, she wrote back straight away, telling him that Irene had showed an interest in the picture on the stamp of his recent letter, so she planned to buy her a little book to keep future stamps in from a little stamp-collecting shop in Fenwick Street. Simon was also taken with the idea, and wanted Grace to ask Ben to send any stamps from fellow recruits who might be receiving letters from the colonies and America. Grace also sent news that, unfortunately, the letters that Alice received from Doc didn't show a foreign stamp, so they had no idea where his ship was, only that he was well. Grace knew from the posters that 'Careless Talk Costs Lives', so she didn't trouble Ben by asking him exactly where his camp was situated. She went on to tell him that the day before she had also received a letter from Milly. Jimmy's moods were improving and that his mother had recovered well from her injuries, and was planning on staying in the Welsh countryside near her convalescent home until the end of the war.

Finally, Grace finished up her letter by telling Ben that the doctor had confirmed that she was with child and that the baby was due sometime around the middle of September. She also told him, that, so far, they had received no more night raids from the enemy since he had left. She signed off, 'Your loving wife, Grace'. She then placed a crayon in her daughter's chubby fingers and guided her to write a line of kisses for her Dadda.

Grace posted the letter on 6th March – a day of clear skies and sunshine. A week later Merseyside suffered its worst onslaught of aerial bombing: thousands of incendiaries were dropped and the resulting fires were so numerous that the military, Home Guard, and firemen from Lancashire, Cheshire and Wales were all called in to assist in the rescue efforts. Following the first nerve-wracking night raid, Grace had gone with Irene and Simon to check on Alice. After telling the elderly Scotswoman about the terrible overcrowding in the local shelter, Alice persuaded Grace to stay with her so she could go down to the cellar for the raids, as another visit from the Luftwaffe was imminent.

With a sinking heart, Grace watched Simon ride away on his bicycle for his messenger shift later that evening. Minutes after he left, the warning siren sounded, and the searchlights lit up the sky, accompanied by the sound of barrage guns booming out. Grace, thanks to Simon's enthusiastic tutorage, recognised the sound of a German Heinkel bomber, followed quickly by the drone of British Defiant, a two-seater aircraft which carried a pilot and an air gunner. She hurried down to the cellar to sit out the duration of the attack with Alice, feeling sick with worry.

As soon as the All Clear sounded, and not able to bear the tension any longer, Grace handed Irene to Alice and left the house to go in search of Simon. As she gazed about her, all she could see all around were flames and smoke stretching into the distance. She decided that she should go and check her and Ben's home first just in case Simon had gone there. On arrival, she was glad to see that the whole street was undamaged. Grace headed for the nearest First Aid Post, thinking they might know where her stepson was. She was in luck, as a neighbour had seen him and informed her Simon was helping with rescue work as the raging fires had made it even more difficult to dig out people than normal and all hands were needed. He told her where to find him at a nearby bomb site, but warned her to tread carefully. Of course, Grace did not need telling, aware of the new life she was carrying, but she had to see that her oldest boy was safe and unharmed.

Eventually, she found him, although at first, she had difficulty recognising him beneath an oversized metal helmet. His young face was covered in dust and filth. For an instant she was reminded of Ben and wanted to weep, but she pulled herself together sharply and said, 'Simon, time to come home.'

The boy just carried on digging carefully with his hands, as if he had not heard her at all, so she touched his shoulder. 'Son, enough.'

Simon glanced up at her, and the whites of his eyes stood out in the filth of the surrounding skin. His face broke into a smile. 'You're all right. I've been so worried for you.'

'Yes, and Irene is wanting you.'

A man's voice called over, 'You go with your mam, lad. You've done your bit. Give my regards to your dad when you write.'

Simon nodded to the man, who Grace recognised as Alf from down the street, and as if in a daze, he went and picked up his bike from the ground, where he had abandoned it. Wheeling it slowly beside him, he then accompanied Grace to the house on Newsham Drive.

'You mustn't write to your dad and tell him about the raid,' Grace said on the way. 'He'll worry.'

'But if I write, he'll know we're alive, so that'll reassure him, Mam,' he said. 'Anyway, I need to pass on Alf's regards.'

She did not respond immediately, as she had a lump in her throat, moved by his calling her 'Mam'. 'Of course, you're right, son. He'll be proud of you. Let's hope there's no raids this evening. You must be exhausted.'

He did not reply, as he carefully navigated his bicycle around a pile of rubble.

Grace's uncle was standing on the step next door and he smiled and waved to them as they approached. 'Glad to see you're all right,' he said as he clamped his hand on Simon's shoulder as he came up the steps. Simon greeted his uncle wearily, and then left Grace talking with Douglas and went inside the house.

'I wonder if Marion will worry and be in touch with Dougie and tell him about the raid to let him know we're all right,' said her uncle. 'Or more to the point, that I'm still alive…'

Grace's heart sank. 'You don't think he'll come and visit you, do you?'

'I'd rather he didn't,' he said. 'Anyway, I'd better let you go in. See you soon.'

Grace went inside and sank into a chair, feeling worn out by lack of sleep and the worry for Simon. She looked up at him standing in the kitchen and saw that he held Irene in his arms. He had removed his helmet and filthy coat and washed his face and hands, by all appearances, because his hands were bandaged. She could only think that was because he had damaged them digging.

She must have nodded off, as she did not wake up until she felt herself being pulled out of the chair and hustled down into the cellar hours later. She gazed bleary-eyed about her and saw that Alice was hugging Irene to her. She could see no sign of Simon and could only think that she had dreamt that she had gone to search for him earlier. She glanced in the direction of the lodgers and said, 'Simon not back yet?'

The words were no sooner out of her mouth than the All Clear sounded and a few moments later, they heard the door open upstairs. 'That'll be him,' said Barbara. 'That didn't last long.'

Barbara and Grace stood up and they went up the cellar steps together. Barbara arrived at the top first and switched on the hall light. She stared at the stranger standing in the hall and only just managed to prevent a scream. 'Who are you?' she asked in a stricken voice.

Grace came up behind her and stared at Dougie. 'What are you doing here? You don't belong here!'

'A nice welcome from you again, Gracie,' he said. 'After me coming all this way last night to see if you were all right.'

'I don't believe you,' she rasped. 'More likely you came to see if your dad was still alive.'

'You do me an injustice, sweetheart,' he said in a saccharine voice. 'Marion let me know that Ben had been called up, so I thought you might need me to keep you warm at night. You used to like my kisses, if I remember correct.' He moved towards her, but Barbara stood in his way.

'Don't be disgusting,' retorted Grace, 'and I'm no sweetheart of yours. Now get out!' An intense anger swept over her and without stopping to think, she went around Barbara and hit him in the midriff. She managed to catch him off balance and Dougie fell awkwardly against the closed front door and hit his head on the doorframe, but not before he managed to seize her wrist and drag her over. Grace fell heavily on the tiled floor, but in that instance, the front door was opened from outside. Dougie toppled backwards, and almost sending Simon flying.

Barbara hurried over to Grace, while Simon tried to make sense of what was happening. Then he moved swiftly and stood gazing down at Dougie with loathing. He didn't know all the ins and outs of it, but he knew his dad disliked this man intensely. His scrutiny then passed to Grace, whom he saw through the open door lying prone on the hall floor with Barbara attempting to rouse her into a sitting position. Simon's first instinct was to kick Dougie where he lay, but then common sense asserted itself, and he bent and dragged the moaning man to his feet and pushed him down the front steps. He then slammed the front door, shut, and locked it, before lifting Grace with the ease of youth, and carried her into the sitting room and placing her carefully on the sofa.

He gazed down at her with concern and said, 'Are you all right? Do I need to fetch a doctor?'

'I hope not. I feel shaken up, but I don't think any damage has been done.' She said in a small voice. She then stared at his right hand and saw his hand was bandaged. 'You're hurt. What happened?'

'You don't remember?' he sounded anxious.

Barbara said, 'She only woke up about a quarter of an hour ago, and I think she hasn't realised she's slept the whole day through. Or do you think she's banged her head and has concussion?'

Simon drew a deep steadying breath and moved away from Grace. 'Before Dad left, he told me she might be pregnant. I was to look out for her. I'm worried that swine could have hurt her and the baby.'

'I see. I'm glad you told me because we can make sure she has enough rest,' said Barbara. 'Perhaps the pair of you should stay here until after the baby is born.' She paused. 'By the way, who is that horrible man?'

'He's her cousin, Beryl's brother. They were going to get married, but he'd gone off to Australia and she was supposed to follow him out there, but she met Dad, and we both liked her, so they got married. Years ago now.' He paused. 'There was some trouble about it though. If you want to know more you should ask Grace. Or Beryl – she doesn't have much time for her brother. Anyway, I'm wacked, I need to hit the sack before my next shift. Can you and your mam help Grace with Irene and see that she's all right?'

'Fine, how was it out there? It didn't sound too bad and you're back early tonight.'

'It was only a light raid. Could be that they threw enough at us the last two nights that they ran out of ammunition, or they've gone somewhere else. Goodnight – see you when I see ya.'

Grace said in a drowsy voice, 'God bless!'

Barbara turned from staring after Simon and smiled down at her. 'Did you hear all that?' she asked.

'Caught the odd sentence. I *am* pregnant, by the way. Baby's due in September.'

'Well, let's hope there'll be no more raids for now,' said Barbara.

Grace agreed, although she doubted that Hitler had finished with Britain. Later that day she asked Alice if they could stay until after the baby was born. Alice had no hesitation in agreeing and was thrilled about the thought of a new baby on the way.

—

For the rest of March, Liverpool was left undisturbed by the Luftwaffe and Grace began to hope that Ben might manage to get some leave and make it home for the Easter weekend. Good Friday was on 11th April this year. She had written to him, but had only mentioned fleetingly about the March raids and Dougie's unexpected appearance. The next time she wrote, it was to tell him that she would be staying at Alice's until after the baby was born and that it would be lovely if he could get home for Easter. Ben replied soon after, saying that he would try and get leave for Easter, but that Grace wasn't to depend on it, as travelling would be difficult and that there were those who had already requested leave. He also mentioned that he had received a long letter from Simon about the

March air raids and Dougie's visit and that she was to let him know immediately if he ever turned up again. He had enclosed an Easter card for Irene, chocolate being in short supply due to the rationing.

Easter arrived, and Grace went to church on Good Friday, and again with the rest of the household on Easter Sunday. Her family next door also accompanied them, and the party was in a happy mood because so far there had been no more air raids on Merseyside; the spring had been kind, and the hens were laying well. Grace had spoken to her uncle and Beryl about Dougie's visit and they had been very apologetic about having told Dougie in passing that Ben had been called up. She told them not to worry, as it was likely that his friend Roddy knew about that because he and Ben had spent some time in conversation just before Ben had left for training.

'I don't think Dougie and Roddie are friends anymore,' said her uncle. 'Marion came to call and she said they had fallen out because Dougie owed Roddy money. Apparently, Dougie tried to cadge money from her as well, but she was skint. She's just asked me for a loan to pay her rent. I told her to tell the rent man to get in touch with me. I wasn't going to risk giving her money and her passing it on to Dougie.'

'So, did the rent collector get in touch?' asked Grace.

He nodded, looking forlorn. 'He set me thinking, though. I'm a fool. She could have given Dougie the money she normally pays to the rent collector when she gets her wages. Dougie's such a bully... I know the two of them have always appeared great friends, but I suspect it is likely due to Marion knowing that it is the best way of stopping Dougie bullying her. Your mother could never see any wrong in him, and I didn't want endless arguments with either of them, but it's gone on for a long time. Anyway, I won't be tricked again. I know it's probably not Marion's fault, but I'm disappointed in the pair of them, and they can keep their distance.'

The days passed. Grace was feeling well and towards the end of April when she felt the baby quickening she was able to write to Ben and tell him that she had felt the baby moving. Also there had been no more raids, and just like a lot of others, Grace had started to believe that Hitler had given up on Britain and was turning his attention on his erstwhile ally, Russia. She was also able to report to Ben that there was no sight nor sound of Dougie.

On 1st May, just after eleven pm, as Grace was thinking of settling down for the night, her thoughts were on Ben and how he might be reading her letter at that very moment, when the air-raid siren sounded a warning. Grace groaned and her heart sank. She stuffed her knitting in her knitting bag and rose slowly to her feet. She was five months' pregnant now, but much bigger than she had been with Irene at this stage. She heard Simon's feet on the hall stairs and a few minutes later she caught the sound of him descending, and Irene's sleepy whimper. She stared across at Alice, who had been keeping her company in the sitting room, and said, 'Here we go again.'

Alice pushed herself up out of the chair. 'Everything is in place downstairs, even some fresh tea and some conny-onny.'

'We've no fresh milk to take down,' said Grace.

'No, it went in Simon's cocoa,' Alice said.

'Never mind chattering,' said Simon. 'Let's get you down to the cellar.'

It was only when they were settled in the cellar and Barbara's mother, Joan, had joined them, that Grace realised that Barbara was not there.

'She's at the hospital,' Simon said.

'Alder Hey children's hospital in West Derby this week,' said her mother.

'At least it's a good distance from the docks,' said Simon. 'Anyway, I'd better be on my way.'

'Watch your step and your head, son,' Grace said.

He winked at her. 'Keep your heads down, ladies, and don't go looking for trouble.' He blew them a kiss and was gone.

Grace prayed that it would be a short raid and Simon would soon return. Hours later the All Clear had still not sounded, so all she could do was pray for courage and Simon's safety. The garden birds were singing the dawn chorus by the time Simon returned, pale beneath the muck. The women fussed around him, pushing him into a chair and handing him a restorative cup of tea and a slice of savoury mincemeat pie.

'I'm going to have to go out again and help down by the docks, although most likely I'll have to push my bike the nearer I get, because the destruction is terrible and vehicles will have a job getting through.' He paused to take a drink and a bite of food. His head nodded, but he jerked it upright again.

Grace's heart went out to him and she thought how it would break Ben's heart if his son were to be injured seriously. 'You need to rest first,' she said.

'No time to rest,' he said, finishing the slice of pie and draining the cup. 'See you later, and give Barbara my best when she gets back.'

But Barbara did not arrive back that day. Her mother attempted to phone the hospital, but could not get through. The tears ran down her cheeks, and it was only when Simon returned at two in the afternoon that she stopped crying as he told her that most of the telephone lines were down and that the regional headquarters and government departments were having to rely on mobile wireless stations in Liverpool. The middle and the northern parts of the docks and Bootle were the worst affected by the bombing – several ships had been sunk in the docks. Hundreds of volunteers were working like crazy to clear the mess and get the docks working again while the fire services put out the hundreds of fires.

'What about the hospitals?' asked Barbara's mother.

'Lots of homes damaged or destroyed. I heard nowt about Alder Hey hospital, and I think I would have if it had been hit, due to it now being a children's hozzie. Most likely Barbara's stayed there because there was no way she could get here except by walking and it is a good old walk home.'

They all decided to try and have a sleep; Grace went upstairs with Irene and took her into bed with her and managed to doze off.

The raid continued ceaselessly, as the Luftwaffe tried to destroy the docks, factories and morale of Liverpool and Birkenhead citizens once again. It was not until the afternoon of 5th May that Barbara arrived home perched on the crossbar of Simon's bike. He had cycled to the hospital to check on her, and as Barbara had worked non-stop for nearly five days, she was told she could go home.

Chapter 33

The next morning Grace heard the sound of a motorbike outside, and curiosity sent her to have a look to see who it could be. To her amazement, there was a motorbike, and as the rider dismounted and removed his helmet, she recognised him – it was Kyle! He spotted her straight away, waved and came towards her.

'What are you doing here?' she asked.

'We heard that Liverpool was having a terrible time and thousands were homeless, with a real shortage of Rest Centres and helpers. I thought of the orphanage standing there empty and brought the keys as it might be a good place to house people who have lost their home. I also thought I could help the workmen with the clearing up process or putting out the fires. The flames can be seen from the top of Clieves Hill, near Ormskirk!'

'It's been terrible the last few nights, but it's so good to see you. Are Jane and the children well – how's Milly, Jimmy and the twins?'

'All well, although worried about you. Jimmy's walking fine now and wanted to come with me, but Milly and Matron wouldn't allow it – said it would set him back. Besides, he's needed there with me being here.' His expression sobered. 'Now where should I go to report?'

Grace barely hesitated. 'I'll wake Simon. He's the one to help you.'

'Simon!' he exclaimed. 'He's only a lad. Isn't he at school?'

But Grace had already vanished leaving Kyle propping up his motorbike against a blackcurrant bush. He removed his gauntlets and made to follow her inside, after a fleeting glance at the front door of his own house, glad to see it still standing and undamaged. Another motorbike with a sidecar pulled up as he was walking inside, and he caught a glance of a man dismounting outside his old home. However, he was distracted as Grace reappeared in the hallway with Simon in tow.

Simon stared at Kyle and his face broke into a smile. Wordlessly, he approached Kyle and put his arms around him. 'I can hardly believe you're here,' he said, hugging him.

'I know how you feel,' said Kyle. 'But I'm thinking there's no time to waste and I need to report to someone in charge of finding shelter for those who are homeless.'

'Righteo,' Simon said, heading for the front door. 'Mam said you had a motorbike, so I can ride pillion and give directions on the way.'

'Great,' said Kyle.

Grace waved them off and again mouthed a silent prayer for their safety. There might not be any bombs falling, but there were craters in the roads, and rubble and unsafe buildings that needed to be avoided. In the meantime, she got Irene ready to go out and noticed that both motorcycles had gone from outside the houses. She knocked on the neighbouring front door and told her uncle about Kyle's visit.

'Will he want us all to move out?' asked her uncle, looking worried.

'I doubt it. He's here to help the homeless or anywhere he can be useful. I think he then wants to return to his job at the orphanage and to his wife and children up in Lancashire,' Grace said, crossing her fingers. 'Anyway, I need to go shopping.'

'But I've something to tell you—' pressed Douglas.

But Grace didn't hear the urgency in his voice, as Irene was fussing her about something. 'Can it wait? I need to get something for Irene's lunch and the queues are terrible at the moment – I'll see you later.'

Grace and Irene walked to the Co-op and joined the queue. An hour later she was told she was entitled to half a pound of stewing steak, and as there had been a special delivery, she could have some liver. She asked the butcher did he have a mutton bone to make soup and after a few minutes he returned with a decent-sized bone which had morsels of meat clinging to it. She thanked him, handed over Alice's, the children's and her own ration books, as well as some money. She also managed to buy some lime jelly before hurrying back to the house.

Once home, Grace set to boiling the bone and adding barley and vegetables. She then stewed the meat and fried the liver and poured OXO gravy over both before making pastry for a pie. Once the pie was in the oven, she poured some of the soup in bowls for Alice, Irene, and herself, and some cut bread to eat with the soup. She called them to the table and they all ate lunch together. Then she debated whether to take Fergie and Irene for a walk in the park or wait in with Alice until Simon and Kyle returned.

She decided that Fergie needed a walk, so she made her way to the park with her daughter and walked to the pond where children could sail model boats. Grace set Irene down, who immediately made a beeline for the water's edge and started playing around. Grace rushed after her and caught her by the hem of her dress as her daughter teetered on the edge of the pond. Fergie capered at their side, yapping.

'That was a close call,' said the voice behind her. It was the last person she wanted to see.

She turned with her arms protectively around her daughter. 'Dougie? Shouldn't you be up north?'

'Haven't you heard? Marion was in Mill Road Hospital when a bomb exploded just outside. I've got leave to see her.'

'No, I hadn't heard. Is she injured? And what was she doing in the hospital?' Grace thought with regret, that this was probably what her uncle must have wanted to tell her earlier. If only she hadn't been in such a hurry.

'She was giving birth,' he said, smirking.

'Go on… You're kidding!'

'Why should I lie about such a thing? Is it that you believe that golden boy Roddy is incapable of behaving like a cad?'

'I don't know him well enough to go about casting aspersions on him,' she said. 'Your dad and Beryl have made no mention of Marion being pregnant.'

'She didn't want them or me to know, but I've been keeping my eye on Roddy. He's still in the city, so I tracked him down when I first arrived in Merseyside, and I have been following him since… but now I've lost him, so that's why I'm here to see if he's at the house.'

'Was it you on a motorbike this morning? Our friend Kyle mentioned someone called on Uncle Douglas.'

His smile vanished. 'Did you see Roddy then?'

'No, only Kyle. He came on a motorbike this morning. He'd heard that Liverpool was having a bad time and wanted to help out.'

'But you're saying there were two motorbikes?' Dougie growled. Grace was silent, all she wanted to do was to get away from him.

'I have to go,' she said.

Dougie seized her by the shoulder. 'What's the rush? Once you couldn't wait to be alone with me.'

'Those days are well over,' she said. 'As you know! Let go!' She struggled to free herself, scared of Irene slipping from her grasp.

'You heard the lady,' said a voice with an American accent.

'Yeah, let her go, Dougie, or I'll punch you,' Kyle said.

Dougie released her and turned and stared at the two men behind him. 'I recognise you,' he said to Kyle. 'I see you aren't in uniform.'

'What's that to do with anything?' said the Yank. 'There's thousands not in uniform who are fighting this war. Now beat it, before I put your lights out.'

Dougie looked at them with hatred in his eyes and then slouched away.

'Am I glad you two came along!' exclaimed Grace in relief. 'But what are you doing here, Kyle? You always come to me rescue by this lake...' Her thoughts turned to that long-ago day in the park with Simon and the runaway bath chair. 'But I thought you were with Simon? And who is this?' She smiled shyly at the other gentleman to show her gratitude again.

'This is Lieutenant Graham Campbell, he's stationed at Blackpool Airport. He's in Liverpool with the American Food Flying Squad. We've just met at the headquarters where the homeless are gathered and are on our way to assess the orphanage's suitability as a possible refuge.'

'Have you seen Simon?'

'He's helping one of the rescue teams,' said Kyle. 'He's a good kid. His father would be proud of him.'

'We're both proud of him. I just wish Ben were here.'

'I can imagine. Maybe he'll make it back for the birth,' said Kyle, nodding to her expanding middle. 'Jane's pregnant too. It'll be a Christmas baby.'

'This one is the middle of September,' Grace said. 'Anyway, I'd better make a move. Alice will be wondering what's happened to me and I also need to have a word with my uncle. Thanks again – you really saved my bacon, I don't know why Dougie won't leave me be.'

'See you later,' said Kyle. The American touched his cap and both men moved on.

–

After she had made boiled eggs and toast soldiers for Alice, Irene and herself, Grace went next door to see her uncle and Beryl to ask whether they had seen Dougie or heard from Marion.

'Have you seen him?' asked Beryl in alarm.

Grace nodded. 'He came up behind me in the park by the lake and frightened the life out of me,' she said. 'He told me some rubbishy tale about Marion being in labour in Mill Road Hospital and that there'd been an explosion.'

'We found it hard to believe too,' said Beryl. 'But apparently she's got married to Roddy! Dad went along to the hospital to check up on her and find out what is going on. Roddy called this morning on his motorbike to tell us.'

Douglas chimed in at this point, 'Yes, I got a telephone call about Marion being in the hospital first thing, and then Roddy turned up on the doorstep not much later, and he told me about them getting married. Said Marion had wanted it kept quiet because she feared Dougie finding out about it and then something about how he would be jealous and lose his temper with her...'

Beryl snorted like a pig. 'Sounds about right!'

'I can believe it,' Douglas said, wringing his hands. 'It's been the same since the two of them were little. I wish I'd done more to help Marion, but your mother always took Dougie's side whenever I tried to step in. Her boy could do no wrong...' He paused. 'Anyway, Roddy and I set off for Mill Road Hospital – he has a motorbike with a sidecar so managed to get us there. I lost mine when the house was destroyed. It was chaotic though when we got there due to the incendiary going off outside – it took me ages to find someone who could help us. We eventually discovered that Marion'd had the baby and the pair of them were en-route to Oxford Street Maternity Hospital with other expectant mothers, so Roddy took us there on his motorbike. It was almost as chaotic there with ambulances and people coming and going.'

Her uncle took a breath again, excited by his tale.

'They wouldn't let us in, and we were just about to leave when Roddy spotted Marion being taken out of an ambulance with the baby. Before I could stop him, he was over there, and the next thing I know, he's half-carrying Marion and the baby towards me. He helps her and the baby into the side car, and then they're off!'

'So, where are they now?' asked Grace, confused. 'Here?'

'You're joking, aren't you? I wouldn't want to have her here to stay!' exclaimed Beryl.

'They've set off to his sister's house for now. I think Roddy's mother was in Kent, but she's moved in with his sister, who is based in Burford in Oxfordshire,' said her father. 'They're crazy, the pair of them travelling with a newborn with the raids going on.'

'It's the war! People do crazy things at such a time. At least she's had the baby and they are both well, but if it was born early, they could both be in need of medical help,' said Grace. 'I hope the three of them make it there safely. I'm glad Marion has Roddy looking out for her—'

'And what about me?' interrupted Beryl. 'I've tried to do everything right, be unselfish and brave, and what happens? I've lost my husband and home, and maybe the next thing that happens is a bomb dropping on me, dad and the kids…'

'Stop being so cheerful, girl,' said her father.

'I'm going back to Alice and check that Irene is still asleep,' said Grace, suddenly weary from the day's drama. 'Keep your chin up, Beryl. You never know instead of a bomb dropping on you, Prince Charming might drop in.' No sooner had she spoken, than the warning siren wailed. She wasted no time leaving and headed to the cellar next door.

'You've been an age,' said Alice, glancing up from her knitting. 'It's a good thing I had company.' She glanced across at Barbara's mother and smiled.

Grace could not keep things to herself and told them what had happened. She had to raise her voice due to the barrage of noise going on from the planes, guns and bombs exploding. Eventually she gave up because her throat was hurting, and she did not want to disturb Irene who was asleep in the corner. Besides, she needed to rest, she was aware of the baby kicking her from inside, and suddenly she felt concerned that her fear might affect the unborn child. She then steadied herself and reminded herself of Simon and Kyle, and all the other men and women working hard, despite the danger, and prayed for them with all her might.

She could not help wondering what Dougie was doing at that moment, perhaps he was actually helping out too. Her thoughts turned to Marion, Roddy and their newborn baby and she prayed that they wouldn't meet with an accident in Roddy's hurry to get his wife and child to his sister's. She thought further about what her uncle had said about Marion being scared of Dougie. Maybe Marion had been putting on an act all this time to persuade Dougie she admired him and was on his side, but was, in fact, just trying to stop him picking on her. Grace's eyelids began to droop as she thought of Ben, and wondered whether he had heard of the battering Liverpool was suffering. Gradually, she dozed off, only to be roused by Barbara's mother shaking her.

'The All Clear has sounded, Grace. I was thinking of going upstairs and having a look outside to see if there's been any damage nearby.'

'I'll follow you up.' Grace yawned.

She checked Irene was all right and then slowly followed Alice upstairs. She went down the hall and eased herself around the vestibule door. The front door was ajar, and she caught a glimpse of a woman standing on the step. Grace thought it must be dawn, because it appeared light outside and she could hear birdsong, but then she realised the light was coming from a glow in the sky from distant burning fires. She looked across towards the park over the road and thought she could hear people talking. She crossed the street to have a closer look and saw that soldiers were erecting a marquee and some smaller tents. At that moment, she thought she recognised one of the soldiers, but told herself that her eyes were playing tricks on her. Then he turned and she saw it was her husband.

Chapter 34

'Ben!' she called, a tremendous wave of joy sweeping over her and she began to run towards him, even as he came towards her. Ben swung her off her feet and kissed her.

'How?' Grace asked, once she got her breath back.

'I had leave due,' he said, smoothing the hair back from her face and gazing into her eyes. 'The Commanding Officer said he was expecting my request and had my travel pass ready. News had been passed on that Liverpool was desperately in need of help.'

'It's marvellous to see you,' she said.

'Likewise,' he kissed her again more slowly and deeply. 'Everything all right?'

'It is now,' she answered. 'Although, I'd like to see Simon arrive back right now.'

'Kyle told me earlier that Simon had been ordered to go home because he was falling asleep on his feet. I thought I was imagining things when Kyle came over to me on Lime Street. I couldn't understand why he was there... Oh, and Lewis's is almost completely gutted.'

'What a shame,' said Grace, thinking of the grand store in happier times.

'St Luke's at the top of Bold Street has been hit as well, some of its walls are still standing, but the roof has gone,' continued Ben. 'Anyway, I can't stand here talking. The marquee is for the homeless and we're setting up field kitchens to feed them. You go back across the road and I'll see you as soon as I can.'

'But what about Simon? I don't think he's back yet.'

Ben bit his lower lip. 'It could be that it's taking him longer to get here if he's tired.'

Grace nodded and then she had an idea. 'Or it could be that he's gone *home*! To our house! It is closer and he'd get to a bed quicker—'

'Is it still standing?' asked Ben, seizing her by the shoulders.

'It was last time I was there,' she said. 'I'll go and see if he's there now.'

He glanced in the direction of the tents and workmen and looked hesitant for a second. 'I'll come with you.'

She beamed at him. 'I was hoping you'd say that. I'd best go and let Alice know what's happening as she's keeping an eye on Irene – she's still asleep in the cellar.'

'I'll come and have a quick look at her,' said Ben.

—

After Ben had pressed a gentle kiss on his daughter's cheek, and received a warm welcome from Alice, they left and hurried in the direction of West Derby Road and then up their street, which once again was unscathed by the Luftwaffe, although there was debris and dust everywhere. They arrived at their house and found the neighbour standing in her doorway, although dawn was still way off. She stared at Ben in amazement. 'I thought you were in training.'

'I'm on leave,' he said. 'Have you seen any sign of our Simon?'

'I don't know if it was him, but I did see someone climbing up your back gate earlier.'

'Maybe he didn't have his front door key with him,' said Grace. 'Hopefully, he had the back kitchen one.' They hurried inside the front door calling his name.

As it was, they saw a body lying flat out on the kitchen hearth rug. Simon's metal helmet had slipped sideways and a trickle of blood was running down the side of his face.

Quickly, they knelt either side of him on the rag rug.

'Simon, can you hear me?' said Ben.

The youth's eyes fluttered open and he groaned. 'Dad?' he said in a strained voice. 'Is it really you?'

'Yeah, it's me, son. What's happened here, then?' Ben choked on the words.

'Help me to sit up,' said Simon.

Grace removed his helmet all the better to see where the blood was coming from and Ben eased Simon into a sitting position against his knee.

'It was him again – that swine Dougie!'

'What was he doing here?' asked Ben.

'I had the impression that he thought he'd find Mam here,' said Simon, glancing at Grace.

Ben stared at his wife. 'And why would he think that?' he asked slowly.

'Wishful thinking,' said Simon, glancing at his father's face. 'You can't really believe that she'd arrange to meet him here, would you, Dad? She has been missing you like crazy.'

'If your father thinks so little of me that he could countenance such a thought, that's up to him,' said Grace hotly.

'I didn't think anything of the sort,' protested Ben, although the thought had entered his head before he dismissed it utterly out of hand.

'Not even for a second? I bet Kyle told you about my encounter with Dougie in the park yesterday and now you're jumping to all sorts of unfounded conclusions?'

'He told me nothing,' said Ben, looking uncomfortable.

'Well, perhaps you'd better ask him…' Grace continued crossly.

Before Ben could ask anything more, Simon said, 'Will you two stop squabbling and pay me some attention? I'm bleeding here! It's a good job I still had my helmet on or he could have split my head open as it is he had a huge splinter of glass in his other hand.' He moaned. 'It's not that long ago since he scarpered. You should get after him, Dad.'

'No, your dad might kill him and end up in prison. We'll phone the police from Alice's,' said Grace.

'I might as well go to the police station in Tuebrook now,' said Ben. 'It's not that much further than Alice's.'

And before they could try and stop him, Ben had got up and left.

Simon said, 'I don't know if that's a good idea. Most of the bobbies could be out helping with the after-effects of last night's raid.'

'But Ben might also find one patrolling on the main road,' said Grace. 'Anyway, there's nothing we can do about your dad now – let me have a proper look at your injury.'

She was relieved to see that although the cut was about two inches long, it was not very deep, so she cleaned it, and then dabbed on iodine and stuck on a plaster. She refrained from asking any more questions after she found a large splinter of glass so instead settled Simon comfortably on the sofa where she could keep her eye on him. Then she found a packet of cocoa in the cupboard and put the kettle on to make a warming drink for him. It was nice to be back in her own kitchen, surrounded by all her things, but all the time her hands were busy, Grace was worrying about Ben and what he might do; that was when she wasn't cursing Dougie and wishing him to high hell.

–

Two hours later Ben returned with a policeman, and he and Grace were able to hear the full story of the attack on Simon. Simon explained that he had returned to the house to get some kip following the raid, but had been confronted by Dougie soon after he had entered the house. He reported that Dougie had been acting oddly – swaying around the place, as though he was drunk. He had been ranting something about being let down by Grace and his sister Marion, and her new fella Roddy, and how he was going to do for them. Grace then spoke to the policeman about her earlier encounter with Dougie in the park and how Kyle and the American lieutenant had come to her rescue. She confirmed what Simon had told them about Dougie feeling duped by Roddy and his sister, and how it appeared that Dougie had been following Roddy all over the city and becoming increasingly outraged.

'He sounds like a right nutter, besides having past form,' said the policeman, staring at the large splinter of glass that Grace had given him. 'I just wish we knew where he was heading.'

'Roddy's mother lives in Kent, so he might head there,' said Grace. 'Although my uncle said earlier that Roddy was planning on taking Marion to his sister's, who lives in Oxfordshire. His mother was going to stay with her daughter, you see. I'm not sure Dougie will know that.'

'You have the address in Kent?' asked the policeman.

Ben took a small notebook out of a pocket and read it out. Grace recalled how he and Roddy had got into conversation way back in February. Then Ben saw the policeman out and when he returned, he sat down and stared at Grace.

'That cousin of yours has a way of twisting things, he is such a b—' he trailed off and tried again, '—but I know you, and I should have known better.'

Grace blinked away the moisture gathering on her eyelashes. 'For a marriage to work one needs to trust – to be trusted – but when Dougie comes on the scene, you behave like… like Shakespeare's Othello.'

'Who is he?' asked Ben in confusion. 'The only Shake speare plays I've heard of are *Macbeth* and *A Midsummer Night's Dream*.

'I heard the play on the wireless,' said Grace.

Simon said, 'I listened to it with you, didn't I? Isn't Othello the husband who believed lies about his wife and ended up murdering her?'

'Good God! You can't believe I'm such a monster as that,' said Ben.

'Oh, I don't know, not really, I suppose, but still—' Grace rubbed her eyes, '—oh, I'm so tired. This baby is taking it out of me.'

Ben said, 'I understand. Me, too, and I know Simon is. Let's get to bed and put this evening behind us.'

Before Grace could say that the beds weren't made up, Ben had pulled her to her feet and lifted her up against his chest and carried her upstairs. Simon, comfortable on the sofa, stayed where he was and closed his eyes.

Upstairs, Ben lowered Grace into a chair in their bedroom and began to make up the bed with fresh bedding from one of the hand-built cupboards. Grace watched him for a few minutes and then she stood up and went to help him.

'So, am I getting an apology?' she asked.

'It's not that I don't trust you. It's that I fear for you when he pops up again, and again, and I'm not here to protect you.'

'Well, he's gone now, and I hope to God that he stays away,' she said, tucking a blanket neatly into the foot of the mattress on her side of the bed. She lifted her eyes and stared at him for a second. 'Do you know, you've never said you love me.'

'I didn't think I had to,' he said, starting to undress.

'It would be good to hear it,' she responded, unzipping her skirt.

'Don't get all sloppy on me. I'd like to hear you apologise for believing me a monster, but I can live without it. Now stop talking and get into bed.'

Grace climbed into bed in her underskirt which clung to the swell of her stomach and her breasts. She drew the covers up to her chin and turned away from him.

'So, this is how it's going to be, is it?' Ben said in a muffled voice, slipping an arm round her, so his hand cupped her belly.

Grace remained silent, tempted to face him, only to be overcome by weariness.

Chapter 35

Grace stood on the bridge overlooking the lake, her arm fastened around her daughter who was standing up, balancing against the metal rail, and dropping bread down to the ducks. Leaves fallen from the trees, some brown, some yellow, were floating on the water, while others formed a rustling carpet beneath Grace's feet. She was aware of a growing sensation in her belly, like period pain, and decided that it was probably time that they made their way back to Alice's. The baby was due any day now, and since Ben's last leave, Grace, Simon and Irene had returned to living in the older Scotswoman's house. Grace eased Irene away from her perch, but her daughter clung on with one hand.

'More bwead for duckies,' she pleaded.

'No – time to go back,' said Grace firmly, unlatching Irene's fingers from the metal bars.

On her way back through the park she saw Simon walking Fergie. She raised a hand and waved to him before calling his name. It was Fergie who responded first and began to pull on the leash. Simon allowed himself to be dragged towards her, coming to a halt a couple of feet away from Grace who was feeling slightly breathless by that point.

'Am I glad to see you,' she said. 'Could you look after your sister, please?'

Irene stretched out her arms towards him. 'Si!' she cried.

Simon took Irene's hand and swapped the dog's leash to his other hand. 'You all right?' he asked, looking at her with concern.

Grace pulled a face. 'I think the baby's started.'

'Heck!' he exclaimed. 'Should I run ahead and let them know to get in touch with the midwife?'

'That's a good idea,' she said, pausing as she felt a contraction.

He gazed at her with a worried expression. 'Perhaps I should try and ring through to get hold of Dad, too.'

'Why bother? He won't be able to make it in time.'

Simon swore beneath his breath. 'I can't understand you. He still needs to know.'

'Tell him then. But I bet he doesn't come,' she said in a small voice.

'That's beside the point,' he said. 'Besides, you know it's more difficult for him now he's on coast-watching duties down south.'

They had come to the road now, as Simon had not gone ahead, but had stayed with her. 'I can't understand why the coast needs to be watched any longer,' grumbled Grace. 'The fight for Britain is over.'

She thought back to early May and how the Luftwaffe had not visited Merseyside since Ben had surprised her that early morning in the park opposite the house. A few days later, on 10th May, Ben had told her that he was being deployed to the south coast. The RAF were now focusing on the war in the desert and also on taking the fight to the skies over Germany, so there were fewer fighter planes to defend the country than during the Battle of Britain. Ben was to be part of a gun placement designed to shoot down any incoming German planes which had managed to sneak past the remaining fighter planes. Relationships between Grace and Ben continued to be strained following Dougie's attack on Simon, although they had kissed goodbye when Ben's leave came to an end, and at least he had been able to spend a little time with his daughter.

Once Simon had informed them that the baby was on its way, Alice, Barbara and her mother hurried Grace upstairs and tucked her into bed almost as soon as she stepped over the threshold. The midwife arrived half an hour later, and in a flurry of activity, Grace and Ben's son was born an hour later. Grace wanted to call him Peter, because in her mind, the names Simon and Peter went together. So, when Simon got Ben on the phone, Grace asked him about the name. He agreed readily, and after telling her to get plenty of rest and to give the small baby a kiss from him, the conversation ended as he was called away. As she put the receiver down, Grace felt close to tears, unsure whether Ben would be able to get leave to come and see his newly born son. Grace guessed it would not be easy to get leave in the run-up to Christmas. But she kissed her baby as Ben had asked and thanked God for a safe delivery for them both.

–

As it was, Ben surprised her by arriving at Alice's four days later. After thanking Alice and her lodgers for looking after his family so well, he ran upstairs to see his wife and their newborn. Grace gazed intently at Ben's expression as he lifted the baby for the first time. She wondered if he could see the similarity of the baby's earlobes to Simon's. But it was the baby's full head of hair and its double crown – which was exactly the same as Simon's – that Ben commented on, smiling as he did so.

'It's almost magical the way family likenesses show up through the ages,' he said. 'My brother had a double crown – so did Mam.'

'So, you're pleased with him then?' Grace said.

He nodded. 'How's Irene with him?'

'She keeps wanting to hold him or put him in her doll's pram.'

'You can't blame her,' said Ben.

'I don't, but it would be foolish to let her treat him like a doll, as she's quite rough with her teddy.'

'You'll have to watch out for her getting jealous.'

'I know, especially where Simon is concerned. She likes to have all his attention as it is.'

He nodded. 'So, are you feeling up to moving back home? I've mentioned to Alice that we might do so soon.'

'Yeah, it's what we planned,' said Grace. 'But I must have a word with my uncle and Beryl before I go.'

'Naturally – does Marion keep in touch with them?' he asked, handing his son back to Grace.

She nodded. 'She also visited with the baby in August.'

'Did she have anything to say about her brother and what happened in the spring after he attacked Simon?'

'She found it difficult to talk about Dougie... after what he did at Roddy's mother's house, and how it all ended.' Grace shook her head in disbelief. 'But I think Marion and Beryl have made a sort of truce. And Uncle Douglas seems warmer towards Marion as well, now he sees that she was just trying to placate Dougie.'

'Dougie was acting crazy. Simon is growing up, but he is still a lad and to have to face down Dougie must have taken guts. And then for Dougie to go on and do what he did, well—'

'Yeah. Well, I'm glad my aunt isn't alive to hear about it,' Grace said, undoing the buttons of her cardigan and blouse to feed the baby.

His face softened as he watched his wife and son. 'I wish I could stay until Christmas.'

She shot him a glance. 'How long can you stay?'

'Ten days. Long enough to get you and the children settled back home, and I thought you might like to go into town and see the damage.'

'Why not? I've yet to go into town. I haven't been there since before the May blitz.'

–

Barbara came with Simon later that day to babysit while Grace and Ben went down into the city centre on the tram. They stood by the Victoria Monument gazing at the empty desolate spaces where once fine buildings and shops had stood. Grace felt tears well up in her eyes and the view blurred so that she could scarcely see the Anglican cathedral still standing in the distance on St James Mount to the southern side of Liverpool.

She said, 'It's going to cost a fortune to rebuild and rehouse all those who have lost their homes. Although work has already started on strengthening the houses still standing. Milly told me. Did I tell you that they're back in Liverpool? Jimmy has been declared unfit for the forces, but he can do rebuilding work. The orphans will be returning soon too.

'That must be a relief for them both,' said Ben. 'How's his mother?'

'Still living in Wales. She's happy there and is looking forward to having her sister stay with her from Southend. And also the whole family once the war's over.'

'Why wait for the end of the war?' Ben asked.

'You should know,' Grace replied. 'Getting about the country is still difficult.'

'So, not impossible.'

Grace wondered if Ben was hinting at something else here, so asked, 'Do some of the other soldiers' girlfriends or wives make the journey across country to see their menfolk?'

'A few, but it's rare for those who have children.'

Grace did not know if she felt relieved or disappointed that by the sound of it he did not expect her to make the effort to come visit his barracks. She thought they needed to talk about what had been said on his last leave and the slight awkwardness that lingered between them. Maybe it was something that would have to wait until the war was over and he was home for good, as what was the use if he was only around for a few days? In the meantime, while he was here, she would put on an affectionate attitude, especially in front of the children. As for coupling in bed, that was out of the question as she was still sore after the birth. But, if she was truthful, it still smarted that he would think she had arranged a clandestine meeting with Dougie. It made her angry every time she thought about it.

They turned away from the viewpoint, and walked down to the Mersey under the Overhead Railway, part of which had been damaged out Bootle way back in May in the raids. It was now fixed so the trains could do their job of getting the dockers and other workers near the waterfront to work. As they gazed across the narrow gap of khaki-coloured water between dock and the landing stage, Grace took a deep breath of salt-laden air and thanked God that Liverpool had survived spring's terrible assault and was still able to play its part in delivering goods and men to fight the Battle of the Atlantic.

–

The following day Ben and Grace took Irene and baby Peter to visit Milly and Jimmy. Milly fussed over both children and asked whether Ben and Grace were hoping to have Peter christened while Ben was home.

'I think that would be a good idea,' continued Milly, who was one of Irene's godmothers; Jimmy was her godfather.

'So, do I,' said Grace. 'I was thinking of asking Simon, Barbara and Kyle to be godparents. What do you say, Ben?'

'I like Barbara, but do you think that hers and Simon's relationship will last? They're only young.'

'I think it will,' Grace said. 'She has a lot of common sense and not only does she care a lot for Simon, but she is great with Peter. I couldn't have done without her help these last few weeks, especially when I went into labour. And the Christian faith matters to them both. I'd like them both to be part of our lives, and Peter's, in the future.'

'Well said,' murmured Jimmy. 'I don't know where my family would be if we hadn't had friends who were prepared to go that extra mile when life got difficult.'

'Point taken,' said Ben, turning to face Grace. 'We best start making arrangements now then, as time is short.'

'First, we ask our proposed godparents,' she said, 'and then we speak to the vicar.'

No time was wasted doing both those things, and Ben was especially touched by Barbara's grateful acceptance, as he saw how much little Peter meant to her. By the following Sunday, with the assistance of the vicar, they were all in St Margaret's Church for the baptism with the godparents and their families, along with Alice, Barbara's mother, Joan, Uncle Douglas and Beryl who was accompanied by the friendly Yank, Graham Campbell, who had helped rescue Grace in the park in May.

'What's the Yank doing here?' Ben whispered to Douglas, as he looked around the busy pub where the party had gone for a celebratory drink after the service.

'He and Beryl have taken a shine to each other, so I don't know how that'll end when the war finishes,' Douglas replied. 'But I won't stand in her way. She deserves some happiness after losing Davy. I don't know what her mother would have said about stepping out with a foreigner, but then she and Beryl were never close.'

'I hear you had a visit from Marion and the baby.'

'Yes, she's a changed person. It's lovely to see. As though a weight has been lifted. Yet, I suppose she would never have met Roddy if it weren't for Dougie, so we're to be grateful to him for that.'

Ben said, 'Roddy's a good bloke.' He sipped his pint.

Douglas agreed, 'It was a shame Dougie took against him. Apparently, according to Marion, he got mixed up again with those blokes he met on the ship going to Australia – the ones that he got into mischief with in South Africa. I suspect he owed a lot of money to the wrong sort of people. I think Dougie thought that Roddy would be able to bail him out, but when that didn't happen, I think he just went mad with fear, which was why he was so desperate to find Roddy back in May and acting so erratically—' Here, Douglas paused, and then added darkly, 'Not that I, or Grace for that matter, ever got any information about what really happened with those "friends" Dougie made on board, but they don't sound to have been good news…' The older man sighed heavily.

'How did he meet up with them again? Was it when he was living in London?' said Ben.

'No, a couple of them joined the navy and he bumped into them again when their ship docked in Hull – they were having a drink in the same pub, so Marion told me.'

'Roddy, Marion and the baby had a lucky escape going to his sister's in Oxfordshire after leaving Liverpool. Dougie must not have known that Roddy's mother had moved from Kent to be with her daughter,' said Ben.

Douglas agreed, 'But I'd never imagine that Dougie would be capable of doing what he did. I know he was half-crazed at the time but attempting to shove a grenade through a letterbox! Of a woman's house too! Poor Roddy's mother – lucky that the house was empty at the time and she was with her daughter, but what must Dougie have been thinking! Foolish boy… And then for the grenade to get stuck and explode before he could put a sensible distance between him and the door. No wonder the explosion killed him…' Douglas trailed off again and stared down at his pint.

Ben, thought about the recklessness of Dougie's last act – as careless in death as he was in life – he sighed too, but with huge relief. As he did so, his eyes involuntarily sought out Grace. They fixed on her across the room, as she held baby Peter and was helping Irene to tie the strings of his baby bonnet. He kept his counsel, but in silence grasped Douglas's arm to acknowledge his loss.

Douglas took a moment, and then changed the subject. 'So, how much longer do you think the war will last?'

Ben said, 'I wish I could say by Christmas, but I believe we're some way off yet, but I doubt Merseyside will be attacked by the Luftwaffe again and that must be of some comfort.'

Douglas nodded towards his daughter and her new American beau. 'Beryl said that Graham reckons the Americans will officially be joining us in the fight soon. Apparently German U-boats have been spotted in the US coastal waters and a couple of American ships have been torpedoed.'

'That doesn't surprise me,' said Ben. 'Anyway, you take care now.' Grace motioned to him from across the bar. 'I'd better mix with our other guests.'

—

The next morning Ben was up early. He took a cup of tea and a slice of buttered toast up to Grace, who was still asleep, before he lifted his whimpering son from the Moses basket. He cuddled Peter to him before sitting down on a chair with him next to the bed, ready for Grace to feed him. The idea of Grace feeding Peter gave him pleasure and reminded him of Christmas cards of the Madonna and the Holy Child. Ben felt a twinge as he realised that he was unlikely to be here for Peter's first Christmas, nor for Simon's birthday this year. He reminded himself that he was more fortunate than many a serviceman, given that he was based in the country and not out at sea or in a foreign land. Even so, he wished he and Grace could have sorted out their problems before he had to leave. Not for the first time, he cursed himself for even entertaining the thought that Grace would have tried to meet in secret with that madman Dougie. It had only been for a split-second, and the idea had left his brain as quickly as it had entered it, on that chaotic evening following Simon's attack. Ben sensed that Grace was still upset by his mistake, and he wanted to clear the air. Yet whenever Dougie's name was mentioned, he somehow found himself losing reason and arguing with his wife. But Ben had had enough of that man coming between them. He readied himself to bring it up now, when Grace awoke, but as she stirred and turned to him, he hesitated. Grace smiled sleepily and reached out for her baby. Ben kept silent, fearful of spoiling the peaceful moment. Instead he handed their son to her and motioned to the breakfast tray at her side, without saying a word. He then stood a moment in the doorway, and gazed at his wife and baby, before going downstairs.

Part 4

1944

Chapter 36

Grace came to a halt outside Milly's house and put on the brake of the pram. She unfastened Peter's straps and lifted him out, and held onto the back of his harness as she set the curious two-year-old on his feet. She thought of her daughter who was now at infant school, and how despite the war and Ben's absence, her early years had seemed to fly by. Milly and Jimmy's children, John and Mary were also at school. Despite the trouble with travelling around the country, Milly and Jimmy had just taken them to North Wales for the Whitsun bank holiday week to visit Jimmy's mother. Jimmy's aunt, who lived in Southend-on-Sea, had also accompanied them, as she was eager to catch up with her sister.

Grace had been invited, and would have enjoyed a few days away with them, as she liked the company of Jimmy's aunt – Ben and her had gotten to know her over the years before the war, whenever she had visited Jimmy and Milly. However, Grace knew it would not be easy coping with her two on holiday without a helping hand, and Milly had enough on her plate with her own family. However, Grace was looking forward to hearing all their news today over a cup of tea. Surely the war in Europe could not go on much longer, she wondered.

Her thoughts soon turned to Simon who had joined the navy just after his eighteenth birthday, a year ago last December. Somehow Simon had managed to get pally with some local sailors who were great admirers of a Captain Johnny Walker, a war hero, known for leading a fleet on escort duty out of Liverpool, with the aim of destroying the German U-boat menace in the Atlantic and the Irish Sea. The Western Approaches Command headquarters was situated in Liverpool and on hearing of Captain Walker's escapades, Simon was determined, as soon as he possibly could, to be involved in destroying the submarines that had ruined so many Liverpudlians' lives. It seemed to Grace that in no time at all, Simon was through his training and on board a vessel under the captain's command. Simon had told Grace with glee that the captain's rallying cry was 'A-hunting we will go!' She smiled when she thought back to Simon's last leave, which luckily coincided with his nineteenth birthday just before Christmas, and how smart he had looked in his new uniform. She was so proud of her stepson, and his joy was clear to see, as joining up had been his life's ambition since the war had started when he was just a young lad.

She did miss having him around, especially now that Fergie, their dog, had passed away. But her young children kept her busy enough and her stepson managed to get home quite regularly to see Barbara who was now a qualified nurse working at Alder Hey hospital. Over the past few years the young couple had continued to be sweet on each other and Grace suspected that they would get engaged soon. Grace was pleased for them, as she liked the young nurse very much, and could only hope Simon would return home from the war, just as she prayed Ben would.

As she sat down for tea with her friend, it turned out that Milly had news for Grace. Jimmy's aunt had spotted Ben in a teashop in Southend. When Milly first mentioned it, Grace could not understand why her husband would be in Southend, and in a teashop of all places.

'At least he wasn't in a pub getting drunk,' she joked, to hide her confusion.

'He was with a woman,' cautioned her friend gently.

'How old did she look?' Grace asked, thinking the woman could have been Anne, the wife of the journalist Andrew. The couple often shared Andrew's press insights into global news events with their friends. Grace felt immediately comforted by this thought. She knew occasionally Ben went to visit Anne and Andrew from his military base in the south, normally when he was granted leave for an afternoon and there wasn't time for him to make the long journey back to Merseyside. But normally let Grace know of his plans. Why hadn't Ben told her about this visit to Anne and Andrew? Besides which, what was he doing meeting the woman *alone* in a teashop?

'Late thirties, dark hair, intense-looking.'

'Not Anne then,' said Grace lightly, having realised seconds before it could not have been Anne with Ben anyway, as Jimmy's aunt would have recognised her, as they were neighbours. A cold shiver snaked down her spine. Her worst fears were being realised. Maybe that was why she hadn't heard from Ben for a while! Who was this woman and what did she mean to Ben? How was she to find out, she thought desperately. No use writing to Ben himself, as she hadn't had a reply to her last two letters. She had assumed he had been too busy to write, or that the post had gone astray, as was sometimes the case, but now… the room spun a little in front of her.

Batting away Milly's concerned questioning, Grace excused herself as soon as she could, and hurried home with Peter. There, with shaking hands, she hurriedly prepared something for the two of them to eat, but found she could not swallow a bite. After clearing away the dishes, she decided to go for a walk in the park to clear her head. On the way, she thought to visit Alice. The kindly Scotswoman remained very fond of Peter and had continued to live, along with her lodgers, Barbara and her mother, next door to Grace's uncle and cousin. Grace's uncle Douglas had found peace tending the large joint vegetable garden, while her cousin Beryl continued to write regularly to her American Prince Charming, Lieutenant Campbell, who was now based at an airbase in the Home Counties.

–

On settling down in her friend's familiar front room, Grace's anger at Ben poured out. Alice listened carefully to Grace's passionate account. She then picked up her knitting and thought a while before suggesting gently that perhaps Grace should be prepared to make the journey down to see Ben before she jumped to further conclusions. Alice had been married a long while before the death of her husband and knew a thing or two about the peaks or troughs in a marriage. She went on to remind Grace that possibly Ben might be a little homesick, which was why he had sought out the company of his friends, before adding quietly that she and Barbara could take care of the children if Grace were to go and visit him alone, if she so wanted.

At first Grace felt dissatisfied with her friend's calm handling of the situation, as she felt herself very much the aggrieved party. However, she promised to sleep on the matter and soon after took her leave with Peter before it got too late.

After a sleepless night, she decided that Alice was right, and she needed to see Ben face to face. She had never doubted Ben's faithfulness to her before, and if she had ever been jealous, it was only of his first wife whom he had lost when he was so young. But why hadn't she heard from him? Besides, if he was feeling homesick why couldn't he have made the journey to Liverpool instead of to Southend? And who was this dark-haired woman?

Later the next afternoon, feeling resolved, she visited Alice again. 'So, you're going to go and visit Ben,' attuned Alice as she saw Grace's set, tired face on opening the door.

'Yes! The only thing I can't decide about is whether I should write and tell him that I'm coming.'

'What reason are you going to give?' Alice asked.

'The truth. I think we need some time alone to talk.'

'I suppose that's fair enough,' said Alice, inviting Grace in, and taking a bottle of sherry from the sideboard cupboard she poured some into two sherry glasses. 'The pair of you need to decide on a date – to make sure he's not on duty and where you're to meet.'

Alice realised that it did no good to meddle in the affairs of the heart, so offered no more advice, yet she had seen how Ben looked at Grace when he thought no one else was paying attention. But Grace needed to discover her husband's intentions for herself. She handed Grace one of the glasses, and looked thoughtfully at her young friend over the rim of her own glass, while she slowly sipped her drink.

Chapter 37

Grace was surprised by how eager she was at the thought of going alone to see her husband after she received Ben's response to her letter in which she raised the idea. In writing, Grace had made no mention of the missing replies to her letters or to Milly's report about Ben and certain women in Southend teashops. She had expected Ben to suggest that they meet in London, but instead he had told her to meet him in Oxford on 10th June. He had requested leave, which had been granted, and had booked a room for them for three nights at the Mitre hotel on the High Street and would wait for her to join him there.

Grace read and re-read his letter, scanning it for clues as to what her husband was thinking. But the most she could take from it was a gruff enthusiasm for the plan. Ben was not a man prone to softness, something which Grace knew well, but for a moment, she thought back wistfully to their conversation following their return from their honeymoon when they had been paddling on the beach. Even then the two of them knew that there would be little time for gallivanting and romantic frivolities once they'd settled down to the daily grind of married life, but neither of them could have foreseen the extent to which the war would pull them in different directions and rob them of being able to decide when to spend time together without asking for permission for it first.

The night before her trip to Oxford, Grace took the children to Alice's and stayed over with them. She was up early the following morning and after kissing Irene and Peter without waking them, she hurried out of the house and caught the tram into town in time to board a train to Birmingham, where she would change for the train direct to Oxford. The journey seemed to take an age, but eventually she arrived in the city, and there she asked the ticket collector for directions to the Mitre hotel. She had no trouble finding it and stood outside for a moment, wondering whether she should carry on waiting outside or go inside, as she wasn't sure when Ben would be able to get there; transport across country being what it was. A few moments later she felt a tap on her shoulder, and she was whirled around straight into a man's arms. As she gazed into Ben's familiar tanned face, she thought his expression was strained.

Her tummy did a flip, and the old fears about the mysterious woman crowded her head. 'What is it? What's wrong?' she asked, alarmed.

'Why should you think anything is wrong?' Ben asked before lowering his head and kissing her firmly on the lips.

Confused by the strength of the kiss amid her tumultuous feelings of anger, Grace's mind reeled as she allowed Ben to take her hand and lead her inside the hotel. Here he paused at reception to introduce her as his wife, before he asked for their room key. It was not until they were inside their room and Ben had helped her off with her creased travelling jacket that Grace's anger and unease from the last few days came to a head.

Without preamble, she blurted out, 'Is it another woman? Tell me, is there?'

Ben's eyes narrowed and he reached for a cigarette and lit up. 'Someone been gossiping?' he asked, smoke escaping from his nostrils, making him close his eyes momentarily.

'Why are you smoking?' Grace asked, distracted for a moment. She used the chance to move away from Ben and went to sit on the stool in front of the dressing table where she could watch his expression.

'I find it helps when out on watch on the gun placement.'

'Surely not more stressful than the blitz was back home?'

'I had you to help me with the stress then. You're a tough woman, Grace.'

'I'm glad you found me a comfort,' she said. 'But for most of the bombing I've had to cope without you,' she said, a tremor in her voice. 'And by all accounts, it looks like I might have to carry on doing that if you've got yourself some sort of fancy woman—' here she broke into a sob.

'What woman? Whatever do you mean?' Ben asked her urgently.

'Jimmy's aunt – she saw you with her – she saw the two of you in a teashop in Southend.'

'Josephine? Did Anne tell you? Or Andrew?' Ben stubbed his cigarette out in an ashtray.

'Anne? No,' Grace shook her head in confusion. 'Josephine – who is that? Is she the woman?' she said, holding her head high despite the tears in her eyes.

'So, that's why you suggested this plan to meet up! I thought you were missing me... but you came down because you didn't trust me—'

'No, I came because I was determined to make you realise what you'd be losing if you made the mistake of tossing me and our children aside.'

He looked incredulous. 'How can you even think I'd make such a mistake?'

'Because you're a man of action, but few words... Because I don't get to see you properly these days, I can't make sense of it. I haven't had any letters from you for weeks and you're so distant... and because—' here, she hesitated, unsure of how to continue, '—ever since you thought I'd tried to meet up with Dougie that night he hit Simon, I don't know, it's just not the same for us...' Grace cried in despair.

At the sight of his wife weeping, Ben crossed the room in one move. 'Grace, Grace, luv, come now – there's no need for this. I am sorry, I never meant to doubt you.' At Ben's words, Grace looked up at her husband's eyes, and realised that there would be no need for further conversation for a while. With her heart singing, and without more ado, she drew Ben close and kissed him.

Later, after a long magical half an hour and a bath together, they lay side by side, holding hands in bed. As she cuddled up to her husband under the bedcovers, Grace said, 'You'd better tell me what you were thinking of sharing a table with this Josephine in a tearoom then. And what's Anne and Andrew got to do with it?'

Ben smiled down at her head nestled below him. 'Josephine is a member of the French Resistance. Andrew knew of her through his press contacts and introduced me to her when I went down to see him and Anne for an afternoon in May. Andrew had met Josephine before and thought her story might be of interest to me. I didn't mention my going to visit them to you, as what happened is not something you can write in a letter – I was saving it for when I next saw you.' He gave her a little squeeze under the covers before continuing, 'Josephine's French, and she's been helping British troops who were parachuted into France gain information about where the Jerries are stationed in her country.'

'Did she fall in love with an English parachutist then? Is that why she's over here? What's this all got to do with you?' asked Grace eagerly, half-convinced Ben was making this story up, as it seemed a little far-fetched, like something she'd see at a movie.

'No, Josephine is already married – to an Englishman she met during the last war.' Again, Ben squeezed her, a little pointedly this time. Grace made a small grimace and buried her face in his chest. He went on, 'That's why she's over here now. I don't know the details, but a returning British soldier brought her back with him when he was flown out.'

'What about her husband?' asked Grace, puzzled.

'He's blind.' Ben's voice quivered. 'Apparently, some-time during the Great War, Josephine found him, wandering lost in a wood on her father's farm in France and took him home with her. The husband couldn't remember his name or where he was from – his nerves were shot to pieces. The French family felt sorry for him and offered him shelter. Before long he had settled down so well on the farm that they decided to let him stay. Besides, they still didn't know his name.' Ben shrugged. 'The rural life seemed to suit him. By then it was the 1920s or early 1930s and he was so much part of the family they didn't want to part with him. Although he couldn't do much to look after the sheep, he learnt to milk their cow, and was good with his hands. Josephine said he could turn a simple piece of wood into different objects – tools and the like, or even a toy dog or a horse for children – things which they were able to sell.' Ben paused.

'Go on,' urged Grace, a vague memory lurking on the edge of her consciousness.

'Then one day they were listening to a football match on the wireless and one of the teams playing was Liverpool. It seemed to trigger a memory in the former soldier's mind and he said the word "Anfield" and something about the colour red.'

Grace could hear that tremor in Ben's voice again. 'So, what caused Josephine to come to England now, as this must have happened a while ago?' she asked slowly.

'The two married, and eventually Josephine gave birth to a son. She wanted to call the boy after her father, but her husband kept saying the baby's name was Ben.'

Grace's eyes widened. 'Did Josephine begin to wonder if her husband was already married and had a son called Ben in Liverpool or something like that?' she whispered.

Her husband nodded. 'The family were – are devout Catholics, but they didn't have the money to start a proper search, and then trouble was brewing with Hitler.'

'So, the search was delayed,' said Grace, fidgeting with the bedcovers.

Ben nodded. 'It wasn't until Josephine was over here as part of her war work that she was able to start looking into things. Somehow, she was introduced to Andrew, I'm not sure how, but you know the circles he moves in. Anyway, they happened to get talking – I think he must have mentioned growing up in Liverpool and—'

'That's it! I remember now, it was bugging me! The wooden toy dog that Irene used to play with – the one your brother made before he went off soldiering which was lying round the house – you mentioned this soldier making some wooden animals. Did Andrew know about you having a brother who had gone missing in the last war? The timings sound about right,' interrupted Grace urgently, reaching out towards her husband to grasp his hand.

'Yes. I have mentioned it to Andrew before now. And, as he said to me, just before I met Josephine at that teashop, he only knew one Ben – so I seemed a good person to start with...'

'So, you think Josephine's husband could be your missing brother?' Grace asked excitedly.

'I believe it's a possibility...' Ben replied. 'Mam always believed Martin was still alive even in those bleak years after the war.' Grace remembered Ben's closed-off face whenever the subject of Martin had come up in the past and knew how much this glimmer of hope about his brother being alive would mean to him.

'Did you tell Josephine that?'

He nodded.

'What happens next?' asked Grace.

'Well, I can't go over there and check if it's him just yet,' Ben said. 'You asked why I asked you to meet me here in Oxford and it's because we wouldn't have been able to find a place to stay close to the south coast.' He lowered his voice. 'The invasion of Europe is imminent.'

Grace turned on her side and looked him in the face. 'Good God, does that mean the war's nearly over?'

He kissed the tip of her nose. 'I think it's the beginning of the end, if all goes well.'

'Where does that leave Josephine and Martin?' she asked.

'Once the Allies secure France,' said Ben. 'I'll explain the situation to my commanding officer and ask permission to go to the farm and see if it is Martin. I've agreed to stay in touch with Josephine and told her I will visit as soon as I can. There's not much I can do for now.'

'Do you think you'll recognise him after all this time?'

''Course! He's my older brother. Then I'd like to bring him to Liverpool and make him an appointment at St Paul's Eye Hospital. Apparently, they've never had his eyes checked and there might be something we can do to help fix his eyesight. He used to paint so well...' Ben trailed off suddenly.

'Will Josephine agree to that, do you think?' Grace asked.

'I'm not going to mention it until I can confirm if it is Martin. No point stirring things up. Josephine's only wanting to make sure he's not married already with a child in Liverpool. I think she's heading back to France soon, once her work here is finished. She's nice, Grace, you'd like her. I know that after the war she wants her husband to stay on the farm with her, and their son. Her parents are getting on and they are wanted there.'

'Of course,' said Grace, her mind spinning with the news. She fell silent, while she digested the unexpected news. To think that she thought Ben might be cheating on her! She could be such a hot-head at times, and her temper could get the better of her, she knew. There was so much to hope for if this mysterious man was Ben's brother! But Grace couldn't bear to think how disappointed Ben would be if it all turned out to be a false lead. To change the subject, she said lightly, 'Now, what about us seeing something of Oxford?'

'Sounds good to me,' Ben said. But instead of throwing back the bedcovers, he rolled over and said, 'Maybe in a little while.' Then he began kissing her again.

Chapter 38

Grace basked in the warmth of those loving days spent in Oxford with Ben during the following turbulent summer months, especially as information seeped into the newspapers about the Allies' advance into Europe. Grace expected any day to hear from Ben telling her that he would shortly be on his way to France too. The thought filled her with dread, as she was terrified of losing Ben, after all they had been through.

She hadn't had a letter from him, and although she tried to quieten her mind, she found one day, when visiting Milly in late June that she could not help but speak of her concern.

'I think you're worrying unnecessarily,' Milly said.

'I hope so, I just don't want Ben delayed too long in France. The Allies have broken out of Normandy now, and the initial D-Day invasion was earlier this month, and I still haven't heard from him!' wailed Grace, fidgeting with a button on her jacket.

'I'm sure he'll get himself back home safely because he'll be wanting to be reunited with you as much as you want to see him,' comforted Milly.

The hot days of July passed slowly but didn't bring any real news from Ben. Grace finally received an out-of-date misdirected letter from him, which was postmarked from weeks before in early June. The letter was brief and gave very little away, other than that he was on the Continent. Although Grace was afraid for her husband's safe return, when she shared his letter with Barbara and Simon, she felt a wave of hope about the outcome of the war that she had not felt before. The Allies were in mainland Europe! And all being well, the young couple were planning an Easter Saturday wedding for the following March, although Simon wanted to get Ben's blessing before he set a firm date with Barbara. Their commitment to each other at such an uncertain time filled Grace with happiness, and she allowed herself to imagine for a moment what it would feel like for the war to be over next year, when Simon and his wife-to-be would be a couple of newly-weds starting a new life together.

As July turned into August, the days went by again with no further information about Ben. Although Paris was liberated on 25th August, Grace could not feel much joy at the news, as she still had no idea about the whereabouts of her husband; or even if he was dead or alive. Sick with worry, she tried to keep a brave face in front of the children but felt world-weary and heartsick. The years of constant war suddenly seemed too much to bear.

Then, unexpectedly, three days before Peter's birthday, as the chill of autumn could be felt in the air, Grace was aroused just before dawn by a hammering on the front door. She rolled out of bed with her eyes still shut and staggered over to the window overlooking the street. She eased up the lower sash window and croaked out, 'What's going on down there? Who's banging like that?'

A moment later she saw a man appear in the road. 'Grace luv, it's me. Could you come down and let me in? I'm tired out.'

Grace could scarcely believe it. Pausing only to put on her dressing gown, she closed the window with a clatter and hurried downstairs. She half-expected to see Simon coming out of his bedroom, as he was currently on leave and might have been disturbed by the noise, but there was no sign of him or Irene. Grace was in the process of shooting back the bolts on the front door when she heard footsteps coming down the stairs behind her. She threw the front door open and flung herself into her husband's arms.

Ben hugged her as she wept on his chest. 'Hey, hey, what's this about?'

'I was worrying.'

'What about?' Ben asked. 'We've pushed the Jerries out of France! We've got them now. It's nearly over! Come, come now, I wasn't in any danger, not really!'

'I was just being silly,' Grace said, pressing little kisses over his face. 'The transportation ship could have sunk or you could have been injured... I didn't hear from you for such a while that I was imagining the worst.'

'I did write, but things were moving so fast over there, I did wonder if my letters would get through. I'm here now – I've got leave for ten days. I was not in the forefront of the invasion but in the rear. I volunteered to go over to Normandy and help unload the ships' supplies and equipment that were to be transported to the advancing troops,' said Ben, holding her away from him and gazing into her tear-stained face.

Grace continued to welcome him warmly, and hugged and kissed him again, before ushering him into the house. By now, Simon stood on the doorstep – he had heard most of the conversation, and wordlessly folded his dad into a great hug.

Grace soon had Ben out of his dirty uniform and sitting down in clean clothes at the kitchen table. She had checked on Irene and Peter who shared a bedroom, and saw that they were still asleep, so decided to leave them be. The kettle was on and she took out cups and saucers, milk and sugar and biscuits for an early morning brew for them all. Simon sat opposite his father, wide-eyed, catching up on all his soldiering news. Ben in turn, asked his son how things were with him. As she bustled in and out of the back kitchen with the tea things, Grace once again noted the similarities between father and son, and gave thanks for this precious time they had together, given that their leave had rarely coincided before.

At Ben's questioning, Simon's expression altered. 'Now the Battle of the Atlantic is as good as won, our ship is being deployed elsewhere, so I won't be able to get home so regular. Don't ask me where, because we haven't been told yet – although we're not to take tropical kit, so my best guess is most likely the coast of Germany.'

Ben's spirits sank. 'Does Grace know you're being deployed away from Liverpool?'

'Not yet, and I haven't mentioned it to Barbara either. But I'm due to go tomorrow, I just heard last night. It's been bad enough waiting for information about you, and this will start them worrying again, so I didn't have the heart to tell them. I'm dreading breaking it to them.'

Ben grimaced. 'So, Mum's the word.'

Simon nodded and turned to face Grace with a smile as she passed him a teacup.

–

The next day, Grace and Simon were up first, and while Grace put the kettle on, Simon lit the fire. It was while they were having a cup of tea that he told her about his ship being deployed. He ended by asking that Grace keep Barbara's spirits up while he was away.

'What about the wedding?' Grace asked her voice a little too bright. 'Will you be back for it? I suppose it's too early to say, all depends on where you end up.'

Simon shrugged in agreement, and his eyes were damp. He was still only a lad after all, and Grace wanted to go to him and hug him and tell him that everything would be all right, but she felt frozen to the spot. What with Ben just back, this felt a hard blow. Simon was the one to come over to her and hug her.

'Pray for me,' he said, his voice muffled against her neck.

'Of course—' she said, and then rallying herself '—but remember when you were in the bath chair and in danger of crashing into a tree? And then that time you were blown off your bike and hit the wall? And what about before we met and you fell out of a tree and damaged your wrists and kneecap, but then made a full recovery? You're a survivor, Simon!'

'Some might say I'm accident-prone, and the day will come when my luck runs out,' Simon said laughing, and he sniffed slightly.

'Luck has nothing to do with it. You're here for a reason. You're needed now and for the future.' She shook him gently by the upper arms. 'And don't you forget it.'

They drew apart and he wiped his eyes with his sleeve. 'I'd better get going,' he said, picking up his kitbag.

'But you've had no breakfast! And what about your dad?'

'I'm going to see Barbara. I want to catch her in plenty of time before she leaves for the hospital. She'll give me something. I said my goodbyes to Dad last night.'

Grace saw him to the door, trying to keep her back straight as she waved the young man off down the street. She was aware of Ben standing behind her.

'He told you then?' he asked.

She nodded and turned and slipped her arms around his waist. 'Hold me tight.'

They held each other, and then still with their arms around each other, they went upstairs and gazed down at their sleeping daughter and son.

Chapter 39

Later that evening when they were in bed and were cuddling up, Grace's thoughts turned again to Barbara and Simon.

'I hope they don't waste their time together worrying about losing each other. When I think of the times that I worried about you and you always arrived back – thank God.'

'Agreed,' said Ben. 'And I'll be posted off again soon. But not long to go now, I can sense that the war's nearly done. I forgot to mention that I had been hoping to sneak off when I was in France and look for Martin, but I just couldn't get away, though I might manage it this time,' he added.

'You might be able to bring him home for the wedding. Simon would be thrilled. That boy thinks the world of you. I take it you gave the Easter wedding date your blessing, didn't you?' Grace said, referring to Simon wanting to speak to Ben before he finalised the date with Barbara.

'Of course,' Ben said. 'They're made for each other, the two of them. Just like we were – your dad realised it before we did,' he said chuckling.

Grace thought then of Norman and how he had given his permission straight away for her to marry Ben – how right he had been to trust Ben to care for her. Norman had been against her and Dougie from the start. Grace smiled. Thank God, Norman had prevented her from going to Australia with him. Suddenly, she thought back to the day on the dock when she waved Dougie goodbye as a fresh-faced girl and she remembered that her father had never told her why he had not been allowed to stay in Australia. That secret had always troubled her for some reason. She couldn't believe that she had forgotten to ask, but with all the drama that seemed to follow Dougie around, she supposed she would never know now, unless Norman had spoken of it to Ben. If he had done so, hopefully he had not sworn him to secrecy.

They were silent for a while, and then Grace spoke up. 'Ben? Do you remember if my dad ever told you why he was kicked out of Australia? Thinking of Simon and Barbara's plans reminded me of our wedding and all that led up to it.' Grace was quiet for a moment, not really wanting to bring up the subject of Dougie, with all that nonsense having been laid to rest. 'He didn't tell me, but I was wondering whether he ever told you.'

'Goodness, that's some time ago now,' Ben said. 'But he did, as it happens. Seems he got himself in a fight with some Aussies over a girl and a knife was produced.'

'By me dad?' exclaimed Grace, shocked, thinking of how mild-mannered Norman had always been towards her.

'Most sailors carried a knife, even if it was just a penknife,' Ben reassured her. 'To cut string, rope, and yes, probably for self-defence in a foreign port. He said that he was a bit of a hot-head in those days. Like someone else

I know, eh?' Grace ignored Ben's gentle teasing, so he continued, 'But he did add that he was thankful to those Aussies because if he had been allowed to stay there, he would never have met your mother, and wouldn't have had you for a daughter.' He put his hand over hers on top of the bedcovers. 'And we wouldn't have each other, or Irene and Peter.'

'Yes, I suppose Dad was right... And our two are as thick as thieves, they're lucky to have each other. Irene defends Peter no end when they play out, it's nice to see.'

'Just like Martin and I used to be,' said Ben thoughtfully. 'I can't wait for the war to end so I can go and visit Josephine's farm and meet her husband. Just imagine if it is him, Grace, after all this time!' Grace squeezed his hand in response.

'I hope Simon and Barbara have children, and Irene and Peter,' said Grace. 'I wonder what they'll have to cope with in the future.'

'We can't know the future. But we can continue to put our best foot forward. The war's got to be over soon, I'm sure of it, and we'll all be back together again before we know it.' Grace sighed contentedly at the thought. 'But, hopefully, our grandchildren will have the best of times, and appreciate them,' murmured Ben sleepily, as he tucked his arm tightly around his wife lying at his side, pulling her close.